PRAISE

"There is
characteriz
all add spi

"Candice

—CATHERINE COULTER

"A unique and welcome new voice in the romance genre. I, for one, am adding Candice Proctor to my 'buy' list."
—*CompuServe Romance Reviews*

"Proctor's vivid characters and elegant style will grab the reader's imagination."
—*The Literary Times*

*Please turn the page
for more reviews. . . .*

SEPTEMBER MOON

THE BEQUEST

NIGHT IN EDEN

By Candice Proctor
Published by The Ballantine Publishing Group

THE LAST KNIGHT

Candice Proctor

IVY BOOKS • NEW YORK

An Ivy Book
Published by The Ballantine Publishing Group
Copyright © 2000 by CP Trust

www.randomhouse.com/BB/

Library of Congress Card Number: 00-190470

ISBN 0-8041-1930-9

Manufactured in the United States of America

First Edition: August 2000

10   9   8   7   6   5   4   3   2   1

For my father, the late Raymond L. Proctor, soldier, historian, and storyteller par excellence, who once taught a little girl to love castles and knights and the power of words.

CHAPTER
ONE

Châteauhaut-sur-Vilaine, eastern Brittany, 1189

The two white candles on the altar filled the night with
a golden, flickering light that shimmered over the painted
walls and high vaulted ceiling of the empty chapel. Letting
go a quiet sigh of relief, Attica d'Alérion dipped her fingertips in the carved stone font of holy water near the door and
went to the rail.

She was glad to find the chapel deserted. In the four
months that had passed since her betrothal brought her
here to the household of the viscomte and viscomtesse
de Salers, the chapel had become a place of refuge. The
chapel and the battlements.

Sometimes, when storm clouds bunched low and threatening in the sky, when lightning split the darkness and
the wind blew fierce and wild, Attica would climb to the
battlements of Châteauhaut's new stone keep and let the
wind whip at her hair and batter her face until she felt as if
the savage night had stolen the very breath from her body.
She would be filled with such an exhilaration, such a reckless excitement, such nameless, soul-deep yearnings that
the sensation both stirred and frightened her. She didn't
allow herself to go there often.

And so she had come here tonight, to the chapel, where she found not wild temptation but peace. Kneeling before the ornate altar with its carved and gilded front, she made the sign of the cross and bowed her head to say a Credo.

She prayed for the easy passing of the Parisian courtier who lay dying in the guest chamber beside the chapel. She sought God's protection for her brother serving as a household knight with the beleaguered English king, Henry II, as he prepared for the peace conference at La Ferté-Bernard. She asked a blessing for her father, old and spending most of his time now in his favorite hunting lodges in Normandy. As an afterthought, she added her mother's name, although she squirmed when she did it, the glazed tiles of the floor feeling cold and hard through the fine wool of her skirt.

Again she hesitated, her gaze lifting to the white plastered eastern wall behind the altar. This was the only section of the chapel yet to be painted. Yvette—the viscomtesse de Salers—was still arguing with the monk from Pierreforte l'abbaye about the subject to be depicted. The good brother thought this section of the chapel should portray the Last Judgment, except that Yvette had a pronounced aversion to the Last Judgment and wanted God Triumphant in Heaven. Privately, Attica agreed with the brother, but she'd had enough sense to keep her mouth shut. Not only could Yvette be vindictive, but she had a long memory. And in one short month Attica would be marrying Yvette's son, a thirteen-year-old boy nicknamed Fulk the Fat.

Attica felt a welling of complex, unwanted emotions at the thought of the wedding day looming before her. Fulk was six years younger than she and sadly inclined to sulk.

He particularly resented the fact that the top of his head didn't even come up to Attica's chin—something he believed was more her fault than his, for she was far too tall and thin for a woman. She hoped he would grow. Quickly.

The melted wax around the wick of one of the candles hissed, filling the air with the scent of hot beeswax and sending up a spiral of dark smoke. Ducking her head, she begged God's forgiveness for her wayward and rebellious nature and asked a blessing for the house of Salers. She saw no need to particularize.

Her duty fulfilled, Attica closed her eyes and let the peace of this place wash over her. Her breathing slowed until it seemed as if the peace became a pulsing thing, as if her heart were beating in harmony with the universe, as if she could feel—

"Ahem."

The harsh and decidedly artificial sound of someone clearing his throat behind her shattered the moment of quiet rapture. Attica's head whipped around. "Oh, Fulk." She schooled her features into a gentle smile. "You startled me."

He stood just inside the doorway in a halo of light thrown by one of the cressets, a fleshy, pale-faced boy wearing crimson silk and purple brocade and an accusatory pout. "You didn't come down to supper because you said you needed to tend that Parisian courtier. So why are you here instead?" He pulled a piece of linen from his sleeve and blew his nose. "It's cold in here."

The walls of the chapel suddenly seemed to press in on her, smothering her. She sucked in a quick breath scented with cold damp stone and the memory of old incense, and pushed to her feet. "Your cousin offered to relieve me while I came to pray," said Attica, who by that time had been sitting with the ailing Parisian courtier for the better part of twelve hours. "I should get back now."

She expected him to go away then, for Yvette refused to enter any sickroom and something of her heightened fear of death and illness had rubbed off on Fulk. But he followed Attica to the door of the guest chamber and stayed there, shifting anxiously from one foot to the other, his fascinated gaze riveted on the long-boned, dark-haired man lying naked and still as death in the big, silk-hung bed.

His name was Olivier de Harcourt, and he was an intimate of the French king Philip II, which is why Yvette hadn't dared hustle him out of her castle the way she would have done with any lesser mortal who collapsed screaming and clutching his belly in her hall. No one could agree on exactly what was wrong with the man, for as his fever climbed, his abdomen swelled up hard and became horribly painful, and he could keep nothing down. The chamberlain said Olivier had obviously swallowed a devil and it was festering in his belly. But the cook said it was putrefaction of the intestines, that he'd seen it before and it had nothing to do with what the man had eaten.

A slim blond girl of twelve had been sitting on a low stool beside the courtier, her elbows on her knees, her chin in her hands. At the sight of Attica she jumped up so fast, the stool went skidding across the rush-strewn floor. "Oh, thank goodness."

"Is he worse?" Attica asked, crossing quickly to the bed. The flickering light of the torches shone over the man's sunken, sweat-slicked face. If it weren't for the shuddering rise and fall of his chest, she'd have thought him dead.

"He's in a faint now," said the girl, "but he is worse, I think. He's so hot, and he seems to be wandering in his mind. He kept asking for a breviary. Only when I sent one of the pages to fetch mine, thinking it might comfort him, he wanted nothing to do with it."

"Did he take any of the tea I asked to be sent up?"

The girl nodded, a lock of her fine hair falling over her shoulder. "Some. But he threw it up again."

Attica sighed. The sour stench of vomit was still there, beneath the sweet, lingering scent of the herbs they'd been using to try to bring down his fever. Angelica root and pennyroyal, hissop and yarrow, elderflower and lavender—she had tried them all without success. "It's getting late," she said, taking the girl's seat on the stool. "I'll sit with him again. You should go."

The girl clasped her hands together, her flat chest lifting with a quickly indrawn breath. "I'll stay, if you like."

Attica shook her head and gave the girl a thankful smile. "No. Go on." Turning away, she dipped a cloth into the nearby basin of lukewarm water and began gently to sponge the man's hot face and thin chest. He was a young man, and handsome in an effete, pale-skinned way. But now his flesh had taken on a grayish tinge, and sweat glistened in the darkly curling hair that covered his thin arms and legs and chest. Attica might not know what was wrong with him, but she had seen enough men close to death to be fairly certain that this one would not live out the night. Already they had had Yvette's chaplain in to give him the last rites.

"Will he die?" Fulk asked, creeping a few steps closer.

"Probably." She didn't look up.

Sullen with resentment at being ignored, the boy began to wander about the edges of the room, fiddling with the buckles on Olivier de Harcourt's leather saddlebags, pushing out his lower lip as he studied the Parisian courtier's fine clothes, his surcoat of deep blue velvet and tunic of fine green wool, his heavy gold neck chain and jeweled belt and dagger.

"Does everyone wear such fine dress at the royal court, do you think?"

Attica paused in her ceaseless sponging to glance at him over her shoulder. "At Philip's court, yes. The English king is a plainer man. I hear Henry likes to wear huntsman's clothes."

"Then I should prefer to go to the French court, I think."

Attica only grunted, for she'd seen the man's lids flutter. Suddenly he reared up, his glazed eyes staring wildly, his chest heaving as he struggled to throw his legs out of bed.

"Lie still," she said soothingly, pressing her hands against his clammy shoulders.

His fist shot out, clipping her chin painfully. Attica threw herself across the man's chest to keep him from lunging off the bed. "Fulk! Help me hold him."

Fulk's small eyes went wide in his puffy face as he backed toward the door. "I don't think Mother would wish it," he said, and bolted from the room.

"Fulk."

"Let me up, you stupid cow," the man snarled, his dry, crackled lips pulling away from his teeth, his thin, sweat-slicked chest shuddering with effort. "I must get there, *I must.*"

He would have hit her again, but Attica jerked her head back out of the way as she tightened her grip on his shoulders and straightened her elbows, holding him down. *"Please* rest easy. You're there, you're there," she said, although she had no idea where he wanted to be.

The man stilled abruptly, his jaw going slack with surprise as he stared up at her. "I'm there?"

"Yes, yes."

He sagged back against the pillows, his feverish gaze searching the shadowy corners of the chamber. "Where is John?"

"John?" she repeated, her voice coming out hollow. Stooping, she picked up the cloth from where it had fallen, dipped it into the water, and began to sponge the man's hot chest and arms again. "Do you mean John Lackland?"

The courtier's face hardened, his shoulders curling off the pillows again as his hand flashed out to catch her wrist in a surprisingly strong grasp. "You said I was there."

"Yes," she lied, using her free hand to press him down again, "you're there."

The man relaxed his grip on her. "I must see him. Must tell him"—his throat worked as he swallowed, trying to ease the fever-seared tissues—"tell him about the conference at La Ferté-Bernard."

In the act of squeezing the cloth over the basin, Attica froze. They would be meeting at La Ferté-Bernard in only a few days, the English king Henry II and the French king Philip, joined in alliance with Henry's son Richard. She knew this because her own brother Stephen would be there as one of Henry's household knights.

"John has gone to one of his hunting lodges," she said, dropping the cloth to scoot her stool closer to the bed and lean into him until her face was only inches from his. "Tell me. Tell me about the conference."

The man's features contorted with a flare of pain. "It will come to naught."

He paused, his chest lifting with another ragged breath, and Attica had to tighten her hands into fists to curb her impatience. "You mean the conference?" she prodded. "Why should it come to naught?"

"Philip and Richard . . ." His head moved restlessly

against the pillow, as if seeking coolness. Attica reached to dip the cloth in fresh water again and pressed it to his forehead. He sighed, his lids drooping. "They do not mean to negotiate. Only buying time . . . shut up the pope and his damned legates."

His eyes closed, his head going slack as if he'd fallen back into a faint. Attica seized him by the shoulders and shook him ruthlessly. "*Tell me.* Tell me about the conference at La Ferté-Bernard. About Richard and Philip."

His eyes fluttered open, looking at her in bewilderment. Attica licked her dry lips. "Tell me," she said again. "Tell me what Richard and Philip plan for the conference."

The dark eyes focused. "They bring their armies with them. When the conference collapses, they'll attack."

"Attack?" Attica let her hands fall to her lap. "What do you mean?"

The edges of the man's lips twisted as if in a smile. "Catch Henry by surprise. Capture him. Force him to agree to their terms." His face quivered with a fresh spasm of pain as he struggled to push the words out. "You know about the Saintly Guido? About the seventh note?"

"What?"

The torch beside the bed sputtered, sending up a flare of golden light that gleamed on the man's sweat-sheened face. With a soft moan, he slid into a faint again. This time Attica let him go.

She sat motionless on the stool, her clasped hands clenched between her knees. "Oh, Stephen," she whispered in dismay.

He was her only surviving brother, Stephen, and she loved him with a fierceness she felt for no one else. He had been consecrated as a child to God, but then their elder brother died and Stephen had found himself yanked from his monastery and taught to be a knight. He made a good knight, Attica thought, even if his heart had never been in it, even if he still yearned to be back in the monastery serving God. A knight like Stephen would give up his life to defend his liege lord. Which meant that if Richard and Philip attacked Henry at La Ferté-Bernard, if they tried to capture him, Stephen could be killed.

Attica felt her stomach twist with fear. Someone would have to be sent to La Ferté-Bernard to warn Henry. She started to push up off the stool, to run for help, only to sink down again, her hands clutching her elbows to her sides, her body rocking back and forth with indecision. For she had no one to run to except Yvette—Yvette and her handsome but ineffectual husband, Gaspard. And Attica did not trust Yvette.

She couldn't say when the suspicion had arisen; she had barely even acknowledged it before now. But there had been too many slight inconsistencies, too many questions raised and not satisfactorily answered, too many conversations halted abruptly when Attica unexpectedly entered a room. All subtle, all perhaps explainable. But she couldn't risk Stephen's life by going to someone she could not trust.

Attica hugged herself, feeling her aloneness like a chill that went bone deep. She was so many miles from home, so far from family and friends, so far from everyone she knew and trusted. She had no one to whom she could turn.

On the bed beside her, Olivier de Harcourt groaned, moving restlessly to throw off the covers. Heat roiled up from his burning, bloated body, and she moved quickly to take up the cloth again and sponge him.

She worked for hours, bathing his hot body, coaxing him to take sips of herbal infusions, holding the basin as he retched and heaved. The long night wrapped itself around

them, dark and hushed and solemn. She worked until her
back ached and her arms trembled with exhaustion, and
still his fever climbed, still he screamed with pain until at
last he slipped into a deep faint from which she suspected
he would never awaken.

She sat back, her hands lying limply in her lap, palms up.

She didn't know how long she sat there, simply staring
into space. Gradually she became aware of some indefinable change in the atmosphere of the room. She shifted her
tired gaze to Olivier de Harcourt's still, lifeless body and
made a quick sign of the cross. She was alone.

A wind had kicked up, rattling the shutters at the window. She lifted her head, listening, but the castle lay still
and quiet around her. Glancing at the fat white candle with
its carefully spaced, incised red rings marking the hours,
she was surprised to see how far down it had burned. It
was almost three o'clock.

She let her breath ease out in a long sigh. So many hours.
So many hours had passed, and she was still no closer to
knowing how she was going to send a message to Stephen.

And it came to her in that moment that if there was no
one in the castle whom she could trust, then the only way
she could be certain that her warning would reach her
brother would be to take it herself.

No sooner did the thought occur to her than she dismissed it. La Ferté-Bernard lay some five to six days' ride
to the east, beyond Le Mans, in Maine; she could never
travel so far alone. The roads were infested with thieves
and outlaw bands of mercenaries; a woman traveling alone
risked not only robbery but rape, torture, death. She felt
her skin crawl at the very idea.

She thought, fleetingly, that she might make up some
ruse, something to tell Yvette so that she might lend Attica

a small party of knights to escort her on a visit to her brother. Except, if she was right about Yvette, if she knew something of Olivier de Harcourt's mission to Brittany, then she might very well guess at Attica's sudden interest in La Ferté-Bernard and refuse to let her go. Worse, she might take steps to make certain that Attica couldn't leave Châteauhaut at all.

Which meant that if she was going to leave, she would have to do it alone, and by stealth.

She thrust her splayed fingers through her disordered hair, tipping back her head as she combed the heavy, tangled mess from her face. So often as a child she had wished she'd been born male. Now she thought it again: *If only I were a man. . . .*

Her gaze fell on the Parisian courtier's clothes, folded in a neat pile beside his saddlebags on the high oak chest near the window. She rose stiffly from the stool, the thought still only half-formed in her mind. Lifting the fine velvet tunic, she shook it out and held it up against her. The Parisian had been a slim man, and tall, but no taller than she. His clothes would fit.

She lowered her arms, crushing the tunic to her in a fierce grip. *I can't do it,* she thought, practically trembling with a rising spiral of panic. *I can't. I can't travel so far all alone.*

And then she realized she had no need to travel the entire distance to La Ferté-Bernard. A day and a half to the east lay the cathedral city of Laval, on the road to Le Mans and La Ferté-Bernard. She had only to make it that far, to her uncle, the castellan of Château Laval. She could trust him to send her warning on to Stephen.

A day and a half. Some ten leagues. She told herself she could do that. She had no choice, really. To save Stephen's life, she thought, she would ride all the way to Jerusalem if she had to, no matter how afraid she was.

She shook out the woolen tunic, looking almost black now in the dimly flickering light of the dying torches. She would have to leave tonight. And she would need to hurry, for in another two hours the castle would begin to stir. Already she could sense that faint lifting of the atmosphere, that breathless hush of wonder as the world awaits a new day.

Ignoring the still, lifeless form in the bed, she crossed the room swiftly to where the scissors they'd used to cut up strips of cloth gleamed dully in the torchlight, beside the basin. Her hair had always been her one vanity; it was long and thick—the color of sunstruck honey, Stephen had once told her with a teasing smile. It made her ill to think of cutting it. But she knew she'd never make a convincing boy if she simply tried to shove the heavy mass up under a cap. Without giving herself time to think about it too much, she grabbed the shears and raised them to the nape of her neck.

Then she paused, letting the scissors go slack in her grasp. She would find it much easier, she realized, to bully her way out of the castle as my lady Attica d'Alérion, future wife of the heir to the viscomte de Salers, than as some unknown lad. Moreover, if she waited to cut her hair and change into Olivier's clothes until after she'd left Châteauhaut, then her disguise would serve two purposes. Not only would it help protect her from any men she might meet on the road, but it would also help to hide her from pursuit, should Yvette chance to guess where Attica was going, and why, and send men after her. Especially if she could find some way to dye her hair, to alter her appearance even further.

Walking swiftly back to the oak chest, she bundled the

scissors up in the courtier's clothes and thrust them into his saddlebags, along with a long strip of the cloth to bind her breasts. She couldn't risk going to her own room, she decided; she would have a hard enough time getting out of the castle without being seen.

It occurred to her, suddenly, that if she left the castle now, in the dead of night and without explanation, everyone would assume she fled her marriage to Fulk. She stiffened, hideously torn, but she could not see that she had any real choice. She had to do this, even if it meant destroying her own coming marriage and the valuable alliance it sealed.

At the thought, she knew a quiver of dismay mixed with a shameful spurt of hope she quickly squashed. The alliance between the houses of Salers and Alérion was too important to be ruptured by the headstrong actions of a mere female. Even if she were, in truth, attempting to flee her betrothal, she would simply be brought back. The marriage contract would endure.

It was a reassurance that, oddly, brought her no comfort.

Catching up the courtier's cloak, she swirled it around her shoulders. It seemed strange and vaguely alarming, wrapping herself in the cloak of a dead man. She pushed the thought from her head, seized the saddlebags, and slipped out the chamber door.

The keep of Châteauhaut was rectangular in form, with four round turrets at each corner. Built of brooding gray stone, it soared three stories above its ground-floor storerooms, with the guest chamber and chapel occupying the top story overlooking the central bailey.

Attica crept down the spiral stairs in the southeast turret, the fibers of the rope banister digging into her fingers as she felt her way through the gloom. She had just reached the second floor when a low, bulky form loomed out of the shadows and a voice said, "Attica? Where are you going?"

She recoiled so violently, she almost tripped on the steep stone steps. "Fulk," she said with a gasp. "You gave me a fright. What are you doing?"

"Visiting the garderobe."

The dim light from the fading torch in the nearest wall bracket showed her a faint line of embarrassment riding high on his cheeks. He wore only a cloak, thrown hastily over a pale fleshy expanse of naked chest and stomach. After that one quick glance, she was careful not to look at him again.

"You're going somewhere," he said, his voice high-pitched and accusatory. "You're *leaving*."

She clutched the betraying saddlebags against the front of the courtier's cloak, her mind racing. "It's my mother. She . . . she's been visiting her brother, only now she's taken ill. Very ill. A messenger came late last night to bring me word. They think she's dying."

Attica's voice quivered slightly on the lie, because lying was an offense to God and already tonight she'd had to be less than honest in her dealings with the dying Olivier de Harcourt. She could only hope Fulk would mistake her agitation as a sign of worry and grief.

He leaned into her, as if studying her closely. "Mother knows of this?"

Attica deliberately made her face go bland. She might not be a good liar, but before she came here, to the household of the viscomte de Salers, Attica had spent six long years at the courts of Aquitaine and Poitou. And at court, even a little girl learns quickly how to hide her feelings and maintain an outward appearance of serenity.

"Yes, of course Yvette knows," she said. "I wanted to set

out for Laval last night, when I first heard, only I couldn't leave your mother to deal with Olivier de Harcourt's illness alone."

"He is dead, then?"

"Yes."

Fulk plucked at the brocade edging of his cloak. "I don't understand why you can't wait until morning to leave."

"It will be dawn soon," she said, anxiously aware of the minutes slipping past.

A sleepy voice came to them from out of the darkness. "My lord? Is something wrong?"

Attica glanced beyond her betrothed, to where a tousle-haired page of about ten had appeared in the open doorway of Fulk's chamber.

Fulk turned. "No, Lady Attica but leaves on an early journey." He tugged his cloak closer against the morning chill. "You will go with her and lend her whatever assistance she requires in her preparations."

"Oh, but I don't—" Attica broke off as she realized, suddenly, that she didn't need to make this journey quite alone after all. She said to the page, "Run ahead of me, please, and awaken my groom, Walter Brie. Tell him to meet me in the stables."

"Yes, my lady."

She caught the boy's shoulder as he rushed past. "Be careful to awaken Walter Brie and no other, do you hear?"

The boy ducked his head, murmured, "Yes, my lady," and disappeared down the winding steps. The wind gusted up, sending an icy draft whistling down the turret. The sputtering torch flickered and almost went out; Fulk sneezed.

"Now look what you've done," he said, his voice turning

back into a whine. "You've made me catch a cold, standing here. Mother won't like that."

"Then you'd best hurry back to bed."

She tarried long enough to hear his chamber door shut with a snap. Then she turned, her feet flying down the stairs. It would be dawn soon.

And she hadn't even made it out of the castle.

Attica paused with one hand splayed against the glossy warmth of the gelding's flank, her head tilted anxiously as she strained to catch any distant sound, afraid Fulk had changed his mind and gone to his mother anyway.

Beyond the half-opened door of the stables, the ward of Châteauhaut-sur-Vilaine lay bleak and empty in the thin, ghostly light of the dying night. From here, the massive new stone keep seemed no more than a black hulk rising menacingly above the smaller shadows of the wooden buildings that hugged the curtain wall—the bakery and alehouse, the armory and blacksmith's and kitchens, all shuttered and quiet now in sleep. She heard only the restless movement of a horse in its stall and the rustle and squeak of mice in the hay.

Turning, she grasped her saddle with both hands and swung it up onto the gelding's back. The chestnut snorted, its shod hooves clattering and ringing on the cobblestones as it danced away. She leapt to lay a restraining hand on its white-blazed nose. "Easy boy," she whispered, stroking, nuzzling. "Easy, Chantilly. *Please.*"

She staggered as Chantilly butted her with its head, lipped her fingers, then swung back to drop its nose into the pail of oats she had brought to keep it quiet. Still caressing the horse's satiny withers, she stooped to reach with her free hand for the girth. She had just thrust the strap home when she heard the sound of footsteps approaching in the ward and the low murmur of Walter's voice.

"If this is a hoax, boy," grumbled Walter, pushing the stable door wide with one out-thrust hand, "the lady Attica d'Alérion might forgive you, but as for me, I'll nail your hide to the—" He broke off, his step faltering as the shaft of faint light cutting through the open doorway fell upon Attica. *"My lady."*

"Well come, Walter," she said, a smile of relief trembling on her lips at the sight of his familiar craggy face and solidly reliable form. A Norman like herself, Walter Brie had served Attica since she'd been a child barely old enough to walk and he a young man in his twenties. It had been Walter Brie who lifted Attica up onto the back of her first pony, Walter who taught her to handle a dagger as well as any boy, Walter who dried the tears on her cheeks as he rode beside her the day she was sent away from Normandy, a lonely girl of twelve, to serve in the courts of the Langue d'oc.

For a long, intense moment, Walter's gaze held hers. She turned to put her hand on the shoulder of the shivering page and give him a warm smile. "You can run back to bed now. Thank you."

"Yon young lad might believe this tale you've spun," said Walter, standing with his legs spread wide, his arms crossed at his chest as he watched the page dash across the bailey, "but you'll never convince me Lady Blanche is dying, or that you'd be setting out at dawn with none but me even if she was." He turned to regard her with narrowed eyes and an impassive face. "Do you flee your betrothal, then?"

"No." Attica reached to buckle the courtier's leather

bags to her saddle. "We go to Laval, but not, I admit, to see my mother." She reached for the bridle. "It's Stephen. There's treachery afoot, and I'm afraid he's in danger."

Walter turned to lead his own gray out of a nearby stall. "Ah. And we're riding to his rescue, is that it?"

Attica went to help Walter saddle the gray, smiling as her gaze met his over the horse's broad back. "That's it. I'll explain the rest later, after we've left the castle."

Grunting, he gave her a boost into her saddle and scrambled up onto his own palfrey.

They crossed to the gatehouse slowly, the clomp of their horses' hooves on the cobbles echoing alarmingly in the empty ward. In the kennels behind them, a dog began to bark, then another. Attica held her reins in a tight, sweaty grip and forgot to breathe.

Beside the open door to the guardroom, a torch fitted to the wall flared and danced in the night breeze, the hissing flame filling the stone archway with a somber glow. At the far end of the passage, the castle's great iron-bound wooden gates stood dark and locked fast against them.

"You, there," called Walter, reining in his palfrey. "Porter!"

A tall, lanky man-at-arms appeared at the entrance to the guardroom, his blond hair rumpled, his jerkin awry. "Who goes there?" he demanded, his thin, bony face closed and suspicious.

Attica thrust her horse forward into the light. She might be inwardly quaking with fear, but all those years of court training had taught her how to keep her features composed, whatever the circumstances. "Mother of God, man," she said with just the right note of imperiousness. "Do you not recognize me?"

The man peered up at her, his pale eyes widening in astonishment. "My lady?"

"Why do you stand there gawking?" she demanded as the gelding sidled nervously in the narrow archway, its big hooves clattering as he danced near enough to the man-at-arms to make him step back warily. "Open the gate and be quick about it."

"But my lady—"

"You dare?" said Attica, doing her best to assume the expression of the comtesse d'Alérion, who had a way of staring down her nose at servants as if they were insects or patches of slime. "You dare to say me nay?"

He didn't, of course. No humble man-at-arms would disobey a direct order given him by the woman betrothed to the future viscomte de Salers. The guard gulped and sputtered, "Never, my lady," and tripped over his own feet in his haste to unbar the gates.

The screech of the great beams being drawn drove away all thought. She glanced nervously over her shoulder and saw, across the open space of the ward, a light show suddenly through a window slit on the second floor of the keep.

The frightened hiss of her quickly indrawn breath brought Walter's head around. She saw his gaze fix on the flickering light, his jaw tighten. Then the iron-bound gate swung slowly inward, and Attica urged her horse forward.

The quick tramp of the gelding's hooves rang hollowly on the wooden drawbridge before being muffled by the dust of the road. Attica drew in a deep breath of air scented with the fragrance of ripening fields and dew-dampened earth. She had never ridden at night like this. As she emerged from the lee of the walls, the full force of the wind slapped into her, whipping loose strands of hair about her face. She hugged the dead man's cloak tighter.

From where Châteauhaut stood, high on the rocky crest

of its hill, the river valley below seemed only a distant mosaic of pale meadows and black clumps of trees shrouded in star-studded darkness. Without a moon, the steep, rocky track downward would be treacherous. But she waited only until Walter drew abreast of her before she dug her heels into the chestnut's sides and sent her horse away at a canter.

She kept listening for a shout of alarm behind her, kept waiting, tensely, to hear the crash of the gates being thrown open again, the bustle of men, hurrying in pursuit. She leaned low over the chestnut's withers, urging it on, faster, faster. Not until they reached the stand of trees growing partway down the hill, out of bowshot of the walls, did she hesitate long enough to throw a quick glance back at the castle.

But by then, even the jagged outline of the walls had been swallowed up by the night.

CHAPTER
TWO

The morning mist crept up from the marshy banks of the river to spread like a thick, sodden blanket over the fields. It brought with it an odd hush, oppressive and unnatural.

Without the sun, the colors of the glade seemed muted and blurred, the pale gray-green of grass and leaf running into the gray-brown of the earth. The only trace of brilliance came from the crackling flames of the burning cottages, tingeing the mist with an orange glow that showed the crumpled, bloody form of a dog lying dead and, beyond that, the lifeless limbs of a woman sprawled in an ungainly tableau of violation.

The knight stood motionless, the reins of his graceful black Arab held loosely in one gloved hand. He wore a leather broigne, but no hauberk or helm, for on this day his mission was one that required speed and intelligence, not arms. Yet he was no stranger to the carnage of the battlefield or the horrors of a sacked town. The flickering flames shone over a sun-darkened, powerfully boned face devoid of all emotion. Only for one brief instant did his nostrils flare as he sucked in a deep breath and smelled the fecund scent of tilled earth, marred by the stink of burning wet timber and freshly spilled blood.

This had been a small village of no more than half a dozen

21

mean dwellings. It had yielded to its attackers—what? A few pigs and cows? A cartful of grain? An iron cooking pot or two? The mist roiled up, so heavy now, he could feel it against his face. Damion de Jarnac's mouth tightened into a hard line and he turned away, gathering his reins. "We can do nothing here," he said, swinging into the saddle.

Beside him, the lithe, light-haired boy who served as his squire made no move to mount. "Shouldn't we bury them?" Sergei asked, his dark, exotic eyes troubled as he glanced around the clearing. "Or at least cover them up?"

Damion shook his head. "I need to get to La Ferté-Bernard. If this conference goes badly, you'll be seeing this scene repeated a hundred times over, boy. From Normandy to Aquitaine."

Still Sergei hesitated, his brooding gaze fixed on the scattered dead. It wasn't an army that had descended on this village, of course. Only a small band of *routiers*—unemployed mercenaries. But Philip and Henry both filled out their armies with mercenaries, and in war, it was usually the villages that burned. Not the castles.

"Sergei," said Damion in the calm, flat voice that all who served under him knew better than to ignore.

The boy scrambled up onto his bay palfrey. But before reaching for the leads of their spare horses, he paused long enough to make a quick sign of the cross.

Damion pursed his lips and blew out a short, exasperated breath. "All right. There's an abbey, not far out of our way. The village probably belongs to it. We can stop and tell the monks what has happened."

Sergei nodded and kicked his horse forward, although his face remained troubled and strained long after they had left the ruined village behind.

Damion spurred his horse on ahead, his own thoughts

already far away from the devastated clearing. At the age of twenty-seven, he had dealt in death and destruction for many years. Too many years spent as a knight-errant, driven by the demons of betrayal and guilt across the battlefields of Europe and beyond. Once, as a boy, he had cherished the kinds of dreams typical of younger sons, dreams of founding a dynasty on land of his own. Dreams that had been shattered in one dreadful night of lightning-split skies and hideous revelations and blood-drenched death.

Yet from the ruins of that boy's visions had emerged a man's ambitions and a man's hunger, not simply for land but for great titles and vast power, aspirations no longer noble and pure but cold and ruthless and utterly determined. Only a king could give Damion the kind of future he had resolved to make his, and so he had attached himself to the service of the most powerful king in Christendom, Henry II, King of England, Duke of Normandy, and lord of more French lands than the King of France himself.

In Henry's service, Damion had undertaken a dangerous four-month mission that had led him from Brittany to the farthest reaches of Ireland. He had learned the names of many of the powerful nobles now poised to join the revolt against Henry, and he had discovered some disturbing indications of just how far the king's youngest son, John, had been pulled into the conspiracy. Damion had even learned something—although not as much as he would wish—of the strange musical code Philip of France was using to communicate with the conspirators.

Now, on his way back to Henry, Damion was acutely conscious of the shortage of time, for the conference at La Ferté-Bernard would be beginning soon. There, Henry would be sitting down to talk peace with a sly French king allied to Henry's own proud, angry son, Richard. And if

Damion didn't reach Henry's side in time, the Old King would be in for some nasty surprises.

But Damion had every intention of reaching La Ferté-Bernard in time. And then he would collect the reward Henry had promised him: the hand of the king's ward, a thirteen-year-old heiress named Rosamund, who would make her future husband the Earl of Carlyle.

Damion had seen Rosamund once. He had a faint memory of a petitely pretty, haughty little girl with blond hair and blue eyes. But it was his prospective bride's lands and titles, not her person, that attracted him. These were the things every knight-errant dreamed of, fought for, killed for: a title and land of his own.

Soon, Damion thought. Soon, he would have both.

The tracks of the *routiers* followed the river eastward, along a narrow path that probably led to some other hapless, isolated village. Damion headed southeast, toward the Abbey of Saint-Sevin, a Benedictine monastery nestled in a green valley surrounded by gently undulating hills densely wooded with oak and scattered chestnut and beech.

The sun rose higher in the sky, burning off the mist and driving away the chill that had kept Sergei wrapped in his cloak. Even with the detour to the abbey, Damion calculated, he ought to reach Loiron by nightfall. Another hard day's ride would see them to Vaiges, then Le Mans, and he'd be in La Ferté-Bernard by Wednesday. The conference—

The voice of an unseen man shouting roughly in anger somewhere up ahead shattered the calm and brought Damion to instant, taut attention.

The woods grew thickly here, the undergrown, taller oaks and chestnuts tangled on either side of the steep, winding track with clumps of flowering hawthorn as impenetrable as a hedge. As Damion reined in, he heard the unmistakable hiss of a crossbow bolt, followed by the scream of a horse in pain.

"Christ." Whirling, he yanked his kite-shaped shield and lance from the squire. "Guard my back," he shouted to Sergei. Then he swung around again long enough to add, "But don't do anything stupid, do you hear?" before he spurred the Arab forward.

The stallion was too light for a proper warhorse, but Damion wore no armor and he was glad of the Arab's fleet-footed intelligence and unswerving courage. He galloped up the slope, the stallion's dainty hooves almost soundless in the deep, spongy humus of the forest track.

At the crest of the hill the undergrowth thinned. From there Damion could look down on a small clearing where some twelve to fifteen raggedly dressed *routiers* formed a shifting circle around a slim, dark-haired youth mounted on a showy, white-blazed chestnut palfrey.

The *routiers* had found a rich young bird for their plucking this time, Damion thought, his eyes narrowing at the sight of the lad's green wool tunic, his surcoat of deep blue velvet trimmed with thick green braid, the jewel that gleamed from the pommel of the short dagger he held clutched in his hand. A rich young bird indeed, and an easy mark, too, left so insufficiently guarded by his family, who should have known better.

Only one other horse stood nearby, a gray, riderless and quivering, its reins caught beneath a man who lay face-down and unmoving in the grass at the side of the road, a crossbow bolt fletched with peacock feathers sticking out of his blood-soaked back. More blood flowed freely from a deep slash on the gray's withers. As Damion watched, one of the *routiers* reached for the gray's reins. The horse spun

about, ears pinned flat to its poll, hooves flashing out as it
reared up, screaming. The *routier* jumped back.

"Stand out of our way and let us pass," said the youth,
his voice husky but surprisingly calm. Yet the chestnut
must sense its rider's well-hidden fear, Damion thought as
he watched the way it danced and sidled nervously, its
powerfully muscled hindquarters swinging in an arc that
kept the *routiers*, on foot and armed mainly with cudgels
and coutels, at a safe distance.

"*Merde*, it's a haughty little lordling we have here, isn't
it?" said one of the men, a thickset, stubbly-faced man
with one ear missing. "Didn't even say please."

The other men laughed.

"I'd say someone needs to teach his lordship here
some manners, don't you think?" said another, and they all
laughed again.

Only one man stood apart, unamused: an archer, who
calmly fitted another bolt and lifted his bow.

"*A moi, de Jarnac,*" shouted Damion, touching his spurs
to the Arab's flanks. It was his battle cry, and he shouted
it now on the off chance that the *routiers* might think he
had a troop of men thundering over the hill behind him—
rather than just one overly sensitive, orphaned squire, late
of Byzantium and Kiev.

Damion grinned at the thought, the smile freezing into
grim determination as he saw the archer swing around. He
was a tall, black-bearded man, better dressed than his companions, his crossbow well made and maintained. Damion's
long lance caught him square in the chest, the force of the
Arab's charge driving the point clean through the man's
body and breaking the shaft.

Damion abandoned it. Jerking his sword from its scabbard, he wheeled toward the pack of *routiers*. "Ride, lad,"

Damion shouted to the white-faced youth on the chestnut. "Get out of here."

Damion had no time to see if the youth did what he was told. The *routiers* swarmed around the Arab, a horde of snarling, spitting, cursing, angry men. Raising his sword high, Damion brought it down, again and again. A man screamed and stumbled away, clutching a bloody sleeve; another crumpled. Damion swung back his blade, aiming for an exposed throat—and saw a cudgel coming at him from the left. *Christ*, he thought, instinctively raising his shield; what he wouldn't give for his armor right now.

Hardly had the thought crossed his mind than he felt the bite of a blade sinking into his right thigh. With a snarl, Damion caught the descending cudgel blow on his shield and spun the Arab on its hocks. He saw the man who had slashed at him with a coutel raise the blade again, then let out a startled gurgle as a jeweled dagger flew through the air to imbed itself in the man's thick neck at the vulnerable point between helmet and jerkin. His eyes already glazing with death, the man went down beneath the charging weight and sharp hooves of the unknown lad's big chestnut.

Damion flung back his head, his gaze meeting the youth's wide-eyed stare. So the boy hadn't run away, Damion thought, and flashed him a quick grin.

Sergei whooped, "They're leaving!"

Limping and dripping blood, the *routiers* melted into the forest. They abandoned behind them four of their kind, lying dead or dying in the glade. Damion watched long enough to be certain they were actually leaving, then swung his head to look again at the white-faced youth who had refused to run when given the chance.

The lad's skin shone pale and clammy with shock, and he was panting, his chest rising and falling visibly with each quickly indrawn breath. But his head was up, his eyes clear. "You saved my life," he said to Damion. "I don't know how to thank you." Urging his horse forward, he held out his hand. "I am . . ." The hesitation was brief, but there. ". . . Atticus."

Damion tossed his shield to Sergei. "Go get my lance point out of that damned archer," he told the squire, and shifted his bloody sword to his left hand so he could return the lad's salute. "Damion de Jarnac."

The hand Damion took felt surprisingly soft and fragile beneath its fine glove, and it trembled noticeably in his grip when Damion said his name. The lad was still very young, Damion decided, looking at him again. He might sit uncommonly tall in the saddle, but his undeveloped shoulders and smooth face betrayed his youth, as did his guilelessly wide brown eyes, lashed thick like a girl's. His mouth was almost feminine, too. If it weren't for his strong, cleft chin, the lad would look hopelessly effete.

Damion's gaze fell to the thick gold chain that hung around the youth's neck and the jewels that studded his belt. Lordling, indeed. Only the lad's hair struck an odd note. A dull, lifeless black, it hung raggedly against his collar, as if it had recently been inexpertly cut.

And dyed.

At any other time, Damion might have been intrigued. But at the moment, all his thoughts were on the conference at La Ferté-Bernard. *Christ.* He couldn't afford this second delay. Dismounting, he wiped his blade on the ragged tunic of one of the dead *routiers* and slipped the sword back into its scabbard. He was tying a torn strip of cloth around his bleeding leg when, out of the corner of his eye, he saw the lad Atticus slide off his horse and sink to his knees beside his fallen companion.

"Walter," the youth whispered, and Damion was surprised to hear his voice crack with emotion.

Damion gathered the Arab's reins.

The youth reached out a trembling hand to touch the bolt protruding from the groom's shoulder, then drew back when the man unexpectedly groaned.

Damion heard the groan and paused. He reached for his stirrup, stopped again, and threw an exasperated glance at Sergei, who had just ridden up. "I suppose you think I ought to help him, don't you?"

Sergei only stared back, his eyes dark and expectant.

"This isn't a verse out of some troubadour's maudlin romance," said Damion tersely. "And I am not a fool knight in shining armor with nothing better to do than gallop around the countryside succoring the weak and unfortunate, and rescuing damsels and lordlings in distress. I am on a mission for a *king*. Everything I've worked for my entire life depends on its success."

Sergei said nothing.

"Sweet Infant Jesus." Damion slammed his open palm against the high cantle of his saddle and swung back toward the clearing. "At this rate, it'll be Midsummer's Eve before I get to La Ferté-Bernard."

I will not be sick, Attica told herself as she knelt in the grass beside Walter Brie's big, bloodied body. *I will not.*

The smell of blood hung thick in the air. Beside her lay a cudgel, lost in the battle, its thick end dark with old stains. She forced herself to ignore it, the same way she ignored the hacked and bloodied bodies of the *routiers* that lay sprawled about the trampled grass of what had once been a gentle glade. It was not the blood that sickened her, or even the sight of death, but the taste of her own fear, raw in her throat.

She rested her hand on Walter's broad, familiar shoulder. He felt so warm and solid beneath her touch, she could not believe he might die. She did not know what to do. She should know, she thought vaguely. She had brought him to this. Somehow, she was going to have to find someone to take care of him and continue on her way alone. But her mind felt numb. She could not think.

A shadow darkened the grass beside her, and she looked up to find herself staring into Damion de Jarnac's vivid green eyes and harshly planed face. *Mother of God*, she thought. *Damion de Jarnac . . .*

Even without a hauberk or helm, this big, dark-haired, brutally powerful man could never be mistaken for anything as peaceful and nonthreatening as a cleric or merchant. He stood well above average height, a battle-hardened knight with broad shoulders and leanly muscled limbs. Years spent beneath the Eastern sun had etched his features sharp and left him with skin burned as dark as any Saracen's.

He had won his spurs unusually young, they said, in the blood-soaked sands of the Syrian desert. The younger son of a powerful Poitou nobleman, he had left France for the Holy Land at the age of thirteen, cut off from his family after a night of such dark and terrible happenings that it was spoken of only in hushed tones and with furtive, sideways glances. They said his merciless ruthlessness in battle was matched only by his brilliance and cunning, so that in Outremer, he had become known as El Sa'eeka—Deathlightning. Some said the Saracens' name had inspired his device—a black shield emblazoned only with a jagged bolt of fiery lightning. But others said he had adopted the shield before, in memory of the storm that had ripped open the skies the night he killed his own brother.

Attica stared up into his darkly handsome face and

knew a fear that hollowed out her belly and robbed her of her breath. He may have saved her from the *routiers*, but Damion de Jarnac was little better than a mercenary and brigand himself. A knight-errant, he wandered the battle-fields and tournaments of Europe and Outremer, living off ransoms and plunder. He was a law unto himself, his sword for sale to the highest bidder. And in his case, the bids were always high, for a man like this was far more dangerous than any band of simple *routiers*.

She stared up at him, speechless, and saw his dark brows lower in a frown. She had the oddest impression that the encounter with the *routiers* hadn't so much endangered his life as inconvenienced him—*annoyed* him, even. And now she was delaying him even longer.

"Here, let me look at your man," he said, his manner brisk and impatient. He sank to his haunches beside her and stripped off his gloves. She found his nearness so intimidating, it was all she could do to keep from drawing back. Yet his powerful, strongly boned hands were unexpectedly gentle as he subjected Walter to a brief, professional assessment.

"He is your groom?" de Jarnac asked, casually wiping his bloodied hands on the grass.

Attica nodded. "Will he live?"

The knight shrugged and pulled on his gloves again. "He might. But the bolt has gone deep. Better to leave it in him now and tie him to his horse while he's still in a faint. There's an abbey just up the road. They'll know what to do with him."

De Jarnac stood in one lithe, athletic motion and turned away, as if he had already dismissed her from his mind. She thought about being left here, in this meadow full of dead *routiers*, to cope with Walter Brie by herself. She thought about the *routiers* coming back—or about others like them waiting on the road ahead. She thought about what had been done to the women of that burned village. And she realized suddenly that no matter how sinister Damion de Jarnac's reputation or how disconcerting she might find him, his presence was infinitely preferable to his absence.

She bounded to her feet. "Monsieur—"

At the sound of her voice, his head swiveled. His gaze focused on her slowly, as if he had been thinking of something else and only now remembered her presence. "Yes?"

"I was wondering if—if you go beyond the abbey? To Laval, or perhaps Le Mans? And if so, if I might ride with you?"

She saw his eyes narrow as he studied her. Something in his expression altered, and she knew a swift stab of panic. If he suspected the truth—

"How old are you?" he demanded suddenly.

She stared at him. "Wh-what?"

"I said, how old are you?"

She hesitated an instant too long. "Sixteen," she said, and knew it for a mistake.

She did not like the light that glinted in the depths of his fierce green eyes. "Liar," he said, his lips curling into something that was not a smile.

It *had* been a lie, of course, only not in the way de Jarnac thought. Attica was nineteen.

"Fifteen," she amended.

The knight's big hand cupped her chin, jerking it up to the sun. He studied her face in the light, and she trembled. "Huh. Fourteen is more like it."

She wasn't about to dispute it. She stood, trying desperately to remain motionless within his grip and terrified of what he might see. But Stephen had once told her that most people see only what they expect to see. It seemed true. De Jarnac stared at her a moment longer, then shook her hard enough to rattle her teeth. "I don't like to be lied to, little lordling. Remember that." He let her go.

He swung away to catch Walter Brie's horse. The gray jerked its head, its flaring nostrils flecked with foam and blood, its eyes wild with fear and pain. "Easy, boy," de Jarnac crooned in a voice so calm and soothing, Attica could only stare. The gelding snorted but stood still while the knight ran a practiced hand down its neck and withers. Attica had the sensation, once again, that she had been dismissed.

She walked to stand beside him. "May I ride with you, then?"

He kept his attention centered on the horse. "I'll see you as far as the abbey. Not beyond."

She felt her throat close with disappointment and a new upsurge of fear. "You mean, you're not going any farther?"

"No. Only that you're not going with me."

Tired of talking to the knight's broad back, she went around to the other side of the horse so that she could look at him over the gelding's gray withers. "Why not?"

This time, de Jarnac met her gaze squarely. "I'm in a hurry."

"I won't slow you down. I promise."

"Yes, you will."

"I'll pay you."

As soon as the words were out, Attica knew they were a mistake. She saw his jaw tighten, saw the dangerous light that leapt again into his eyes. He straightened, his inspection of the horse finished. "I have no need of your money."

All she could do now was push ahead. "I'll give you this"—she lifted the heavy gold chain from around her neck—"if you'll agree to act as my escort."

He didn't even bother to look at the chain. "Sorry. Not interested." He ran his hand one last time down the gelding's sweat-stained neck. "The gray's not mortally injured, but it's lost a lot of blood and is dangerously skittish besides. I think we'd best put your man on one of my horses."

"Then what of this?" Attica asked in desperation, yanking the ring from her thumb and holding it out to him.

Fire shimmered in the palm of her hand. Made of gold in the shape of an eaglet and studded with pearls and sapphires, the ring was the most precious thing she owned. Not because of its monetary value—although that was considerable—but because Stephen had given it to her. It was an exact replica of the ring their father, the comte d'Alérion, had given his only son on the day of his knighting. Stephen had had his own ring copied as a gift for Attica at the time of her betrothal. It cost her a pang even to think of giving it up, but she held it out determinedly.

"I told you," said de Jarnac, "I don't want—" He broke off, his gaze narrowing as he moved suddenly to pluck the ring from her outstretched hand. He stared at the ring for a long moment, then lifted his frighteningly intense gaze to Attica's face. She could not even begin to guess at his thoughts. "You're a d'Alérion," he said. It was not a question.

She just managed to swallow her surprise. She hadn't expected him to recognize the ring. "Yes."

An unpleasant smile curled the knight's hard mouth. "The comte d'Alérion has but one son. And you, my fine young friend, are not he."

"I . . ." Attica swallowed. "I am the comte's natural son."

De Jarnac tilted his head. "Indeed?" His gaze traveled significantly over her fine clothing. "Your father appears to be unusually generous with his bastards."

"He . . . he loved my mother very much," said Attica, almost choking at the thought of what the comtesse d'Alérion would say if she could hear her daughter now. She wondered which would insult Blanche the most—the suggestion that she had given birth to a natural child or the idea that there existed even a hint of affection in her union to Robert d'Alérion.

"I see," said de Jarnac, and Attica was afraid he saw far too much. "And exactly why, M. le Batard d'Alérion, are you so anxious to reach Laval?"

Attica cast about wildly for some probable explanation. The problem with always priding yourself on your truthfulness, she thought in despair, is that when you really, truly, do need to lie, you're not very good at it. "My uncle," she said finally, borrowing a portion of the tale she had told Fulk. "He is dying. We have always been quite close, so he is asking for me now."

"Oh?" De Jarnac crossed his arms over his chest. She had the sudden ridiculous sensation that he was enjoying himself. "And exactly who is your uncle?"

Too late, she realized she should have left her uncle out of it. But then, if de Jarnac did agree to escort her, he would find out who her uncle was in any case when they reached Laval. "He is the castellan of Laval," she said, making up her mind to tell the truth.

It was another mistake. De Jarnac's gaze locked on hers. "Renouf Blissot is your *uncle*?" He began to advance on her with slow, menacing steps. "Are you telling me your mother was a Blissot? That Richard d'Alérion got one of his bastards on a woman from the same family as his own comtesse?"

Attica almost groaned out loud. Who would have dreamt,

she thought despairingly as she retreated before de Jarnac's steady advance, that the man would know so much about her family? She cleared her throat and said in a wooden voice, "My mother also is a bastard."

If she didn't stop soon, Attica thought with a nervous inner bubble of amusement that she suspected verged on hysteria, she was going to end up bastardizing her entire family. But to her relief, the statement at least stopped him in his tracks.

"Indeed?" he said, his brows rising. "Another bastard. Also acknowledged, apparently, if your uncle Renouf not only recognizes the connection but holds you in such esteem that he sends for you from his deathbed."

Attica eyed the knight suspiciously. There was no doubt that he was amused. She could see the glint of quiet laughter in his eyes—along with something else that was not laughter at all. "My mother and her half brother were very close as children," Attica said cautiously.

"What a loving, congenial family you have, lordling. You are fortunate."

For some reason she could not have explained, Attica felt suddenly, irrationally annoyed. "Does this mean you will escort me to Laval?"

Damion de Jarnac bounced Attica's ring up and down in the palm of his bloodstained glove, then closed his fist around it. "Yes. I believe I shall."

She expected to feel relieved. She should have felt relieved. Instead, she had the most sinking sensation that she had just made a terrible mistake.

CHAPTER
THREE

The monk from Pierreforte l'abbaye had wanted to paint the ceiling of her bed with scenes from the martyrdom of Saint Agatha. *Imagine*, thought Yvette with a lazy yawn, *having to wake up every morning to the sight of a defiled virgin having her breasts cut off.*

She let her gaze travel lovingly over the woodland scene of flowers and trees and prancing unicorns that now decorated the great oak panel over her head. *Beautiful.* With another yawn, Yvette Beringer, viscomtesse de Salers, stretched her arms up over her head and smiled. *Next*, she thought, *I'll have him paint the—*

A frigid gust of morning air rushed in as the bed's brocade hangings flew open with a harsh squeal. Yvette yelped and swung about. "Odette, you fool," she began, but broke off at the sight of the handsome face and Viking-like proportions of her husband.

Gaspard Beringer, viscomte de Salers, stood well over six feet tall, a great, strapping man with long, elegantly formed limbs and an awesome physique. Pale blond hair framed a face of exquisitely shaped bones, a wide brow, glowing blue eyes, and sensitively formed lips: the personification of beauty in hose and tunic.

Yvette smiled as a warm tingle coursed through her the

way it always did at the sight of this gorgeous man. Being so plain herself, she had a special weakness for beauty, and she never tired of looking at her husband. "Gaspard," she said, yawning again. "You are making me cold."

"But, Yvette—" Gaspard opened and closed his lovely mouth in distress. "She's gone!"

With a sigh born of experience, Yvette sat up and yanked her chemise from beneath her pillow. "Who is gone?" She tugged the fine linen over her head and goose-bumped naked shoulders. "Your goshawk? Your favorite hunting bitch? That new mare you bought last week?"

"No." Gaspard let go of the curtains and spun away to where a ewer of wine stood warming on the exquisitely inlaid and carved table Yvette kept beside the hearth. "Attica," he said over his shoulder as he hunted for a cup. "Attica is gone."

"What?" Yvette froze for an instant, then scrambled to thrust her plump white legs over the edge of the big bed and push upright with a grunt. "What do you mean, Attica is gone? Gone for a walk? Gone riding? Gone—"

"I mean, she's simply gone." Gaspard swung around to point the hand holding the ewer at her. "I told you she'd never agree to this betrothal. Didn't I tell you?"

"Don't be ridiculous." Yvette jerked the ewer from his slack grip. "She *has* agreed to this betrothal. And Attica d'Alérion is too determinedly honorable, too sensible of her duty to her family to ever do such a thing as flee her betrothal to Fulk."

"Then where has she gone, you tell me that? Because gone she has." He regained possession of the ewer and poured himself a drink. "I heard it first from one of the pages, and then the guard at the gate confirmed it. She rode out of here before dawn, accompanied only by that Norman groom of hers."

Throwing a cloak around her shoulders, Yvette walked, silent and thoughtful, to stand at the open window, her gaze on the turmoil of activity in the bailey below. Suddenly her hand tightened on the edge of the window frame, her head coming round to stare at Gaspard over her shoulder. "That Parisian courtier—Olivier de Harcourt—does he still live?"

"No. The servants found him dead this morning."

Yvette chewed her lower lip. "I wonder . . ." Banging the window against the wall, she turned to where her women waited, their eyes hooded and wary, their arms full of silken and velvet gowns for her to choose. "Well, don't just stand there, you fool women," Yvette snapped, waving her arms at them. "Help me get dressed. And have that guard and page sent to me."

As the women rushed to do her bidding, Yvette glanced up to find her husband standing gape-mouthed. "Gaspard, why are you still here? Send for that page and guard. Now. And when I'm through with them, I want to see Fulk."

Gaspard Beringer might be the viscomte de Salers, but he knew the limitations of his own intellect, and there had never been any doubt where the real power in their marriage lay.

He hurried to do his wife's bidding.

An hour later, the viscomtesse de Salers, now splendidly attired in gold silk trimmed with crimson velvet, settled back in the wide, carved chair reserved exclusively for her use and subjected her son to a coldly critical stare.

She noted with satisfaction that he had dressed for his interview with her in gold velvet and crimson brocade, her own favorite colors. Some people might think the flamboyant combination had the effect of making the boy look like an overdressed (and overfed) field mouse. Fulk's mother decided he looked as impressive as could be expected, given the circumstances. She'd often thought it sadly ironic that the only things Gaspard Beringer's son had inherited from his gorgeous father were the traits one couldn't see: a weak will and an addled intellect. Poor Fulk had come out of her womb looking every bit as plump, brown, and pudding-faced as Yvette herself.

As if aware of the unpleasant train of his mother's thoughts, the boy began to fidget. "Stand still," she barked.

Fulk froze.

Yvette leaned forward in her chair. "One of the pages tells me you knew Attica left the castle this morning. Why did you not come at once to tell me?"

Fulk opened his mouth, closed it, then opened it again in a movement reminiscent of his father. Only, without Gaspard's beautiful mouth, the same habit in Fulk had the unfortunate effect of making the boy look like a beached fish.

"Fulk."

He sucked in a gasp of courage and blurted out, "She said you knew!"

"I knew? She said I knew. And you believed her?"

Fulk's face went so white, she could have counted every freckle on his pug nose. He wisely kept his mouth shut and hung his head.

"You believed her," said Yvette again. "You actually believed that I would let your betrothed set out for Laval before daybreak and accompanied only by one groom? *God's death, Fulk; where was your head?"* Grasping the carved arms of her chair, Yvette heaved herself onto her feet with such uncharacteristic vigor that the boy went scuttling backward in alarm. She whirled away from him. "*Idiots.* I am surrounded by idiots."

"But why would she lie?" Fulk asked in a small voice.

Yvette swung to face him again and forced herself to take a deep, calming breath. "I understand you visited her while she was tending Olivier de Harcourt."

Fulk's small, already protuberant eyes bugged out even further in alarm. "I didn't get close to him, I promise. I was very careful."

Yvette waved one hand through the air. "Never mind that now. Did he say anything while you were there?"

"No. He was in a faint."

Yvette pressed her lips together in disappointment. A tense silence descended on the chamber, during which the steady snap and crack of a whip, punctuated by a man's screams, could be heard wafting through the window on a balmy breeze.

Fulk glanced nervously toward the bailey. "What's that noise?"

"The guard at the gate was negligent," said Yvette, her concentration devoted to picking a speck of lint off the crimson velvet sleeve of her kirtle. "He is being punished." She lifted her gaze to her son again. "This is important, Fulk: Did Attica tell you anything the courtier might have said?"

Fulk shook his head vigorously from side to side. "No, nothing. Although Judith said he'd been asking for a breviary." Fulk's lip curled in disdain; he didn't think much of his pretty little cousin. "The silly girl tried to give him *her* breviary, but he obviously wanted his own. I saw it in his saddlebags."

Yvette stared at her son. "De Harcourt had a breviary?"

"Yes, although it was only a small, plain thing," said

Fulk, obviously disappointed. "I'd have expected it to be something magnificent, but it had only a simple green leather binding and almost no gilt."

Yvette's gaze flew to meet Gaspard's, but it was Gaspard who said, his voice hushed, "A Sainte-Foy breviary."

Yvette nodded. "Send someone to the guest chamber. I want all Olivier de Harcourt's things brought here to me."

A new silence descended on the room as they waited for Gaspard to return, a silence undisturbed this time by the screams of the guard, who had presumably finished receiving his chastisement and been carried away. Yvette was relieved; his screams had given her a headache.

Gaspard was back in a moment, his handsome face slack with concern. "They're gone—his clothes, his saddlebags, everything. The servants searched everywhere."

Yvette's hand closed into a tight, angry fist. "She's taken them."

"But why would she take de Harcourt's clothes?" asked Fulk, his head swiveling back and forth from his mother to his father to his mother again.

Yvette shook her head. "She must have known he was carrying something, but she wasn't certain exactly where it was hidden, so she took everything."

"I still don't understand," said Fulk, his voice rising in a whine. "Why would Attica be interested in something Olivier de Harcourt was carrying? Carrying to *whom*?"

Both his mother and father ignored him.

"Where would she have taken it?" said Gaspard, his broad forehead wrinkling with the strain of thought. "To her father?"

"No, he is too far." Yvette began to pace up and down the chamber, kicking the rushes and dogs out of her way as she went. "She's much more likely to have taken it to her brother Stephen, at La Ferté-Bernard."

"La Ferté-Bernard?" wailed Fulk.

"Unless . . ." Yvette stopped short. "That's it. She *has* gone to Laval. But, not to see her sick mother. She's taking the breviary to her uncle. She would trust him to deal with it from there." She swung around so fast that Fulk jumped. "Go, quickly," she told the boy, "and have the master of arms come to me here. I want search parties sent out immediately. In all directions, but especially toward Laval."

"But . . ." Gaspard protested as Fulk hurried from the chamber. "Why would Attica take the breviary to Renouf Blissot? I mean, he's been conspiring with Richard and Philip against Henry for years. Longer even than we have."

"We know that." Yvette smiled as a rare ripple of amusement bubbled up from within her. "But Attica doesn't."

She could always change her mind, Attica told herself as they wound their way down into the valley. Her decision to travel to Laval in the company of Damion de Jarnac was not irreversible; once they had delivered Walter into the care of Saint-Sevin's infirmarer, she could always change her mind and continue on alone.

Comforted by the thought, she narrowed her eyes against the glare to study the distant monastery, its cluster of golden-white buildings looking solid and comforting in the midst of ripening fields striped yellow and green with wheat and barley. The afternoon had turned hot, the sun a golden ball that beat down to fill the air with the scents of baking earth and steaming green leaves and lush grass. She glanced back anxiously at Walter Brie, slumped unconscious over the neck of de Jarnac's roan. He had not stirred.

They had tied him to the saddle with strips of cloth torn

from the tunics of the dead *routiers*. The squire led Walter's injured gray and de Jarnac's second spare mount, a bay, but Attica herself had taken the roan's lead rope. Her arm was beginning to ache from the strain, although she barely noticed it, since it was only one small ache lost amid the shrieking agony of sore thighs and stiff back and raw knees. She considered herself an accomplished horsewoman, but she had been riding now for hours, and she was exhausted.

She shifted her gaze to the broad, smooth back of Damion de Jarnac, trotting ahead of her. He sat easily in the saddle, one gloved hand resting negligently against a solid thigh. He had his dark head up, his strong-boned profile sharp and alert as he scanned the road ahead. He looked as if he could ride to the ends of the earth, Attica thought, and never suffer any discomfort. Watching him, she felt herself fill with a wistfulness that was part admiration, part envy, and part something else she could not name.

A warm wind gusted up, rustling the oak leaves overhead and billowing the hem of the dead courtier's surcoat out around her. She watched the summer breeze ruffle the knight's dark hair where it lay against the taut, tanned column of his neck, and she knew a strange, swift sensation, as if everything in her world had shifted suddenly, then realigned itself in an unfamiliar, frightening, yet somehow exciting pattern. Perhaps it was the male clothing she wore or the strange company with which she rode, but she felt . . .

She felt as if she were someone else, she decided. As if she were moving through someone else's life. A swift thrill of exhilaration tingled through her at the thought. She knew it made no sense; she had never been more frightened in her life than she was at that moment. She was worried about the threat to Stephen's life and to his liege lord, the English king; she was worried about Walter's wound and about her own safety. And yet she also knew that she hadn't felt this alive, this free in years. She felt as if she had escaped. Which was odd, since she hadn't even realized, until now, just how hedged in she'd come to feel as she'd grown from the rather wild young girl she had once been into the affianced wife she had become.

A flock of swallows arose from the valley floor ahead to dart screeching across the sky. Looking up, Attica saw the knight check the black Arab for a moment, his hand resting on his sword, and she realized there was a definable edge to his watchfulness. She cast a quick, nervous glance around and spurred her horse up beside his. "You don't think they're still about, do you?" she asked. "The *routiers*, I mean."

He brought his gaze to her face, the edges of his lips lifting in a wry smile that flashed, then was gone. "They're still around. They wouldn't leave without robbing their own dead back there, if nothing else." His eyes narrowed as he stared off down the valley. "We'll ride across the fields from here, I think, rather than follow the road past that clump of trees. No reason to present ourselves for an ambush simply because they've prepared one for us."

She straightened in her stirrups, trying to peer in the direction he'd indicated. It might have been her imagination, but for a moment she thought she saw something move in the stand of birches that stood just where the road flattened out into the valley. A brown, shifting shadow that appeared, then was gone.

All the soft warmth and heady sense of adventure she'd known just moments ago suddenly vanished from the afternoon. She remembered the chilling hiss made by the crossbow bolt as it flew through the air to sink into Walter's flesh. She remembered the *routiers'* ugly taunts and the savage malice twisting their faces as they reached for her. She remembered the ripped and bloodied bodies of the women in that burned village, and before she could stop it, a violent shiver shook her.

She darted a quick glance at de Jarnac, hoping he hadn't noticed that betraying moment of weakness, but to her dismay, she discovered him watching her. "Don't worry, little lordling," he said, his voice unexpectedly soft, his expression unreadable. "I'll see you to Laval."

She found she could not say anything, perhaps because there was, after all, nothing to say. She was afraid, and he knew it. Their gazes met and held, and it was as if she could feel his eyes upon her, piercing her, judging her. It unnerved her, the way he looked at her. She found it unsettling enough, simply being near him. He was so fierce and intense, he frightened her. And yet she knew, in that moment, that she would not change her mind. Whether she was comfortable with him or not, she desperately needed his escort to Laval.

She could only hope that he would not change *his* mind and decide to leave her at the monastery after all.

They came to the Benedictine monastery of Saint-Sevin shortly after terce.

The monastery lay at the edge of a wide water meadow flanking a broad stream that flowed slowly down toward the Vilaine. Creamy white sandstone walls, still new enough to show their crisp chisel marks, encircled a compound dominated by the great stone mass of the church tower rising up as tall and solid as any castle keep.

Above the dull tramp of their horses' hooves in the dusty road, Attica caught the distant pearling of the stream, just visible as a ribbon of sparkling light through the trees and rushes. Cattle lowed in the pasture, brown heads swinging up to stare solemnly at the riders as they passed. From somewhere out of sight came the high-pitched shouting of children—the *nutriti*, dedicated as young boys to a life of seclusion, holiness, and scholarship.

She had not expected the air of peaceful serenity that hung over this place, for she had heard the terrible tale of its founding often enough since coming to eastern Brittany. How some threescore years before, during the reign of Louis VI, a darkly handsome but ruthlessly ambitious knight by the name of Lothar had murdered his brother, raped his brother's wife, and blinded their son—his own nephew—in order to seize the boy's inheritance. According to the tale, Lothar had lived a long and prosperous life, untroubled by either repentance or punishment. Only on his deathbed did the dark knight begin to fear retribution for his hideous crime. And so he had endowed the monastery of Saint-Sevin to buy his way into heaven. As they drew to a halt before the monastery's new gatehouse, Attica stared up at that massive church tower and wondered if it had worked.

A crow wheeled, cawing, above them. She turned her head, watching it, only to have her gaze captured by the dark, restless knight beside her. A knight who, like Lothar, had killed his own brother.

A profound sense of disquiet rippled over her, a fear that she tried to calm with reason. She told herself that, unlike Lothar, de Jarnac had not mutilated his nephew or seized the boy's inheritance. The nephew still lived, secure in his castles, while it was de Jarnac who roamed the world, dispossessed, haunted. He was not like Lothar. He was not.

"Porter," he called, tipping back his head, his gaze assessing the monastery's gate and walls. His voice was not loud, yet Attica wasn't surprised to see the porter come hustling out of his lodge, his tonsured sandy head bent, his long black robes hitched up with one hand as he hurried. Few men, even monks, she thought, would fail to respond to the implacable authority in that smooth, cold voice.

"Do you need shelter for the night?" asked the porter, his fingers still anxiously clutching his robes as he skidded to a halt a safe distance from the big knight. He was a young monk, with the soft white face of a man who has spent most of his life indoors, and he peered up at them with pale, myopic eyes that widened at the sight of Walter, slumped unconscious over the saddle.

De Jarnac's elegant black horse fidgeted. "No, but we have a wounded man. Might we enter and entrust him to your infirmarer?"

"Yes, yes, by all means," said the porter, his pale eyes opening even wider as he stepped back quickly. "The infirmary lies just beyond the gardens, to your left. I will have Brother Infirmarer sent for, if he is not there already."

De Jarnac nodded and nudged his horse forward through the gatehouse.

Clicking to the roan, Attica followed him into a forecourt littered with great piles of sand and stone. Dust and the scent of freshly cut timber filled the air, along with the familiar *thwunk-chink* of mallet striking chisel that echoed across the court from the mason's lodge hugging the south side of the nave. She remembered having heard it said that most of the immediate funds provided by Lothar had gone, at his insistence, into constructing the monastery walls and gate and the massive stone church that crowned the black knight's tomb—as if all that masonry might somehow serve to protect him from the wrath of God. They said the monks were still struggling to finish their cloister and replace the temporary buildings scattered about the compound. As her tired horse picked its way across the court, Attica looked around at the tumble of old timber buildings and decided the rumors were true.

But the monastery gardens, when they came to them, were extensive and well tended. A heady mingling of scents wafted up to greet them, sweet lavender and pungent rosemary and an unidentifiable but delicious medley of other rich fragrances that washed over her like a cleansing balm. Attica felt some of the strain of the past hours begin to ebb away, and in its place came an exhaustion so complete as to be almost numbing.

"The good brothers of Saint-Sevin appear to be building themselves a new kitchen," said De Jarnac, nodding toward the half-erected walls of brilliant white, newly cut stone rising on the far side of the gardens from the timber-built infirmary that stood looking quiet and empty in the afternoon sun. "I wonder if Brother Infirmarer is here"—reining in, the knight slid from his saddle in one graceful motion—"or if we must wait for Brother Porter to fetch him."

Attica didn't say anything. She couldn't. She suddenly felt so tired, she wondered if she had enough energy even to dismount. She watched in an envious kind of amazement as de Jarnac ran up the three short steps to the infirmary and disappeared through the open door. Her own body felt so weighted, her brain so sluggish, that it took an enormous effort of will simply to swing her leg over the cantle. As she lowered her weight, the ground came at her in a rush and she stumbled awkwardly, grasping the stirrup leather for support. She was glad de Jarnac wasn't there to see it.

But his squire was.

"Give me a hand with your groom; then I'll take care of the horses," said Sergei.

She lifted her head and looked at him. She had never seen anyone quite like this small squire. He had a strange, wide-boned face, with fair hair and skin still surprisingly pale despite the hours he obviously spent in the sun. But it was his eyes that fascinated her. Dark and tilted upward slightly at the corners, they seemed to stare at her almost unblinkingly, as if he had seen too many horrors, too young, to ever recover. She had no idea how old he was—surely no more than thirteen or fourteen, she thought, from the size of him. But looking at him, Attica could understand why de Jarnac had thought her so young if he had compared her to this lad. The squire might have the ruddy cheeks and smooth forehead of a boy, but his eyes were old.

"Thank you," she said. By gritting her teeth with determination, she managed to find the strength to push away from the chestnut and go help untie the bonds that held Walter to the back of the big roan.

The sudden cessation of movement had brought Walter to semiconsciousness. As she reached his side, the groom groaned and lifted his head. His eyes fluttered open, then rolled back in his head.

"Watch it," she heard de Jarnac say from behind her. "He's going to fall."

She stretched out her arms to stop Walter Brie slipping sideways from the roan's back, but he came crashing down on top of her, buckling her beneath the impact of his unconscious weight.

She heard the click of de Jarnac's spurs on the stairs and felt the overwhelming power and size of his man's body as he came up behind her, his strong arms enfolding her, his hard chest pressing against her back as he lifted Walter from her. "I've got him," de Jarnac said, his face close enough to hers that the warmth of his breath ruffled her hair. "Move out of the way."

She ducked beneath his arm and backed away, oddly shaken.

"I'll get his legs," said the infirmarer, hurrying down the steps. He was an incredibly tall, thin monk with a long but gentle face and the almost emaciated form of a hermit. As Attica watched, the two men lifted Walter Brie's unconscious body between them and carried him up the steps.

She followed them through the infirmary door, which opened directly into a small hall lit by four long, tall windows, their shutters thrown open to the midday sun. "Put him in here," she heard the infirmarer say as he backed down a dark corridor to the curtained doorway of a small cell. They hefted the groom up onto the low pallet and he groaned again, a dark rivulet of fresh blood gushing from his wound to run over de Jarnac's supporting arm and drop in bright red splotches at his feet.

At the sight, Attica made a thin, strangling sound in her throat. De Jarnac's head fell back, his brows lowering as he realized she had followed them into the cell. "There's no need for you to see this if it distresses you." He straightened. "You might as well make use of the time to find yourself something to eat. You look as if you're ready to collapse yourself."

Attica shook her head. "I should stay with him."

De Jarnac shrugged and turned away to help the infirmarer, who had already begun to strip off Walter's tunic. "As you wish," he said, no longer looking at her. "But be warned. I leave as soon as his wound is tended. And if you become too tired and hungry to keep up with me, I won't wait for you."

He would do it, she thought, staring at his hard, implacable profile. She could see nothing but ruthlessness in every set feature. Wordlessly, she turned on her heel and left.

Attica knew she needed to eat, but it wasn't until she neared the door of the abbey's old timber kitchen and smelled the enticing scents of roasting meat and simmering pottage that she realized just how hungry she was. Her stomach rumbled louder than a waterfall, and it occurred to her that she probably felt faint almost as much from hunger as from exhaustion.

In the end, she ate far more than she had expected, leaning against the warm trunk of an apple tree in the orchard and washing the food down with several droughts of watered ale. She might even have dozed, if the distant lowing of a cow hadn't brought back to her the passage of time.

"Mother of God," she whispered. She leapt to her feet, seized by the sudden terror that de Jarnac had already left, without her. Her heart pounding in her chest, she raced across the abbey's carefully tended garden and entered the infirmary at a quick half run.

After the bright blaze of the June afternoon, the darkness of the hall almost blinded her. Her momentum had carried her halfway across the rush-strewn floor before she realized that the room was not empty.

She saw the long, thin back and bowed tonsured head of the infirmarer first. He stood beside a table at the far end of the hall and was grinding something in a wooden mortar and pestle. But what brought her skidding to a shocked halt, the breath leaving her lungs in a noisy rush, was the sight of Damion de Jarnac, stripped down to nothing but his white linen braies and sprawled in arrogant negligence on a bench pushed up against the near wall.

He had a magnificent knight's body, she thought, his shoulders broad, the muscles of his chest hard and exquisitely defined by hours spent at practice in the tilting yard. Against her will, her gaze roved over him, over the strong arms that could wield a sword to such deadly effect. Over the taut, smooth line of his stomach. Over the lean hard thighs that could ride a horse all day and never get tired.

And then she saw the long, ugly cut that disfigured one powerful leg. She had forgotten that he, too, had been wounded in the fighting with the *routiers*.

She wrenched her gaze up to his face to find him regarding her quizzically. As well he might, she thought. For here, she realized with a numbing sense of shock, was one aspect of her disguise as a boy that had not yet occurred to her. Traveling with Walter had been comparatively simple, for the groom knew her for a lady and had treated her accordingly. But it would be a far different matter to travel with this man. For this man—this big, virile knight— thought her just another male. And as Attica stood, frozen with chagrin, her imagination conjured up for her a host of embarrassing and potentially disastrous possibilities.

She became aware of the silence between them lengthening, becoming awkward. Frantically, she cast about for some explanation for her seemingly odd behavior. "I . . . I was afraid you had left without me," she finally said.

Which was true enough, as far as it went.

He gave her an easy, fierce smile. "Not without warning, lordling." He jerked his head toward the corridor. "Your man is awake, if you care to see him before we leave."

"Yes. Thank you," she murmured, ducking her head as she hurried toward Walter's cell.

She found him looking drawn, but awake and surprisingly lucid. "Thanks be to God," she said, sinking down onto the rush-seated stool beside his pallet. "You look far better than I ever hoped you might."

Walter shifted awkwardly against the pillows that held him lifted up to one side to keep the weight off his wound. "It's not me I'm worried about, my lady—"

"Sshhh." She cast an anxious glance toward the partially curtained door. "No one here knows me for a woman. You must not give me away."

Walter jerked. "But you can't still mean to continue to Laval? Not alone."

"Lie still," she said softly, resting a restraining hand on his shoulder. "You'll start your wound bleeding again. And you needn't worry. I won't be alone. I have found a knight to escort me."

"A knight? What knight?" Walter demanded, trying to twist his head around so that he could see through the doorway.

"Stop moving. You can't see him. He was wounded slightly in the fighting and the infirmarer is binding his leg."

Walter brought his gaze back to her face. She saw his eyes, sunk deep with pain in their blue-tinged sockets, narrow with suspicion. "What knight?" he said again.

In spite of herself, she almost smiled. Walter knew her too well. "The knight who saved us from the *routiers* and brought us here. Did you not see him? He helped the infirmarer tend you."

"No. Only the monk was with me when I awoke. Who is this knight?"

Still Attica hesitated, although she could not have said

why she found herself so reluctant to utter his name. "Damion de Jarnac."

She saw Walter's already pale face go a shade whiter. *"God the Father and all the holy saints preserve us."* He tried to sit up again, gasping for air as if he'd just had the wind knocked out of him. *"Damion de Jarnac?* My lady, *you cannot."*

"Shhh," she hissed again, pressing him back down against the pillows. "I have no choice, Walter. You must see that. With a knight such as de Jarnac to protect me, I should have no difficulty reaching Laval. Whereas alone . . ."

"But my l—" He broke off to dart an anxious glance toward the empty doorway and dropped his voice to a hoarse whisper. "Who is going to protect you from de Jarnac? Do you *know* the things he has done?"

His words brought a peculiar dreadful ache to her stomach. She had heard some of the tale, but she had always suspected there was more to it, told only in whispers and never to an unmarried maiden. "He does not know who— or what—I am, Walter," she said, keeping her voice calm and level with effort.

"But if he should guess and . . ." Walter broke off and swallowed the rest of his sentence, his eyes bulging out as if he were strangling on whatever it was he couldn't bring himself to say aloud to a gentlewoman.

"Walter, the man is a knight, not a common brigand."

The groom's fist tightened over the edge of the rough monastic blanket, his normally congenial face hardening. "A knight he may be, yet I have heard it said he openly laughs at the codes of chivalry. You will not be able to rely upon his honor, should he learn the truth."

Attica ignored the chill his words sent coursing through her. "He won't. I'll make certain of that."

Walter's gaze drifted awkwardly away from her as he struggled with something he obviously felt he needed to say. "You will not reach Laval today. You realize that?"

Attica nodded. She knew it, but if she let herself dwell on the intimacy of all those hours she would be spending alone on the road with that man—if she thought about tonight—she would never find the courage to ride on. "If possible, I'll try to convince him to ride through the night without stopping anywhere. I'll—"

She broke off at the sound of footsteps coming toward them down the corridor. She barely had time to leap to her feet like some guilty conspirator before de Jarnac's strong hand swept the curtain to one side.

His big body filled the doorway, his gaze traveling from where Attica stood, her color probably betrayingly high, to Walter, who looked so much like a cornered wolf determined to guard its only cub that Attica might have laughed if she'd been in a different frame of mind.

Then the knight's cold green eyes swung back to Attica, and any thought of laughter fled. "If you still plan to come with me, it's time to leave." He held her gaze for a long, tense moment, as if he were issuing some sort of challenge.

"I am ready," she said, careful to keep the fear she felt out of her voice and face. "Only give me a moment to say farewell."

Nodding, he spun on his heel and left the cell. She could hear the quick tread of his boots echoing down the corridor.

Walter reached out to grasp her hand, jerking her attention away from the empty doorway where the curtain still quivered. "You don't need to go with him. You could stay here, in the monastery, where you'll be safe. Surely there must be someone you could send in your place?"

Attica gently slipped her hand from his grasp. "You know I can't, Walter. How could I trust such a secret to some stranger?"

Walter's gray brows twitched together in a troubled frown. "Do you think Stephen would want you to do this thing you are so set upon?"

A wry smile twisted Attica's lips as she thought of what her big brother would say if he knew what she were about to do. "Probably not. But he would do it for me."

"He is a man."

Attica's chin came up in an unconscious gesture of pride. "He is a d'Alérion, and so am I. Just because I am a woman doesn't mean that loyalty and honor are nothing to me. Or that I can't be brave."

Walter let his breath out in a long sigh. "I know how brave you are. That is why I am worried."

CHAPTER
FOUR

They were being followed.

A thicket of tall beech trees grew beside the track, their slender leaves quivering and rustling in the late afternoon breeze that skimmed along the top of the rise. Damion drew aside into the sheltering shadows of trunks and overhanging branches before he wheeled the Arab to face the way they had come.

By squinting hard against the westering afternoon sun, he could count four mounted men, maybe five, in the distance. Armored men, riding fast. He could see the glint of sunlight on their helms, the cloud of dust raised by the thundering hooves of their horses. They were only half an hour behind, maybe less, and gaining fast.

He turned to survey the road ahead and swore softly to himself at the sight of gentle countryside lying open and vulnerable beneath a wide blue sky. Striped, rolling fields of golden-green grain and cleared pasture stretched on for miles, broken only here and there by a few scattered copses of mixed brush, a hamlet or two, and, not too far ahead, the strung-out line of a merchant caravan, its pack horses heavily laden with goods bound for the summer fair in Laval.

Damion pursed his lips and blew out a long, slow breath

as he turned to stare again at that armed party of men. His mission for Henry had been cloaked in secrecy and known only to the king's most trusted inner circle of men. But Damion had learned young not to trust anyone, had learned well the dangerous lesson that things are often not what they seem.

His hand moved unconsciously to the hilt of his sword as he considered the hard-riding men behind him. It was always possible, of course, that they were simply headed, like the merchants, to Laval. Then again, he thought, setting his teeth in annoyance, they could very well be after his mysterious little lordling. Whoever they were, they obviously had orders to kill their horses, if necessary, to get where they were going.

"What is it?" asked Atticus, riding up to him.

Damion shifted his gaze to the slim, dark-haired youth reining in beside him. "Is there any reason to think someone might be following you?"

The youth's face went admirably blank as he blinked into the sinking sun. "No," he said, drawing the syllable out. "Why? Is someone behind us?"

Staring down into that fine-boned, attractive face, Damion felt a smile pull at his mouth. At some point, the lad had managed to pick up the courtly trick of making his features go completely smooth and expressionless, thus hiding whatever betraying thoughts and emotions might be boiling behind the public mask. With most people, it probably worked. Except that in Atticus's case, the studied lack of animation formed such a marked contrast to the lad's natural, open expression that its assumption was a betrayal in itself.

Damion felt his smile fade. In the three hours that had passed since they left the monastery, he had studied the

youth closely and come to several confusing conclusions.
Despite his fine seat on a horse and his undeniable skill
with a dagger, the boy nevertheless had the pale face and
soft hands of one dedicated to scholarship and the church
from an early age. Which made him a peculiar choice,
Damion would have said, to play a role in a treasonous
plot. While there was obviously nothing wrong with the
lad's courage or determination, anyone who knew the boy
well enough to trust him must surely realize that he was
too sensitive, too inexperienced, too compulsively honest
and forthright to ever succeed at something as dirty and
unprincipled as a conspiracy to depose a king.

But Damion didn't believe in coincidences, and for the
natural brother of one of the English king's household
knights to be on the road to La Ferté-Bernard, at this time,
and not be involved in some way in the plot against Henry
would be simply too much of a coincidence for anyone to
swallow. True, Damion wouldn't have picked Stephen
d'Alérion as one of the conspirators, but then, one never
really knew what lay in another man's heart.

"I can't see anything," said the lad, peering into the
distance.

"It's a small party. Four, maybe five men. Riding hard
and fast."

And then the boy must have seen them, for he jerked
suddenly, swinging the chestnut away abruptly before
Damion could see his face.

Touching his heels to the Arab's sides, Damion followed
the boy thoughtfully down the hill to where Sergei waited
with the spare horses at the base of the slope. They had almost reached the squire when Atticus drew up sharply.

"Something wrong?" Damion asked, reining in beside him.

He found himself confronted with Atticus's courtly mask of a face. "It's Chantilly—my mount. He keeps favoring his right foreleg. I think he must have a stone caught in his shoe."

Damion watched the lad swing his leg over the cantle and drop to the ground. He moved stiffly and awkwardly, Damion noticed, as if he were unaccustomed to such long hours in the saddle and was sore as a result. "Sergei can look, if you like," offered Damion.

"I can do it," said the lad, running his hand down the gelding's right leg. He lifted the forehoof up on his thigh and bent to scrape at the caked mud with the point of his dagger. His movements were careful and slow, as if he hadn't done this too many times before. From just over the top of the hill, a flock of swallows took flight, twittering loudly. Damion's head fell back, his gaze following the birds as they wheeled away to the south, the golden sunlight gleaming on their outstretched wings. The riders must be gaining on them.

Atticus let the hoof drop and carefully wiped his blade in the grass before straightening. "I don't see anything. But I've pushed him hard today." He looked up at Damion with wide, overbright eyes. "Perhaps I could ride your roan for a while?"

There could be no disguising the mingling hope and fear that sharpened the boy's features and quickened his breath. Curious, Damion studied the big chestnut. It was an unusually fine animal, with a distinctive white blaze and four white socks. A horse such as this, he thought, a man would notice—and recognize if he came upon it again. But not more readily, surely, than this finely dressed, patrician-boned youth?

Damion's gaze shifted back to the boy, to those thick

black lashes and smooth, rose-touched cheeks. There was something ethereal, almost unnaturally beautiful about his face. Something that nagged at Damion, like an elusive thought or a memory half-forgotten.

As if uncomfortable with Damion's scrutiny, the boy swung his head away, showing Damion only his classic profile. Still watching him, Damion raised his voice. "Sergei. Bring up the roan for our lordling here. His chestnut seems to be favoring its right forefoot."

"Oui, messire," said the squire, slipping out of the saddle. "I didn't notice a limp," he added, moving quickly to help Atticus transfer the saddle from the chestnut to the roan, "but that chestnut does have the look of a horse that's spent too many months doing little beyond eating its head off in the stables, I'd say."

Damion stood in the stirrups to stretch his legs and glance around. "I can hear a stream running somewhere, probably at the base of that hill over there. Perhaps you should take the chestnut and bathe its legs in cool water for, say, an hour or so?"

Sergei glanced up from fastening the saddle girth. His black, knowing gaze met Damion's and held it. "I understand," he said, and turned away to gather up the chestnut's lead.

"If you're quick," Damion said to Atticus, who hauled himself up onto the big roan's back, "we should have time to catch that merchants' caravan and blend ourselves in with them before your friends overtake us."

The boy's wide brown eyes flew to Damion's face. "They're not my friends."

Damion reached out to close his gloved hand over the small, fragile fingers holding the roan's reins. He exerted just enough pressure to make the boy wince, and returned his frightened, breathless stare with a deliberately cold, mean look. "Friends or enemies, it matters not what you call them. But make no mistake about this, lordling. Once those men have passed us, you and I are going to have a reckoning."

They overran the merchants on the far side of the nearest small hamlet.

The company was a large one, Spanish by the looks of it, preceded by a standard-bearer and flanked by crossbowmen and pikemen. An impressive display, Damion thought, as he spurred the Arab past the lumbering line of burdened pack animals and tired men—although one probably intended as much to advertise the value of the shipment as to guard it, since he could see only one knight, a fat, graywhiskered cavalier dozing in his saddle with his double chin sunk against his hauberk. The man half strangled on a snore, his head jerking up as Damion drew in beside him.

"Good evening," said Damion with a lazy smile. "You're late on the road."

The knight sat up straight and wiped his nose on the back of his hand. "As are you, my friend."

Damion stared off into the distance, as if surveying the land. "I was hoping to find an abbey where we might stop. But I've seen no sign of one for hours now."

The knight shook his head. "Nor will you, in this country. But there is an inn, at the crossroads outside the gates of a small town called Ravel, not too far from here." A look of wondrous longing crept over the man's mottled face. "They serve the most wonderful, garlic-roasted milk-fed lamb there."

The knight—who introduced himself as Sir Odo—had

obviously traveled this road often. Damion listened, his expression politely interested, his attention on the road behind them, as the old knight discoursed at length on the quality of the inn's food and wine and then moved on, by natural extension, to the relative merits of the whores who frequented the establishment.

"But if you like your women with big tits," said Sir Odo, "you'll want to ask for Rose. Now, her face isn't much to look at, I admit. But the things she does to a man with those—"

Out of the corner of his eye, Damion saw the fast-rising dust from the west gradually solidify into five horsemen— three knights and two servants, wearing the livery of the house of Salers.

"She takes them in her hands, see," Sir Odo was saying, "and squeezes them together. Now remember, they're big. As big as the watermelons of Jerusalem—"

The riders passed the plodding pack horses as Damion had done, at a canter. Watching them come on, Damion caught a brief glimpse of Atticus's dark hair and pale, strained face near a cluster of mules loaded with what looked like bags of alum, but after that, Damion took care not to glance in the boy's direction again.

The unknown horsemen paused several times to speak to various merchants, then spurred on to where Damion and Sir Odo rode at the vanguard of the cavalcade. "I tell you," Sir Odo was saying, "you've never felt anything like it—"

He broke off as the men approached. Two of the knights were young yet, fair-haired and fresh-faced. They hung back as the third, a dark-haired man with small, sharp eyes and a hawklike beak of a nose over a tight-lipped, hard mouth, drew rein beside Damion and said, "We're looking for a gentlewoman. Tall, slender. Brown-haired. Young. Have you seen her on this road?"

"A gentlewoman?" repeated Sir Odo, fingering his wiry gray face whiskers. "No. Don't think so."

Damion didn't let the surprise he felt show on his face, although the man's words were hardly what he had been expecting. *A gentlewoman,* he thought. Now what the devil would a monastery-bound youth like Atticus have to do with a gentlewoman—a *young* gentlewoman—from the house of Salers?

He studied the closed, guarded face of the hawk-nosed knight. The man had obviously been ordered to keep his inquiries short and discreet. But there were ways around that.

"A gentlewoman from the house of Salers has gone missing?" Damion said with just enough surprised amusement in his voice to provoke a reaction.

He got one. "Not missing," Hawk Face snapped. "The viscomtesse de Salers simply wishes her future daughter-in-law to travel with a larger escort."

"Ah. Well, you'd best hurry, then," said Damion, obligingly drawing the Arab closer to the grassy verge of the road. "Because the future viscomtesse is surely still ahead of us."

He waited, one hand resting on the pommel of his sword until the knights and servants of the house of Salers were little more than specks on the eastern horizon. Then he said farewell to the talkative Sir Odo and cantered back to deal with Monsieur le Batard d'Alérion.

Whatever relief Attica felt at escaping detection by the men from Châteauhaut-sur-Vilaine vanished immediately at the sight of Damion de Jarnac thundering toward her.

She had no way of knowing what the knights from Châteauhaut had said to him, but it had obviously been enough to enable him to guess that she had deceived him in some way. And one did not lightly deceive a man such as Damion de Jarnac.

Her stomach twisted with fear at the thought. She turned her head, the late-afternoon breeze fluttering the ragged ends of her cropped hair about her face as she stared at the distant hills. She knew an almost hysterical impulse to dig her knees into the roan's sides and gallop off across the fields, not caring where she went as long as she got away from him. She even collected her reins. But then she remembered that the roan she rode was *his* horse, not hers. And it occurred to her that even though she might have a head start and a fresher horse, she wouldn't put it past de Jarnac and that indefatigable Arab of his to ride her down anyway.

If he didn't simply borrow one of the archers' crossbows and shoot her as she fled.

Abruptly abandoning all thoughts of wild flight, she considered instead the possibility of throwing herself on the mercy of the nearest merchant and asking for his protection. But when she glanced about at the disinterested, self-absorbed faces of the fat, overdressed Spanish burghers, she knew that no man here would dare to stand up against a knight such as Damion de Jarnac. Especially not for the sake of some unknown woman caught masquerading as a man.

He was almost upon her. Lifting her chin proudly, her heart pounding painfully in her chest, Attica drew the roan onto the grassy verge and waited as the dark knight rode right up to her.

His hand flashed out to grasp the roan's reins below the bit. "Get down," he ordered, as if he knew how close to flight she'd come. "Now."

Her gaze focused on the cruel, mean slant of his mouth. Wordlessly, she slid out of the saddle.

To her chagrin, her knees buckled as soon as her feet hit the ground. She couldn't have said whether it was from fear or exhaustion, but she simply no longer had the strength to stand. The grass rose up to greet her, cool and soft and familiar in a world suddenly gone strange and frightening. She made no attempt to stand up. She was aware of de Jarnac on his black horse, looming over her like some evil nightmare, but she kept her gaze fixed on the passing pack horses. He would do nothing as long as the Spanish traders were here.

The Spanish caravan was a long one, but eventually the last steel- and leather-laden mule and the last curious pikeman plodded past. The setting sun caught the dust of their passing as it hung in the air, shimmering in the slanting light like gold. In the distance she could hear the lowing of cattle being driven back to some village for the night. The grass suddenly felt damp through the blue velvet of the dead courtier's surcoat, and she shivered.

She heard the faint scrape of de Jarnac's prick spurs as he swung out of the saddle and stalked up to her, but she kept her gaze fixed on the now empty road. She could not bring herself to look at him.

A long black shadow fell across her. "Stand up," he said.

Her head tipped back almost of its own accord until she found herself staring up into his darkly handsome face. *The devil must look like this,* she thought, *when he's come to collect the soul of a sinner.* His eyes were the strange iridescent green of some enchanted forest well, mysterious and unholy.

She could not move.

She saw two white, angry lines bracket his mouth as his lips tightened. "I told you, lordling, that I don't like being lied to. Yet you seem to have done little else since we met."

Lordling. Whatever the men from Châteauhaut had said, it obviously hadn't been enough to enable de Jarnac to guess her sex. Attica let out her breath in a long sigh as the largest part of her fear broke away—then flooded back, tenfold, when his hand closed around her arm and hauled her up until her face was within inches of his. "Tell me again why you want to go to Laval," he said, his lips curling away from his teeth. "Only make sure I believe it this time."

Attica stared into that dark, disturbing face and swallowed hard. "I told you the truth."

Still holding her arm, he wrapped his other hand around her neck, tight enough that she could feel her own pulse beating against his palm. "Think again."

She fought desperately to keep a sob from shuddering her body. She was brutally aware of the killing strength of those hard fingers holding her throat. His man's body seemed to tower over her, big and powerful and dangerous. She sucked in a half-hitched breath, filling her nostrils with the scent of dust and wind-tossed grass and him.

"Would you die, then, to protect the fair name of your lady?" De Jarnac's mouth slanted into a smile that was pure meanness. "An impressive display of chivalric virtue, lordling, but foolish."

Attica licked her dry lips. "What do you mean?" Her voice came out husky. "What did those men say?"

"Only that the future viscomtesse de Salers is traveling with an insufficient escort."

"That is all?"

"It was enough." De Jarnac's gaze swept over her, and she was surprised to see a gleam of what might have been amusement warming the shadowed depths of his disconcerting eyes. "I had you pegged for a traitorous cleric, lordling, but obviously I was mistaken. It seems you had seduction, not treason, on your conscience." He let go of Attica's neck to cuff her hard on the shoulder. "The next time you decide to run off with your lord's betrothed, don't involve me."

Attica staggered back beneath the blow. Then, realizing what he must think, she sprang quickly to catch his arm when he would have turned away. "You are wrong. The future viscomtesse de Salers does not flee her betrothal."

De Jarnac swung to face her again. Something that was not amusement glittered now in the icy depths of his hard eyes, and she wished she had simply kept her mouth shut and let him think what he would think. "No?" He took a step toward her. "Then why did you fear what those men might have to say to me? And don't try to deny it," he added, when Attica opened her mouth to do just that, "because I saw the worry in your eyes when I rode up to you after I spoke with them. You feared what I might learn from them the same way you feared they might recognize your horse. Your *horse*, mind you, but not you."

He leaned into her until it seemed that his broad shoulders filled the sky. "So tell me, my little lordling, if you are not assisting her to escape her betrothal, then what the devil have you to do with the future viscomtesse de Salers?"

"She is my sister," said Attica with a gasp. "My half sister. Stephen's sister." She was blathering now, desperate to think of a name to call, well, herself. If only she hadn't told de Jarnac that her name—as a base-born son of the house of d'Alérion—was Atticus, she could have named the future viscomtesse de Salers as Attica d'Alérion. If he—

"Your sister," said de Jarnac.

Attica made herself hold his gaze. "Yes."

"And you expect me to believe that tale? Let me tell you something, lordling. Every time you have something to hide, your face goes blank. You might think you deceive me, but you may as well turn red and stutter, for all the good it does you."

"She *is* my sister," Attica insisted, determined to brazen the lie out. "Her name is Elise, and she is betrothed to Fulk the Fat." Once, Attica had had a sister called Elise. A pretty little child with sparkling gray eyes and a merry laugh. She had died at the age of five from the flux.

De Jarnac gave a startled bark of laughter. "Fulk the Fat? *Fulk the Fat?*"

"Yes," said Attica, the word coming out as an angry hiss.

"What kind of a father would betroth his daughter to a man named Fulk the Fat?"

Attica felt her skin grow warm. "The alliance is very valuable to the d'Alérions."

"It must be," said de Jarnac, his gaze flicking over her oddly. "And your sister must be a very dutiful daughter to agree to it. How old is she?"

"Nineteen."

De Jarnac grunted. "Ah. I see. Not dutiful, then, but just plain ugly if your father still has her on his hands at that age."

"She is not ugly," said Attica indignantly. "She was betrothed as a child to Ivor of Chauvigny. But he took the Cross before she was old enough to marry, and died just last year in Antioch."

De Jarnac grinned. "Not ugly?"

"No."

He crossed his arms over his chest. "All right. What does she look like?"

"She is tall. With light brown hair. And brown eyes," Attica added, hoping she wasn't saying too much.

He stared at her, his gaze so hard and flat, she decided she must have imagined that brief moment of amusement. "Well, at least you're not lying about that," he said.

He moved then, so swiftly she saw only the blur of his hand as he reached for the sword that hung against his lean left hip. The blade came out of its scabbard with a practiced hiss. Polished steel flashed in the sun as he brought the sword up until it pointed at her breast.

She stood transfixed by the sight of death held steadily only inches from her heart. The blade was double-edged, at least three feet long, and inlaid with a peculiar inscription of what looked like Saracen writing. Red and gold leather wrapped the grip, which ended in a heavy ball-shaped pommel made of a rock crystal that seemed to glow and pulse in de Jarnac's hand as if he had snared the lightning from the sky and harnessed it to his deadly sword.

As she watched, his wrist flexed and the tip pressed against her breast. A peculiar, half-strangled hiccup escaped from her throat before she could swallow it.

The sword was not as finely pointed as a dagger, for this was a battle weapon, made for cutting and thrusting more than piercing. But it was sharp enough to dig into her skin painfully every time her chest lifted on another breath. Sharp enough to slice through flesh and sinew and take her life, should he simply lean his weight into it.

She raised her gaze, slowly, from that cold, deadly length of steel to the dangerous man who held it.

"Now," he said, his voice a lazy drawl that somehow managed to sound as lethal as a crossbow bolt whispering through the air. "You, my finely feathered young friend, are going to tell me why not only Stephen d'Alérion's bastard half brother but also his beautiful nineteen-year-old *sister* are chasing each other down the road to Laval."

The pressure of the blade against her chest increased. Attica stopped breathing.

"And before you open your mouth," continued de Jarnac, "you are going to remember that like the Spring of Saint Ide, I can tell when you are being less than truthful. And I don't like being patronized with falsehoods."

She stared up into his stark, harsh-featured face, at the flaring line of his high cheekbones and the ruthless slant of his mouth. She wondered what he would do to her if she did tell him the truth.

A man like Damion de Jarnac, his loyalty belonged to whoever bought his sword. The dynastic squabbles of the house of Anjou probably interested him not at all, she thought—unless, of course, he had reason to hate Henry. Or unless his sympathies lay with Richard or Philip. In which case he would surely kill her, she thought with despair, to keep her silent.

Yet if she refused to speak, he would kill her anyway.

Attica's heart thumped painfully in her chest. She would have to tell him the truth, she decided—or at least part of the truth. She saw his eyes narrow suddenly in a decisive way that sent shivers curling up her spine. She opened her mouth. But nothing came out.

She watched, wide-eyed, as his grip tightened on the hilt of his sword, his fingers long and powerful, his leather gloves worn and bloodstained from past killings. The movement caused the rock crystal that formed the blade's pommel to catch the rays of the setting sun. It flashed in her eyes, as brutal and raw as the promise of death she read in his face. "No, please," she whispered. "I'll tell you. I'll tell you."

His jaw tightened. "Then tell me." The sword point never wavered.

She sucked in a half hitching breath that lifted her chest and pressed the sword's tip into her flesh deep enough to draw blood. "Several days ago, a—a man rode into Châteauhaut-sur-Vilaine. A man from the court of Philip of France." Her voice came out thin and scratchy, hardly her own voice at all, as if all of her fear had lodged in her throat and was strangling her.

"What was his name?" de Jarnac demanded when she paused.

She lifted her chin in a probably pitiful gesture of defiance. "I can't breathe with your sword digging into me."

The edges of his lips tightened. He curled his wrist a fraction, and the pressure of the blade eased—but only slightly. "What was his name?"

"Olivier de Harcourt." She studied his face. "Why? Do you know him?"

"I know of him." Neither his features nor his voice betrayed his reaction to what she was saying. He was obviously much better at maintaining a mask than she was. "Go on."

She swallowed, but the knot of fear remained tight in her chest. "He had a high fever and died in great pain. Near the end, he did not know where he was. He . . . said things."

"What things?"

The slanting rays of the dying sun cast a strange, fiery-red light across the knight's fierce, strong features, making him look like some kind of demon, sprung from the fires of hell. She felt the urge to make the sign of the cross, although she didn't dare move a finger. "He said that Philip and Richard attend the conference at La Ferté-Bernard in bad faith. That they do not intend to try to seek peace but will launch an attack when the conference ends."

She waited, tense, her heart pounding hard enough to make her feel almost physically sick. The silence stretched out, became unbearable. "You don't believe me," she said incredulously.

He shook his head. "I didn't say that. What else?"

"He said something about someone named Guido and a seventh note, but it didn't make sense."

"A seventh note?"

"Yes," she said, surprised by the gleam of interest in the shadowed depths of his eyes. "Does it mean anything?"

He didn't answer her. She watched his jaw harden, and decided she must have imagined that brief flicker of reaction. "How do you know all this?" he demanded. "Were you at Châteauhaut when de Harcourt died?"

For a moment, the question confused her. Then she realized he still did not know who she really was. "Oh. Oh no. My sister—Elise—told me. For it fell to Elise to nurse the man, you see. Yvette—the viscomtesse de Salers—has a great fear of illness and death."

By now the sun had disappeared behind the rise, taking the light and warmth of the day with it. She became aware of the wind, gusting cool and sweet around them. As she watched, the shadows on de Jarnac's face darkened and he tightened his grip on his sword, lifting it just enough to make her heart skip a beat. "I am not an excessively tolerant man, lordling, and you are definitely trying my patience with this tale of yours. Tell me quick, now. Where is your sister?"

"At—at Pierreforte l'abbaye." Attica closed and unclosed her fists against her thighs in a spasmatic, unconscious gesture. Until she'd had to mention Elise again, she'd been able to tell the truth, essentially. Now she was going to have to start lying. Again. And she didn't need de Jarnac to tell her she wasn't very good at it.

"I was on my way to—" *To where?* Attica thought frantically. She remembered de Jarnac's words, *I had you pegged as a traitorous cleric,* and continued in a rush, "—to Paris. To study at the university. I had stopped at Pierreforte for a few days to visit Elise at Châteauhaut and—and to rest my horse. So when de Harcourt died, Elise came to me at the abbey. She told me what she'd learned, and we decided that I should carry word of it to our uncle in Laval, so that he might warn Stephen. I—I had to take Elise's chestnut, you see, because my own horse was a bit lame."

Attica closed her mouth and glared at the black knight, almost daring him not to believe her. The string of falsehoods she'd just unleashed almost took her breath away. The next time she went to confession, she thought in despair, she was going to find herself loaded down with such a penance that she'd be on her knees for a week saying it all.

The wind gusted against her again, hard enough this time to make her lose her balance. She staggered slightly, then straightened and faced de Jarnac, her head up, her heart quaking. "So now, Monsieur le chevalier, it is my turn to ask you a question. Will you help me to warn my brother and King Henry of this treachery? Or are you fond of the king's enemies? Will you slay me here, by the side of this road, to keep me silent?"

She waited, her knees shaking, her mouth dry. Waited for him either to lower the sword or thrust it into her heart. Instead, he said, "Why did your sister run to you with this secret? Why not to her betrothed?"

"Because she is not convinced that the viscomte and viscomtesse de Salers are as loyal to Henry as one might wish."

All he did was grunt. Finally, she could bear his fierce, steady gaze no longer. "And what about you, Monsieur? To whom are you loyal?"

He smiled then, a brief, fierce smile that showed his teeth and never touched his eyes. "To myself," he said, and lowered the sword.

Attica's relief was so total, the release of tension so sudden and complete, that she would have fallen if de Jarnac had not thrust home his sword and caught her by her shoulders as she sagged.

"Steady now, lad," he said, the warmth of his breath brushing her cheek. "I don't know whether you speak the truth or not, but I'm not about to ignore information such as this. I'll see your warning reaches La Ferté-Bernard."

The firm pressure of his hands on her upper arms felt oddly comforting. She knew a strange impulse to lean into the protective warmth and strength of his big, masculine body—an absolutely absurd impulse, she thought with a wave of self-disgust, considering that he was the one who had just threatened to kill her and scared her out of her wits in the process.

She jerked out of his grasp, fury and righteous indignation rushing in to take the place of stark terror. "I thought you were going to kill me," she screamed at him, her hands gripped into tight fists, her entire body quivering. "You scared me half to death."

His eyes narrowed, his nostrils flaring wide as he leaned into her. "Did I? Well, good. Because you lied to me, my young friend, and your lies could easily have gotten me killed." He thumped her shoulder with one crooked finger, hard. "If I decide to risk my life, that's one thing. But I don't like other people doing it for me without my knowledge or consent. Is that understood?"

She glared up at him, a flush heating her cheeks as she realized he was right. By asking him to accompany her without telling him she might face pursuit more serious than that offered by a band of ragged *routiers*, she had placed him in far greater potential danger than he had bargained for. She opened her mouth to apologize to him, then thought about those hideous, heart-stopping moments she had spent staring down the length of his naked sword and changed her mind.

"So," she said, her voice brusque. "Now you know." She peered up at him. "Will you still accompany me to Laval?"

He swung away from her, growling a string of oaths that made her eyes widen and her jaw drop. She watched anxiously as he reached out to snatch up the Arab's reins. He stood for a moment, staring down at the leather in his hands. Then his head jerked up and he dropped the reins to spin around again so unexpectedly that she took a hasty step backward. She would have retreated farther, only his fierce gaze fastened on her, trapping her like a deer caught in the glare of a lantern.

"What else are you not telling me?" he demanded.

She stared up into his hard, accusing face and felt her breath and her wits both desert her. "N-nothing."

When she said it, she honestly believed it to be true—in the sense he meant, at least. Surely neither the truth about her sex nor her true identity could place him in any more danger than the knowledge she had already given him.

She saw his lips twist into a half sneer that flicked her on the raw. She straightened her back and lifted her chin. "I know you might find my words difficult to believe, sir knight, but I am normally a very truthful . . . person. I pride myself on my honesty and honor."

"Do you indeed?" He took a step that brought him right up to her. "Well, then, let us hope for your sake that neither your honesty nor your honor are found lacking. For if that should prove to be the case, then make no mistake about this, lordling: You shall heartily rue the day our paths crossed."

She drew in a deep, shuddering breath, her head falling back as she stared up into his shadowed eyes. She heard in the distance the clip-clop of hooves and the gentle purring coo Sergei used to talk to the horses. But she could not tear her stricken gaze away from de Jarnac's cold, cruel face. Every muscle in her body seemed stretched taut, as tense as the air that shimmered between them.

He held her gaze for another endless moment. Then she saw his lips twist into a chilling smile as he said, "And you have my word on *that*."

CHAPTER
FIVE

The last of the light leached from the sky, turning it first to pink, then pale gold, and finally a somber bluish gray that was not so much any particular hue as a simple absence of color, a harbinger of the darkness to come. And still they rode on.

Once more in the saddle, Attica hunched her shoulders and tried not to shiver, for the heat of the day had disappeared with the sun and a bitter wind kicked up. In her exhaustion, the cold seemed even greater than she knew it really was, became one more enemy to be borne, like the scream in her back and the ache in her legs. She clutched with numb fingers at the wooden pommel before her, afraid that she might slip unknowingly into sleep and tumble from the saddle, but even more afraid that her endurance would crack and she would open her mouth and beg de Jarnac to stop for the night.

She pressed her lips together and rode on.

"You're very quiet," he said, his voice coming to her out of the wind-tossed darkness, and she realized he must have reined in to allow her to catch up with him.

She felt her body tense with strain and anger and something else she couldn't even begin to identify. "What do you expect?" she snapped, weariness and simmering fury both sharpening her voice. The roan would have paused, but she kneed it determinedly forward without even glancing at the man beside her.

The soft huff of his laugh curled toward her through the night. "You're still angry with me," he said, and brought his horse in beside hers.

"Did you think I would not be?" She turned to look at him. To her eyes, he was little more than a shadow in the moonlight, a dark silhouette of broad shoulders and lean, athletic grace. Yet she was intensely aware of him beside her, of the sheer energy of his being and the dangerous power of his masculinity. Riding through the cool, starlit night, with the wind blowing her hair about her face and this man by her side and only the faint following patter of Sergei leading the spare horses, she felt again that sensation of dislocation, as if she were someone else, not herself at all.

She looked away from him to the distant, gently rounded hills glowing dimly in the moonlight. "My mother tells me I have an unforgiving nature," she said. "But I doubt even she would expect me to forgive too quickly someone who held a naked sword to my . . . chest." She only just managed to catch herself before she said "breast."

"Huh. If you're going to move through the world of men, lordling, you must expect to be treated accordingly." The clatter of their horses' hooves filled a slight pause before he added, "Or would you rather I had taken my belt to your noble backside?"

His words sent such a wave of heat blazing through her that she was thankful for the darkness hiding her face from his gaze. "The world of men?" she said, imbuing her voice with all the scorn she could muster. "Is it a manly thing, then, to draw steel upon an unarmed . . . boy?"

He let out a sharp laugh. "You think it feminine, do you?"

She slewed around in the saddle to face him. "What I think it, is unchivalrous. I would expect you, as a knight, not to take unfair advantage of one in no position to defend himself."

She couldn't see his features, but she could hear the hardness beneath the heavy mockery in his voice as he said, "Now, whatever made you expect such a foolish thing as that?"

"There are codes—"

"I don't follow them." The Arab snorted and tossed its dark head with a jangle of its bridle as he abruptly drew rein and turned to her. "What do you think? That because I am a knight, I live my life by some idealistic code of chivalry articulated by fat old priests, who tell me that I must be not only brave, strong, and true but also generous to the weak and an unthinking, unquestioning servant to the Holy Church?"

She stared at him. "You would question the teachings of the Holy Church?"

"When I've seen countless thousands of Saracen women, children, and old men put to the sword by the unthinking and unquestioning servants of that Holy Church—the same Holy Church, mind you, that teaches its adherents that *Thou shalt not kill*—then, yes, I question it."

"But a knight's honor—"

"Honor?" He let out a harsh laugh. "Believe me, the thought of young men dying needlessly because of their allegiance to some abstract concept of honor and loyalty might be noble. But I decided a long time ago that when it comes down to a choice between me fighting fairly and

dying or me gaining an unfair advantage over my opponent by stabbing him in the back first, the dagger in the
back wins every time."

"You're just saying that," she whispered.

He leaned closer, close enough for the faint moonlight to show her the stark planes of his sun-darkened
face, close enough that she could see the faint flutter of
his black hair as it moved against his strong throat in the
night wind. "Don't you believe it. You'd best get this
straight right now, lordling: I am loyal to no one but myself, and the only code I follow is my own." He urged his
horse forward and left her there to follow or not, as she
pleased.

She sat staring after him, the reins slack in her hands,
a strange, lonely ache burning fiercely in her chest—an
ache that was part sorrow, part yearning for some nameless thing she could not grasp. She didn't know how long
she would have sat there, lost to exhaustion and her own
private, suffocating wants and confusion, if Sergei hadn't
come up beside her. The roan began to move of its own
accord, following the other horses down the pale ribbon
of road.

"Why are we stopping?" Attica asked, lifting her head
to glance about in sudden confusion.

She realized she must have dozed, because to her surprise she found herself staring at the timber and wattle and
daub facade of an inn that stood at a crossroads just outside the dark wooden palisade of some town. The gates of
the town itself had long since been shut and barred against
the night. But welcoming light and the enticing scent of
roasting meat and good soup spilled from the inn's open

door. Attica's stomach rumbled loudly, reminding her just how long it had been since she'd last eaten.

"Smells good, doesn't it?" Sergei said, from so close beside her that she realized he must have been pacing her, watching carefully, ready to catch her if she started to slip from the saddle.

She turned her head to smile at him. "Yes, except . . ." Her gaze traveled beyond the squire to de Jarnac, who slid out of his saddle with an enviable ease that told her he could have ridden through the night without pause. "Why have we stopped here?" she asked as the knight came at her out of the darkness.

"Because you look as if you're about ready to topple off that horse," he said dryly. "Let me give you a hand down."

He started to reach for her, but she touched her heel to the roan's side to send it dancing away. "I can keep going," she insisted.

She heard his grunt of disbelief. "I doubt it," he said, stepping back to plant his hands on his hips in that way he had that caught strangely at her breath. "Besides, I lied. We're here because the horses need a rest and I'm hungry. Now get down."

He would have turned away then, but she stopped him by saying hotly, "We can't stop; you know that. I must reach Laval in time to send a warning on to my brother."

De Jarnac swung to face her again, his head tipping back as he grinned up at her. "Sweet Jesus. You're as worrisome as a woman. I've more than enough time to reach La Ferté-Bernard before anything happens. And I'll be of far more use to Henry when I get there if I haven't half killed myself on the road."

She stared at him. "You? *You* are going to La Ferté-Bernard?"

"I told you I'd see your warning delivered. But right now I'm going to have myself a good supper and drink a horn of wine in a gesture of thanks to poor old Sir Odo, who is probably camped at this very moment in some damp meadow full of quarrelsome Spanish merchants and dreaming wistfully of milk-fed lamb and big-titted whores."

Attica had never heard of Sir Odo, but the casual reference to whores conjured up alarmingly lurid images that caused her to sit bolt upright in the saddle. "Whores?" she said with a gasp. "*Whores?* I . . . I do not think I wish to stay at this inn."

De Jarnac was already turning away from her, his gaze scanning the upstairs windows as he said, "Stop fretting, lordling. The inn might be full, but I ought to be able to get a private chamber for us. I won't make you sleep in the attics with the riffraff."

At the words *private chamber*, Attica's stomach did a curious flip-flop. She threw herself off the roan so fast, her wobbly legs almost collapsed beneath her. "No, wait," she cried.

But he had already disappeared through the door of the inn.

Some quarter of an hour later, Attica stood rooted to the doorway of the private chamber, the dead courtier's saddlebags clutched to her bound breasts like a shield as she let her gaze drift around the low-ceilinged room with its freshly whitewashed walls, its close-shuttered window, its glowing charcoal brazier adding a warm red hue to the golden flickering light of the cressets.

"Not a palace, I admit," said de Jarnac, kicking off his boots. "But at least it's surprisingly clean." He unbuckled his sword and tossed it onto the bed while Attica made an incoherent gurgling sound in her throat.

Oak framed and hung with crimson-dyed linen, the bed was wide—wide enough to sleep five, which it doubtlessly often did. She knew she should consider herself lucky to be given even this limited amount of privacy. After all, she could have found herself sleeping on a pallet in the loft along with the assorted book peddlers, cock masters, tinsmiths, jongleurs, and pilgrims who seemed to make up the majority of their fellow guests for the evening. Or she could have been expected to bed down in the hay of the stables with Sergei and the other guests' grooms and squires. But those alternatives, which had once loomed frighteningly, now seemed oddly preferable to this . . . this . . . intimacy with this man.

"Stop dawdling and close the door," said de Jarnac, pulling his tunic off over his head. "The landlord's boy should be here soon with my water, and you're letting in the cold."

His hands dropped to the laces of his braies. Attica turned in a barely disguised panic and fled.

She washed as best she could at the well in the yard. The water was shudderingly cold and the night air chilled by the gusting breeze, and she had to be careful not to wet her hair, in case the dye she'd rubbed into it after leaving Châteauhaut should come off. Quickly drying her face and hands on a length of linen from the courtier's bags, all she could think about was how she longed to strip off her dusty clothes, as de Jarnac had doubtlessly done, and wash the dirt and sweat from her body with a basin of warm water. Or better yet, sink into a deep, sweetly scented, steaming bath.

Sighing, she bent to tuck the towel back into the satchel. The light from the torch near the stable flared, catching on the edge of what looked like a book. Curious, she pulled it out, oddly affected to find herself staring at a small, plain breviary. *So this is what Olivier de Harcourt was asking for,* she thought sadly. With an unexpected twinge of sadness, she thrust the book back into the satchel and buckled it closed.

Tossing the bags over her shoulder, she crossed the manure-strewn yard toward the noise of the common room. At the bottom of the inn steps she paused, one hand on the railing, to stare uncertainly at the muted golden light that glowed through the cracks around the shuttered windows.

When the comtesse d'Alérion traveled, she stopped the night at abbeys or in the manor houses and castles of her class, where beds were always made available to noble travelers. Never in her life had Attica sat down to eat in the common room of an inn. On those rare occasions when Blanche did have need to pause at such a place, the comtesse would remain in her litter, resting in the shade of a tree, while servants were sent running to bring any required refreshment out to the yard.

Attica herself was too much the daughter of Robert d'Alérion—a rough, hard-drinking, loud-mouthed Norman knight—to have grown up to share her mother's haughty arrogance. Yet there was no denying that the room before her was an alien world, and the thought of having to keep up this wearing pretense of maleness in front of so many people—so many *men*—made her heart sink.

Before she could give way to the cowardly impulse to retreat without supper to her bed, Attica ran up the three shallow steps to the door and pushed it open. A blast of warm, noisy air slammed into her with an impact that was almost physical. She found herself confronting a strange, dimly lit masculine world, murky with smoke from the torches and thick with the smells of damp wool and male sweat and the fumes of spilt wine and ale. A confusing medley of rough voices and ribald laughter and one un-inhibited, high-pitched feminine squeal swirled around her. She pushed herself forward, searching the room for a familiar pair of broad shoulders and a darkly handsome face amongst the unkempt heads and huddled forms of the strangers who jostled one another on the rough benches.

She saw an aging knight, his tunic tattered and shiny, his dark beard threaded with gray, and a ruined monk, his black hair bristly and stiff over the relic of his tonsure. Then a man's laugh rang out, deep and clear and blessedly familiar. She felt a flood of warm relief and turned.

De Jarnac sat at the table in the far corner, his back to the wall, the flare of a nearby rushlight glazing his high forehead and the sharp lines of his cheekbones. In place of his leather *broigne*, he wore a dark wool tunic that molded itself to his broad chest. As she watched, he lifted his cup and tilted back his head to drink. She saw his jaw bulge and the muscles of his tanned throat move as he swallowed. Then he lowered his head and his gaze met hers across the length of the room.

She watched his face break into a lazy, welcoming smile that was a wonder to her. Looking at him now, she thought, no one would ever suspect that only an hour or so ago he had held his naked sword pointed at her breast and threat-ened to kill her. She had always known men for strange, in-comprehensible creatures. But as she wove her way toward him through the crowded trestle tables, Attica decided that a woman needed to dress as a man and go among them as one of their own for at least a day in order to truly under-stand just how illogical and absurd men really were.

"There you are, lordling," he said, his gaze flicking over

the dark water stains on her velvet surcoat, his senses doubtlessly noting the cold night air that clung about her still. "I
was beginning to wonder if I should ask the innkeeper to
drag his well. Best take a seat before they run out of food.
There's a full house tonight."

Suppressing another craven impulse to flee, Attica
dropped her bags to the floor and gripped the edge of the
table. Threading one foot in between board and bench, she
swung the other leg over and sat down opposite him. It was
an amazingly easy movement, without the hampering en-
cumbrance of long skirts, and it occurred to her that, in
some ways, at least, she could almost begin to enjoy this
disguise.

"Where is Sergei?" she asked, her gaze sweeping both
sides of the board and finding only strangers, several of
them other knights.

"In the small chapel near the base of the town walls,"
said de Jarnac, raising his cup and taking a slow, deep
swallow.

"In the chapel?" she repeated. "Now? Whatever for?"

He lifted his eyebrows. "Praying, one presumes. For the
souls of the day's dead, both those dispatched by my own
sword and some others we came across in a burned village
this morning."

"I saw them," Attica said, her voice hushed as she remembered the crackle of the flames, the smell of burning
wood and freshly spilled blood. She had seen the dead and
been troubled by them. Yet it hadn't occurred to her to pray
for them. And she certainly felt no compulsion to pray for
the souls of the dead *routiers*.

"He is unusual, your squire." She accepted a cup of wine
from a buxom, red-headed young woman who gave her

a beckoning smile that had Attica looking away quickly.
"Where did you find him?"

"Sergei? At a slave market in Acre."

Caught in the act of swallowing a mouthful of wine,
Attica choked and fell to coughing. "You *bought* him?"
she said when she was able.

He had his attention focused on a juicy pork joint he
was selecting. "I bought his mother. The boy came with
her. He was only about six at the time."

"He is Saracen, then?"

"No. He's from a place known as Kiev. He and his mother
were taken by nomads who raided their town and sold
them down the Dnieper to some Byzantine traders." De
Jarnac glanced up, his lips twisting into a cynical smile at
the sight of Attica's horror. "Did you think only Muslims
were killed and enslaved in Outremer? Believe me, we're
not particular."

Attica took another quick swallow of wine. "Why did
you buy her, this woman from Kiev?"

De Jarnac's grin broadened in a way that made Attica's
heart begin to beat in odd, unsteady lurches. "Why do you
think, lordling? She was a very beautiful woman."

As he spoke, his voice softened and his eyes darkened,
as with old, sweet memories. Attica watched him take another long drink from his cup, the red wine wetting his
lips, and she found she had to drop her gaze from his face.
Only then she found herself staring instead at his strong
brown fingers, curved around the base of his cup.

She realized that she was suddenly intensely aware of
him as a man. A man who had fought and killed beneath a
scorching foreign sun. A man who had once bought a beautiful woman in a noisy Eastern slave market and laid down
with her beneath a hot, star-brightened desert sky.

"Was?" Attica said, her voice husky.

This time he was the one who looked away. "She died of a fever in Egypt."

Attica studied his averted face. She could see no sign of emotion, only a closed, cold kind of detachment. And yet . . . "You kept the boy?" she asked. "And trained him as your squire?" It was unusual. Knights typically took only the sons of other knights as their squires.

De Jarnac shrugged. "Sergei's good with horses. Although I'm beginning to think he'd be happier as a priest."

Attica laughed softly. On the far side of the room, the inn-keeper's servants were already moving among the tables, clearing away trenchers and platters. One of the minstrels stood up and strummed his lute. Attica turned her head to see better and found herself staring into the massive cleav-age of the red-haired young woman.

"Here you are, monsieur." With deliberate, provocative slowness and an enticing smile, the serving woman leaned over, her breasts pressing almost into Attica's face as the woman placed a trencher overflowing with choice meat cuts on the table before Attica.

Attica didn't know where to look.

"My name is Rose, when you're ready for something more," she said with a giggle, and whisked herself off be-fore Attica had time to clamp shut her dropped jaw.

"*Ha!* You see," said the man on de Jarnac's left, a thin, long-boned knight with a lined face and the blue eyes and fair hair of a Norman. "It's the soft, pretty boys that women like." He waved one arm expressively through the air in a grand gesture that tottered the ewer of wine at his elbow. "Not mature, battle-tested men like us."

The other men at the table all laughed while another

knight with black hair and a bulbous nose said, "I'll drink to that," and called for more wine.

De Jarnac quietly settled back until his shoulders touched the wall and he could cross his arms at his chest. "What do you think, lordling?" he asked teasingly, slanting a look up at Attica from beneath lazy lids.

Attica shifted uneasily on her bench. She never, ever should have come in here, she thought despairingly. "What do I think about what?"

His lips curled into a faintly malicious smile that told her he hadn't entirely forgotten their confrontation on the road, either. "What do you think women want?" he said.

She ducked her head and feigned a sudden, intense interest in her supper. "How would I know?"

"Ah, look at the lad blush, the sly thing," said the long-faced Norman knight, displaying a mouthful of half-chewed pork. "He's had himself a few pieces of tail already, and that's a fact. Go on, lad. You tell us what makes the women happy."

Attica flung up her head, her cheeks burning, her determination to keep silent forgotten. "I can tell you what women *don't* like," she said, her voice rising higher than she'd intended. "They don't like being referred to as *pieces of tail*."

To her chagrin, the other men at the table all looked at her and laughed, including the Norman, who washed his food down with a swig of wine and grinned. "All right then, lad. You tell us. What *do* women like?"

From the far side of the room came the drunken jongleur's rough baritone, raised in song. *"En cest sonet coind'e leri . . ."* he sang.

"What's the matter, Roger?" someone said with a snicker. "Had so little luck lately, you're looking for pointers?"

There were a few catcalls and lewd suggestions, but the general noise quieted down, and Attica realized they were all looking at her. *Oh, God,* she thought wildly. *Why didn't I keep my mouth shut?*

"Go on, lad," said de Jarnac softly. "You've let yourself in for it now."

"Fauc motz e capuig e doli . . ." sang the jongleur.

She glanced, panic-stricken, down the row of expectant and faintly hostile male faces staring back at her. "I should think," she said, her voice sounding uncharacteristically prim and dangerously feminine, "that most gentlewomen wish for nothing more or less than a good Christian knight." Her chin lifted as she felt de Jarnac's sardonic gaze upon her. "A man who is courageous and loyal and—and charitable toward the weak and unfortunate."

"I thought we were talking about tavern wenches," said Sir Roger, sloshing more wine into his cup. "Not gentlewomen. Gentlewomen listen to too many damned troubadours and expect us all to be damned Rolands."

"Oh no, not Roland," said Attica with a quick shake of her head. "For does Roland think of his lady, the Fair Aude, at the moment of his death? No, his last thoughts are of Durendal, his sword." Some of the men laughed, but she pushed on, her gaze locked with de Jarnac's. "A woman dreams of a knight who is not only brave and honorable but also gallant and chivalrous."

"Bah," said the bulbous-nosed knight. "You've been listening to too many troubadours along with the ladies, lad."

"Aye," agreed Sir Roger, nodding his head sagely. "What a gentlewoman wants is a rich, powerful lord. It doesn't matter how he acts, or even what he looks like, as long as his estates are grand enough."

"It's not that simple," said Attica, her voice lost amid the general chorus of agreement.

"No?" said de Jarnac, sitting forward so that his words reached her alone. "Just ask your sister Elise."

Attica felt her breath leave her body in a painful rush that brought her splayed hand up to her chest in an unconsciously feminine gesture. "You say that as if you fault her for her betrothal. Yet she only does what her father wishes."

De Jarnac's eyebrows rose in a mockery of polite incredulity. "And if her father had wished to marry her to a poor man known as Fulk the Fat, would she have agreed so readily?"

"Women have no choice in such matters."

But de Jarnac wasn't about to let her get away so easily. "Are you saying she would have agreed?"

A ridiculous and wholly incomprehensible threat of tears stung Attica's nose, taking her by surprise and filling her with terror, lest she give herself away utterly. "You speak as if a woman's interests in marriage are different from a man's," she said, seizing on anger as a desperate antidote to this dangerous weakness. "Yet tell me, Monsieur le chevalier: What does a knight want?"

De Jarnac's lips curled away from his teeth in a quick smile. "An heiress, of course."

His laughter seemed to break the strange, inexplicable seriousness of the moment. She folded her hands on the tabletop and looked down at them. "How did we come to speak of marriage, anyway? I thought we spoke of love."

The jongleur's voice warbled in the background. *"Qu'Amors marves plan'e daura . . ."*

"Of love?" De Jarnac reached for the wine ewer. "Hardly. A knight can't afford love. At least not a knight-errant."

She drew in a deep breath and pushed it out again before she could trust herself to speak. "I think you're wrong."

He paused in the act of pouring his wine and looked at her from beneath quirked eyebrows. "Do you, indeed?"

"Yes, I do. I think a knight must learn to harmonize his knightly virtues with love—"

"Sweet Jesus. Not the knightly virtues again."

"Laugh if you want." She leaned forward, her weight on her elbows. "But it's true. Without love—without *fin'amors*—a knight will never truly achieve what he seeks."

"Here, here," said Sir Roger, startling Attica by lifting his cup high. "To the eternal quest."

"To the eternal quest," rang the chorus up and down the table.

"Which quest?" called someone from the far side of the room.

"The quest for love," shouted Sir Roger, the wine sloshing over the edge of his cup. He looked down at it, startled; then his eyes rolled back in his head and he slowly sank beneath the table. The room rang with laughter while the minstrel, abandoning the sweeter rhymes of Arnaut, strummed a new chord and raised his voice gleefully.

> *"I quest for love*
> *O'er hill and dale*
> *Yet ne'er do I find*
> *A willing female.*

> *"Or if I find her*
> *And she's generous*
> *Her lord's a miser*
> *And her cons gardatz."*

Attica felt her cheeks flame with embarrassment at the crudity, but the men in the room all let out a bawdy whoop that turned into a chorus of laughing boos as the jongleur staggered drunkedly and, clutching his lute to his breast, closed his eyes and began to howl like a hound baying at the moon.

"Here, give me that," said the bulbous-nosed knight, rearing up to pluck the lute from the drunken minstrel's grasp. He turned. "You play for us, de Jarnac."

Attica ducked as the lute sailed through the air. Standing, de Jarnac deftly caught the instrument around the neck and began almost absentmindedly to tune it. She found herself staring at him in astonishment, for he held the lute as easily and naturally as he held his sword.

"Sing us a song about a knight," called someone.

"Oui," said someone else.

"De Jarnac," chanted a third, thumping the table in front of him.

Tilting his head, de Jarnac looked up from the lute and smiled, a smile so open, so boyish even, that it took Attica's breath away. His fingers began to move, coaxing from that battered lute a sound so beautiful that the entire room fell silent. Then, as she watched, his smile broadened and became faintly rakish. *"Ferai un vers, pos mi sonelh,"* he sang in a clear, rich tenor.

A roar of appreciation rose from around the room, then quieted as he launched into the familiar, lighthearted tale about a knight who pretends to be a deaf-mute in order to enjoy the carnal favors of two obsessively discreet ladies.

At the end of the last verse, he started to put the lute down but paused amid shouts of "More!" and "Don't stop now." His gaze met Attica's for one intense instant. Then he laughed and, clearing the table with an easy leap, landed lightly on the balls of his feet in the center of the room, his fingers already plucking the strings as he launched into a classic *vers* about a valiant knight and his beautiful, wise, and courteous lady.

A lithe shadow moved along the near wall. Turning, Attica felt a breath of cold night air and caught the faint echo of incense as Sergei slid onto the bench beside her. By now, de Jarnac had changed songs and moods, shifting gracefully into a hauntingly beautiful canso that she realized with a jolt of surprise was about love. Not lust, but the kind of tender, eternal, ennobling love this man claimed he had no use for.

> *"I die for you.*
> *You are my hope*
> *My life*
> *My love."*

"I've never heard this before," Attica whispered to Sergei, pushing the trencher of meat toward him. "It's beautiful."

Sergei nodded, his gaze on de Jarnac. "It's one of his own."

> *"In you alone*
> *I see*
> *I hear*
> *I breathe."*

Attica swung her head around abruptly to stare again at Damion de Jarnac. *His own.* The torches in the wall brackets sputtered and flared, casting a rich reddish-gold glow over the roomful of upturned, enraptured faces. She felt the rough edge of the table pressing into her side, felt a strange, enveloping heat that spread over her as she looked at this man.

In the torchlight, his eyes seemed almost black—mysterious, unknowable. She let her gaze drift over the line of his jaw, the flaring elegance of his cheekbones. She watched the graceful, athletic movements of his body, the broad line of his shoulders beneath the rich dark cloth of his tunic, the lean length of hip and thigh as he strolled slowly about the room. She watched his long, tanned fingers move effortlessly over the lute's strings, watched him make sweet, beautiful music.

She thought what it would be like to take a man such as this to husband. Not a plump, weak, sulky boy but a man grown. A man who was big and strong and brave, a man who could be brutal with a sword yet was capable of composing such heartbreaking poetry and coaxing such magic from a battered old lute.

Her breath caught painfully in her throat as she realized the wayward direction of her disloyal thoughts. Not only disloyal but sinful, too, for she was a lady betrothed before God and man.

And yet . . . and yet she could not stop herself, for it was not so much a thought as a heartfelt yearning, a bittersweet ache that swelled her breast and made her want to reach out and stop this moment and make it last and last.

> *"Without you,*
> *My sun dies*
> *My prayer falters*
> *My song ends."*

He swung around then and found her watching him. Their gazes met, and it was as if he sang to her, as if he knew what was in her heart and soul better perhaps even than she knew herself. As if he saw her secret sorrow and despair, and called to it.

> *"Give me yourself.*
> *If not your body,*
> *Then your heart.*
> *Make me your soul."*

The song ended and the room erupted in cheering. And still he looked at her, his gaze sharpening with an unmistakable gleam of understanding, his jaw hardening with dangerous intent.

She stared into his dark, strong-boned face and felt a wave of panic that welled within her, stopping her breath and setting off a fine trembling from someplace deep inside her. *He knows,* she thought wildly, watching him hand the lute back to the drunken jongleur without dropping his probing, frightening gaze from her.

Mother Mary, help me, she prayed. *He knows I am a woman. He knows.*

CHAPTER
SIX

The wind had increased until it blustered against the inn's thick walls with an insistent howl that seemed to Attica to accentuate the unnatural silence between them as she followed de Jarnac's broad, dark-clad back up the stairs to their chamber.

She could hear the tossing branches of the big old chestnut that sheltered one corner of the courtyard and the flapping of a loose shutter somewhere in the unseen night. A draft eddied up from below, flaring the torch he carried and flinging huge, misshapen shadows across the narrow whitewashed walls of the stairwell. She watched him shove open the chamber door and thrust the torch into a wall bracket, and had to tense every muscle in her body to stay where she was rather than bolt back down the stairs.

He had scarcely spoken to her or even looked at her since handing the lute back to the jongleur along with an easy smile and shake of his head that quietly refused the crowd's roar for more. "We start early," he'd told Sergei, resting a light hand on the boy's shoulder. "Don't linger too long over your supper." Then he'd pinned Attica with a frighteningly intense gaze and said, "Come."

It never occurred to her to refuse. If he had somehow guessed the truth about who she was, Attica decided she would far rather he confront her with it in the privacy of their chamber, rather than downstairs before a ragged assortment of half-drunken, unruly, and unpredictable men. Only now she wasn't so sure.

Pausing halfway across the room, he glanced back at her over his shoulder, his brows drawing together, his eyes lost in dark shadows. "Splendor of God, must you always hold the door open?"

She moved quickly, the latch catching with a snap as she leaned back against the heavy planks, her wary gaze following him as he crossed to the laver and reached to wash his hands. His dark, simple tunic had been made of fine cloth and cut to fit well, so that she could see plainly the intimidating bulge of every toned muscle in his shoulders and back as he bent to splash his face.

Since she'd closed the door he had not looked at her again, and she felt the breath ease out of her in a long sigh. She told herself she must have imagined what she'd read in his face earlier, when their gazes met across the crowded common room below. No matter how hard she tried, she could think of nothing she had said or done in that moment that might have led him to guess the truth about her. She must have been mistaken.

In which case, she thought with a renewed upsurge of panic, she should not be arousing suspicion where none existed by standing with her arms splayed against the door, as mute and motionless as if she had been crucified against it.

"For a knight who does not believe in love," she said, striving to keep her voice light and relaxed as she pushed away from the rough panels, "you sing of it very beautifully."

He swung away from the laver, his wet skin gleaming in the torchlight, his eyes dark above the white of the length of linen he used to dry his face. "All troubadours sing of love, just as all priests prate about the mercy of God." He tossed the cloth aside. "How many believe in it is another matter."

She looked up from setting her saddlebags on the bench beside the bed. "Don't you believe in the mercy of God?"

He unbuckled his sword belt as he walked toward her, and she tried not to tremble at the rattling scrape of the scabbard as it came to rest on the floor on the far side of the bed. He faced her across six or seven feet of plain coverlet. "Do you?"

The intensity of his gaze made her uncomfortable. She sat down on the bench and yanked at her boots, keeping her head bowed. "Of course I believe in God's mercy."

"So you embrace your vocation willingly, do you?"

She paused, one boot still in her hand, conscious of a sense of edginess that had somehow crept into the conversation. She did not know how to answer him. In the course of this long and hideous day, she had uttered more falsehoods than she could remember, yet she could not bring herself to lay claim to a religious vocation she had not received. "I should make a poor knight," she said, choosing her words carefully. "And the life of scholarship does appeal to me."

"Indeed? I had thought it perhaps an obligation laid upon you by your father."

Something stirred within Attica, something unacknowledged and unwanted and quickly suppressed. "I should be proud to serve my father in any way he deemed necessary," she said, keeping her voice steady with effort.

De Jarnac grunted. "And does Elise d'Alérion go to her fat bridegroom as willingly as Atticus goes to his cloister?"

Attica swung her head to look at him. He had already removed his boots and mantle. As she watched, he tugged off his tunic and tossed it aside. He looked big and frightening and magnificently male, standing there in his shirt, hose, and braies. She felt a queer trembling start, someplace deep inside her, but she could not look away. "My sister knows that women of her station do not marry for love," Attica said slowly. "She has never expected nor wished for anything different."

He pulled off his shirt, baring his smooth, muscular chest to her fascinated gaze. "I wonder if she'll still feel that way on her wedding night, when she finds herself spreading her naked legs beneath him."

The crudeness of his words conjured up shudderingly vivid images of the one aspect of her betrothal Attica rarely allowed herself to dwell on. Once, shortly after she'd been sent to Salers to prepare to become Fulk's bride, she had come upon him swimming in the river with a couple of his father's squires. She had gazed in a kind of sick despair at his white, sagging chest, his grossly distended stomach, his quivering buttocks. And for one hideous, disloyal moment, she had looked into her woman's heart and thought, *I cannot do this. I cannot.* She could imagine moving through her days at his side. She could imagine helping guide him as he grew and matured into a man. But she could not imagine laying herself down and taking his naked, rutting body into hers.

"It is a woman's duty to bear her lord's heirs," Attica said, her throat so tight, she could scarcely push out the words. "Her duty and her honor."

"You d'Alérions take great pride in your devotion to duty and honor, do you?" The words came out smooth as silk, but his eyes had turned brittle. She could scarcely bear to look at him.

Her chin came up. "Do you doubt it?"

His lips curled away from his teeth. "Is there a reason why I should?"

The uneasiness she'd felt earlier came rushing back in full force, threatening to swamp her. For the length of one burning, endless moment, they stared at each other, Attica and this brutal, frightening man she had asked—no, God save her, *bribed and begged*—to accompany her. And now he knew—what?

With an abruptness that caught her by surprise, he swung away to stand with one arm braced against the wall, his head thrown back, his eyes squeezed shut. "I should like to retire some time before dawn," he said, his voice sounding suddenly tired. "If you could see your way to finish your preparations?"

Attica dropped her gaze to the boot she still held in her hand. She had considered suggesting she make up a pallet so that she might sleep on the floor, then dismissed the idea as impossible. If de Jarnac did indeed suspect her sex, such an action would only confirm his speculations. Yet what was the alternative? She could hardly strip off her clothes and crawl into bed naked, the way a lad would do.

Slowly, she unlaced her blue velvet surcoat and pulled it over her head. With trembling fingers, she reached beneath her wool tunic and linen shirt to fumble with the points that held up her chausses. The air felt cool against her bare legs as she pushed the hose down and she shivered. Still clad in tunic, shirt, and braies, she leapt for the bed and quickly pulled the linen sheets and coverlet up under her chin. Not daring to look at de Jarnac, she resolutely squeezed her eyes shut.

An ominous silence descended upon the room. She felt rather than saw him shift his position to stare down at her.

"Do you normally go to bed in all your dirt, lordling?" he asked, still in that smooth voice she did not trust. "Or are you concerned, perhaps, that I might have designs on your virtue?"

Attica's eyes flew open wide to discover him standing with one shoulder propped against the far bedpost, a hand resting on his lean hip in an intensely masculine pose she found intimidating. He gave her a smile that showed his teeth. "Would it reassure you to know that I only ravish females?"

She felt her heart crack up against her ribs with a resounding thump. "I . . . I was raised in a monastery. We . . ." She tried to swallow the tremble in her voice. "We do not disrobe for bed."

He pushed away from the post to come around the great bed toward her. "Indeed," he said, his voice lightly mocking, his eyes hard. "And do they wear silk and velvet at your monastery?"

She felt her muscles tighten up, ready to fight him off if she had to. But she realized he walked not toward her but to the flickering torch. He reached up to extinguish it, and the room suddenly plunged into darkness.

She listened to the rustle and crunch of the rushes beneath his feet as he crossed back to his own side of the bed. Her breath eased out of her in a long sigh, then caught again when she felt the straw mattress give beneath his weight and heard the creak of the leather supporting braces as he lay down beside her.

The room was suddenly so quiet, she imagined she could hear her own pounding heartbeat. Even the wind seemed to have died. She lay beside him in the darkness, afraid to move, afraid even to breathe. Every sense seemed achingly alert, every nerve on end. She had never been so intensely aware of her own body, of her bare legs against the sheets and her swelling breasts, pressing painfully against their bindings.

She did not know how long she lay there, tense and waiting in the darkness, quiveringly aware of the man beside her. But gradually she began to realize that he was no threat to her. That she had done him an injustice by fearing him tonight, just as she had wronged him by lying to him today. True, he had been angry with her and suspicious of her—but justifiably so. And she had never even apologized.

She cleared her throat. "Monsieur le chevalier?" she said softly.

She heard a whisper of movement, as if he turned his head to stare at her. "Yes?"

"I am most heartily sorry for having deceived you."

She held her breath, listening, waiting for his response. After a long moment, he said, his voice unexpectedly tight, "It's late, lordling. Save your confession for the morning and go to sleep."

His words had an ominous ring to them that worried her. Exhaustion pulled at her. She fought hard to stay awake, to force her sluggish mind to think. But the bed was soft and warm, her body sore, the night dark and quiet.

Oblivion rolled over her, and she slept.

Damion lay beside her in the darkness, his body tense, his mind alert and wakeful. He listened to her breathing drift into the unmistakable rhythms of sleep, and still he held himself rigid, waiting. Waiting for his eyes to adjust gradually to the dim glow of mingling starlight and moonlight that shone around the closed shutters. Waiting for her to sink so deeply into sleep that he would not risk waking her.

Gently, he propped himself up on his elbow and gazed down at the still figure beside him. Sensitive lips, too soft and feminine ever to belong to any boy, parted with the soft breath of sleep. He saw a high, smooth forehead, a thin, delicate nose, soft cheeks. A woman's face, belied by its strong cleft chin.

His exhalation stirred the hair beside her ear as he let his gaze drift lower, over the neck and shoulders of a woman. A woman built tall and slender like a boy. But a woman, nonetheless.

A woman.

Yet he hadn't seen it. Not when he'd ridden beside her through the long and danger-filled day. Not when he'd held his sword to her breast in an obviously unsuccessful attempt to intimidate the truth out of her. Not until tonight, when he'd turned, lute in hand, and found her watching him across the length of the common room.

One moment he had looked back at a boy, Atticus. Then something had shifted. Even now he could not say what had caused it—a trick of the torchlight, some unconsciously feminine gesture that she'd made. He didn't know.

Perhaps it had been none of those things, only something in the way she looked at him, something in the way he had responded to her. But he had known, in one blinding flash of revelation, that he beheld not a lad destined for the church but a girl. A woman. Unbelievably brave and strong, but a woman nonetheless.

And in that moment it had all made sense. All the subtle inconsistencies, the nagging doubts that had bothered him throughout the day. Everything that had not quite fit, fell suddenly into place. And he had known an anger so intense, so gut-deep and blood-boiling, it had taken his breath away.

Part of it, doubtless, was injured pride. She had deceived him. She had lied to him. She had *used* him. And he had let her do it. Yet he also felt betrayed on another, more personal level. For he had actually come to *like* that brave, sensitive, funny youth, Atticus. A youth who did not exist.

He was still angry, although his anger had cooled now to a kind of controlled, lethal purposefulness. Yet when he gazed down at her, lying asleep so close beside him in the still of the night, what he felt was desire. Unbidden and unwanted, but desire, nonetheless, swelling his body, heating his blood.

With a muttered curse, he pushed himself away from her and flung back the covers. Crossing the room with long, swift strides, he cracked open the shutters and windows and let the coolness of the night soothe his hot, naked body.

The wind had almost died. Their chamber overlooked the courtyard, so that he stared down on the dark shifting shadows of a chestnut tree and an expanse of cobbles that gleamed silent and deserted in the blue-gray light of night. A bell tolled in the distance, then another, calling the observant to matins and counting out the passage of the night for those too restless to sleep.

He swung his head to look back at the woman in his bed. She lay still and unmoving, lost in exhaustion. He wondered who she was. Elise d'Alérion? He supposed it could be possible, for she doubtless rode Elise's chestnut gelding. But when he tried to imagine a lady as gently reared and sheltered as the comte d'Alérion's daughter cutting her hair and dressing as a boy to ride bravely into the dangers this woman had faced, he knew it could not be.

Doubtless Elise herself had sought shelter at some convent and sent one of her servants—this woman—instead.

But to what purpose? To what purpose, he wondered, tapping his fingertips on the wood of the windowsill. He remembered the girl's eyes, so huge and dark with terror when he held his sword to her breast. She had told him part of the truth, he was sure. But obviously not all of it.

Pushing away from the window, he moved softly to the side of the bed. He had a vivid image of Atticus hovering just inside the door of their chamber, the saddlebags clutched against his chest—no, *her* chest, Damion reminded himself with a private, fierce smile that boded no good for the slim figure sleeping so peacefully in the faint shaft of moonlight.

He crouched down beside her. Whatever this unknown woman carried for her mistress, he thought, she doubtless bore it secreted either about her person or in her saddle-bags. Tomorrow, when he had her in some isolated place where no one could hear her screams, he fully intended to search the woman herself. Now he carefully lifted the leather satchels from where she'd left them on the bench.

He subjected the bags to a quick, thorough search. One side yielded a woman's dress, stockings, and chemise, all made of exquisitely fine material. The other side contained a change of male clothing, a scattering of items for personal cleanliness, and a book.

His breath caught, for he knew what he held the instant his hand closed around the soft leather binding. He drew the book out slowly. In the dim light from the half-opened window, the deep forest green cover looked almost black, the incised lettering too small to read.

But he did not need to flip through the pages to know it for a simple breviary, copied diligently by the nuns of the convent of Sainte-Foy-la-Petite, near Saint-Denis, and sold in vast numbers to the students who came from all over to study at the University of Paris. A common book—so common that for years now, books such as this one had been used by the courtiers of King Philip of France to transport those official documents their royal master wished kept secret.

Using the unknown woman's own dagger, he carefully slit the edge of the leather covering the board that faced the manuscript, then slipped the blade tip beneath to catch the white edge of a sheet of velum that crackled softly as he eased it out and unfolded it. *"My God,"* he whispered, staring unbelievingly at the document in his hand.

Somewhere in the distance a dog barked. Quickly refolding the document, Damion slipped it back beneath the binding, just as the breeze gusted, swinging the open window against the wall with a creaking *bang*. Damion's head jerked up. In the bed beside him, the girl murmured something, her head shifting restlessly against the pillow. Then she fell silent.

He stayed where he was, every muscle in his body tense as he gazed down at her. The moonlight etched the tumble of her hair and emphasized the dusky curve of her lashes lying against her cheek. She looked so young and inexperienced and yet oddly, fiercely brave. And he felt it again, that strange twist of confusion, that unfamiliar sensation composed of equal parts anger and loss and hot desire.

He wanted to dig his hands into her shoulders and shake her awake. He wanted to make her tell him who she was—not tomorrow but *now*. He wanted to know why she carried one of King Philip's treacherous documents in her saddlebags. He wanted to crush her to him and cover her soft, lying mouth with his own. He wanted to rip away the lie of that man's tunic and hose and reveal the slim woman's body they hid. He wanted to pin her to the bed and feel her laying naked beneath him.

God help him, he thought, reeling away from the bed. He knew nothing of this woman, only that she was involved in treason against the lord he served. And still he wanted her with a fierceness that left him aching and sleepless for most of the night.

The late afternoon sunlight filtered down through the high branches of the forest, casting dappled shadows over the girl's slim, straight shoulders.

"Why do we stop?" she asked when Damion reined in and waited for her to come up abreast of him. He rode the bay today to rest the Arab. Unfortunately, he'd had to mount her on his roan again, because whatever her real reason for wanting to keep the chestnut from the sight of the riders from Salers, there was no denying that the horse, while a splendid animal, had been pampered of late and was in no shape for the kind of relentless journey she had subjected it to.

He watched her thoughtfully as her alert gaze scanned the birch and poplars that pressed in on both sides of the track. "Is something wrong?" she asked. Her face looked pale and vulnerable in the gloom. Strain etched her features sharply, and exhaustion had lain dark smudges beneath her eyes, for dawn had been little more than a pale promise on the horizon when he'd dragged her out of bed and out onto the road that morning. He'd wanted to be certain they would reach Laval before nightfall and still have time for this.

"Nothing's wrong," he said, pressing the heels of his palms against the pommel to give a deceptively lazy stretch.

"But it's hot, and I would rid myself of the dust of the journey before we reach Laval. There is a pond"—he nodded toward the base of the hill that fell away steeply to their right—"just out of sight of the road."

"I do not wish to bathe." He heard the nervousness she normally managed to keep out of her voice, saw the muscles in her throat work as she swallowed.

He gathered his reins and touched his spurs to the bay's sides. "Then guard my back while I do," he said, and swung away from her.

After a moment of hesitation, the bay struck through the brush that grew thick at the side of the track. A shower of dirt and small stones tumbled downhill as the horse picked its way down the slope toward the vale below. He was aware of Sergei, ambling along behind, leading the spare horses toward the water. He did not look back to see if the girl followed.

A warm breeze wafted around him, sweet with the scents of grass and scattered white daisies. From deep in the forest came the repetitive call of a cuckoo and a distant, muffled snort that might have been a wild boar but was more likely just a pig, wandered from some isolated hamlet. He was aware of the woman, hanging back another moment. Then he heard the crash of the roan hurtling through the underbrush behind him, and he smiled to himself.

"Surely this is unnecessary," she called after him.

"You may have an aversion to cleanliness, lordling," he said, lifting his voice so that it would carry back to her. "But I am considered quite fastidious."

"I do not have an aversion to cleanliness," he heard her mutter beneath her breath.

Grinning, he drew rein beside a small pool formed by a fall of rock that had caused the stream to back up behind it.

He threw his leg over the cantle and slid to the ground but caught Sergei's eye before the boy dismounted, too. Sergei paused and sank back into the saddle.

"I want you to go ahead," Damion said, his voice low as he walked up to his squire. "Find someplace to stable the horses on the road to Le Mans, on the far side of Laval." He glanced behind him. The girl had reined in some distance beyond his bay. She had not dismounted but simply sat, her horse shifting restlessly beneath her as she stared at the pond.

He continued, "Then I want you to ride Atticus's chestnut back to Laval and wait for me there, at the fountain near the castle gates. Do you understand?"

Sergei's dark, exotic eyes searched his face. "You're expecting trouble?"

Damion shrugged. "No, but it's better to play it safe." He glanced at the girl again. She had dismounted now and gone to stand on a large, flat shelf of rock that jutted out over the pond.

He wondered how he had ever mistaken her for a boy, for she moved with a grace that was all woman, long-legged, slim-hipped, and sinuous. Beneath their bindings, her breasts would be small, he decided. Small and high and round. He watched as the wind ruffled the surface of the pond, the gentle waves catching the sun to throw sparkling flashes of light across her face. She had a boyish face, for a woman, with that strong chin and straight nose. But her mouth . . .

Her mouth was all woman. Not the mouth of a lady like Elise d'Alérion, born to silks and feather beds and passionless, arranged marriages, but the kind of lush, full-lipped mouth that made a man think of laying a woman down in a sun-kissed meadow and taking her with swift, hot lust, all sweat and moans and naked, panting bodies entwined in raw, violent passion.

"Messire?"

He jerked his attention back to the squire. "I'm not certain what to expect," Damion said again, his voice rough. "I should have a better idea after I've had a private conversation with Monsieur le Batard d'Alérion there."

"Don't hurt her," Sergei blurted out as Damion started to turn away.

Her? Damion spun about, his boots crunching in the sand that lined the pond's edge. *"Splendor of God—"* He broke off, took a deep breath, and said with deliberate, low-voiced calm, "How long have you known she was a girl?"

Sergei did not meet his gaze. "Almost from the first."

Damion walked back to stand at the boy's stirrup. "I won't ask how you knew," he said, looking up at his squire through hard, narrowed eyes. "But what I do wish to know is, *why in the name of all the saints didn't you see fit to mention it to me?*"

A faint flush stained the boy's cheeks. "I was afraid you might hurt her."

"She deserves to be hurt," Damion hissed, feeling again that strange twist of angry betrayal and fierce lust, deep inside.

"Messire," said the boy with a gasp of alarm that startled his horse. "You would not!"

Damion pursed his lips and blew out his breath in a long sigh. Having a squire with the instincts of a priest could be a sore trial at times, especially for a knight-errant with his own way to make in this brutal, cut-throat world. "I only intend to frighten her, lad," said Damion, keeping his voice level with effort. "Just enough to make her tell me what I need to know." *Of course,* he thought, *if she refuses to answer me . . .*

"Oui, messire," said Sergei, his face still dark and troubled as he gathered the spare horses' leads.

Once more, Damion started to turn away, then swung back again as a new thought occurred to him. "How did you know?" he asked, his head tilted against the harsh afternoon sun. "I mean, how did you know I'd finally figured it out?"

Sergei swallowed. "I saw it in your face. When you looked at her."

"Ah," said Damion into the short, heavy silence that followed.

"You won't—" Sergei began, then cut himself off.

"Force myself on her?" Damion felt his lips twist into a hard grin. "I already said I didn't intend to hurt her, didn't I?" He slapped the boy's mare on its hind quarters. "Go on. Get out of here."

Damion saw the girl's head come up, her troubled gaze following the horses as Sergei left the clearing. He walked toward her.

"Where goes your squire?" she asked, her breathing so high and rapid, he could see the quick rise and fall of her chest.

"I sent him ahead." Damion planted himself in front of her, close enough that his body threw a long, dark shadow across her. "To prepare for our arrival in Laval."

She stepped back, one hand coming up across her chest to nervously clasp the other arm at its elbow, her face turning away so that he saw only the fine line of her profile.

His gaze still on her face, Damion slowly unbuckled the belt that supported his scabbard and sword and set it on the rock, where it would be within easy reach of the pool.

"Best hurry." He pulled off his boots and unfastened his girth. "I don't want to be here all day."

She didn't move.

"Don't tell me," he said, his voice mocking as he stripped off his leather *broigne*. "You've taken a vow against bathing." He watched a gentle flush suffuse her damask cheeks as he went to work on the points of his chausses. "Or is it just against taking off your clothes?"

Her head snapped around, her lips parting on a quickly indrawn breath as she watched him pull his shirt over his head. "In the monastery," she said, swallowing convulsively, "it was discouraged."

"Oh?" He tossed the shirt aside. "And which monastery was that?"

He saw her go still, as if she were drawing deep into herself. He already knew how much she hated to lie; she always got the same expression on her face, every time he cornered her and forced her to answer a direct question—a sort of hunted look, quickly smoothed into a semblance of courtly serenity that made him want to smile.

"Saint-Hervisse," she said in that husky, boyish voice of hers. "The monastery of Saint-Hervisse."

He untied his braies and let them fall. "Oh? And where exactly is that?"

He watched her nostrils flare in alarm as her wide-eyed gaze took in the sight of him naked before her. Her nose was sunburned, he noticed; she might not be a grand lady like Elise d'Alérion, but she obviously wasn't used to being in the sun all day.

"In Aquitaine." She kept her dark brown eyes determinedly fixed at some point over his left shoulder. "I was raised in Aquitaine."

And that, he decided, watching her closely, was probably the truth. *Christ*, he thought; Aquitaine. Home of Henry's high-spirited, hardheaded, treasonous queen, Eleanor, and more rebellious and treacherous nobles than in the rest of Henry's realm put together.

Damion swung away from her and walked, naked, to his horse to retrieve the ball of soap and length of linen he kept in his saddlebags. When he came back, it was to find her sitting scrunched up on the rocky shelf, her arms wrapped around her bent knees, her gaze discreetly lowered.

"Here," he said, looking down at her determinedly bowed head. "Hold these for me."

He watched her gaze shift to the bare male foot he'd planted beside her, then lift slowly to midthigh—but no higher. She reached out one hand, blindly, and managed to snag the linen. He let the soap fall in her lap.

He stood a moment, looking down at her and listening to the shifting of the leafy branches up above and the sibilant hiss of the marsh grasses blowing in the wind. The sun felt hot beating down on his bare skin. The ruffled surface of the pool beckoned, cool and glistening, the water so clear he could see the sandy bottom, far below. Curling his toes over the edge of the rock, he sucked in a quick breath and dove.

The water was colder than it looked, a vibrant shock that sent a delicious shudder through his naked body as he plunged deep. He kicked out, his arms cutting in an arc that brought him back to the surface.

He broke through to the air above and tossed his head, shaking water and a tumbled lock of hair out of his eyes. He found her watching him, a wistful, almost envious expression on her face. The heat had flushed her cheeks until they were almost as red as her burned nose, and as he watched, a bead of sweat formed to trickle down beside her ear.

"You look hot," he said, bobbing lazily amid the waves of his own creation.

He was surprised to see a wry smile curl the edges of her lips. "I am."

"So, come in," he invited, rolling forward to swim back to her.

She shook her head.

He laughed. "Then take off those boots and put your feet in the water. Monks wear sandals, don't they? Even Jesus Christ wasn't averse to baring his toes."

"Surely that's blasphemy," she said, still smiling. But she must have been hot indeed, because she hesitated only a moment before reaching down to grasp one boot and tug it off.

Which was a good thing, he thought, watching her kick off the other boot and then, more shyly, her chausses. Because he knew damned well she didn't have a spare pair of shoes in her bags.

And she was about to get wet.

CHAPTER
SEVEN

Yvette ran her fingertips over the tightly matted carpet of thyme beside her. She'd had the bench built only last year, along the eastern wall of her garden, and she'd come to love sitting here on days such as this one, when the air was crisp and clean and filled with the sweet song of birds. Sighing contentedly, she rested her shoulders against the sun-warmed stone wall behind her and closed her eyes to breathe in the heady scents of crushed thyme and honeysuckle and jasmine mingling with the rich, fertile odor of damp earth.

There had been no garden in the old motte and bailey castle in Normandy, where Yvette grew up. Just a dark, dank wooden tower on a windswept hill and a muddy, manure-filled yard crawling with scrawny chickens and squealing pigs and the three-dozen scrambling, half-wild children her father had got upon his succession of seven wives.

People used to whisper about old Alain Pardue, about the wives he'd buried. He'd been a brutish man, her father; short but stocky and thickly muscled, with a flowing gray-brown beard and great, bushy eyebrows.

He knew what people said about him, but it only made him laugh. "God's bones," he used to say, pounding the dais table with one meaty fist while throwing back his head to roar for more ale. "Why would I need to murder the bitches? I just breed them to death." And then he'd laugh, and the rough men-at-arms he liked to surround himself with would laugh, too. Only Yvette, who'd been the death of her own mother, Alain's third and shortest-lived wife, never joined in the laughter.

She'd been a serious child, Yvette, and never pretty or winsome, even when small. She'd never won the favor of any of that succession of ill-fated and often surly step-mothers, which meant she'd had to grow up fast, dodging kicks and blows, and hungry, always hungry. Not just for a good, filling meal but for other things, elusive things she yearned for even before she learned their names. Things like solitude and beauty.

Especially beauty.

There was little solitude and even less beauty at Alain Pardue's castle, but Yvette still managed to find it. She could stand alone in the middle of a wheat field after har-vest and marvel at the grandeur of the clear blue sky, or the graceful arc of a sparrow's wing, or the vivid, unexpected brilliance of the beech tree near the crossroads after the first frost had touched it.

Of her father, she saw little. Alain was proud of his sons—"my own private army," he liked to call them—and he trained them well in the arts of war. But he had no use for his daughters, didn't know half of their names, and scarcely noticed when one or the other of them—those less stubborn and determined than Yvette—would simply give up and die.

Most of Alain's daughters knew well enough that they had little to live for. Alain didn't have enough land for his sons. His daughters had to see to their own futures, and with-out dowries, they had no hope of ever securing knightly husbands. The best any of them could look forward to would be to find herself married off to some peasant, who would work her like a mule and get her quick with his sons, year after year, until he killed her the way her father had killed all of his wives.

By the time Yvette was thirteen, she had already seen four of her older sisters suffer that fate, and she'd made up her mind that it wasn't going to happen to her. She wasn't exactly sure how she was going to avoid it, since she certainly had no intention of spending the rest of her days as an unpaid drudge to her father and brothers. She didn't know enough yet to know what she wanted; she only knew what she did not want.

And then Gaspard Beringer came into her life.

She'd been out picking strawberries on the hill that brilliant May morning when she walked into the yard, her pail swinging at her side, and saw him. He was mounted on his big white destrier, and although only eighteen, already he was taller by far than any of her brothers, broader in the shoulder, longer in the leg. The sun shone golden on his silken fair hair and kissed his handsome cheeks with a healthy flush, and she knew, in that moment, that she had never seen anything so fine. It wasn't until she'd beheld the subtle hues of Gaspard's expensive woolen surcoat and tunic, until she'd discovered the intricate workmanship of his saddle, the delicate metalwork of his rings and brooch, that it even occurred to Yvette that beauty could be found not just in nature but in things made by man. In the *person* of a man.

He was the fourth son of the viscomte de Salers, and Yvette couldn't begin to understand why he had been sent as squire to such a poor, out-of-the-way castle as Château Pardue, until later, when she heard her father say, "He's as close to being an idiot as a man can come without actually *being* one. Which is why the old viscount sent him here, of course. I mean, he could hardly send him to court, now could he?"

But Gaspard didn't fit in well at Château Pardue, either. It wasn't that Alain's sons were so much brighter than Gaspard, because most of them weren't. But they were harder and cruder, as well as being sly and vicious and mean.

Less than two weeks after his arrival at the castle, Yvette came upon the young viscount's son quietly sobbing in a dark corner of the hay barn. Until then, she'd found him simply too magnificently beautiful to approach. But after she'd held his hand in comfort and dried his tears, she discovered that he was just a boy—a shy, malleable boy, who looked at Yvette Pardue and saw not a plain, worthless female but a clever, strong person who could guide him and protect him and care for him.

It wasn't long before Yvette discovered other things about Gaspard. She discovered that his skin was as smooth as it looked, and that when she touched him, her breath hitched and her own skin felt all warm and tingly, as if she'd stood too close to the kitchen hearth.

Gaspard stayed at Château Pardue for three years. With each passing year, he grew both closer to Yvette and more dependent upon her. So that when word came one day that he must return to his family's principal estate at Châteauhaut-sur-Vilaine, he ran straight to her to pour out the terrible tale he'd just heard: that his father and eldest brother George had both fallen victim to a deadly fever, just days after learning of the death of his brothers Louis and Francis in a shipwreck off the coast of Marseilles.

Gaspard was now the viscomte de Salers.

"But what shall I do, Yvette?" he wailed, his head buried

in her lap as she stroked his heaving shoulders. "I don't know how to be a viscomte. No one ever taught me to be a viscomte. I was never meant to be a viscomte. How shall I manage? I won't even have you there to tell me what to do."

Yvette sat on a stool beside the bubbling cauldron of wash she'd been boiling in the yard, her red, work-roughened hands clutching his broad, wonderful shoulders, her heart aching almost unbearably, as if someone were trying to rip it out of her chest.

And then it came to her, how she could both keep Gaspard and at the same time grasp at everything she'd always dreamed of. "You can take me with you, Gaspard," she said, hearing her own words as if they were coming from a long ways off. "Marry me, and then I'll be able to go to Châteauhaut with you. I'll help you learn to be a viscomte."

He raised his head, so that she was looking into his anxious blue eyes, shining now with hope and gratitude.

"You can do it, Gaspard," she told him. "With me there beside you, you can do it."

And so Yvette Pardue, the plain, dowerless daughter of a poor Norman baron, became the viscomtesse de Salers.

Except that when the new viscomte and viscomtesse arrived in Brittany several weeks later, it was to discover that Gaspard's second brother, Louis, hadn't died in the shipwreck, after all. He was alive, although suffering from a crushed leg, which had made the journey home both slow and painful. Gaspard was overjoyed to see his brother, and more than happy to abandon his claim to the family's titles and estates.

Gaspard's new sixteen-year-old wife had different ideas.

Louis might have died anyway; he was so weak, and his wound refused to heal. But Yvette had to be sure. So one night she fixed him a warm drink, sweetened with poppy syrup, to help him sleep. And later, when the castle was quiet, she crept into his chamber, covered his handsome face with a pillow, and held it there until he died.

After that, she never went near a sickroom again.

"Yvette?"

Awaking with a start, Yvette opened her eyes to the sight of Gaspard weaving his way toward her through the intricately planted beds of lavender and dianthus and stocks, of hemlock and henbane and nightshade, the late afternoon sun casting a bronze sheen across his damp handsome face.

"Yvette," he said again with a gasp, for he'd obviously run the length of the castle compound. "I've just heard from one of the men-at-arms that you've taken Attica's groom, Walter Brie."

"Yes." Pushing up from the thyme bench, she bent to pluck an aphid from the stem of a nearby white rose. "I found him at the monastery of Saint-Sevin," she said, and squashed the insect between thumb and forefinger.

"But you *took* him, Yvette." Gaspard's voice trembled with the horror of it. "You had the men seize him. With violence. From a monastery."

She swung about, the soft leather soles of her slippers hissing over the stone flagging of the garden path as she walked up to rest her hand on his arm and pat it lightly. "He was in the infirmary, Gaspard. Not the church. There is no question of a violation of sanctuary. Besides, Saint-Sevin has no powerful protector. The monks might sputter and complain, but no one will pay them much heed."

"But what has happened to Attica?"

Yvette wrinkled her nose at the sight of a drop of sweat cascading down his hard cheek. "Gaspard. You are perspiring."

He swiped his silk sleeve across his face. "I ran. Fulk has heard, you see. The man-at-arms said Fulk was very upset when he found out about some knight Attica seems to have met—"

Yvette frowned. "This man-at-arms of yours has a loose tongue that needs fixing. Which one is he?"

Gaspard's soft blue eyes shifted to a sight in the distance. "I . . . I am sure I could not say. They all look alike to me."

"Never mind," said Yvette, looping her arm through Gaspard's to draw him up the path beside her. "I shall find him."

"But this knight with Attica—" Gaspard swallowed. "Do you think in truth that she might have run away with him? That perhaps we were wrong when we thought she had learned something from that courtier—"

"No, I do not think I was wrong." Yvette lifted her gaze to the South Tower. "But I shall know more, soon. I told Wolf to report to me here."

"Wolf?" echoed Gaspard, following her gaze. "You've given the groom to Wolf to question?"

Yvette picked a spray of rosemary, her nose quivering at the pungent scent it released. "And why not, pray tell?"

"The last man you gave to Wolf to question died before he had a chance to say anything."

Yvette frowned. She would like to have denied it. Except that Wolf could sometimes be unfortunately heavy-handed in his methods.

She saw the door at the base of the South Tower swing open. The tower was old, square-built and little-used, for it had stood on this bluff overlooking the Vilaine for a hundred years or more, since before the viscomtes de Salers had come here and built Châteauhaut. A man filled the darkened entrance. A big man with an enormous head, as square and thick as a battering ram, and a body as solid and

forbidding as the tower behind him. He had stripped down
to his braies, his naked torso gleaming with sweat, as if
he had been standing beside a hot fire. Yvette's frown
darkened as she watched the man visibly hesitate. But Wolf
knew better than to avoid her, and after a moment he cut
across the ward to where she stood, waiting for him, beside the tunnel arbor at the entrance to her garden.

"My lady." Wolf dropped to his knees before her and
bowed his head. "I fear Walter Brie's wound proved to be
more severe than we thought."

A tense silence hung over the garden, broken only by
the buzzing of bees and a distant hammering from the
smithy. Then Yvette's breath exploded out of her in a savage curse. "God rot you, Wolf, you've killed him."

Wolf trembled and wisely kept his head bowed. "I do
think he told us the truth, my lady. That the lady Attica asked
him to escort her to Laval, and the knight came upon them
by chance, when they were attacked by a band of *routiers*."

Yvette pursed her lips and blew out a huff of annoyance.
"Did he tell you this knight's name?"

"No, my lady. He said he did not know."

Yvette swung away, dismissing the man with a wave of
her hand.

"So? So? What do you think?" Gaspard asked as soon
as Wolf had taken himself off.

She stared thoughtfully at the gentle hills falling away
toward the east. "I think Walter Brie knew more than he
would admit," she said slowly. "He was very devoted to
Attica."

"Yes, but where has she gone? To Laval, as we thought?
Or has she simply run away to meet this strange knight?"

Yvette glanced at her husband. "Don't be a fool, Gaspard. Attica is a d'Alérion, not some village maiden. She

would never bring shame upon her house by seeking to avoid a marriage arranged by her father. She has gone to Laval."

"Then the men we sent might already have overtaken her," he said hopefully.

Yvette shook her head. "According to the porter at Saint-Sevin, Walter Brie was left in their care by a knight traveling in the company of his squire and a well-dressed youth. A tall, slim youth with dark hair. Riding a white-blazed chestnut."

Gaspard's elegant forehead puckered in confusion. "I don't understand."

Yvette turned to stroll slowly through the tunnel arbor, her silken skirts swishing about her feet. It was dark in here, and cool. She lingered for a moment, her hand caressing the velvety petals of a rose, her thoughts far away.

"Yvette," said Gaspard again. "I don't understand."

She brought her gaze back to her husband's face. "Attica has dressed herself as a boy, of course. That is why she took de Harcourt's clothes. It sounds as if she's cut and dyed her hair as well. Our men would simply have passed her unknowingly on the road."

"Then shouldn't we send a message to warn Renouf Blissot to be on the lookout for a lad?"

Yvette laughed softly. "Think, Gaspard. She will be in Laval herself long before another messenger could reach there. Don't worry; she will hardly fail to reveal herself to her uncle."

"Then we do nothing?"

"No, we pack," said Yvette, swinging toward the keep.

"Pack?" Gaspard stood staring after his wife in open-mouthed astonishment, then hurried to catch up with her. "But . . . where do we go?"

Yvette's voice drifted back over her shoulder. "To Laval, of course."

Self-consciously aware of her bony knees and long, narrow feet, Attica scooted quickly to the edge of the rock. In the golden sunlight of the afternoon, the skin of her legs shone almost indecently pale. She poised her feet above the surface of the water only for an instant before plunging them in.

An icy shock tore through her body. "Aahh," she yelped, and jerked her legs up. She heard de Jarnac's low, throaty laugh as she held her feet, dripping, above the pond. She glanced up accusingly to discover him treading water only an arm's span away from the rock shelf where she sat. "You didn't tell me it was *this* cold," she said, and he laughed again, his dark eyes flashing.

The slanting rays of the afternoon sun sparkled on the rivulets of water that ran down the planes of his face and dripped from his dark hair onto his bare shoulders. She stared at him, and her world sharpened and grew more vivid until it seemed as if she had never seen the clouds billowing so white and high in such an achingly blue sky. Never known the warm caressing whisper of the wind, so rich with the scents of deep forest glades and sunlit water meadows. Never felt so aware of herself as a woman—the strange fullness of her lips, the swell of her breasts beneath the unfamiliar male clothing.

She looked at him and saw the laughter slowly fade from his face until he regarded her with a still, intense expression that made her shiver. Slowly, she eased her feet back into the water and kept them there.

"Throw me the soap, would you?" he asked, his voice rough.

She had left the soap farther back on the rock, so that she had to stretch, twisting sideways and tottering, to reach it. She just managed to close her hand over the ball when she felt the hard strength of his fingers grip her ankles.

"What are you—" She whipped back around, trying to regain her balance, but it was too late. He gave a sharp tug, and she shot off the edge of the rock and hit the pond with a splash that sent water spraying up into the air.

Attica yelped but quickly shut her mouth as the cold water closed over her head, and she plunged into a billowing green world that bubbled and swirled around her, silent and slow.

When she was a little girl, she had spent long, lazy summer days with her brother Stephen, swimming in the ponds and streams that abounded near her father's various castles and manor houses. She hadn't been in anything deeper than a tub for years, but she still moved naturally, kicking out, aiming toward the light above. Her head broke the surface, and she drew a quick gasp of air, laughing. Then she saw de Jarnac's face. Saw his narrowed eyes and the hard, uncompromising line of his lips. She knew a quick stab of uneasiness, so that when he reached for her, she jerked away from him—just as the water-sodden weight of the thick velvet surcoat she wore pulled her under again.

She opened her mouth to let out a cry of alarm and took in water instead as the pond swallowed her. She clawed wildly at the weight of the surcoat to try to free herself from it, but it clung to her like a dead man, dragging her down.

Panic exploded inside her, cold and paralyzing. She felt de Jarnac's strong arm close around her waist, felt him pull her back against his big, strong body, felt him lift her up, up. Her head reared into the air, and she sucked in great, choking breaths.

"Hellfire," he said, his deep voice close to her ear, his hard arm still around her, digging into her ribs as she sagged against him. "You're not supposed to try to scream under water."

She realized her feet could now touch bottom. She pushed away from him and swung about, staggering clumsily in the waist-deep water. "You—you . . . *salaud*!" she spat, hunching over as she coughed up water. "You tried to drown me!"

His fist closed on the shoulder of her surcoat, hauling her upright as he leaned into her, his dark face dripping, his wet, naked chest heaving as he sucked in air. "If I wanted to drown you, lordling, you'd be dead. All I wanted to do," he said, bringing up his other hand to tangle his fist in the short crop of hair that hung wet and ragged against her cheek, "was to see what color your hair really is."

She jerked her head back, drawing her hair through his fingers, fingers now stained dark with the dye she had used to blacken her hair. She raised her gaze, slowly, to his face.

He stared at her, accusation sharpening every feature. "It's brown, Atticus. Not black but brown. Light brown. But then, Atticus isn't your real name, is it?"

In the sudden stillness, she could hear the water lapping around their legs, hear herself breathing. She backed away from him, backed away from the purpose she read in his hard green eyes. Her bare feet sank into the deep sand that edged this part of the pool and she stumbled, the wet weight of the sodden velvet hanging about her legs, tripping her, as she swung around and waded into shallower water. With an exclamation of annoyance, she tore off her girdle and the surcoat and flung them both onto the bank.

"I think," de Jarnac said, his voice as soft and dangerous as a silk garret, "that you and I need to have a little talk."

"We have nothing to talk about," she said, her voice shaky as she bent to try to squeeze some of the water from the hem of her tunic.

"Don't we?"

She heard the splash and slap of water from behind and spun around just as his weight slammed into her.

He bore her down into the sandy, grass-strewn bank and covered her with his big, naked man's body. "Unhand me," she cried, rearing up against him, suddenly frantic as she realized his intent. She twisted sideways, pushed against his water-slicked bare chest, tried to claw his face.

"God damn it," he swore, catching her wrists and pinning her arms to her sides as he leaned into her. She felt the weight of him, felt the power of him, felt the anger in every taut line of his hard body pressing her down. She stared up into dark green eyes, as cold and empty as a primeval sea. And she knew a terror that seemed to incapacitate every muscle, so that she couldn't move, couldn't even speak.

"Now," he said, his warm breath washing over her as he brought his wet face down until it hovered less than a hand's breadth above hers. "I think it's time you tried telling me the truth for a change."

She gazed up at him, at the creases beside his mouth that deepened as he pressed his lips together into a hard line. "I have told you the truth," she whispered.

"Have you?"

She saw a muscle jump along his jaw. His fists clenched tighter, and she let out a sharp cry as he yanked her arms high over her head and brought them together so that he could encircle both her wrists with one hand. She felt the back of the knuckles of his other hand brush down her neck and press into the base of her throat as his fingers tightened around the neck of her tunic and shirt.

"Have you?" he said again, his own breath coming hard and fast. "And if I rip this cloth, what shall I find beneath?"

Attica felt her heart slam up against her ribs with a resounding *thump-bump*. "I don't know what you mean," she said, her voice catching on a tremble.

"Don't you?" He leaned into her, so close that she could see herself reflected in the dark pupils of his eyes. "Don't you, *demoiselle*?"

She licked her suddenly dry lips, then regretted it when she saw his gaze fasten onto her mouth. "No," she whispered. "You're wrong."

"Am I?" He shifted his weight. "Let's see, shall we?"

She felt the beat of her pulse, tight against the heel of his hand, read the purpose in his eyes, saw the tightening of his jaw. "No," she said with a gasp, lunging up against him, twisting her hands in his grip. "No. Don't. Please, don't." She swallowed convulsively, twisting wildly beneath him. "Oh, God. I'll tell you. Just—please don't."

He stared down at her. She was agonizingly aware of him as a man, of the weight of his wet, naked body, bearing down on her, his hips pressing intimately against hers, his knees thrusting between her spread thighs. He seemed to loom over her, a black, dangerous silhouette against the sunlit pond. "Who are you?" he demanded.

"Attica." His face was so close to hers, her mouth almost brushed his when she spoke. "My name is Attica. Attica d'Alérion."

His lips curled into a mean smile. "You would have me believe you're the natural sister of Stephen d'Alérion?"

"No." She sucked in a deep, ragged breath. "I am his full sister. Lawfully born of the marriage of Blanche Blissot and Robert d'Alérion."

"You are sister to Elise d'Alérion?"

Attica shook her head. "I once had a sister named Elise, but she died as a young child. Many years ago now."

"So who is betrothed to the future viscomte de Salers?"

"I am."

The silence hung between them, filled with the slap of water against the bank and the sibilant hiss of the breeze through the marsh grasses. A heron flew by overhead, croaking harshly, its shadow knifelike and swift.

"You are hurting me," Attica said, feeling suddenly crushed beneath his weight.

"Huh. You deserve it." He shifted in a way that took some of the pressure off her hips even as it seemed to nudge her thighs farther apart. He gazed down at her, his expression hard and unreadable, and she knew a new rush of fear that seemed to radiate up like a slow heat from the depths of her belly.

"Do you honestly expect me to believe you?" he said.

She stared up into his shadowed eyes. "No. But I swear before God and all the saints that it is true."

He brought his other hand up to her wrists, letting his fingers slide along her arms in a movement that was almost a caress. "Then why all the lies?" he asked, his face still set. "Why didn't you simply tell me the truth from the very beginning?"

"Tell you what? That I am a woman? I was afraid you would—" She broke off, her gaze shifting uncomfortably away from him.

He spanned her jaw with one hand, forcing her head around and bringing his face so close to hers she had no choice but to look at him. "Afraid I would—what?" His brows drew together in a dark frown.

She swallowed. "I saw what the *routiers* did to the women of that village yesterday."

He let go of her wrists and reared back, his thin nostrils flaring as he breathed in. "Splendor of God, what do you take me for?"

She propped herself up on her elbows. "You said yourself that you acknowledge no rules but your own. That the codes of chivalry are nothing more than poetic inventions. You even threatened to kill me. Why shouldn't I think you capable of anything?"

His eyes narrowed down into two unpleasantly glittering slits. "Because, unlike the *routiers*, I do have some rules I live by, even if they happen to be my own. Because— Oh, hell."

He pushed away from her and sat up. She lay still, staring at the blue sky above, her heart pounding, her breath coming in great, catching gulps. But after a moment she swung her head and looked at him.

He sat turned half away from her, his forearms resting on his bent knees, his man's body naked and splendid. And even though she burned with angry resentment over the way he had treated her, even though she knew it was wrong, she let her gaze rove over him, over the tight cords of his strong neck, the muscular curves of shoulder and chest, the lean line of waist and hip, the shadowy recesses now hidden from her gaze.

She jerked her head away, staring out over the shining, undulating surface of the pond. The silence between them twanged out, became tense.

"I only lied to you about who I am," she said softly. "And I think you can understand why. Everything else I told you was true."

She felt him staring at her but kept her gaze firmly fixed on the cool, shifting water before her.

He grunted. "About what? The courtier your *sister* Elise cared for?"

"Yes." She curled into a sitting position, bringing her knees up to her chest so that she could wrap her arms around her legs. "Except, of course, that I was the one who tended him in his fever."

She paused, but this time de Jarnac didn't even grunt. She had to force herself to go on. "After he died, I didn't know what to do. I was desperate to get some kind of warning to Stephen, but there was no one at the castle I could trust. I realized the only way I could be certain that Stephen would receive my message would be to go myself."

She bent her head to rest her cheek on her knees. "When I heard about Philip and Richard's plans for the conference, I was so afraid for Stephen, afraid he'd be killed trying to defend his lord. But when I thought about what it would mean, riding all the way to La Ferté-Bernard by myself . . ." Her voice quavered. "I was even more afraid. For myself."

She sighed. "Then I realized that I only had to go as far as Laval, to my uncle, and I thought, I can do that. So I took the courtier's clothes, and once I got away from Châteauhaut, I cut and darkened my hair."

The wind blew over the surface of the pond, filling the silence with the rustle of leaves and the fluttering of her damp hair against her cheek. She turned her head to find him regarding her, his expression dark and unreadable.

"Do you believe me?"

"I might," he said. "Except for one thing."

He stood abruptly and walked, naked and beautiful, to where their horses grazed beside the pond. She watched as he pulled something from his saddlebags. Then he swung back to face her, and she jerked her gaze up and kept it focused on the treetops swaying against the blue sky until a sudden flick of his wrist sent something spinning through the air toward her.

She jumped as a book thumped onto the grass beside her, a small book, its green leather binding now ruined by a long slit. She stared at it, then raised her gaze, slowly, up the long line of his naked body to his face. "Where did you get this?" she asked.

"From your bags. Last night."

She reached to pick up the slim volume and turn it in her hand. "Why have you slit the binding?"

"Why do you think?"

She shook her head. "I don't know."

"You don't know that Philip's courtiers use breviaries such as this to transport the king's secret correspondence?"

She swallowed. "No."

"Then why did you bring it?"

She lowered her gaze to the ruined breviary in her hands. "I brought Olivier's saddlebags because I needed his clothes. It was with them."

His voice came to her, harsh, threatening. "And you knew nothing of what it contains?"

She fingered the slit in the leather. "Does it contain something?"

He grunted. "Letters patent. From Philip to John, promising that the French king won't make peace with Henry until John receives what he seeks in the settlement."

She sucked in a quick, startled breath. "Mary, Mother of God," she whispered. She set the breviary down on the grass before her, her fingers knitting together, her head falling back as she looked up at him. "I swear to you, I did not know."

The silence stretched out, filled with the chattering of

birds in the trees and the slap of gentle waves against the reeds. "Don't you believe me?" she said at last.

He shifted his weight, his arms coming up to cross at his chest in a way that seemed to accentuate the size of his big male body. "I don't want to." He let his breath out in a long sigh. "But your face doesn't lie."

The warm afternoon sun filtering down through a leafy oak tree overhead cast interesting patterns of golden light and dusky shadows across the hard planes of his naked body. She felt her cheeks begin to flame with unwelcome heat, but she could not look away. "If you found the breviary last night, why did you wait until now to confront me?"

"Why do you think?" he said, and she caught the gleam of dark, dangerous fires deep in his eyes. Something built within her, something unfamiliar and painful. She was aware, once again, of the isolation of this place. Of his man's body, so naked and powerful. Of her own vulnerability. The breeze gusted again, bringing with it the scents of lush green grass and damp earth, and she shivered, her wet clothes lying cold and clammy against her skin.

"So you see," he said, one corner of his mouth lifting into a mocking smile, "you were probably right to keep your true identity from me."

He went to unbuckle her saddlebags from the roan's back. "Here." He tossed the leather satchels to her, his smile widening when she caught them neatly in midair. "You might be able to catch like a boy, and throw a dagger like a boy, and you can even look like one for the most part." His gaze drifted over her in a way that stopped her breath. "But not," he added, his voice becoming oddly rough, "not when you're bare-legged and all wet."

She glanced down and noticed for the first time how the fine wet wool clung to her body, revealing the subtle curves of waist and bound breasts. She wrapped her arms around her chest, hugging herself, and heard him let out a huff of breath that might have been a laugh as he turned away.

"Better put on some dry clothes quickly," he said over his shoulder. "Before I forget what few rules I have."

The future viscomtesse de Salers knelt beside the pool, her aristocratic head bent, her arms raised as she used Damion's soap to wash the rest of the dye from her hair.

It was a feminine pose and a feminine occupation, even if the hair ended abruptly at her chin. Watching her, Damion found himself wondering what she would look like dressed in a woman's fine, fitted robes—or better yet, he thought with a private smile, in nothing at all, with her hair still long and unbound and—

With a muttered oath, he pulled his shirt over his head and fumbled with the laces. But he couldn't seem to stop his gaze from drifting back, inevitably, to where she knelt, totally oblivious, he knew, of the seductiveness of the image she presented.

She had a boyish body, long-legged and slim hipped, yet soft. He remembered the way she had felt flat on her back beneath him, remembered the sweet, water-slicked scent of her, the petal-like delicacy of her flesh beneath his rough grip, the erotic tangle of her legs with his. He remembered the way her brown eyes had seemed to glow and darken as she stared up at him, and the way her lips had parted, the breath easing between them in a soft sigh.

She had been aware of him as a man, he knew. Aware of him and afraid. But it hadn't all been fear, and he had come so close—so close to dipping his head and tasting the sweetness of that impossibly seductive mouth. Just the thought of it now was enough to make his body throb with such an unexpected rush of desire that he swore again and turned away.

She was the comte d'Alérion's daughter, he reminded himself, not the simple servant he'd assumed her to be. A comte's daughter, betrothed to the future viscomte de Salers. What in the name of sweet Jesus was he doing, thinking about kissing her?

Moving quickly, he jerked on his broigne, swiftly fastened his belt, and reached for his sword. She had been wise to dress herself as a boy, he thought, buckling on his scabbard. There was a reason ladies of her station traveled closed up in litters and surrounded by armed men. A reason they were kept away from hot-blooded, lusty young knights. It was a wonder to him that she had dared to set off alone with him as she had, trusting only in her disguise to keep her safe from insult or assault. She must love her brother very much indeed, Damion thought. But then, Damion had loved his own brother like that, once, before—

He abruptly closed his mind against the thought.

She had finished washing her hair now and disappeared behind the rocks, presumably to change into dry clothes. Damion pulled on his boots and went to tighten the girths of the saddles. He was leaning against a rock and watching a bee investigate an orchid when he heard her come up behind him.

"I can't find the breviary," she said in that husky voice of hers. "Did you take it?"

He swung to face her. She had changed into a fresh surcoat of dark crimson velvet trimmed with midnight blue damask, the same color of blue as the wool tunic beneath it. Her freshly washed hair framed her face in soft, honey-brown curls that seemed to accentuate the delicate bones of her face.

"You made a better boy before you washed your hair," he said, his voice coming out harsh.

He watched, bemused, as a light band of color stained her fine cheekbones. "Perhaps I should not have done it," she said, glancing away. He was aware of an awkwardness hanging in the air between them, a kind of ambiguity and uncertainty that hadn't been there before. Before they had been simply a knight-errant and a youth, traveling together in that rough camaraderie that can form so quickly between men. Now they were a man and an unescorted maiden, each aware of the drastic change in their association. More, each carried the memory of that burning moment when she had lain beneath his wet, naked body in a posture so evocative of the familiar position for lovemaking that neither of them could forget it.

And they both knew that the only thing that had kept him from taking her then—the only thing that kept him from taking her *now*—was a code of conduct he himself professed largely to scorn.

"Don't worry," he said, pushing away from the rock and straightening. "We should be in Laval in an hour. I don't expect much trouble."

He took a step toward her and she skittered backward, as if she were afraid to tempt fate by letting him come too close to her again. "And the breviary?" she asked.

He brushed past her to where he had tied the horses. "I have it."

She followed him. "I will take it back now, please."

"I don't think so," he said, gathering the bay's reins and reaching for the stirrup.

"And why not, pray tell?" she demanded haughtily as he swung up into the saddle, the leather creaking as he settled himself.

His laugh was low and a bit ragged as he stared down at her tense white face. "You play the grande dame very well, my lady." He rested his forearm along the high pommel of his saddle and leaned into it. "But I'm still not giving you the breviary."

He saw her hands clench into fists at her sides, and kept a careful eye on her. He hadn't forgotten the way she'd thrown her dagger at that *routier*.

"And what would you do with it?" She tilted back her head so she could stare down her nose at him.

"Take it to Henry, of course."

He watched her forehead crease in a surprised frown. "Why?"

"What do you mean, why?"

"I mean, what possible motive can you have? You, who scorn the conventions of chivalry and acknowledge no lord?"

He gave her a smile that showed his teeth. "Greed, of course. Henry will reward me well."

Her chest lifted sharply on an indrawn breath. "How do I know you won't take the breviary to John or Philip, rather than to Henry, as you say?"

He let his smile turn mean. "With all due respect, demoiselle, I'm not the one who's spent the last day and a half pretending to be something and someone I'm not." Then it occurred to him that he hadn't been exactly honest with her, either, for he hadn't told her of his own association with Henry. Tightening his jaw, he straightened and said roughly, "Now, are you going to mount up, or not?"

Belatedly, he thought he probably should have offered her a leg up. As much as he was aware of her as a woman, in some ways he still thought of her as Atticus; it would take some adjustment to remember to treat her as my lady Attica d'Alérion.

Her cleft chin jutted forward. "I hired you to escort me to Laval, not to interfere with what I am doing."

He stared at her, his gaze narrowing. Without taking his eyes off her, he reached two fingers into the purse that hung at his waist. "Here." He sent the ring spinning toward her.

She brought up her hand, catching the ring deftly in her fist. She looked down at it, then up at him.

"I'm glad you reminded me. Now get on that horse."

Her nostrils flared. "If you would be so good as to direct your squire to deliver my chestnut to the castle at Laval, I shall see that your roan is returned to him." She stepped back. "I thank you for your escort and wish you well on the remainder of your journey."

There could be no mistaking her meaning. An icy silence opened up between them. He heard the gentle trickle of the stream that fed the pool and a faint rustling in the bushes as something moved—a deer or perhaps a fox. A fly buzzed; the bay shook its head, rattling the bit.

Damion knew their discord had less to do with the breviary than with what had happened between them as a man and a woman lying tangled in each other's arms beside that pond. But that didn't make his anger any less intense. He tightened his jaw. "As you wish. *My lady.*" He pulled the bay's head around and touched his spurs to the horse's sides.

And left her standing there, looking haughty and righteous and just a bit scared.

CHAPTER EIGHT

Left alone in the forest with only her raging emotions for company, Attica cast a quick, uneasy glance about the small vale where she stood.

The forest grew thickly down to the edge of the pool's small clearing, the great chestnuts and oaks undergrown with dense brush. She heard the splash of a frog hitting the water and a faint rustling, as if something moved through the bushes. Something heavy.

Attica froze, her imagination conjuring up wolves and bears and desperate, hunted men. "Don't be a fool," she whispered through her teeth, annoyed with herself for this weakness, refusing to give way to it. She closed her eyes and lifted her face to the sun. She felt its strength pour down on her golden and warm out of a vivid blue sky, and some of the uneasiness began to drain out of her.

She sucked in a deep, steadying breath. "God rot you," she said aloud, although the man to whom she spoke was no longer there to hear it. She opened her eyes. "God rot you all the way to hell, Damion de Jarnac," she said again, her voice echoing about the clearing to drift away with the breeze.

Running her fingers through her wildly curling hair, Attica walked to one of the boulders that had tumbled down from the hillside above and sat upon the hard, warm surface.

Gripping her elbows with her hands, she hugged herself, hunching over, trying to stop the fine trembling deep within her, trying to make sense of the confusing tumult of emotions that swirled through her.

She thought about the men she had known—her father, that rough, uncouth warrior that her mother hated because she had never been able to look beyond his lack of letters and refinement to see the brave, honorable man Robert d'Alérion was; she thought about Stephen, so intense and devout, so loyal and brave—everything a chivalrous knight should be. She thought about all the clerics and knights, the lords and squires who had passed through the courts of the Langue d'oc where she had grown to womanhood. But she had never known a man like Damion de Jarnac, so wild and lawless and ruthlessly ambitious. No one she had ever known had prepared her for him.

She didn't understand the way he stirred her, the way he made her feel. The things he made her want. The things he made her need. Wants, feelings, needs she had no place for in her life, bound as she was by duty and obligation and honor.

"Oh, God," she whispered, pressing her fingertips to her lips. It was wrong, all wrong, the way she had responded to the shock of finding herself beneath his naked man's body. The way her senses had reeled with unexpected delight, her insides clenching with a swift, searing need as unwanted as it was undeniable. She felt betrayed by her own woman's flesh.

Oh, he had angered her, with his arrogance and his high-handedness and the way he used that big male body of his to threaten and intimidate her. Yet she knew it was her own shame that had made her turn on him afterward, that had led her to drive him away. Her shame and confusion and fear—not of him but of her own treacherous, unexpected impulses.

The sound of de Jarnac's roan pawing restlessly at the soft earth brought her head around. The horse stood alert, its head up, its ears pricked forward, listening. Watching that proud, well-bred animal, Attica thought of the man who owned it, thought of the things she had said to him, the way she had treated him. And she felt suddenly small, less than the person she liked to think of herself as being.

She slid off the rock. The day was growing late, and she wanted to be in Laval before the shadows lengthened into dusk. She wondered if de Jarnac would stop the night in Laval, then decided he probably wouldn't. He was too anxious to reach King Henry, too intent on claiming his reward—whatever that might be. She would probably never see him again.

It was a thought that brought with it a savage wrench of sadness, of loss. Attica pushed it away and went to check the girth of her saddle.

The roan moved skittishly, tossing its head, snorting. Attica laid a calming hand on the warm satiny neck. "Easy boy. What is it?"

And then she smelled it. A faint but unmistakably familiar sour stench that brought her head up and around.

It stood at the edge of the trees, a great black boar, bristly and grizzled and mean. Giant tusks, thick and long and lethal, curled up from an open mouth of sharp teeth dripping saliva. As Attica watched, it dropped its long snout, routing for a moment among the dirt and dead leaves at its feet. But its eyes—its beady, pink-rimmed eyes, remained fixed on Attica.

She forgot to breathe. Once, on a hunt, Attica had seen a man gored by a boar. The animal's great tusks had caught him in the groin and ripped up, gutting him. She would never forget the way that man had screamed.

She moved her hand slowly, inching her fingers over to slip her dagger from its sheath. But it was a pitifully small weapon, less than a third the length of the boar's tusks. And the boar watched her every move.

She thought that perhaps, if she were lucky and remained quite, quite still, the boar might amble along on its way and leave her alone. Behind her, the roan danced nervously, throwing its head, pulling at the reins that tethered it to the sapling. The reins suddenly snapped. With a high-pitched squeal, the roan lunged sideways and, finding itself free, cantered up the hill.

The boar shook its head, snorting, its ugly tusks waving in the air, its gaze fixed on Attica, its small hooves kicking up dirt and grass as it savaged the soft ground. Attica's sweaty fingers tightened around her dagger. She could throw it, she thought. Although, even if the thin blade did manage to penetrate the bore's thick hide, she knew it would simply enrage the beast without doing any serious damage.

Her only hope was to try to run—to make it to one of the larger trees in time to scramble up into its branches. Or into the depths of the pool, she thought, glancing sideways. The problem was, the water was shallow here. And boars were good swimmers.

She had sucked in a deep breath and tensed her muscles, ready to sprint, when she heard de Jarnac's calm, cool voice say, "Don't move. If you try to run, you'll only provoke it into charging you, and you'll never make it deep enough into the water or to the trees in time. It'll simply gore you in the back."

She stiffened, not believing at first that he could be there. Yet he was, at the edge of the forest, still astride his big bay, one knee hooked around the pommel in a casual pose belied by the coiled alertness of his well-trained body.

"Then, what should I do?" she somehow managed to ask, her voice gritty, her gaze flicking between the man on the horse and the restlessly intent boar between them. "Can you reach me in time to swing me up onto your horse?"

"No. Boars are fast, and it's closer to you than I am." He shifted his weight slowly, carefully. "I'm going to have to distract it. Get it to charge me. And when it does, I want you to run."

"But you don't have a spear."

"I know. I'll face him on foot. With my sword."

She shook her head. "You must be mad. You'll be killed."

Unbelievably, he threw her one of his reckless, devil-damn-the-world grins. "Then you can have the breviary back," he said. And slid out of the saddle.

"Hey," he shouted, clapping his hands and waving his arms. "You big, ugly piece of pork. This way."

The boar swung about, grunting angrily, its great head lowering threateningly.

"That's right," said de Jarnac, falling back a step, luring the boar farther away from Attica. "Come to me, piggy-piggy." He took another step back, his right hand on his sword. He had the blade half out of its scabbard when a loose stone rolled beneath his boot heel and he went down, landing with a thump on his side—just as the boar collected its powerful haunches and charged in a great snorting rush.

"De Jarnac!" She threw herself forward, knowing it was too late, knowing she could never reach him in time, knowing her only hope was to distract the animal long enough to give de Jarnac time to get back on his feet. She shouted again. Then she remembered the dagger she still clenched in her fist, and she drew back her hand to send the blade whistling through the air.

The boar squealed and spun around, Attica's dagger

embedded in its left shoulder. De Jarnac was already scrambling to his feet, his sword singing as he swung it from its scabbard. "God damn it, Atticus. *Get out of here,*" he cried as the boar, shaking its great head, crazy now with pain, charged straight at him again.

Attica bit down hard on the scream that rose in her throat. In horrified fascination, she watched, helpless, as he simply stood there, deathly still, his mighty sword held aloft in both hands as he calmly awaited the boar's rush. It seemed to her as if time had slowed and stretched out, her world narrowing to this sunlit patch of grass, to this dark, motionless knight, defiantly facing the bunching muscles and gleaming, deadly tusks of the animal hurtling toward him. The thud of the boar's hooves digging up the ground seemed to jar through her, its heavy, labored breathing keeping time with her own as de Jarnac waited, waited. At the last possible instant, when she knew he would surely be gored, he leapt sideways.

The boar's momentum carried it forward, past de Jarnac, who pivoted about, driving his great sword down, deep into the juncture of the boar's neck and shoulder blade as it rushed past. The boar screamed, staggered, swung about, its ugly head shaking, blood streaming from the sword protruding from its thick hide.

De Jarnac faced it, weaponless, vulnerable, his chest heaving as he sucked in breath, his face hard and expressionless. *"No,"* Attica screamed as the boar gathered itself again, prepared to charge. And collapsed in a groaning heap.

A silence so complete that it almost ached hung over the clearing. She felt the gentle wafting of the breeze, brushing her cheek and bringing her the smell of sun-warmed earth and the coppery stench of freshly spilled blood. Slowly, she lifted her gaze from the now still boar to the knight who had killed it. They stared at each other.

"You saved my life. A second time. And after I behaved so churlishly toward you." She tightened her face against a sudden rush of foolish tears and forced herself to go on. "Thank you."

She saw his jaw harden, as if he had remembered something that angered him. "And this is the second time I've told you to run," he said, "and you didn't."

"I don't run."

Something flashed in his eyes, something that was there and then gone, hidden by the lazy droop of his eyelids. "No, you don't, do you?"

She looked at him, standing there with his feet planted wide apart, his gloved hands resting on his lean hips. "Why did you come back?" she asked suddenly.

"I am a man of my word. And I said I would see you safely to Laval."

"So you did." She felt a queer, trembling smile pull at her lips. "Not only brave and strong but also true. I fear perhaps you are a more chivalrous knight than you care to pretend, monsieur le chavalier." Then her voice cracked, and she had to turn away before he saw just how close to tears she had come.

"Attica," he said softly, and she knew he had come up behind her, for she could feel his presence. It was more than just the heat of his body; it was an awareness of this man's very essence. She waited, afraid he would touch her, afraid he would not.

She felt his hand, strong on her shoulder, pulling her around, gathering her into his arms. A shudder ripped through her and she went to him, as naturally as a river to the sea. Her hands slid around his waist, clutched him to her, his body hard and hot beneath the fine cloth of his tunic and shirt.

"I am not normally so weak," she said shakily as she buried her face against his broad chest.

"Weak?" he whispered in disbelief. He stripped off his gloves, his big hand cupping her head, his fingers tangling in her hair. "Splendor of God, woman. Whatever possessed you to throw your dagger at that boar?"

She simply shook her head, glad he could not see her face. "You called me Atticus when you were swearing at me."

He laughed softly, and she felt the rumble of it, deep in his chest. "Believe me, I don't think of you as a lad."

She caught the change in his inflection, the subtle quickening of his breath, and knew she should pull away from him. But it felt so wonderful to be held like this, breathing in the sun-warmed scent of his skin, surrounded by the strength of his arms. She had received casual, affectionate hugs from her father and brother; even her mother had embraced her on rare occasions. But in all her life, Attica couldn't remember anyone actually *holding* her— simply holding her, offering comfort and the tangible proof of their caring.

"Look at me," he said.

She felt his fingers tighten in her hair, coaxing her head back until she was staring up at him. She smiled softly and saw the creases beside his mouth deepen. He had a beautiful mouth, delicately sculpted. Before she'd thought it hard and maybe even a bit cruel. But now it seemed almost soft, full, and she found herself watching his lips move as he spoke.

"Was it Stephen, then, who taught you to handle a dagger?"

She shook her head. "No. Walter, my groom. Indeed, Stephen never forgave the poor man for it. My dear brother has always claimed that it's an unseemly talent for a lady. But the truth is, he's simply jealous."

She saw his lips quiver, and held her breath, waiting for another smile. "It was the summer after he first went as squire to Sir Baldric," she continued. "Stephen came home for a visit, insufferably full of himself and showing off. I was very envious."

His eyebrows lifted in surprise. "You wanted to be a knight?"

She felt her cheeks heat. "I had always spent more time wandering about the countryside with Stephen than my mother considered seemly. His newly refined talents bothered me more than you might expect."

"So that's when you decided to become a master of the short blade."

She nodded. "I knew I couldn't tilt or swing a heavy sword, but I didn't see any reason why I shouldn't be able to throw a dagger, and I pestered Walter until he taught me. I practiced every moment I could. And the next time I saw Stephen, I bet my dagger against his saddle that I could beat him."

"Did you?"

"Oh yes," she said, feeling shyly proud of herself even as she added modestly, "Stephen is a bit shortsighted, you know, so it wasn't all that difficult. But he didn't take well to being bested by his little sister. He immediately challenged me to a different contest, and . . ." She hesitated, remembering the nature of that contest. "I lost. In fact, I conceded defeat without competing. I didn't have the right equipment, you see."

"And what kind of a contest was that?"

Attica pressed her lips together and shook her head, an uncomfortable warmth enflaming her cheeks.

"Go on," he said. "What was it?"

She couldn't look at him and say it. So she swung her

head away, her gaze fixing on a blue dragonfly hovering over the breeze-ruffled surface of the pond. "A pissing contest." She pushed the words out with difficulty.

He laughed then, a deep, husky laugh that brought her gaze back to his face. Her ignoble defeat hadn't seemed funny at the time, but it did now, and she laughed, too, the lighter notes of her voice entwining with his richer tones to drift away on the breeze. And then he wasn't laughing anymore. He was staring at her mouth, and she saw that his face had taken on an odd, tense quality, as if the dark skin had been pulled taut, accentuating the sharp line of his cheekbones, the strength of his jaw, the determined slant of his lips.

His fist tightened in her hair, drawing her toward him. She read desire in his face. Desire and a strange kind of wonder. And she was very much afraid that what she saw in his face was reflected in her own. Her heart pounded fiercely with want and fear and the painful knowledge of what she must do. His head dipped.

She drew back, gently pressing her fingers to his mouth, stopping him. "No," she said, her voice hushed and thick. "You mustn't."

His fierce green gaze caught hers and held it, and she knew a strange shifting inside her. His eyes were like the forest around them, she thought: deep and mysterious and dangerous. And for a moment she lost herself in them.

Still holding her gaze, he brought his hand up to capture hers and cradle it against his lips. "There is a reason," he said, his mouth moving softly against her fingers. "A reason lovely damsels are kept locked fast and well guarded in their castles, far away from dark, dangerous knights." He let his lips trail down her fingers, pressed a kiss to her palm. "You would be wise to remember what that reason is." He curled her hand into a fist still held within his own.

"I don't believe I have anything to fear from you," she said, her voice husky.

She saw something leap in his eyes, something hot and reckless. "Believe it, my little lordling," he said. "Believe it, and guard yourself well." He kissed her hand again, his breath soft and warm against her flesh.

And let her go.

They faced each other, the wind blowing hot and dry between them. She stared at him, at the hard tilt of his mouth and the heat that still glowed like a banked fire in his eyes. He was like lightning, this man. Wild and free and dangerously, frighteningly attractive. She knew an ache in her chest, a fierce wanting for something that would never be. Should never be.

But oh, God, she had glimpsed it, and she knew with a painful kind of certainty that her life would never be quite the same again. Once, she had faced her coming marriage to Fulk with a fatalistic resignation sustained by the knowledge that her choice was the honorable one, dictated by duty and God. Only she had never truly understood either the nature or the extent of her sacrifice. Now she had been allowed to suspect what could be, what she would be giving up. And she was terribly afraid she was going to spend the rest of her life wishing and wanting and regretting.

It was after nones by the time they dropped down out of the hills into the broad valley of the Mayenne River and saw the walls of Laval in the distance.

It had taken time for them to find the frightened roan, and de Jarnac had gutted and hung the boar before leaving the pond. And then he paused at the first hamlet they passed to tell the villagers where they might find the meat.

"What are you grinning at?" he asked, catching her eye upon him as he swung back into the saddle.

She let her grin broaden into an open smile. "I'm looking at a dark, dangerous knight, so lost to the virtues of chivalry that he succors the helpless and goes out of his way to be generous to the poor and weak."

He grunted and cast her an exaggerated scowl that only made Attica laugh out loud.

As they crossed the valley of the Mayenne, high clouds began to appear on the horizon, bunching up to become thicker and darker. "Looks like a storm coming in," said Attica, lifting her face to the wild caress of the wind.

Something in the silence that followed—some strange, tense quality—made her swing her head to look at him.

She found him staring at her, his face oddly dark and fierce, his eyes glittering with a man's longing, a man's hunger. She felt her cheeks flush, her breath catch in her throat. But she could not look away. *He warms me with the heat of his gaze,* she thought in wonder. *He looks at me and my breath quickens, and I feel such stirrings within. Such wild, impossible wants.* And still she could not look away.

Thunder rumbled low and distant over the mountains behind him. His gaze swung away from her, and the moment shattered, became a memory.

The cathedral city of Laval rose up before them on the crown of a low hill on the western slopes of the river. Side by side, they rode toward it through cleared pastures and vineyards, through gardens and orchards and ripening fields. The traffic on the road became increasingly thick as they joined the steady stream of fair-goers headed for Laval: knights and their ladies on richly caparisoned palfries; black-robed monks on trotting donkeys; farmers in roughly woven tunics, their feet brown and bare in the dusty road.

"Have you ever been to the fair at Laval?" de Jarnac asked.

"Only once." She steadied the roan as a flock of geese fluttered, honking in protest, out of her way. "My mother brought my brother and me when we were children. It's not as large as the Champagne fairs, of course. But many merchants come here on their way to the Hot Fair in Troyes."

By now they had reached the cleared space before the town walls to find the open meadows filled with brightly striped tents and wooden stalls and a colorful, noisy, shifting sea of people. A stiltwalker in a bright yellow-and-red-skirted tunic trundled by on wooden legs taller than de Jarnac's head. Attica threw the white-masked lute player behind him a coin and laughed when he tilted his head and yapped like a happy dog. "Pepe the stiltwalker thanks you!" he called after them.

They entered the town between the twin towers of the porte de Rennes, the clatter of their horses' hooves on the cobbles echoing loudly through the dark archway. The gate opened onto a wide, sunny street paved with smooth stones and swarming with people. Housewives haggled over fluttering chickens and squealing pigs. Peddlers hawked their wares—wine and sweetmeats, garlic and milk and cheese. Shrieking children chased hoops and balls and each other. Attica let the tired roan follow de Jarnac's bay through the press, the smells of the city rising up to envelop her—manure and woodsmoke, cellar-stale damp air, and the rich, tantalizing aromas of roasting meats and baking bread.

He reined in at the entrance to a side lane running up the hill toward the castle and waited for her. "You've grown very quiet," he said as she rode abreast of him.

She tilted back her head, studying the outline of the

castle above them. "I'm trying to decide what I should tell my uncle."

He nudged his bay forward, and they turned into the lane. Most of the houses here were three and four storied, built mostly of timber post and beam, their upper floors jutting out to cast the lane into shadow, their ground floors forming shops with horizontal wooden shutters thrown open to make a counter and the awnings above. "Why shouldn't you tell him what you came here to tell him?" de Jarnac asked, his attention seemingly caught by the shop they were passing.

She drew up the roan as it stumbled over some mal-odorous rubbish in the street. "I came here to ask Renouf to send a warning to my brother. But the sense of urgency is gone now, isn't it, when you keep the breviary and ride to La Ferté-Bernard yourself."

He swung to look at her. "Attica . . . I know you must tell your uncle about Olivier de Harcourt because you can hardly justify your coming here in any other way. But I ask that you not let him know where I am going, or why, or about the breviary. Let him send his men to La Ferté-Bernard; it will do no harm."

"But why would you not want—" She broke off, her head jerking, her eyes widening with comprehension. "No." She kept her voice steady with difficulty. "You are wrong. My uncle is Henry's man. He would never betray you."

His gaze never faltered. "Possibly. Perhaps even prob-ably. But why take a risk?"

She held herself stiffly. "Why should I trust you more than I trust my own uncle?"

"Because I didn't kill you."

At that moment the dark lane emptied out abruptly into a sunwashed square with a fountain and a long, low stone trough. Small knots of townswomen with buckets and pitchers dangling empty from their fingers loitered near the pool while others moved away with stately grace, their full jars carefully balanced atop their heads. A chestnut horse tethered near the trough lifted its head and whinnied at Attica in recognition.

She slid from her saddle to run her hand over the gelding's satiny withers. "Chantilly?" She staggered as the horse gave her a welcoming nudge with its velvety white nose. "What are you doing here?"

"Waiting for you," said de Jarnac, coming up behind her, her saddle over his arm.

Laughing softly, she turned to catch a glimpse of a lithe, fair-haired boy with flashing dark eyes who stepped back and tucked something out of sight up his sleeve. Then the chestnut butted its head against her hip, momentarily reclaiming her attention. When she looked again, the squire along with the roan she'd been riding had both disappeared.

"Why would you have killed me?" she asked as de Jarnac tightened the girth on her saddle.

"What?" Spanning her waist with his big hands, he threw her up onto the chestnut's back and handed her the reins.

"You said I should trust you because you didn't kill me," she said, watching him vault easily into his own saddle. "What did you mean?"

His eyes crinkled with amusement as he laid his reins against the bay's sweat-darkened neck and turned into the winding, shadowed rue leading to the castle. "If I were part of the conspiracy against King Henry, or at least interested in aiding it for my own gain, then I would have killed you to keep you quiet. Since you're still alive and here to tell your tale to your uncle, you can take it as a given that I'm not involved." The amusement left his face. "It's only your kinship with Renouf Blissot that causes you to trust him."

"Isn't that enough?" Attica asked softly.

"When it comes to treason—and your brother's life—I'd say no."

She rode beside him in silence for a moment, thinking about it, before she said, "Yet, if you should prove to be right about my uncle—if he has indeed sided with Richard and Philip—then haven't you put yourself in danger by bringing me here?"

He glanced at her. "Now you sound as if you do suspect him."

"No. But you do."

From the doorstep of a house on their right, a serving woman tossed a bucketful of slops to a couple of hogs rutting in the gutter. "I said I would see you safely delivered to Laval." He let his bay dance fastidiously around the mess, then added, "Besides, in my experience, grand ladies are not normally in the habit of confiding their secrets to their escorts. Renouf Blissot is unlikely to give me a second thought, Attica. I'm just a humble knight-errant, strong of arm and short of brain."

She let out a trill of laughter. "Knight-errant you may be, and strong of arm. But humble and short of brain you are not."

"You don't need to tell your uncle that."

The pale walls of the castle rose up before them. Attica checked her horse. "I could tell him," she said quietly. The chestnut shook its head, bothered by flies, and she patted its glossy neck. "He is my kinsman. Are you so certain I wouldn't that you are willing to hazard your life on it?"

He swung his head to look at her. "You won't tell him."

She met his gaze. "I could say something unintentionally. Something stupid."

He nudged his horse forward into the sunlit open space before the gate. "You're not stupid."

Wordlessly, she followed him into the Forecourt. The massive, stone-built walls of the castle loomed over them, and she tilted back her head, her gaze drifting over the familiar battlements. She became aware of a sense of heavy melancholy, pressing in on her, weighting her down, hurting her chest. It seemed so strange; she'd spent the past two days desperate to reach this place. Now she was here, and she wished she weren't.

The chestnut cavorted beneath her, as if sensing her reluctance. She steadied him unthinkingly, her gaze shifting to the dark knight riding ahead of her. She had felt such fear these past two days. She could still feel the residue of her fear, like a buzz beneath her flesh. And yet she'd also felt gloriously alive. Alive and free. In a few moments it would all be coming to an end. She would be safely within her uncle's care and tomorrow, or the next day, she would be returning to Châteauhaut. She would never see Damion de Jarnac again. And in one month's time she would become the wife of Fulk the Fat and spend the rest of her days as his viscomtesse.

The pain in her chest increased until it seemed as if she were smothering, as if the ominous weight of the future were crushing her. She sucked in a deep, gasping breath, but there was no escaping it. No escaping what would happen. No escaping this truth she had now acknowledged to herself: She did not want the life that stretched out before her.

Once, she had consoled herself with the knowledge that her sacrifice would serve the interests of her house, that this was the way of her world. Once, she had resigned herself to her fate. But the past two days had shattered that resigned complacency. And she was very much afraid she could spend the rest of her life trying to regain it.

The tunnel-like arch of the castle gateway rose up before her, blocking out the light. She glanced back at the sunlit forecourt, aware of a spiraling sense of despair. If she were a different person, she thought fleetingly, she might seek to escape her fate. But she was who she was, and she knew she could not live with herself, were she to shirk her responsibility to her family and attempt to escape the vow she had made to Fulk. She could not live without honor.

She felt de Jarnac's eyes on her and turned her head to meet his gaze. He waited for her on his big bay, a dark knight, tall and lean and so splendid, he made her heart ache just looking at him. In some ways he frightened her still. He was so fierce and ruthless, so enigmatic and hard. Yet she knew him better now, knew that he could be not only kind and generous but also astonishingly honorable. And she felt an intense, useless wish that she could have come to know him better. That she might somehow have gained a glimpse into his dark, secret man's heart.

She looked into his terrible green eyes and found them hooded. "It's over now, lordling," he said, as if sensing her thoughts. "Will you go back? To Salers?"

"Yes," she said, hearing the clatter of their horses' hooves, echoing together over the cobblestones as she rode on beside him.

"To Fulk the Fat?"

She gripped her reins in hands that had suddenly, unaccountably, become cold and shaky. "To Fulk the Fat. If he still wants me."

"He'll still want you."

He swung his gaze away from her. Their stirrups almost but not quite touching, they rode out the gateway and into the court of her uncle's castle.

CHAPTER NINE

"Attica! Praise God you are safe."

Attica paused just outside the entrance of the castle's stables, her head turning toward the sound of her uncle's joyous shout. She could see him now, hurrying down the stone steps from the castle hall, his short fur-lined mantle billowing out behind him in the cooling breeze kicked up by the coming storm.

"You go ahead," said de Jarnac, taking the chestnut's reins from her loose grasp. "I'll see to the horses."

She hesitated, her suddenly anxious gaze searching the hard, inscrutable features of the man beside her. She felt a great sadness sweep over her, squeezing her heart with the ache of impending loss. "You won't leave the castle without seeing me again, will you?"

She watched his lips curl into a wry smile that only seemed to make the ache in her chest worse. "No." He nodded toward her uncle. "Go on now. Go on," he said again when she still hesitated.

With another quick, backward glance, she hastened across the castle yard.

Renouf Blissot was Blanche's youngest brother, and in his early thirties yet. A small, wiry man, he had dark brown hair, sharp features, and a dark, neatly clipped beard. He was smiling broadly as he caught Attica by the shoulders and held her at arm's length, his gray eyes widening as he took in her lopped hair, her man's hose and tunic. "Holy Cross, child. I almost didn't recognize you. What have you done to yourself?"

She laughed and leaned forward to kiss his cheek. "You've no notion how much easier it is to travel as a man than as a woman, Uncle."

"Easier?" Renouf shook his head, his smile fading. "I think you mean safer, don't you?" He broke off to give her a hearty embrace. "I've been frantic with worry ever since I received word from Châteauhaut that you'd left there yesterday with only an old groom as an escort. Whatever possessed you, child?"

Attica studied his face carefully. "What did Yvette tell you?"

Her uncle threw an arm around her shoulders and drew her up the stairs beside him. "Something about you thinking your mother lay here ill. But, Attica, you must know Blanche is in Aquitaine, where I've no doubt she enjoys her usual good health." He paused within the shadow of the arched doorway to the hall and turned toward her again, his brows drawing together with worry. "Child, why have you come here?"

She touched his sleeve. "I must speak with you in private."

She watched his eyes narrow with concern and something else that was there in a flicker and then gone before she could identify it. "Of course," he said, glancing toward the far end of the stone-built hall.

She followed his gaze, half expecting to see Yvette's men from Châteauhaut lounging about the hall. But the room was empty except for a small knot of women at the far end who were carding and spinning wool while keeping an eye on several small children playing with a litter of half-grown pups. Renouf snapped his fingers; the women looked up, their happy chatter dying instantly.

"Leave us," he said with a jerk of his head.

Quickly gathering their distaffs and wool, the women rounded up the children and shooed them down the passage between the buttery and the pantry. "Come away," said one of the women, a broad, middle-aged dame with graying wisps of hair escaping from beneath her wimple as she bent to catch a dawdling boy's hand. "Your papa is busy."

Attica smiled as she watched her small cousins scamper out into the sunshine. "I'm surprised you have not yet remarried, Uncle."

"I haven't found a woman with a fat enough dowry who'll have me." Grinning, he reached for the earthenware ewer resting on one of the sideboards and held the wine up questioningly.

"Yes, please," she said, walking over to take the cup he poured for her. "How long has it been since Matilda died?"

"She died just after Landri was born, so it's been . . ." He paused. "Three years now."

Attica watched the three laughing children and their nurses disappear down the steps. The children were dark-haired like their father. But whereas Renouf was slightly built, all of his children seemed to have inherited the big-boned proportions of their mother.

"Dress those children in rags and plop them down in the middle of the meanest village, and they'd all look perfectly at home," Attica's mother, Blanche, was fond of saying, usually with one delicately arched, aristocratic eyebrow lifted in disdain. Blanche had never quite forgiven Renouf for marrying Matilda, whom she considered a far from suitable match for a Blissot. Not only had Matilda Carmaux been the granddaughter of an Auvergne peasant, but she'd looked it, with her big, blunt hands, her stocky build, and her wide-set, slightly protuberant eyes.

Of course, old Jacques Carmaux hadn't been your average peasant; not only had he managed to get his son and grand-sons knighted, but he'd also acquired enough landholdings to tempt Renouf into overlooking Matilda's dubious origins in exchange for the prosperous manors she'd brought with her to her marriage. Too many younger sons such as Renouf spent their entire lives as *"jeunes"*—knights-errant, deprived by their birth order of land and therefore unable to marry and have a family and home of their own.

Younger sons such as Damion de Jarnac.

Attica brought her gaze back to her uncle to find him re-garding her quizzically. "Don't tell me you rode all this way to talk to me about my marriage, Attica," he said.

"Uncle"—She set aside her wine and clenched her hands together before her. "I came because I need your help."

He took her hands in his. "Child, if it's your coming marriage to Fulk that has driven you here, then you must know that however much I might dislike this match Robert d'Alérion has arranged for you, there is nothing I can do about it."

Attica's hands twisted in his. "No, it's not that—not that at all. I know my duty to my family, and I could never in all honor attempt to withdraw from a betrothal I have ac-cepted. I came to you about a different matter entirely."

"Here," he said, drawing her toward the scattering of simple, rush-seated stools beside the hearth. "Sit." He pushed her down on one of the stools and propped his booted foot up on another so that he could lean one elbow on his knee. "Now tell me."

Her hands still clenched together tightly in her lap,

Attica told him. She told him about Olivier de Harcourt's arrival at Châteauhaut, about Count Richard's plan to launch an attack on his father when the peace conference collapsed, and about her fears for her brother's safety.

But she did not tell him about Damion de Jarnac, or about the dangerous secret he'd found in the Sainte-Foy breviary.

"And so I made up my mind to come to you," she said slowly, her gaze fastened on her uncle's face, "and beg you to send some of your knights to La Ferté-Bernard to warn Stephen and King Henry."

"I'll send someone off tonight, of course. Only . . ." Draining his cup, Renouf dropped his foot and walked to the sideboard to pour himself more wine. "There's one thing I don't understand," he said after a moment, his back to her. "Why did you not simply take this information to the viscomte and viscomtesse de Salers and have them send word from Châteauhaut? I mean—God's teeth, why put yourself to the danger of coming to me? Do you have any idea of what could have happened to you, alone on the road?" He swung to face her.

"I know," she said, her voice hollow with the memory of everything that had happened—and almost happened— over the past two days. "I came to you because I felt you were the only person I could trust."

Even as she said it, Attica remembered the Sainte-Foy breviary and felt shame touch her cheeks with a faint heat. It was a wonder to her now to think that she had allowed herself even for a moment to doubt her own uncle. But she had given de Jarnac her word, and she would keep it.

The sound of the children laughing and calling to one another out in the yard wafted back through the open door. She watched her uncle's eyes narrow as he set aside his own cup untasted. "Are you telling me you have reason to suspect that Salers is involved in this conspiracy?" He searched her face carefully. "Why? What have you overheard?"

She shook her head. "Nothing, really. Only . . . How could I trust Yvette and Gaspard to warn Stephen of this conspiracy when I could not be certain they were not a part of it themselves? I mean, I hardly *know* them."

Pushing away from the sideboard, Renouf came to crouch at her feet and take her hands in his again, his gaze hard on her face, worry shadowing his fine features. "Attica, I know you have been affianced to Fulk for only four months, but he is your future."

She searched her uncle's concerned gray eyes. "What are you saying? That my loyalty now belongs to Salers and not to my own house? How can that be?"

A soft, sad smile played about her uncle's lips, lifting the edges of his mustache as he reached to touch her hair lightly with gentle fingers. "Child. You have always been so—so *fierce* in your beliefs. So determinedly steadfast and uncompromising. Seeing the line separating loyalty from betrayal as something clearly delineated, and the choice between them as easy to make. But it's not. It's not."

He dropped his hand to her shoulder and squeezed it, then stood up with a lithe, graceful motion and drew her to her feet beside him. "Come. The servants will be wanting to prepare the hall for supper soon. I'll have hot water sent to the ladies' chamber for you and ask the women to find you something more suitable to wear than these Parisian courtier's clothes." He drew her toward the small, arched wooden door set into the far wall of the hall, his arm resting lightly around her shoulders. "Although where they are to find women's garments long enough to fit you, I know not. God's blood, I believe you are taller than I am."

Attica laughed softly. "Thank you, Uncle, but I was able to bring one of my own gowns with me. Will you also send someone to see that the knight who accompanied me here is suitably housed in the Knights' Tower?"

Renouf paused, his brows lifting in surprise. "What knight is this? I thought you came with your old groom?"

"I did. But, Walter was wounded when we were attacked by *routiers*. The knight who rescued us agreed to escort me the rest of the way here. I owe him my life."

"Routiers?" His mouth tightened. "God's Cross, Attica, the risk you put yourself through in coming here! Stephen will no doubt threaten to beat you soundly when next he sees you. And you'd best pray to God your mother does not set eyes upon you again until your hair grows out. When is your wedding to be?"

"In one month, after Fulk turns fourteen." She felt the chill of the stairwell hit her like a slap in the face. "Uncle," she said hoarsely as she followed him up the torch-lit spiral steps that led to the tower chambers. "I would ask that I might ride with your men, when they go to Stephen."

Renouf swung to face her, his fist tightening around the rope banister, the torch high in its wall bracket casting his sharp-bearded shadow over the dressed stones behind him. "I thought you said you do not flee your marriage, Attica?"

She paused with one hand splayed flat against her chest, her head falling back as she looked up at him. "I do not. I know my duty to my house, Uncle, and I shall do it. Only . . ." She turned her face to the narrow window beside her and let the cooling breeze caress her cheeks. "I have not seen Stephen much of late, and I find myself anxious to spend at least some small time with him before my marriage."

Renouf rested his shoulders against the curving stone wall, one hand coming up to rub the back of his neck in a distracted gesture. "Ah, Attica, I wish I could, but . . . how can I in all conscience send you to La Ferté-Bernard now? If what you say is true, you could be riding straight into a war. Besides which you will find it difficult enough to make amends with Salers for your lack of faith without running off to Stephen now."

"But what if Salers truly has joined those who take up arms against Henry?"

Pursing his lips, Renouf let his breath out in a long sigh. "Then you'd best pray this peace conference at La Ferté-Bernard succeeds."

The constant lamp on the altar glowed red and comfortingly familiar in the chapel's gloom, the flickering golden light thrown by the blessed candles beside it dancing over the gilded painting of the crucified Christ that hung darkly from the wall above. Breathing in the scent of incense and hot beeswax, Attica knelt on the hard, glazed bricks that paved the floor and drew her mantle close against the damp chill that seemed so much a part of these thick stone walls that she doubted it could ever be warm in here.

She paused for a moment, her head tilted back, her gaze on the crucified Christ, her breath coming slow and shallow as she let the peace of this place seep into her. Through the narrow, arched windows she could see the pale summer light fading from the sky with the setting of the sun. Swallowing a sudden surge of emotion, she bowed her head and closed her eyes in prayer.

Her lips moving silently, her hands clasped together against her chest, she gave thanks to God for bringing her here, into her uncle's protection, safely. She prayed for the departed souls of the dead villagers they had passed and—after a slight internal struggle—found it within her to ask

God's mercy, also, for the fallen *routiers*, especially the one she had killed with her own dagger. She prayed for Stephen's safety, and for the health of the English king and the security of his realm. And then she paused, for she could find no words for the rush of raging disquiet and desperate wanting that welled up within her.

She opened her eyes, the candle flames on the altar blurring as she sucked in a deep breath and then, when that wasn't enough, another. *Oh, God,* she cried in silent anguish. *Deliver me. Deliver me from this pain and these disloyal thoughts. From this sinful, impossible wandering of heart and will . . .*

Deliver me.

She wasn't even certain precisely what she was praying for. She only knew that the peace she'd found before, when first she knelt in prayer, now seemed to have slipped away from her. She lingered, trying to recapture it. But in the end she had to admit it was gone.

She pushed to her feet, her knees stiff and sore from so long on the cold floor. Genuflecting before the host, she crossed herself with holy water from the font near the door and stepped out into the coming evening. It would be time to go back for supper, soon.

Only instead of turning toward the hall, she swung away, her lagging footsteps carrying her through an open gateway into the castle's privy garden. And it was there, amid the sweet scents of honeysuckle and rose, of lilies and thyme and lavender, that he came to her.

Damion stood beneath the small porch of the empty chapel, his gaze narrowing as he stared through the open wicket gate to the castle gardens. The rose-tinted golden light of the setting sun spilled down the network of brick pathways and turned the surrounding beds of rosemary and lavender and apothecary roses into darkly shifting shadows, worried by the growing wind.

She sat on a turf-topped stone bench built against the garden's eastern wall, an elegant young woman in a rich crimson gown. Pushing away from the chapel's stonework doorway, he walked toward her.

It seemed strange to realize he had never seen her dressed as a lady before. He had imagined she would look like this, cool and slender and remote. And he thought what a wonder she was, this pale, delicate-looking woman. For he knew well that her porcelain-like air of fragility was deceptive; she was strong. Strong and brave and too beautiful, inside and out, for words.

He left the shadows of the narrow path and walked up to her. She had her face tilted up to the sun, her eyes closed. A gleam of moisture shone against the pale flesh of her cheeks, and he reached to run one knuckle gently along the ridge of her cheekbone, catching her tear. "Ah, Attica," he said softly.

Her eyes flew open, her long lashes clumping wetly as she blinked up at him. He saw her chest hitch on a quickly indrawn breath, saw her press the fingertips of both hands to her lips in a gesture he was coming to know well.

"How did you find me?" she asked, gripping her hands together and letting them fall to her lap.

He wanted so desperately to touch her, to gather her in the circle of his arms and hold her slim, young body close to his. Instead, he sat down beside her, his back to the rough stone wall, and fixed his gaze on the gathering clouds highlighted with vivid shades of purple and cerise by the setting sun. "I asked one of the women in the yard. She said she'd seen you going into the chapel."

"I wished to give thanks for our safe arrival here . . ." He heard the slight hitch in her voice before she added, "And to pray for those still in danger."

He swung his head to look at her. The strengthening wind ruffled the light brown curls framing her face. He wanted to tangle his fingers in her hair. He wanted to lift her face to his and kiss away those tears. He wanted . . . Ah, God. What he wanted.

He dug his fists into the turf at his side, his nostrils filling with the scent of crushed grass and night-blooming flowers and this woman. "And your uncle?" he asked, although he didn't think it was disappointment in Renouf that had brought those silent tears to her eyes.

She raised her chin in that way she had, a faint hint of color staining her cheeks. "My uncle's reaction was everything I had hoped it would be. It was wrong of me to doubt him, even for a moment."

"I wasn't aware that you had." He saw the confusion on her face, and let his lips curl into a smile. "Doubted him, I mean."

She stared at him, her eyes wide and solemn. "I promised not to tell him about the breviary, didn't I?"

"Ah. And now you're feeling guilty. Is that it?" He reached out to take her hand in his. "Don't."

Her gaze dropped to their linked hands—his so big and dark, hers pale and slender and bone-thin. He felt her tremble within his grip, but she made no move to slip her fingers from his. All around them the walls of the castle had taken on a fiery hue, lit by the last rays of the dying sun. In the distance he could hear the honking of geese and the lowing of cows being driven back into the castle for the night. It would be dark soon.

"Will you walk with me?" she asked, looking up suddenly. "In the garden?" In the gathering gloom, the deep crimson of her bliaut seemed to emphasize the fairness of her skin and the unexpected contrast of her big brown eyes. She looked beautiful, and hurting.

He brought her hand to his lips, his gaze never leaving hers. "With pleasure. *My lady.*"

He watched the quiet smile spill over her face and bring a sparkle to her eyes, and he thought he'd never known anyone whose emotions and thoughts showed so clearly on their face. She was too honest, too transparent. It made her vulnerable. And it filled him with an unprecedented and wholly unwanted urge to protect that fragile vulnerability, to protect her from the ugliness that could be life.

He stood and swept her a grand courtly bow that brought a gurgle of laughter to her lips. She was still smiling as she slipped off the bench and stepped toward him. Then the laughter died from her face as she stared up at him, her eyes deep and luminous now with some emotion he could not name.

The last rays of the setting sun caught the honey-toned highlights in her light brown hair, making it glow like gold. He watched her suck in a quick breath that lifted her unbound breasts. Her breasts were small but high and firm, just the way he had known they would be. He wondered what they would feel like beneath a man's hands. Beneath his hands.

And then he wondered if his thoughts showed on his face, for he saw her lips part, felt her hand clench in his. It was as if the very air between them heated, became tense with expectation and need.

If they had been anywhere else, he thought. If they had been anywhere but in this garden, in the open, he would have bent his head and kissed her. This time, he knew, she would not have stopped him.

He swung away, breaking the spell. He was aware of her falling into step beside him, although he was careful not to look at her again. Across the darkening castle grounds he could see a man lighting the torches that bracketed the gatehouse. The stiffening wind carried the hot, resiny odor across the yard to them.

"I asked my uncle if he would allow his knights to act as my escort to La Ferté-Bernard," she said after a moment. "But he said it would be too dangerous."

"He's right. Besides, you have no reason to go there now."

They passed between two rows of neatly espaliered pear trees that formed an allée. "I know. But . . ." She paused to pluck a leaf from one of the carefully pruned trees and stood for a moment staring down at it. "I would like to have been able to spend some time with my brother before I returned to Châteauhaut."

The wind gusted surprisingly strong, bringing with it the scent of coming rain and the low rumble of distant thunder. She had her head bent, her concentration seemingly fixed on the task of curling the slender green leaf between her fingers.

"Attica," he said, so near to her that he could see his breath wash over the bare skin at the back of her neck, raising the fine hairs there. "Delay will only make what you must do that much more difficult."

Her head came up, her eyes wide as she swung to face him, her lips open in surprise. He felt a sad smile tug at the edges of his mouth. "Did you think I couldn't guess why you don't want to go back to Salers yet?" Reaching out, he brushed her cheek, where a dried tear glittered silver in the vanishing light. "Did you think I wouldn't know what these are for?"

She bowed her head and half turned from him, her shoulders held straight and rigid. "I was sitting here tonight, remembering when I was a little girl. My mother . . ." Her voice broke, and she had to swallow hard. "My mother has never made any attempt to hide the fact that she dislikes me. It's because I look nothing like her, you see; she's very small and dainty, with almost black hair and gray eyes. While I look like my father."

Damion rested one hand, lightly, comfortingly, on her shoulder.

"At first, when I was very little, I couldn't understand why she didn't like me. I tried so hard to make her like me. But eventually I came to realize that every time she looks at me, all my mother can see is my father. And because she hates him, she hates me."

She seemed suddenly to become aware that she'd torn the leaf she held to shreds. Opening her fingers, she let the bruised pieces flutter down to the brick paved walkway. "Because of that, I avoided her as much as I could. My father was kind enough, in his way, but he was always awkward around females and I was, after all, a girl. The only person who ever had any time for me was Stephen, and I used to follow him everywhere, like a shadow."

She smiled sadly at the memory. "I must have been a sore trial to him, but he rarely told me to go away. I grew up running at his heels, playing rough boys' games, swimming, climbing trees. I thought I made as good a boy as any of them, so one night, when I overheard my mother talking to Renouf about a possible betrothal, I went to my father and told him very seriously that I didn't want to be a knight's wife; I wanted to be a knight myself."

He shifted his hand to rub the side of his thumb, ever so

gently, over the nape of her neck. "And what did old Robert d'Alérion say to that?"

"He laughed, of course. But then he took me on his knee, and he was even kind enough to tell me that he was convinced I'd make a splendid knight. Only, he also explained that I couldn't become a knight, because I was a girl. Girls grow up to become gentlewomen, and gentlewomen serve their families not by fighting but by making strong and useful marriages."

He felt her quiver beneath his touch, and let his hand slip upward, his fingers tangling in the short curls at the base of her head. He heard her breath leave her throat in a low, keening sigh. She leaned against him, her head falling back against his shoulder, her gaze on the storm clouds gathering over the battlements.

"So, you see," she said, "ever since I was a little girl I've known that I could not expect to marry for love. Women of my station do not. But I grew up watching the hell that was my parents' marriage and I used to hope—pray even—that the man chosen for me would be someone I could at least come to love."

"The heart is a wayward thing," Damion said very softly. "It never loves where you would will it."

She turned her head until she was looking at him over her shoulder. He saw the surprise in her face, and the wonder. "I thought you said you don't believe in love."

He stared down at her, his gaze roving over the fine bones of her face. "Oh, I believe in the existence of love all right. But not as something beautiful and glorious. Love is a dangerous thing, Attica, a powerful, destructive force that can shatter lives. Far more lives than the two people involved ever imagine."

"It doesn't have to be that way," she whispered.

He cupped the side of her head in his palm, drawing her around to face him completely. "For the peasants in their fields and the artisans in their shops, perhaps not." He gave her a wry smile. "It's ironic, isn't it? Their lives might be more harsh and precarious than ours, but at least they're able to love—and wed—where their hearts lead them. Whereas men and women such as you and I . . ."

He let his fingers trail down her throat to linger at the point where her pulse beat hard and fast. She stood utterly still beneath his touch. "We marry for land," he said, his voice a rough expulsion of breath. "For land and power and alliances. There's no room in those neat arrangements for love. And if love does come . . ." He brought his head down until his forehead touched hers, his hands framing her face, his thumbs brushing back and forth across her cheeks, their breath mingling hot and close. "If love does come, it brings tragedy, not joy. And death. Not life."

She leaned into him, her hands coming up to wrap around his wrists. It was as if he were falling into her, as if they were falling into each other. The wind gusted hard and fast around them, but he was lost in her, lost in the magic of this last, stolen moment with her.

He tightened his fingers in her hair, tipping her head back so that he could look into her eyes. She stared up at him, her face pale and still, her slim arms sliding up to curve around his neck, drawing him closer, until their lips were but a murmur away from touching.

He watched her nostrils flare on a quickly indrawn breath. Felt the fine trembling going on inside her, a trembling that matched his own as he whispered, "This is madness, Attica. It cannot be."

"No. It cannot." She swallowed, her voice tight and raw. "Not tomorrow, or the day after, or the day after. For I will return to Châteauhaut and do what I must do. Yet for now—for this one moment out of time, it can be."

He saw the need in her dark brown eyes. The need and the want. With a groan, he surrendered to both.

Pulling her up to him, he covered her mouth with his. He meant it to be a gentle kiss, a tender brushing of lips that would comfort her without frightening her. But her lips were so soft. So soft and warm and sweet as they moved beneath his.

It was a virgin's kiss, untutored, yet unhesitant. He heard her breath leave her body in a low, keening rush, felt her hands roving over his shoulders, his back, as she pressed herself against him. He felt the warm, yielding flesh of the woman beneath the fine cloth of bliaut and kirtle, and all the desire for her he'd held in check for so long burst suddenly into flame.

He tilted his head, slanting his mouth back and forth against hers as the kiss caught fire, became something raw and wild and all consuming. She opened her mouth to him hungrily, greedily, and he felt her quiver of shock and delight as his tongue entered her. She welcomed him, her tongue mating with his in a way that tempted him, tormented him with a need so great he was aching with it, trembling with it. Burning with it.

The night wind moaned around them, dark and stormy and sheltering in its secrecy. She flung back her head, her eyes open wide to stare at the storm-filled sky above, her fists clenching the cloth at his shoulders as he rubbed his lips down the curve of her neck, pressed a kiss into the hollow of her throat. *"Attica,"* he whispered hoarsely, feeling his breath wash hot over her skin. *"Je n'y puis rien . . ."*

His hands were at the small of her back now, holding her close, close enough that she could surely feel the heat of him, feel the hardness of him. But instead of pulling away, she pressed herself closer. And he wanted . . . he wanted to lay her down in a flower-strewn garden with the petals soft on her skin and her body naked to the sun and his hot gaze. He wanted to touch her warm flesh everywhere with his hands, with his lips and his tongue. He wanted to watch her neck arch, her lips part, her trembling body open to him in welcome as he entered her. He wanted . . . It was all wrong, what he wanted.

"Attica . . . dear God." A shudder wracked through him as he tightened his hands around her waist and set her away from him.

She stumbled backward until she was leaning against one of the espaliered trees of the allée, her hands flung out to grasp the straight branches, her face pale and stricken, her lips swollen from his kiss, her eyes huge. Lightning flashed across the sky, vivid and jagged; the wind whipped at her hair, tossing it across her face until she had to put up one hand to hold it back.

For a long moment, they simply stared at each other, her breath coming hard and fast, his chest heaving. He could see the pulse in her neck beating wildly, in time to his own throbbing desire. And somehow . . . somehow, he found his voice. "I'm sorry."

"No." She shook her head violently, reaching out to him. He took her hand in a tight grip, although he did not draw her close. "Don't be sorry," she said, her voice a raw ache. "Although it might have been better for us both, I think, if we had never met."

He ran his thumb along the back of her knuckles, his lips lifting in a tortured smile. "Easier, perhaps. But I would not wish for it."

He watched an answering smile touch her face. "No. Nor would I."

They stared at each other, sharing a long, silent moment. Then the sharp blast of the horn, announcing the meal, cut through the night.

She swung her head to stare at the distant hall.

"Come," he said, linking his fingers with hers. "We must go."

She looked at him, her eyes deep and dark with pain. He saw a quiver pass through her, and it was all he could do to keep from sweeping her into his arms again and telling her that he never wanted to let her go.

How had it happened, he wondered. It had begun so simply, as an amused liking for a brave, winning lad named Atticus. Then he'd discovered her secret and with that discovery had come a swift, unexpected rush of desire. And now, somehow, it had come to this, to this wanting that was more than liking, more than desire, so much more than either of them had room for in their lives.

"Yes." Her hand clutched at his. "We must go."

He held her hand as they walked through the darkened garden. But at the wicket gate they moved apart, walking sedately side by side across the yard. As they turned to go up the steps, the flickering light from the mounted torches threw their shadows out before them, separate, contorted.

And he thought, *This is how we are both fated to go through our lives. Disjointed and alone.*

He knew something was wrong as soon as he entered the hall.

The trestle tables had been set up and spread with fresh white cloths, the fire on the central hearth fed against the growing chill, the oil lamps suspended from their wall-mounted brackets lit against the night. Outside, the wind howled around the castle, billowing through the high wooden rafters of the hall and creaking the chains of the lamps until they swayed back and forth, their flickering flames casting grotesque shadows into the darkest corners. Damion glanced about, his gaze sharpening. There were too many men in the hall. Too many men simply standing around the door.

And they were all armed.

He pivoted warily as Renouf Blissot stepped forward, his face unsmiling, the draft-tossed light accentuating the point of his beard and the hollows beneath his cheekbones. His hand rested on his sword. "Are you Damion de Jarnac?" he asked, his voice a rough challenge.

Ahead of him, Attica whirled about, her face white and startled in the flaring torchlight. "What is this, Uncle?"

Renouf kept his gaze fastened on Damion. "Are you?"

Regretting the broigne and sword he'd left in the Knights' Tower, Damion rested his hands on his hips, and smiled. "Yes. Why?"

Turning to the men-at-arms, Renouf gave a curt nod. "Seize him."

Attica lunged forward. "No!" Her uncle's hand snagged her arm, drawing her up short. "Mother of God," she said on a gasp, struggling against him. "What is this?"

Dagger in hand, Damion dodged sideways as the men converged on him. A heavyset blond man with short legs screamed and fell back, clutching his shoulder. Another man doubled over, his hands to his guts. Then Damion staggered back as some half a dozen men threw themselves on him.

He realized dimly that they must not want him dead, or he would have fallen more quickly. He managed to slash two more before they wrested the dagger from him.

He didn't see the blow that knocked him senseless.

CHAPTER
TEN

Thrust unceremoniously and without explanation into her uncle's solar, Attica stuffed her hands into her sleeves and clutched her forearms against the dull ache in her midriff. Forgotten hunger gnawed at her stomach. Hunger and a rising spiral of anxiety she tried desperately to tamp down.

Two braziers stood, one at each end of the long, narrow room, but they had only recently been lit. The room was cold, the wind slamming against the castle with enough force to stir the fine wool hangings on the outside whitewashed plaster walls and rattle the closed shutters in the deep window embrasures. On the long, dark oak table in the center of the room, the flames of the beeswax candles in an ornate silver candelabra flared and fluttered with a shivering violence.

Still hugging herself, she prowled the richly appointed chamber, pacing past carved chests and cushioned stools, her gaze sliding almost unseeingly over the expensive collection of inlaid and jewel-incrusted swords, daggers, and maces that adorned one inner wall. But no matter how she tried to reconstruct the events since their arrival, she could not make sense out of what had just happened.

The sound of the door opening brought her spinning

180

around. *"Mother of God,"* she exclaimed, starting forward at the sight of her uncle's elegant form and handsome, un-smiling face. "What is the meaning of this, Uncle?"

He shut the door behind him with a snap and leaned against it to fix her with a cold stare. He had always been her favorite uncle. In those lonely years after Blanche sent Attica south to the courts of the Langue d'oc, he had come to visit her even when her mother did not. Not nearly as often as Stephen, of course, but he had come, a handsome, charming young knight, bringing gifts of sugarplums and gaily colored ribbons. For a few shining, memorable hours, he had lit up her young girl's life and made her feel special.

Only this was not the smiling young uncle of her child-hood but a harder, more formidable man. "Tell me, At-tica," he said, yanking something from his sleeve and tossing it onto the high oaken chest beside them. "Have you ever seen one of these before?"

She found herself staring at a breviary. A green, leather-bound breviary from the convent of Sainte-Foy-la-Petite, its cover whole and unsplit. "It's a Sainte-Foy breviary," she said.

"That's right. A very common little book. There was one in Olivier de Harcourt's bags when you took them from Châteauhaut-sur-Vilaine. It's not there now."

She raised her gaze to his face. "How do you know?"

"How do I know?" He pushed off the door and walked away from her to the far end of the room, where the howl-ing wind battered the shuttered window. "I know it's no longer there because I've just had the bags searched. I know it *should* be there because Yvette tells me Olivier de Harcourt was carrying one." He stopped, drawing in a deep breath as he turned to face her again. "This is impor-tant, Attica. *Where is the breviary now?*"

Her heart began to thump so wildly in her chest, she wondered her uncle couldn't hear it from across the room. "I don't know."

"You don't know," he repeated.

"No. It's just a simple breviary. Why is it so important?"

"It's *important* because Philip of France uses these breviaries to transport secret state documents. And it's *important* that whatever document Olivier de Harcourt was carrying not fall into the wrong hands." He walked back toward her until they were separated only by the narrow width of the table. His voice rose. "What have you done with it?"

Attica stared at him. "How do you know these things?" she asked. A tense silence tightened between them, filled only with the rush of the wind throwing itself against the castle walls outside. She saw her uncle clench his jaw, a muscle jumping along his cheek where it showed smooth above his beard. *"Grand Dieu,"* she whispered. "You've joined him. You and Yvette both. You've joined Philip against Henry."

"Not Philip. Richard."

Her lip curled. "That makes it acceptable, does it?"

He pressed the palms of his hands onto the polished surface of the table between them and leaned into her. "Where is the book?"

She forced herself to return his gaze calmly, steadily. "I don't know. I knew nothing of its importance when I brought the courtier's bags with me. I took them for his clothes, that is all."

He pushed away from the table with a violent shove. "Then the knight must have it."

She let out a startled laugh that sounded false even to

her own ears. "Don't be ridiculous. I must have left it at Châteauhaut."

"No."

"Then I must have lost it. It was dark when I changed into the courtier's clothing, and I was nervous. I had no reason to take care with it. I could have dropped it."

"Dropped it?" He shook his head. "I don't think so."

She watched, silent, as he walked to where an earthenware ewer stood, warming beside the brazier. "Why didn't you tell me the knight you brought with you is Damion de Jarnac?" he asked, his attention seemingly focused on the task of selecting a silver-mounted drinking horn and pouring himself a cup of wine.

"What do you mean? He is simply a knight-errant I hired to escort me. Why should I have named him?"

"A simple knight-errant? Is that what you think?" He raised the cup to his lips and took a deep swallow. "For the love of God, Attica, nothing has ever been simple about Damion de Jarnac. And he is no longer a knight-errant. He joined Henry's household months ago."

The wind gusted up, flaring the candles on the table and filling the room with the scent of hot wax and leather and oiled wood. "That's ridiculous," she said. "Why wouldn't he have told me?"

"Why should he?" he asked, throwing a glance at her over his shoulder. "What exactly did you think, anyway? That he agreed to escort you here out of the goodness of his heart? A true chivalrous knight, succoring the weak and unfortunate and rescuing damsels in distress? *Damion de Jarnac?*" A humorless smile twisted his lips as he gazed down at his cup. "My God."

"I tell you, he knows nothing of this."

"Nothing? On the contrary, niece. Damion de Jarnac

probably knows more about Philip's correspondence with John than I do. That *simple knight* of yours has been to Brittany and Ireland on King Henry's business, trying to learn from nobles close to John the extent of his involvement with Philip of France."

She wouldn't have believed what he was telling her except that she couldn't seem to get past the memory of de Jarnac standing in that glade surrounded by the bodies of the dead *routiers*, his gaze narrowing as she held Stephen's ring out to him. No wonder he had recognized it and known so much about Stephen and her family.

"What have you done with him?" she asked, her voice low and quivering.

"Nothing so far." He set aside his cup. "My men locked him in the North Tower. He hasn't talked yet. But by the time I am finished with him, he will."

Her legs trembled oddly beneath her, so that she had to grip the edge of the table before her for support. One of the candles in the intricately wrought silver stand hissed, drawing her attention to the flickering golden flames. As she watched, a trickle of wax spilled out of the liquid pool around the wick to run down the taper and harden in the cold. "You will torture him?" she said, the words coming out in a hoarse whisper.

"If I have to."

"And me? Will you torture me, Uncle, to be certain I tell you the truth?"

He smiled and came around the table toward her. "I don't think that will be necessary. But I'm afraid I'm going to have to lock you up, Attica. It's worth my neck to leave you wandering around the country, knowing what you know."

"You think I would betray you?" she asked, pivoting to face him.

"Given the chance, yes. Which is why I don't intend to give you the chance."

He reached for her arm, his grip tightening as she tried to pull away from him.

"Don't touch me," she cried, hitting out at him with her free hand. Her nails caught his left cheek and ripped through the flesh deep enough to draw blood. He let her go.

"God's teeth, Attica." He swiped at his face with his sleeve as he backed away from her.

"Don't touch me," she said again.

"Very well." He dropped his hand to his side, his gaze cold and angry. "I will leave you here while a separate, more secure room is prepared for you. Hopefully by then you will have calmed yourself. But be warned, Attica: I'll have my men-at-arms drag you there if necessary."

He turned on his heel and left her.

She watched him slam out the room, then stood quite still, staring at the closed door and listening to the murmur of voices as Renouf posted a guard at the door. Her heart beat hard and fast within her, but an odd kind of calm had settled over her.

She walked with deliberate purpose to study the wall containing Renouf's collection of inlaid and jeweled weapons. After some thought, she selected a jewel-encrusted mace that looked as if it had probably been made for a bishop, and a poniard, handsomely sheathed in silk-wrapped leather. The mace proved to be heavier than she'd expected, and the poniard long. It wouldn't be easy to keep them concealed in the sleeves of her gown. When her uncle came back, she would go with him quietly.

* * *

He awoke to a sense of pain and cold.

Damion lay unmoving for a moment, his eyes closed while he waited for full consciousness to return. He found that his cheek rested against hard-packed, rush-strewn earth, which he supposed meant he must be lying on a dirt floor somewhere. He felt trickles of moisture running over his flesh and a pool of wetness beneath him; he assumed both were his own blood. He could taste the metallic tang of blood in his mouth. He stretched his senses, listening. But the silence around him hung empty and absolute, stirred only by the distant thrashing of the wind. He was alone.

He opened his eyes to darkness. His head and his ribs ached from the beating he'd received, although he didn't think anything was broken. By gritting his teeth against a wave of dizzy nausea and levering up with his hands, he managed to sit. He kept still for a moment, his ears filling with the sound of his own ragged breathing, his head bowed as he gathered his internal forces. Then his vision cleared, and he lifted his head and looked around.

The room contained only one small barred window, open to the night and placed high up near the ceiling. Through the opening the night sky shone black and starless, but some unseen torch in a bracket on the castle walls cast a faint, flickering golden light that revealed unwhitewashed circular stone walls. A tuff of rank grass hung down through the bars to move fitfully in the wind. There was no furniture except for a bucket. He could see only one door, which doubtless gave onto the stairwell.

By inching carefully backward, he was able to brace his shoulders against the coarse wall. He was in the lower room of a tower. A tower somewhere in Laval Castle, he supposed, but probably uninhabited, since he could hear no movement above. Although that might simply be because of the hour; he had no way of knowing how long he had lain unconscious.

He wrapped his arms around his legs, drawing them up close to his body for warmth as he assessed his situation. It wasn't difficult to guess the reason for his imprisonment. And it wasn't much of a stretch from there to the realization that his chances of release were slim, and the possibility of escape or rescue, even less. Only Sergei and Attica knew he had come to Laval. Sergei was already on his way to warn Henry at La Ferté-Bernard, while Attica . . .

Damion tilted his head back against the stone wall, the chill of this place striking deep within him. He told himself her uncle wouldn't hurt her, had no reason to hurt her. But it didn't stop fear for her from churning his gut and bringing an icy sweat to his face.

He closed his eyes and tried to think, except his head ached ferociously. He only realized he must have dozed when he jerked suddenly awake and found himself shivering with cold and listening alertly. His body tense, he heard the sound of footsteps on the circular stone steps outside the heavy plank door. A bolt shrieked as it was drawn back on the outside of the door.

He would not meet his captor like this, curled up in a shivering huddle against the wall. It might not be easy to retain his dignity through the events to come, but he would preserve it as long as possible. So he pushed himself upright, slowly, his breath hitching as a searing pain grabbed at his side. Then, using the wall as a prop, he pivoted to face the door.

The castellan of Laval came in carrying a horn lantern and flanked by four burly men wearing helmets and mail hauberks.

"Four men," said Damion, pursing his lips. "And decked out in armor, too. You must think I'm dangerous."

A touch of color rode high on Blissot's cheekbones, one of which now bore an interesting series of scratches. "Shackle him," he said, standing back to let his men past.

Damion watched the golden light from the lantern play over the bare, irregularly cut stones of his prison to reveal several sets of fetters bolted high on the walls. He knew fists weren't much of a weapon against men wearing mail shirts and helmets, but he fought anyway, the breath leaving his body in a painful huff as the men seized him and flung him back against the wall. His arms were yanked brutally over his head, the rough stones scraping his flesh as iron bands, cold and abrasive, clanged closed around his wrists.

He lunged once, uselessly, the chains ringing, the metal biting into his wrists, wrenching painfully at his shoulders. Then he hung still, setting his teeth against the rush of panic and the animal-like impulse to continue to pull wildly, mindlessly.

"I would have thought you had enough bruises already," said Blissot, smiling faintly from across the room. The smile faded as he nodded to his men-at-arms. "Leave us."

"Is that wise?" said Damion, tossing his head to throw the tumbled hair out of his eyes. "I'm only fettered and beaten half-senseless."

Unexpectedly, Blissot laughed. Turning, he hung the lantern from a hook near the door. "Your reputation is formidable, I admit. But unless you number witchcraft amongst your skills, I fail to see how you expect to escape your fetters. They are quite solid, believe me."

"Test them regularly, do you?" Damion said, wrapping

his fists around the chains to ease some of the stress on his arms. "Have you turned robber baron? I hear capturing innocent pilgrims and holding them for ransom under threat of hideous tortures and painful deaths can be lucrative."

Blissot shook his head. "You are no innocent pilgrim. Although I might be persuaded to allow your family and friends to ransom you."

Damion bared his teeth. "Well, we both know that the members of my family aren't likely to take you up on any offers. But I do have friends. And some personal resources, if you're not too greedy."

"Don't worry," said the castellan of Laval, coming to stand in front of Damion beyond the range of his feet. "The price won't be excessive. Say, five hundred livres? And one small piece of information."

Damion met the other man's gaze steadily. "I can't imagine what I could possibly know that you don't."

"Flattering. But unfortunately inaccurate. You see, a book has gone missing. A Sainte-Foy breviary that Attica by chance brought away with her in Olivier de Harcourt's saddlebags. Attica claims she knew nothing of the importance of the breviary and that she has no idea what has become of it. And do you know what? I'm inclined to believe her."

"Well, I'm glad to hear you're such a trusting fellow, because I'm afraid I don't know what you're talking about either," said Damion.

Blissot sighed. "We could play these games all evening, de Jarnac, but I have other things to do with my time. So let us say simply that I know you have joined Henry's household, I know you have been to Brittany and Ireland, and I even know why. Which leads me to the inevitable

conclusion that if the breviary and its incriminating documents have disappeared, then you are probably the one
responsible."

With effort, Damion kept his face impassive. There should
have been only three, perhaps four people outside of King
Henry himself who knew the true purpose of Damion's
recent travels. Yet someone had told Renouf Blissot, and
Damion was suddenly quite sure he knew who that person
was. Slowly, he smiled. "Documents, you say? Now that is
interesting. Do you mind if I ask whom they are for?"

Blissot tssked. "Monsieur le chevalier, if you continue
in this vein I shall be forced to order my men to apply certain persuasive techniques that are both unpleasant and
permanent in their affects. And in that case, I fear there
may not be much left of you for your friends to ransom."

Damion had seen men tortured. Smelled the sickening
stench of burned flesh. Heard their unending screams of
terror and unbearable agony as the knife cut, destroyed,
took from a man everything he held most dear . . .

He tilted back his head to look at Blissot through slitted
eyes. He felt light-headed from the beating, his mouth dry
from blood loss and a range of emotions held in check by
willpower alone. "Would that be wise?" he said, somehow
managing to keep his voice level. "I mean, no one is likely
to be willing to pay much for a blind eunuch lugging about
bloody misshapen stumps instead of the usual hands and
feet."

What might have been a reluctant gleam of admiration
lit the other man's pale eyes. "I would prefer to ransom
you whole," said Blissot, walking to the door. "But I will
have that breviary, and I will do whatever is necessary to
obtain it."

Damion tightened his jaw. "I'm afraid I still don't know what you're talking about."

Blissot paused to look back, a bemused expression on his fine-boned, handsome face. "Why? Why persist? How could Henry possibly compensate you for what I will do to you?"

Damion said nothing. Blissot shrugged and reached for the lantern. "I'll give you the rest of the night to reconsider."

He turned toward the door again, the light playing across his face. Damion said provocatively, "Get too close to a cat?"

"My niece," said Blissot, his fingertips going self-consciously to his scratched cheek. "I always thought Robert d'Alérion betrothed her to Fulk unwisely. Now I know it. That boy will never be able to handle her."

"Does she know you've turned traitor to your liege lord?"

"What an ugly word that is, 'traitor.' " Blissot smiled. "I prefer to say I've altered the direction of my loyalties."

"To Philip?"

The smile hardened. "No. To Richard. He will be the next Duke of Normandy and King of England, you know."

"I know," said Damion. "I simply have problems with his impatient attempts to hurry the process along, that's all."

"Indeed? I should think rather that you and he had much in common. But no—" He paused, as if struck by a thought. "It was your brother you killed, not your father, was it not? Or was it?"

With a snarl, Damion lunged forward, to be pulled up by the fetters digging painfully into his wrists.

He expected Renouf Blissot to smile again, but he didn't. He simply turned and left Damion there, with his memories of the past and his fears for the future.

* * *

The room to which Renouf escorted her turned out to be the last in a series of small chambers on the second floor of an old, disused timber dwelling that backed onto the curtain wall. It wasn't exactly a prison, but it was small and cold and meanly furnished, and it had obviously been only hastily and not very thoroughly cleaned. The door was stout and could be barred from the outside.

"It won't be for long," he said, his hand still on the door as she stood alone in the center of the bare floor, her gaze quietly surveying her surroundings.

"Why, Uncle?" she asked, her brows drawing together as she turned to face him. She felt such an ache in her chest, the pressure of so many emotions—fear, betrayal, and a fierce, determined anger—that she wondered that her heart could contain them all without ripping apart. "Why have you joined the rebellion against Henry?"

His jaw tightened. "Henry is old."

"Not so old."

"Too old to win against Richard. And I plan to be on the winning side, Attica."

"Is that what's important? Winning? What of honor?" Her voice cracked. "And loyalty?"

"Honor and loyalty?" He smiled wryly. "They're words, child. Pretty words, beloved of troubadours and fresh-faced, eager young knights. But still only words."

She thought she caught a faint timbre of regret in his voice, a trace of the young man he had once been. "They were more than words to you once. They were part of the code by which you lived."

"Perhaps. When I was young." His face looked strained, and she saw the lines left there by all the years that had passed since he had been that laughing young knight, bringing sugarplums and ribbons to the innocent little girl she once had been. "I'm not so young anymore, Attica. And in my experience, there is no honor. Anywhere. So that a man is wise if he is loyal only to himself."

The sentiment was bitter. Bitter and angry, and it so closely echoed something de Jarnac had said to her that she knew a swift rush of what she thought might be despair. She had the most peculiar sensation—as if her entire world, everything she believed in, was collapsing around her. "What kind of world would we live in, if all men thought thus?" she said scornfully.

His head reared back, his nostrils quivering, his hand tightening on the edge of the door. "You're a woman, Attica. You should be seeing to your bride clothes and preparing to take your vows, rather than concerning yourself with these matters."

"Well, I should have plenty of time to meditate on my womanly obligations while I wait for you to release me from my prison, shouldn't I, Uncle?"

The room shook as he slammed the door behind him.

She stood quite still, listening to the grating of the bolt being drawn across the door and the brisk tramp of his receding footsteps. She forced herself to count very slowly to fifty before she eased the mace and poniard from her sleeves and went to hide them beneath the thin straw-filled mattress on the bed.

She was surprised to see that whoever had cleaned the room had also brought her saddlebags from the ladies' chamber. She tore them open, a smile touching her lips at the sight of the courtier's clothes carefully folded within.

Setting them aside, she hurried to the room's single window. She pulled the pin from the shutters and gasped as the wind whistled through a rent in one of the old, oiled parchment windowpanes and practically whipped the wooden panels from her grasp.

Biting her lower lip, she carefully braced back the shutter, then eased open the window, holding the frame tightly against the howl of the incoming storm. The room overlooked not the bailey itself but a narrow, noisome alley running between the timber building and another structure, made of stone, that she thought was probably the kitchen. The smell of roast meat and old woodsmoke hung heavy in the air, and she could hear a confusion of voices and the rattle of pots and pans in the big barrels used for washing. As she listened, someone began to sing a silly ditty about a lovesick pig, which made the knaves and pages laugh.

The wind gusted again, bathing her face with fresh air and the smell of coming rain. She said a small prayer and looked down.

The timber-framed building had been constructed over a stone undercroft, probably used for storage, so that the drop to the muddy path below was one of at least fifteen feet. She could never jump so far. She twisted around to look back at the bed. She couldn't jump, but dressed again in the courtier's clothes and with the aid of a rope, she could climb down. Later, after the castle had settled into sleep.

Renouf would never have locked up a male prisoner so carelessly, she thought, refastening the window and shutters before turning to the task of ripping up her coarse, stout sheets. He considered her a mere woman, a mistake Damion de Jarnac would never have made.

The thought brought a faint smile to her heart as she set to work.

* * *

Alone once more in his dark, cold prison, Damion leaned his head against the stone wall and squeezed his eyes shut.

He found himself oddly aware of small things. The sharp links of the chains, digging into the palms of his hands as he clutched the fetters as if clinging to them for support. The rising roar of the storm, sweeping in on the city. The pounding of his own heart, beating loudly in his ears. He could not think of what was about to happen to him. He could not risk tapping into the dangerous well of emotions that lurked within him.

It wasn't that he particularly feared death, although he had always hoped that his death, when it came, would be quick and painless. It was obvious, now, that it would be neither. But what bothered him more than anything was the sense of incompleteness, of unfulfillment. He was not ready to die.

He thought of all the things he had wanted to accomplish in his life and now never would. The grand ambitions, the determination to win for himself both land and titles, to prove that he didn't need the birthright he'd discovered he never really had. But what cut him even more was the realization that his restless, futile search for relief would never end, that he would die still tortured by the all-consuming guilt and anger that had tormented him since that dark and deadly night fourteen years ago. . . .

Thunder rumbled in the distance, a long, low reverberation that seemed to shake the very walls of the tower. Damion smelled dust and the promise of rain upon the restless wind. He pulled the damp air into his chest and pushed it out again, aware of a sharper sense of regret as his thoughts turned to Attica. He knew he could never have had more with her than what they had shared together these past two days, and yet the sense of loss he felt when he thought of her was bitter and tragic. He wondered if she realized yet that her brother had most likely turned traitor to the king he served, and he thought with pain of how the disillusionment would shatter her, when she did learn the truth.

Thunder boomed again, louder this time. So loud that for a moment it drowned out the sound of quick footfalls on the steps, a low voice, a thump.

Damion's gaze flew to the small square of black sky that showed through the window, his breath coming shallow and rapid in his throat. It was too soon, surely? It couldn't possibly be dawn yet. Not yet. He heard the grating of the heavy bolt being drawn back, the creak of the door swinging inward, and he tightened his grip on his chains, his grip on himself.

And then, out of the darkness, came a whisper. A woman's voice, cultured, husky with strain, saying, "Damion? Are you there? You must come away quickly."

Attica.

The relief he felt was so total that for one intense moment, it obliterated all thought. Then he gave a hoarse laugh that came out almost like a groan and said, "Unless you have the keys to these fetters, my valiant little lordling, I'm afraid I'm not going anywhere."

CHAPTER ELEVEN

Attica breathed in the dank, foul air of the tower room and felt her stomach roil. The curving walls of the room seemed to close in on her, blanketing her with a mindless, primeval fear of dark, close places. She could see nothing.

"Fetters?" she said, the words echoing hollowly in the stony emptiness. "You are chained?"

His voice came to her from out of the storm-blackened void, along with the clank of metal, as if he had given his shackles an angry yank. "To the wall. A time-honored and highly effective means of preventing prisoners from wandering off into the night."

A flash of lightning sliced through the darkness to show her a bare prison room with dirty rushes on the floor and a man hanging in chains against the damp stone wall. Blood matted his head and trickled down one side of his face, while his clothes hung in tatters on his leanly muscled frame.

"Mon Dieu," she whispered as thunder rumbled in the distance. She went to him, close enough that she could have touched him, although she did not. "Are you badly hurt?"

Her eyes were beginning to adjust to the blackness of the room. She could see a square of wind-tossed sky through the high, barred window, and the quirk of Damion's swollen lips that might have been a smile. "Bruised and battered, but whole. So far. Your uncle plans to start carving up bits of me in the morning."

The thought of what had been done to him—of what would be done to him if she couldn't get him away from here, tore savagely at her heart. She heard herself make a strange sound, almost like a whimper, deep in her throat. And then she was touching him, her fingertips coursing lightly over his forehead, his cheeks, hovering over his mouth for one intense moment.

"I'm all right. Truly," he said softly, pressing his lips to her palm.

Trembling, she let her hands slide along his arms to where the irons bit into his wrists. "How can I get you out of these?"

He pressed his forehead against hers, his breath warm against her cheek. "It won't be easy without the key. And unless the guard has it, it's with your uncle."

She took a quick step back. "The guard? Of course." Whirling about, she stumbled across the uneven floor. From the base of the tower, a tight spiral of worn stone steps curved up toward a glimmer of light and a fresh gust of night wind. She ran up the stairs to where a bunch of keys lay on the stone lintel of the doorway, beside the curving, still hand of the guard. She snatched up the ring without looking at the man's face, or at the dark patch of blood she'd left on the back of his head. Her heart pounding in her chest, she raced back down the steps and hurried across the cell.

"I hope these are the right ones," she said, reaching to try one of the keys in the fetters.

It didn't fit.

Stifling a small gasp of dismay, she shifted to try another key. Her breasts pressed against Damion's chest as she leaned into him, the heat of his body rising up to her, close and intimate.

She heard the swift, hissing intake of his breath, and for a moment, she froze. "I'm sorry," she said, her voice unusually husky as she moved again to struggle with the lock. "I can't reach otherwise."

He murmured something incoherent that sounded halfway between a laugh and a groan. Then the key clicked home, and the iron band at his wrist sprang open.

He lowered his free arm, his teeth clenching against the pain as blood rushed back into his numb hand. She reached quickly to unlock his other wrist. "Where is Sergei? How can I find him?"

"You needn't worry about Sergei." He winced as his second wrist came free. "He's already on his way to La Ferté-Bernard."

He bent forward, rubbing his sore wrists, so that he didn't see her hand coming until her open palm caught his cheek with a sharp crack that sent his head jerking sideways under the impact. "Sweet Infant Jesus, Attica! What was that for?" he demanded, his hair tumbling over his eyes as he stared at her.

"For not telling me about you and Henry."

He straightened. Then, to her surprise, he laughed. "Let's get out of here," he said, and grabbed her hand.

The air was fresher in the stairwell. He paused at the foot of the steps, his back to the curved wall, his hand still in hers as he sucked in great, gasping breaths. "Is there a guard?" he asked, his left arm pressed to his ribs as if they hurt.

"Not anymore."

A faint, wavering patch of moonlight broke through the wind-blown clouds to reveal the dark bulk of her uncle's man-at-arms sprawled half on the entry landing, half on the steps that continued up into the darkness of the tower. "Is he dead?" de Jarnac asked in wonder, inching carefully up the stairs with Attica behind him.

"I do sincerely hope not. Although I fear I hit him hard."

"Exactly what did you hit him with?"

"A mace. I borrowed it from my uncle's collection."

He grunted, turning to study the yard beyond the narrow doorway. "How well do you know this castle?"

"There's a sally port between the stables and the armory. It has but one guard."

He brought his still, intense gaze back to her face. "Do you come with me?"

"Yes," she said simply, holding his gaze. "I can't trust my uncle. He may be my kinsman, but that didn't stop him from imprisoning me tonight. I don't know what he would do to me for helping you escape."

She thought, for a moment, he meant to say something. Instead, he swung abruptly away, his head falling back as he cast an appraising glance up at the sky.

The rain still held off, but dark clouds hung low overhead, massive and thick and turbulent above the jagged crenellations of pale sandstone towers and walls. The darkness of the night rendered the details of the castle indistinct, the various buildings ringing the yard showing only hazy, muted shades of charcoal and lead and ash. Then the wind gusted up, scouring the bailey, sending dried leaves and a scared, white-tailed cat scuttling across the hard-baked ground as boot heels clicked on the wall walk above.

De Jarnac's hand tightened on her arm, drawing her further back into the shadows as the helmet of a guard appeared, silhouetted against a flash of lightning as he moved along the wall walk. The castle might be asleep, but it was still guarded. And escaping from the castle itself would only be the beginning, Attica thought. Once they were clear of the castle, they would still need to traverse the city and find some way through its high walls and locked gates.

She watched Damion reach instinctively to put his hand on his dagger, then heard him swear softly, because the guards had of course taken it from him before flinging him into the tower. "Christ," he muttered under his breath. "What I wouldn't give for a sword right now."

She slipped the poniard from her sleeve and held it out to him. "I brought you this."

His teeth flashed in a smile. "More of Uncle Renouf's collection?" he asked, strapping the dagger to his belt.

She caught his arm, drawing him around to face her when he would have moved. "I would ask that you avoid using it, if at all possible."

He grunted. "Do you bring your mace?"

"No."

His gaze lifted once more to the guard approaching on the wall walk.

She held on to his arm. "Promise me?"

He let his breath out in a long sigh. "I'll try." He took her hand in a tight grip and leaned forward until his lips almost touched her ear. They watched the guard above pause, then swing about. "Now," De Jarnac whispered, and darted through the doorway.

They kept to the shadows of the wooden buildings that lined the castle wall, their movements smooth and wraith-like, their soft boots noiseless on hard earth and rounded cobbles, on straw and soft, squishy things neither of them

cared to identify. In the darkness of the night, they navi-
gated mainly by sense of smell, recognizing the fermenty
tang of the alehouse, the lingering scents of charcoal and
raw metal that marked the blacksmith's, until at last they
came to the mingling odors of warm horseflesh and hay
and manure that told them they had reached the stables.

Damion could see the sally port now, a small arched
opening set at the base of a square tower, its heavy, iron-
banded oak door barred fast against the night. A flambeau
thrust into a nearby bracket on the wall smoked badly, its
dancing yellow light revealing a man-at-arms, his helmeted
head tilted back as he anxiously surveyed the jumbled
clouds above.

Reaching out, Damion put his hand on Attica's shoulder
and whispered softly in her ear. "Walk up to the guard and
talk to him."

She jerked her head around to stare at him. *"Me?"*

He threw her a reckless grin. "Simply act as if you have
a right to be where you are. I'll take him from behind."

Her wide, solemn eyes, black as the night around them,
gazed back at him. "You won't kill him?"

Damion pursed his lips and shook his head.

She eyed him a moment longer. Then she sucked in a
deep gasp of air, as if to steady herself, and crept to the
corner of the stables. Damion watched her hesitate, visibly
throwing off the skulking furtiveness of a shadows-bound
figure. Chin up, her shoulders back, she strode forward
with an arrogant masculine strut that was such a caricature
that Damion smiled softly into the night.

"Do you think it will rain?" she asked, throwing her already husky voice low as she sauntered up to the guard.

The guard swung about, his hand tightening on his pike
as he stiffened, then visibly relaxed at the sight of Atticus's

fine clothing and friendly, smiling face. "What the devil are you doing here, lad?"

"Meeting Juliana." Attica edged closer to the port. "You do know Juliana, don't you?" she asked, drawing the guard around to face her. Leering suggestively, she cupped her hands a good foot in front of her chest and thrust her hips back and forth in a rudely suggestive motion that made the guard chuckle and led Damion, watching her, to wonder where she got *that* from. "The new dairy maid with the big tits?"

"No," said the guard, sounding interested. "Juliana, you say?"

Attica nodded. "She promised to meet me in the square, by the fountain." Her smile faded suddenly, and she dropped her hands in a gesture of despair. "Except she said she wouldn't come if it was going to rain. Do you think it's going to rain?"

The guard, his back now to Damion, squinted up at the night sky and growled, "It always rains when I'm on guard duty."

Damion crept forward. A swift, lethal twist of the neck or a knife blade expertly drawn from behind across the throat would have been quick and quiet. But Damion had promised. Setting his jaw, he brought the heavy jeweled pommel of his borrowed poniard down on the back of the guard's helmet with a thumping *clang* that echoed around the yard like a kitchen dinner gong. The guard collapsed at Damion's feet, just as someone shouted an inquiry from out of the darkness.

"Shit," said Damion, leaping forward to yank back the bolts on the portal. He threaded his hand through the iron grip and yanked.

The door swung inward with a betraying shriek of grinding hinges that seemed to fill the night. Swearing again, he ducked through the doorway, one hand curling around the stone frame as he reached back for her. "Attica?"

She hesitated, the wind whipping the hem of her surcoat and fluttering the curls at her cheek, her eyes huge in a pale face, as if she had only now realized the enormity of what she was about to do.

Another shout went up, this one from the wall walk above. A torch flared hot and bright; running feet pounded toward them across the yard. "Attica," he said, his gaze shifting away from her, then back again, "if you're coming with me, my love, now would be a good time."

She came at him in a rush. He caught her hand, and they ran together through the open portal and into the darkened city beyond.

Her feet flying over the hard-packed ground, her heart pounding painfully in her chest, Attica clung to the strong, capable hand of the man beside her and ran.

A wild wind whipped the hair across her face as lightning shattered the dark sky and the earth shook with the rumble of thunder. They fled through the storm-charged darkness, down a steep, curving street of tightly packed timber and stone merchants' houses, past windows shuttered now in sleep. The patter of their running feet echoed hollowly through the deserted space, the sounds of shouting growing fainter behind them until she thought for one brief, hopeful moment that they might actually get away.

Then a shrill clang rang out over the sleeping houses, the first deafening stroke followed by another and another as the alarm bell sent its warning to all the guards of the city. A dog somewhere up near the castle began to bark, then another and another. A man's sleepy voice called out, his words lost in the bang of a shutter being thrown open against the house wall over their heads.

"I think," said de Jarnac, his teeth flashing in a devil-damn-the-world smile, "that they've found your mace-felled friend."

"Huh." She threw a quick glance over her shoulder, half expecting to see the dark armor and menacing pikes of the guard pouring out the castle gate in pursuit. But the jagged rooftops of the curving rows of stepped houses had already hidden the castle from her sight.

"My compliments to your uncle," said Jarnac softly. "His men are quick."

She swung her head back around and bit off a gasp of dismay at the sight of a coppery glow wavering over the upper stories of the houses below. A shower of sparks flickered up into the night, and she knew it came from the wind-blown torches held high by the hands of hurrying men.

Glancing about wildly, she saw the black mouth of an alley yawn enticingly up ahead on their left, and knew it was too far away. Already the bobbing helmets and thrusting pikes of the first line of men-at-arms rushing up the hill in answer to the castle's alarm were visible around the bend in the street.

"There!" One of the men drew up momentarily in surprise, his fist tightening on his pike. "See them there?" he cried, his sweat-sheened face highlighted in orange by the flaring light of a flickering torch as he charged forward again. *"Seize them."*

Attica's step faltered, her feet stumbling over the lip of the foul-smelling, stone-lined gutter that ran down the center of the street. "We're trapped."

"Not yet," said de Jarnac. He caught her before she fell,

yanking her arm as he dragged her into the darkness of a
deep porch that turned out to be not a porch at all but an
arched passage piercing the facade of the merchant's establishment beside them.

The stone tunnel closed in around them, dark and dank
and close, then emptied into a long, narrow yard flanked
on one side by the long ell of the house, on the other by the
high wall of its neighbor. The yard itself was a mosaic of
dark, mysterious shapes that soon identified themselves as
de Jarnac tripped with a clatter over the pole of an un-
horsed cart and Attica catapulted, arms outflung, into a
huge pyramid of empty barrels. She careered sideways,
scraping her elbow, losing her footing to land on her backside with a teeth-rattling thump as the barrels wobbled
precariously beside her.

"*Juste ciel.* It would be a wine merchant," she heard de
Jarnac say in soft amusement, as if they didn't have a troop
of armed men hard on their heels, as if the insistent peal of
the alarm bell wasn't still ringing out to rouse the entire
city against them.

"I think I prefer a wine merchant over a pig farmer," she
said, pushing herself up onto wobbly legs. She heard the
low huff of his laugh as she groped her way toward him.
He seemed to be doing something with the barrels. She
had only just grasped what he was about to do when a low,
throaty growl brought her spinning around.

Sharp canine teeth gleamed white and deadly from a large,
furry shadow that crouched menacingly beside a nearby
shed. "De Jarnac," Attica whispered, just as the huge mastiff
growled again and hurtled itself forward.

"Christ," said de Jarnac, grabbing her arm as he kicked
loose a carefully positioned lever that sent a shudder through
the looming pile of wine caskets. She didn't see the chain

until the dog hit the end of its tether with a blessed clang of metal links and a snarling, frustrated fury that was all but lost in the thunderous roar of the barrels as the pyramid collapsed.

Leaping forward, the great casks bounded and rattled across the courtyard, a rolling, charging cylindrical army of dark oak to the rescue. She heard a quickly cut off crude expletive and a startled yelp from two of the men-at-arms who had just burst through the passage from the street only to disappear in a confusion of upflung arms and smashing staves and burst iron bands.

"Ha," said de Jarnac, his laughing voice close to her ear as they ran together toward the back of the yard. "You're right: much better than a pig farmer."

They pelted over the uneven paving blocks, past a startled, white-headed goat and a squawking, ruffle-feathered aviary, before they came upon the outside corner stair that they followed up and up, to the house's third-floor gallery. From there, it was an easy matter for Attica to follow de Jarnac's lead and swing her legs over the gallery's wooden railing for the leap to the gently sloping roof of the two-story workshop that abutted the back of the house.

Balanced on the top of the railing, she hesitated, her head jerking toward the sound of heavy feet pounding up the steps behind them. One of the soldiers, quicker than his fellows, was closing on them fast. Glancing about in a panic, she seized one of the pots of scraggly geraniums that decorated the railing and sent it hurtling downward to shatter with a cascade of dirt on the crest of the helmet that had just appeared on the steps below her. The helmet abruptly disappeared.

"Got him," said Attica, pushing off the railing into de Jarnac's waiting arms.

"You have a talent with blunt objects." He laughed as he caught her. But then the laughter faded from his face to be replaced by a strange intensity she'd never seen there before as he held her close to him. "This is getting dangerous, Attica. I'd rather you'd left me in that prison room to die than that something happen to you because of me."

She watched, her head thrown back, as the wind ruffled the sweat-dampened hair at his temples. Against the darkness of the storm-driven night sky, his face shone pale, the flaring bones of his cheeks, the strong line of nose and chin striking her as both achingly beautiful and oddly vulnerable. She looked at him and felt deep within her the heavy beat of her heart as it seemed to slow and then stop for one momentous, unforgettable instant of revelation.

I love him, she thought with quiet, piercing wonder. *That is why I am here, running through this storm-filled night, my heart light with a wild excitement that can find a source for laughter even in the face of death. Because I love him, and I cannot bear to let him leave without me.*

She reached up to touch his cheek, her hand trembling. "Whatever the outcome," she said softly, "I could never regret what I did."

Unexpectedly, his smile flashed, wide and cocky and stealing her heart all over again. "The outcome is still ours to make." He seized her hand in his sinewy grip. "Come, my mace- and flower-pot-wielding lordling; the sky at least is open before us."

Hand in hand they ran, across the slippery, slanting slate roofs of the houses that descended the hill of Laval Castle like a series of giant, ragged steps so tightly wedged together that the short distances between them could be leapt, the differences in height not so great she couldn't scramble up them with the aid of jutting gargoyles and de Jarnac's strong, helping hand.

Their progress was not quiet. Ever conscious of the pounding feet and hoarse shouts of their pursuers, they moved with no thought to stealth but seized whatever could be enlisted in their defense: loose tiles snatched and thrown on the fly, unripe plums plucked from a big old overhanging tree, yesterday's washing, carelessly left drying across some upper gallery, now cut free to whip through the air and momentarily blind and trip the men who slogged determinedly after them.

Stumbling and cursing, the men-at-arms plowed on through the wind-whipped, lightning-charged night, only to blunder into the clutches of outraged townspeople awakened by the ruckus. To the missiles of the fugitives, the good citizens of Laval unwittingly added their own impediments as they took their fury out on those nearest at hand. Renouf's faithful soldiers found themselves splashed with the contents of slop buckets and dodging flying boots as they fended off broom-wielding middle-aged matrons in flowing white shifts and night caps whose shrieks redoubled in intensity when the cloud-filled skies above parted and the rain came pouring down.

The rain fell in big, hard drops that filled the air with the sharp scent of wet earth and stone. The slates and tiles underfoot, already dangerous, now became wet and deadly. The wind sent the rain driving into Attica's face, blinding her. She fell to her hands and knees, creeping along slowly, her heart in her throat. And then the long, curving row of houses they followed ended abruptly at a triangular plaza cobbled in gleaming, rain-washed gray stones toward which the wall of the last house dropped a straight three stories. There was no way down.

They stood together at the edge of the tiles, Attica's breath coming so hard and fast, her chest ached. Rain ran down her face, dripped off her hair, soaked her torn, filthy clothes. She felt as if she were drowning in failure and despair.

"I can try to lower you over the edge," said de Jarnac, his own breath ragged. "Or we can jump together."

Through the driving, roaring rain, she looked up into his strained face and thought for one tormented moment that he must have decided to choose death on the cobbles below over inevitable capture. But then his hand tightened in hers, and he was dragging her along the wet slates, and she saw what he had already noticed: a lean-to barn built in a shadowy corner against the house wall.

She stared down at the barn's thatched roof, some fifteen feet below, then glanced over her shoulder at the men rushing across the roof toward them through a swirling blaze of torches. An arrow whizzed through the night, so close she felt the wind of its passing. She met de Jarnac's questioning gaze and said, "Jump."

They jumped hand in hand, the thatch absorbing much of their momentum before giving way to spill them through rough-hewn rafters into the straw-strewn bed of a very startled cow.

Scrambling up, winded but unbroken, they erupted out the barn door into the empty plaza, straw plastered to their wet clothes, the cow interested, ambling behind as they considered the rain-washed darkness before them.

Three streets, two wider than the other, opened off the small plaza. They chose the narrow lane that wound around the base of the hill toward the river, and set off again at a run.

But they had lost the freedom of movement they'd found on the rooftops, and Renouf Blissot's men had had more than enough time to spread out over the twisted network of streets and alleyways around the castle. Within twenty-five paces, the reddish glow of torchlight gleaming through the rain up ahead showed them the dim silhouette of armed men, blocking the lane.

Too late, now, to turn back, for a stream of curses and pounding feet announced the imminent if limping arrival of their caprioling companions of the rooftops. Damion spun round in the narrow, muddy rue, searching for a way out, but this was an old street and a poor one, with ancient houses leaning drunkenly against one another and no friendly dark archways to welcome them into hidden courtyards.

Swearing, Damion began to throw himself first against one door, then the next, pounding on the locked, metal-studded panels until, to his surprise, one gave way before him, and he found himself stumbling down a shallow flight of stone steps, with Attica yanked in behind him.

A swirl of soapy steam enveloped them in warm wisps that floated away between row after row of stone columns and drifted up in a golden, lamp-lit mist to hover beneath round arched stone vaults that reminded him vaguely of the ancient ruins he had seen half-buried in the hot shifting sands of eastern deserts.

The baths were old, very old, and once, doubtless, respectable. They were not respectable now. Perhaps by day the poorer citizens of Laval still came here to wash away the dirt of their honest labors. But by night the place was obviously given over to the kind of activities that had made bagnios and stews bywords for brothels all across Europe.

A second look showed him that paint darkened both the

lush lips and the pertly bared nipples of the woman who
had opened the door to them and now stood gape-mouthed
with surprise, staring at them. Beyond her, the whirls of
steam floating over the lapping surface of the large central pool parted to reveal the brawny back and thrusting
naked buttocks of a man who coupled openly with a
white-limbed woman he held pinned to the marble steps
descending languidly into the waters.

"What is this place?" Attica whispered, her eyes wide
and round.

"Don't look," Damion told her. He grabbed her hand
and ran with her around the foggy edge of the pool, just as
the first man-at-arms burst through the open doorway.

Unprepared for the stairs, the soldier somersaulted down
the ancient steps to crash into the Lady of the Painted
Breasts, who recovered her voice and her wits at the same
time and fled screaming.

"Shit," said Damion, ducking between a row of secluded
alcoves. It was here that those too modest to expose themselves in the public pool bathed instead, in wooden troughs
set upon raised stone platforms and curtained with heavy
silks and brocades rather the worse for age and long exposure to damp air and careless frolicking.

The sound of boots pounding across the tiles behind
them echoed through arching stone vaults already ringing
with the panicked splashes of bathers and staccato bursts
of sodden female shrieks. "I do not think," said Attica, as
Damion yanked down a moldy blue velvet curtain to throw
into the path of their nearest pursuer, "I do not think these
gentlemen came here simply to bathe."

"I told you not to look," said Damion, whirling to confront a slim, dark-haired soldier whose sword was already

singing free of its scabbard to flash naked and sharp through the misty air.

Leaping out of the way, Damion caught the still swinging sword with a looped towel plucked from the waist of an indignant bather. The bather fled, pink bottom waddling, as Damion jerked the towel-wrapped blade and sent it arcing through the air to land with a ringing crash on the tiles. Grim-lipped, the soldier reached for his poniard, just as Attica hit him from behind with a three-legged stool.

"I wondered where you were," said Damion, breathing heavily.

She was better with flower pots and maces than with stools. The soldier only staggered, grabbing for support at the splashing edge of the recently vacated trough. With a splintering rip, the old wood gave beneath his weight. Eyes widening, he pitched over backward, still clutching the side of the trough, which tore loose in his grip.

Like a steaming miniature tidal wave, the hot, soapy water poured forth, washing over the tiled floor to knock the next soldier off his feet and send another skidding across the slippery tiles to crack his forehead against a column.

"It's getting crowded in here," said Damion. "There must be a way out to the yard."

"I thought I saw a door at the end there," said Attica, tossing away her stool as she ran down the curtained corridor.

She *had* seen a door, only it was now blocked by a white-robed wraith of a woman with a pointed chin and improbable red hair, who said calmly, "The yard is already full of soldiers. You can't get out that way. Follow me."

Damion's gaze met Attica's for one significant moment. At some point during that long, danger-filled night, they had moved beyond the need to communicate with words.

Their minds had leapt together, just as their bodies had moved in concert across the rooftops and alleyways of Laval.

And so he knew her thoughts, even though she did not speak them. He knew that she realized, as he did, that their options were rapidly being reduced to nothing. This strange woman with her diaphanous gown and overbright hair and beckoning candle had no reason to help them, and they had no reason to trust her. Yet they followed her.

They followed her down a mean passage grimy with the debris of untold centuries' carelessness with overflowing coal scuttles. The woman's translucent gown seemed to glow ethereally in the darkness, the faint, golden light of the candle she carried throwing their shadows, long and grotesque, across the soaring walls.

At the end of the passage, she stopped abruptly to raise the flickering candle and say simply, "Behind the chest."

Damion leapt to put his shoulder to a large coffer that stood against the ancient ashlar wall. Made of oak and strapped with iron, the chest moved more easily than he had expected, sliding noiselessly over a surprisingly clean stone floor to reveal a low gap in the masonry.

The sound of hurried footsteps, growing closer, left no time for hesitation. Attica scooted through the dark hole on her hands and knees, her head bent. Damion pelted in after her, pulling the chest in place behind him as best he could.

He saw a drift of white gauze. Then the coffer thumped back solidly against the wall, eclipsing the last faint glimmer of light thrown by the woman's single candle and plunging them into total darkness.

CHAPTER
TWELVE

The rain drummed hard and fast on what sounded like a shingled roof, low over their heads.

Damion crouched on his haunches, his gaze assessing the dim outlines of a surrounding jumble of barrels and crates before settling on the faint, distant line of gray light that outlined what looked like a door. He decided they were probably in a cellar or storage shed of some sort. The floor was of packed earth, the air around them damp and unused, the walls thick enough that he could hear nothing except the pounding of the rain and their own strained breathing.

Attica's low voice came to him out of the darkness. "What do we do now?"

He reached out to her, his fingers closing over the delicate bones of her wrist. Her flesh felt cold and wet and trembling beneath his grasp, and he drew her to him, shifting his weight as she settled into the V of his spread thighs. "We can't stay here," he said. "When they don't find us in the baths, they'll start searching the surrounding area."

He felt a shudder pass through her, and put both his arms around her thin frame to draw her closer to his chest and envelop her with his warmth. She let out a long sigh, her hands clutching the wet cloth of his torn tunic as she leaned into him, her face buried in his shoulder, her voice muffled as she said, "I suppose this means we take to the rooftops again?"

She said it lightly enough, but he heard the tight thread of fear in her voice, and he knew what she was thinking, knew she was remembering the brutal lashing of cold wind and driving rain, the treachery of steep, slippery slates, the dizzy, heart-stopping, body-smashing distances to pavements below.

He laid his cheek against the wet tangle of her hair, breathed in the scent of rain and woodsmoke and this woman, knew again a bitter sense of regret at the danger she now faced because of him. "Attica," he said softly, his heart aching in his chest, "I swear before God, if there's a way to get you out of this safely, I will. I never should have—"

He felt her shift within the circle of his arms, her head falling back as she pressed the tips of her fingers against his mouth, silencing him. "I did this because I wanted to. Don't make me say why."

The touch of her fingertips to his lips shocked them both into sudden, quivering awareness. In the darkness her profile was only a faint shadow, delicate and fine-boned and strong. He felt something catch deep inside him, something so sweet and rare as to be almost unbearable.

"You do realize," he said, his lips moving against her fingers, "that there could be a dozen men-at-arms waiting for us on the other side of that door? That we could walk out of here and die?"

"I realize it."

He felt the deep trembling going on inside her, felt her

chest lift against his as she sucked in a quick breath. "Damion?"

The question in her voice hung in the stillness between them. He didn't need to ask what she wanted, and in that moment, all the reasons that made it wrong didn't matter.

He drew her to him. She opened her mouth to him, her slim young body pressing wholly against his, her hands bracketing his head, drawing him closer, closer, as if she would make them as one. He thrust his tongue into her mouth, and she met him in an endless, gasping, aching kiss, a kiss driven by fear and need of a raw passion that went beyond carnality to a total immersion of body, mind, and spirit such as he had never known.

"Attica," he murmured, his mouth still moving against hers. He kissed her trembling eyelids, her hair, her throat. Then he took her hands in his and pulled her to a stand with him. "We must go."

He saw the sweet curve of her smile in the faint gray light. "I still don't regret it," she said, her eyes wide and shining. "No matter what happens, I'll never regret knowing you."

He looked down at her shadowed features and felt his chest tighten. He could have told her he'd lost his heart to her that first day, when he'd looked across a crowded common room and recognized her for what she really was. He could have told her she'd always been his heart, his fire, even before he'd met her, perhaps even before he'd been born. But some things were better not said, could never be said between them. He kissed her fingers where they entwined with his and said simply, "Nor will I."

And then, her hand in his, they turned together to face whatever awaited them on the other side of that door.

* * *

Attica watched de Jarnac's hand tighten on his dagger as he pushed open the stout plank door.

She found herself staring out at an overgrown garden filled with the roar of the rain teeming down in great slashing silver sheets. A garden filled with rain and wind and nothing more.

Weak with relief, she followed him, creeping up a short flight of broken stone steps and into the storm-racked darkness. The rain pelted them with oceans of water that cascaded down their faces in blinding streams as they splashed their way to the back of an old, half-tumbled-down dwelling barely visible through the gloom.

"How do we get up?" whispered Attica, staring up at the low roof. "There's no steps, not even a ladder."

"No. But there is an old grapevine." He tested his weight on the weathered trellis and grunted when it snapped in his hands. "The wood is rotten, so make sure you use the vine itself."

"But I haven't climbed a tree since I was—" She broke off as his hard hands closed on her waist, hoisting her up into the wet foliage. She found the thick central trunk of the vine and clung to it.

Sharp twigs snagged her clothes and scratched her skin as she scrambled up, moving stealthily from one foothold to the next, de Jarnac behind her. Craning back her head, she could see the line of roof tiles thrusting out above her. She reached for them, her fingers closing over the edge.

And then the tile she grasped crumbled within her grip, just as her left foot shot off the slippery trunk of the vine.

She let out a small gasp, her fingers clutching frantically for the vine again as she felt herself begin to fall. "Christ," said de Jarnac, his big body lunging upward in a rush that slammed her to the wall, holding her there, surrounded by his strength and warmth.

"Oh, God," she whispered shakily.

"Wait here."

She pressed her face into the wet leaves and branches, her fingers gripping the vine as he clambered past her. "Give me your hand," she heard him say, and somehow she found the courage to let go of the vine and let him pull her up.

She rolled onto the wet, mossy tiles, her breath coming in quick pants as she lay pressed facedown on the sloping roof, the rain beating down on her back. He touched his hand to her cheek in a butterfly caress, then moved on. She forced herself up onto her hands and knees and crawled after him.

He stopped just below the point of the roof. She inched up beside him to peer down through the smoke of hissing torches at the men-at-arms filling the streets below. The men stood with their backs hunched against the rain, their attention still focused on the bathhouse. No one even bothered to glance up.

Damion touched her elbow, and she turned her head to look at him. The rain ran down his cheeks, dripped off his nose, plastered his dark hair to his head. His once fine clothes, already torn from her uncle's rough handling, now hung in rags, smeared with moss and mud. It suddenly occurred to her that she must look the same, and the thought brought a smile of unholy amusement to her lips.

He saw it and, as if recognizing the source of her amusement, flashed her his rogue's grin. Then the smile faded and he mouthed, "Let's go."

They slithered down the sloping tiles to the next roof, then the next, then the next. They moved stealthily, the cold, wind-driven rain enveloping them in a protective darkness even as it turned slate and tile into slippery death traps.

Attica moved through a hazy agony of grazed palms and bruised shins, of aching muscles and gasping lungs as they leapt from house to house, working their way around the base of the castle hill toward the river. Three times they had to flatten themselves against a sloping roofline as a troop of soldiers passed by below. When they came to a narrow street, they didn't dare climb down but used overhanging balconies and jutting dormer windows to cross the yawning gap.

At the edge of the city, the houses grew small and mean and so scattered that they were finally forced to come to earth. There were gardens here, and an orchard, and the low, solid bulk of the church of Saint Suplice, overlooking the River Gate. When her feet touched the soft, spongy earth, Attica sagged forward, trembling with exhaustion, her hands braced on her knees, her head bowed as she sucked in air.

"Wait here," de Jarnac said, gently pressing her back into a protected corner where a decrepid wattle-and-daub house and some half-ruined outbuilding came together. "I'll see if I can find someplace dry and out of the wind where we can spend what's left of the night."

Her head came up with a sudden fear that if she let him out of her sight, something might happen to him and she'd never see him again. She caught his arm when he would have turned away, her hand tightening on his sleeve. "I'll come with you."

He swung back to face her. A blue streak of lightning cracked through the dark sky, followed quickly by the boom of thunder. The wind whipped at his torn tunic, exposing the edge of his white shirt and the dark, bare flesh beneath. Rain dripped from his hair.

"I'm not leaving you." His features were drawn with a strange kind of intensity that left him looking wild, almost brutal. "I'm not leaving you, Attica," he said again, and vanished into the rain-washed night.

She leaned her shoulders against the rough wall, her arms crossed as she hugged herself, trying to keep warm. Away from the crowded houses at the center of the city, the wind seemed stronger, howling through the eaves of the hovel and thrashing the surrounding trees until the shadowy canopies of their leaves whipped frantically back and forth in the storm.

She had to grit her teeth and fight down a shiver. The windblown night had always unsettled her; it was so wild, so uncontrolled, so unpredictable and irrationally, dangerously exciting. It seemed to call to something within her, something she always fought to hold down. Yet here she was, abandoned to it. Lost to it.

She hugged herself tighter, her gaze drifting past the trees to where the hulking tower of the church thrust up boldly against the roiling sky. Beyond that, the city walls loomed, an ominous, silent reminder of the fact that they weren't safe yet. They might have managed to escape the castle and evade her uncle's men-at-arms tonight, but they were still in Laval, still trapped behind the city's high walls and locked gates. When the gates swung open tomorrow with the dawn, every portal would be watched, every person passing through carefully scrutinized. There was no way out.

She squeezed her eyes closed and let her head fall back against the rough hovel wall, hating herself for the sick fear and despair that surged through her. She wished de Jarnac would come back.

The sound of careful footsteps, dangerously close, brought her to instant, quivering attention. She jerked her eyes open to discover the misshapen outline of a man's body moving stealthily through the night toward her. But then she relaxed, for there could be no mistaking de Jarnac's catlike grace. The strangeness of his silhouette came from the objects he carried: a lute, a bundle of clothing, and something else. Something long and thin and vaguely familiar.

She pushed away from the wall to meet him. "What is it? What have you found?"

The soft huff of his laugh came to her out of the darkness. "A way through the city gates."

She stared at him. *"A lute?"*

He handed it to her, along with a bundle of gaily colored clothes. "You can play, can't you?"

"Yes, but . . . I don't understand. What else is that you're carrying?"

She saw his smile flash white in the storm-darkened night. "It's a pair of stilts."

Attica stood beside the squat western tower of the church of Saint Suplice, the pilfered pile of cloaks and colorful tunics clutched to her chest as she stared down into the dark, yawning void before her. "You want me to hide in there? *With the dead?"*

De Jarnac's voice floated up to her, along with the echo of his footsteps receding down the stairs before her. "It's a crypt, Attica. Which might be similar to but is not exactly the same as a grave. Besides, which are you more afraid of? The malevolent spirits of the unquiet dead or your uncle's very alive men-at-arms?"

She threw an anxious glance across the dripping church-yard to the empty streets beyond. The rain had slowed to a thin drizzle, but the wind that buffeted her was still cold, and it carried to her the faint but unmistakable sound of tramping boots and curt, raised voices. She tightened her grip around the stolen clothing and ducked through the low archway.

"Don't forget to shut the door," said that disembodied voice from below.

She gave the heavy, iron-banded plank door a hard push that drew a shrill shriek from its hinges. "Mother of God," she whispered as the door slammed into place, plunging her into an echoing darkness so total, she felt for one hideous moment that it might smother her.

"Want to ring the bell in the tower while you're at it?" said de Jarnac dryly. "They might not have heard you."

"Hmph." She groped along the cold stone wall until her hand closed over the scratchy rope of the banister, then worked her way carefully down the stone steps.

It was not completely dark down here, she realized as her feet reached the base of the staircase. She traced a faint graying of the gloom to a series of arched light wells, set high on the rough stone walls. The crypt seemed to run the length of the central nave, although it looked old, older even than the church above it. The double rows of fat columns supporting the low vaulted ceiling were plainly carved of sandstone and fretted with age. Yet the crypt appeared surprisingly little used, the regular square sand-stone paving blocks that covered the floor being inter-rupted only here and there by a long funerary slab or the few flat-topped stone tombs she could faintly see scattered at random among the columns.

"Couldn't you find a nice, warm barn?" she asked, her voice echoing away into the darkness.

De Jarnac's low chuckle came back to her. "I'm afraid that in this part of town, lordling, the houses *are* the barns. Besides, the soldiers will never look for us in here. Not tonight, at any rate."

"Why not?" she asked, leaning against the cold, hard edge of the nearest tomb.

She heard the smile in his voice as he walked up to her. "Because they're too afraid of the malevolent spirits of the unquiet dead. Here—" He reached for the bundle of clothing she still clutched. "Give me those. You're getting them all wet."

She realized she'd virtually forgotten the clothes she held, and surrendered them unresisting. She was so cold and tired and sore. The tomb behind her beckoned like a bed, and she knew an overwhelming urge simply to lie down and close her eyes. Hitching her hips higher, she eased sideways until her upper body lay prone along the elevated slab. Her feet were still dangling over the edge, but she didn't care. It seemed more of an effort to swing them up than it was worth.

"Oh no you don't," said that irritatingly energetic voice beside her. "You've got to get out of those wet clothes first."

She groaned. "I can't."

Strong hands seized her feet and swung them up onto the slab. "In case you hadn't noticed," he said, working off first one boot, then the other, "it's dark in here, Attica. I won't be able to see a damned thing, if that's what you're worried about."

It wasn't. She was simply too cold and tired and stiff to move, let alone struggle with knotted ties and heavy wet cloth. "I will take them off," she promised vaguely. "I'll just sleep awhile, first."

She heard him swear under his breath, then felt his

hands at her belt, opening it. When he went to work at the tangled ties at her throat, she did not resist, only murmured an incoherent protest when he forced her to lift her shoulders so that he could draw first surcoat, then tunic and shirt over her head. She was dimly aware of his swift, sure touch untying the points of her hose and easing the wet cloth of her braies down over her naked hips. She thought vaguely that she should feel some embarrassment, but she didn't. Only profound gratitude and a sweet, unfamiliar sense of being cared for and cherished as he wrapped one of the purloined cloaks around her.

"Thank you," she murmured, and rolled over onto her side, hugging the warm, dry cloth to her.

Again she felt the touch of his fingers, on her cheek this time. Felt their gentleness and an odd, unexpected tremor as he smoothed her wet hair away from her face.

"Go to sleep, lordling."

She awoke to the clear, melodious notes of birdsong and a luxurious sense of warmth she gradually realized came from the large male body cradling her.

She lay on her side, her back snuggled against de Jarnac's chest, his hand resting on her hip. All her life, Attica had slept alone. A luxury, she knew, for many slept five or six to a bed. And yet it was a fine thing, she thought, to wake up next to someone. To a man.

To a man she loved.

She kept her eyes closed a little longer, drawing out the moment, reveling in the warm intimacy of his hard man's body so close to hers. Still faintly smiling, she opened her eyes, then felt her heart lurch at the sight of the pale glow lighting the vaulted gloom. Dawn was breaking.

She squeezed her eyes shut again. She didn't want morning to come. She knew a futile sense of wishing she could reach out and stop time, hold off the coming of the dangerous day and cling to this moment. This moment of peace and warmth and safety.

He hadn't moved, yet she somehow sensed from the aura of coiled alertness about him that he was awake. "Is it time?" she asked quietly.

"Not yet."

He drew back, as if he meant to put some distance between them now that she was awake. She caught his hand, stopping him. "Hold me. Please."

There followed a tense pause filled with the quiet exhalation of his breath and a strange, quivering tension. Then he said, as if to break it, "That's only false dawn you're seeing. Try to go back to sleep."

She shifted her shoulders until she lay flat on the hard stone beside him. Her body ached with scrapes and bruises and an intense physical weariness such as she'd never known. She closed her eyes. But sleep seemed to elude her.

"De Jarnac?" she said softly, glancing toward him. He lay with his head resting on his upflung arm. His eyes were open, and he was looking at her.

"Yes?"

She let her gaze rove over him. She could see him now in the growing light, see the darkly brooding eyes, the fiercely beautiful line of cheek and jaw. His neck was bare, and his shoulders, and she realized suddenly that he was as naked as she beneath the covering of cloaks. The thought brought her a strange, forbidden thrill that sent heat surging into her cheeks, so that she found she couldn't look at him anymore.

She stared at the stones of the vaulted ceiling above them.

"Do you think it will work?" she asked. What she meant was, Do you really think we'll be able simply to walk through the city gates unchallenged, dressed as Pepe the Stiltwalker and his lute-playing companion?

But she didn't need to say all of that, because he knew exactly what she was asking. "I don't know," he said. "How good are you on the lute?"

She let out a low, nervous laugh. "Good enough, I think. How are you on stilts?"

"Well, I have used them before."

She swung her head to look at him in surprise. "You have?"

"Mm-hmm. At Acre, in Outremer. When I was serving as squire to Sir Rauve. I think I was fifteen."

"Sir Rauve? Is he the knight with whom you took the cross?"

"Yes. He had the devil's own temper when roused, but I stayed with him because he was one of the best men with a horse and a sword there ever was." He shifted his weight so he could glance down at her. "I wanted to be the best myself, you see."

She imagined de Jarnac as a brash fifteen-year-old and smiled. "So what happened?"

He lay on his back beside her, his elbow bent behind his head. "I had some free time one Sunday afternoon, so a couple of the other squires and I decided to go into the city. To the market. That's where we saw him."

"A stiltwalker?"

De Jarnac nodded. "Ponce and Sigibert—that's the other squires with me—they knew I had a pretty high opinion of my athletic abilities—"

"You mean, you were insufferably cocky?"

"Something like that. At any rate, the other boys bet me that I couldn't walk the length of the leather souk on those stilts without coming to grief."

"So of course you took them up on it," she said, unable to keep the laugh out of her voice.

He frowned at her, but she saw the wicked gleam in his eyes. "Well, I couldn't hardly not, now, could I? I mean, I had a reputation of my own to keep up."

She rolled over onto her side so that she was facing him. "And you did it?"

"*Mais oui.* I paid the stiltwalker a few coins for the use of his stilts and some quick pointers. It's not as hard as you'd think, if you know what you're doing and if your balance is good."

"*If* your balance is good."

"Mine is. I put on quite a show. Before I was halfway through the souk, I'd collected a considerable crowd around me, heavy on dogs and little boys. The boys were all laughing and yelling, and the dogs were all barking—which wouldn't have been a problem, except for this camel."

"A camel," repeated Attica, not sure whether to believe him or not.

"A camel. Right at the end of the leather makers' alley. I came charging out of that leather souk on my stilts, with all those barking dogs and shrieking boys leaping around me, and that camel, she took one look at me and knew she wanted nothing to do with me. She threw back her braying head, showed me an ugly mouth full of yellow teeth, and bolted."

"She?"

"Of course it was a she. She ran right into me."

"And?" Attica prompted, trying hard not to laugh.

De Jarnac sighed. "It's a long fall from up on stilts. I

went flying. And when I came down, I was on top of a pastry stall. Smashed the stall, of course—not to mention all of those sticky pastries, *and* the pastry seller's head, too. Oh, and I broke two of my own ribs. But not the stilts."

Attica let out an ungenteel sound, rather like a snort. "And Sir Rauve?"

"I was his squire, so he was held responsible for all the damage and had to pay for it. Of course, he took every last sou of it out of my hide. But at least he waited until my ribs healed before he thrashed me."

At that, she couldn't help it: She laughed out loud. But as her laughter floated away into the dark columned recesses of the crypt, she sobered suddenly, her fingers clutching at his hand. "If this doesn't work," she said, her voice low and earnest, "if something goes wrong and they take us at the gate, you must tell my uncle what he wants to know."

He sucked in a hard breath that lifted his bare chest. "I can't, Attica."

She sat up, hugging the cloak to her breasts as she turned toward him. "But—he'll torture you! *Torture you to death* if you don't."

"I know. He took some pains to outline the entire procedure for me in great detail, presumably on the assumption that knowledge of the particulars might increase my willingness to cooperate."

She searched his features and dark, shadowed eyes, looking for some sign of the fear he must surely—*surely?*—be feeling. But she saw nothing. Nothing except a wry, bitter kind of self-mockery. Her own fear for him trembled through her. "I don't understand. Why not tell him? Whatever reward Henry has promised you for your loyalty, it won't be of any use to you if you're dead."

He shoved himself up on his elbow, the cloak falling away from his broad, naked chest as he leaned into her. "Sweet Infant Jesus. Is that why you think I'm doing this? For some damned royal reward?"

She stared at him. "Why else? Don't tell me it's out of loyalty to Henry, because I won't believe it. You're the one who is always saying you're loyal to yourself and no other. The documents in that book aren't worth you dying for."

He sat up completely, swinging his legs over the edge of the stone slab and taking one of the cloaks with him in a swirl of dark cloth as he stood up. "It's not a matter of what's in the book." He reached for his braies. "It's who has it."

"Sergei," she whispered in sudden understanding. "You're protecting Sergei. You gave him the breviary when he met us in the square, and then you sent him ahead to warn Henry of Richard's plans for the conference."

De Jarnac paused to throw her a hard glance over his shoulder. "Do you really think I'd send your uncle's men after that boy, just to save my own hide?"

She felt the blood drain out of her face, her gaze falling away from his to her own, clenched hands. "No. No, of course not."

She could feel him staring at her, even though she was no longer looking at him. Then he picked up one of the gaily colored tunics and tossed it to her, along with her own underwear. "You'd best get dressed. We need to get through that gate before Pepe and friend wake up and find their clothes and the articles of their profession gone."

Attica caught the bundle of clothes. "But we paid for them. Far more than they're worth."

De Jarnac grunted. "Making me go back to leave your gold necklace at Pepe's bedside might have eased your conscience, lordling, but somehow I doubt it'll stop him from setting up a howl when he finds he's nothing left but his underwear."

Wordlessly, she pulled on her shirt and braies, then suppressed an inward cringe when she reached for the lute player's red-and-yellow tunic. The wool cloth was old and coarse; it reeked foully of cooking fat and woodsmoke and stale sweat, and it was doubtless infested with lice and other vermin. Gritting her teeth against a wave of revulsion, she jerked the tunic over her head, pulled on the coarse hose, and stood up.

The tunic had been made for a much broader man. It hung on her awkwardly, so that she had to pad it out with her own clothes and de Jarnac's, too, wrapped about her torso and tied in place with their hose. The effect was less than realistic.

This is never going to work, she thought, fastening the lute player's worn leather belt with fingers that suddenly began to shake violently. *It's not going to work.*

"De Jarnac?" she said quietly.

"Mmm?"

She swung to face him. "I'm scared."

He came to her, his gaze intensely serious as he searched her face. "I know," he said softly, resting his hands on her shoulders. He took her mouth in a swift, sweet kiss. Then he smiled. "Look at it this way."

She cocked her head. "How's that?"

His grin widened into a low laugh. "At least there are no camels in Laval."

CHAPTER
THIRTEEN

Pepe the Stiltwalker was in fine form that morning, unfazed, it seemed, by the light drizzle that fell incessantly from out of the low, dull sky.

His long sticks flashing, his tall, athletic body unbelievably lithe and controlled, he charged down the hill from the church of Saint Sulpice, a circle of laughing, excited children darting around his stick-extended legs like ragged brown bumblebees about a giant yellow-and-red flower. Behind him came Benno the Lute Player, his white mask a frozen grin of black thread on coarse linen, his cold-numbed hands working hard to coax a tune from the battered old lute.

"Look at that," said the younger of the two guards at the River Gate. "Now, that's one way to stay out of the mud." But the other guard, wet and chilled and foul-tempered after a long night spent chasing shadows across the rooftops of Laval, simply grunted and retreated farther beneath the sheltering archway of the gate.

"Hey, Benno," called the younger guard, bobbing up and down on his toes to keep warm.

The lute player, looking dumpier than ever in his ill-fitting yellow-and-red tunic, spun about to face the guard and froze.

The guard grinned. "Play something by Isabelle d'Anjou."

The masked head nodded, the sewn black starbursts around its eyeholes seeming to explode in a parody of alarm. He swung away, his fingers flying over the lute strings, while Pepe the Stiltwalker, not content simply to walk, began to dance, his long stick legs moving in a stately parody of a courtly promenade that brought shrieks of delight from the children.

The young guard laughed. *"Merci bien,"* he called, and tossed the lute player a coin.

Benno caught the coin neatly from the air and threw back his head to yap like a happy dog. The yapping could still be heard, growing fainter in the distance, as the two performers twirled their way through the gate to be lost in the tangle of tents that filled the open fields between the city walls and the wood beyond.

"Mother of God, you—you cocky—" Attica sputtered, searching desperately for the right word.

De Jarnac's eyes sparkled at her through the slits of his mask. *"Méchant diable?"* he suggested, then ducked as she snatched off her masked hood and used it to whack him across his shoulders.

She felt almost breathless with lingering fear and a queer, trembling sense of triumph. "What in the name of God did you think you were doing?" she demanded as he pulled off his mask and backed away from her, his hands up as if to ward off more blows, a smile tugging at his lips. She wanted to reach out and trace the curve of that smile. She wanted to hit him hard enough to wipe that smile off his face. "There I was, so afraid you were going to come tumbling down on top of one of those guards that I could scarcely play the lute, and you start *dancing*?"

Laughing, he feinted sideways as she threw her hood at him. "I told you I was good, didn't I?" He tugged off Pepe's parti-color tunic and tossed it aside, his hands settling on his lean hips as he paused a moment to stare at her. "Besides, I wanted to put on a good enough show that neither of those guards would get the bright idea that they ought to make us take off our masks."

"Huh." She yanked off Benno's filthy tunic and reached for her own, her hands still shaking so badly, she found it difficult to do up the laces. They had paused to change in the shelter of a small grove of leafy green poplar trees some half a league from Laval. The rain still fell in a light drizzle, pattering softly on the overhead branches. But the mist was lifting from the low ground and the sky had lightened until the wet leaves and vivid green grass seemed to sparkle with jewels.

She looked up from tying her laces to watch him bend over and pick up his own tunic. The great rents in his shirt showed her a back strapped with muscle and marked with purpling bruises. "Don't tell me you learned to dance like that after one pass through the leather souk?" she asked.

He swung to face her as he pulled on his torn tunic. "Not exactly. You remember that stiltwalker in Acre I told you about? Well, after I came to grief with the camel, he set up a screech that I'd cracked his stilts. I hadn't, of course, but in the end, Sir Rauve bought the things, just to shut the man up."

"You mean, you used them more than just the once?"

He looked up from tying the points of his chausses and grinned. "That's right. By the time we left Acre, all of Sir Rauve's squires could do a jig on stilts."

"You could have told me."

"Huh. Then what excuse would I have had if I had fallen off?"

She scooped up his boots and threw them at him. He caught them neatly. "Where is Sergei supposed to meet you, anyway?" she asked.

Balancing against the trunk of a nearby tree, de Jarnac tugged on first one boot, then the other. "He's not. When I gave him the breviary, I told him to take his own mount and the Arab, and kill both horses if necessary, as long as he reaches La Ferté-Bernard in time to warn Henry about Richard and Philip's plans to attack after the conference."

She felt as if someone had just kicked all the wind out of her. "You mean, we have no horses?"

"One, hopefully. Sergei was supposed to leave the roan at a cottage not far from here." He finished lacing his boots and straightened. "Are you ready? We need to put as much distance as possible between us and Laval before your uncle realizes we've left the city and organizes his men to come after us."

She swung one of the purloined cloaks over her shoulders and turned toward the road. "But we'll have only one horse between us."

"That's right," he said, keeping to the grassy verge that flanked the muddy track.

She stopped. "Then you must go on without me."

"Keep walking, Attica," he said, not missing a step.

"Listen to me." She caught his arm to jerk him around.

He swung to face her, his eyes hooded, his jaw set. "All right. I'm listening."

"If Renouf catches you, he'll *kill* you."

He flashed her his devil's grin. "*If* he catches me."

He would have turned away again, but she stopped him,

her grip tightening on his sleeve. "He'll be far less likely to catch you if I'm not with you."

She watched the smile leave his face. "That's true." He took a step that brought him right up to her. "But if you think he will be gentle with you, I wouldn't count on it, Attica. His life's on the line here, and by helping me to escape, you've shown yourself to be his enemy."

"He is my kinsman. He would be angry, and he might very well beat me. But I doubt he would kill me."

"That's not what you thought last night, when you fled the castle."

She brought her chin up. "It doesn't matter. I'm willing to take the chance."

"Well, I'm not." Something flashed like quick lightning in the depths of his fiery green eyes before he hooded them with his drooping lids. "I might have to stand by and watch you sacrifice your happiness out of a sense of honor and duty to your family, but I'll be damned if I'll have you sacrificing your life for *me*."

She took a step back, her hand coming up to hold the edges of her cloak together at her neck. "Oh? And what makes you think I'm willing to let you risk your life for me?"

He gave her a slow, unexpected smile that clutched at her heart. "I'm a knight, remember—even if I do seem to have temporarily misplaced my horse, armor, and sword. Rescuing damsels in distress is what I do."

Her breath caught on a startled laugh as he reached out to snag her around the neck with the hook of his elbow and draw her to him. "Ah, lordling," he said, his breath wafting warm against her cheek. "I'm not abandoning you, so you'd best make up your mind to it."

She leaned her head against his shoulder, her gaze on his hard face outlined against the low gray clouds above

her. Beneath her cheek, she felt his heart beat, felt him
live. And she was suddenly so terribly afraid for him—
afraid for them both. "At least we know that even if we
don't make it, Sergei will have warned Henry."

He touched his sword-callused fingers to her lips, silencing her. "We'll make it."

Attica watched de Jarnac lead the saddled roan across
the muddy farmyard toward her. The rain had settled in
hard again, pounding on the broad leaves of the old oak
overhead and splashing into the broad brown puddles that
littered the yard.

Through the gloom, she saw a jagged blaze of red that
confused her until she realized it came from the lightning
bolt of de Jarnac's shield, dangling from the saddle. She
supposed it made sense for Sergei to leave the knight his
shield. But how did one explain the simple sword now
buckled to de Jarnac's hip?

"Merci bien," de Jarnac called to the peasant woman
who shuffled back to her thatched-roof cottage, her
hooded head bent against the rain, her fist clutched tight
around the coins he had given her.

The horse's hooves made little sucking noises in the
mud as de Jarnac stopped before Attica. She caught hold
of the cheekpiece of the roan's bridle. "Where did you get
the sword?"

"You'll have to ask Sergei that," he said, vaulting into
the saddle. "He left it."

"But how could he know you'd be needing it?"

De Jarnac shrugged. "I stopped asking myself questions
like that a long time ago." He slung his shield by its strap
across his back and reached down his hand to her. "Here."

She hung back, staring up at him through the driving

rain. She thought she'd probably never wanted to do anything in her life as much as she wanted to take his hand
now. "I still think you ought to ride on without me," she
said, her voice husky but calm.

"Très bien." He leaned his right forearm on the pommel
as the horse moved restlessly beneath him. He was no
longer smiling. "You've told me what you think, and I am
impressed with your nobility even if I'm not particularly
flattered by the implication that I am so lacking in honor
that I'd even consider riding off and leaving you to face
possible death. Now give me your hand and put your left
foot on mine."

She held out her hand. His big fist tightened around her
wrist, and she scrambled up into the saddle in front of him.

"You are a fool," she said, clutching the gelding with
her legs as de Jarnac's arms came around her to hold her
close against him. His body felt so warm and comforting
around hers. She tilted her head back against his shoulder,
felt his chest hard and strong against her spine.

His breath tickled her ear as he pressed his lips once
against her neck. "Don't worry," he said, his voice deep
with amusement. "When the horse gets tired, I'll make
you walk."

She laughed softly as he spurred the reluctant roan out
of the yard.

The direct road to Le Mans and La Ferté-Bernard ran in
an almost straight line to the east, down a slope to the
broad valley beyond. They turned instead toward the grass-
covered hills that would lead them to the higher, wilder country stretching northeast in a wide arc to Sille-le-Guillaume
and Beaumont-sur-Sarthe before curving back toward No-
gent and down to La Ferté-Bernard.

Raising her hand to shield her face from the rain, Attica

studied the distant hills. Even without the rain and with two good horses, the roundabout route was a journey of at least five or six days. But with only one horse between them and the need to stay away from the main roads . . .

"Why are we stopping?" she asked when he drew up beside a copse of chestnut and beech, not long after they'd dropped over the rise from the farm.

He jumped down to the wet, spongy ground and handed her the reins. "I'll walk from here."

She reached out to grab his shoulder when he would have strode ahead. "But you can't."

He swung to face her, the rain running in rivulets down his hard, tanned cheeks. "Attica, this horse will never last carrying us both."

She grabbed a handful of mane, ready to scramble down herself. "Then we'll take turns. I'll walk first."

His big hand closed over hers, stopping her. "Oh you will, will you? And can you walk eight leagues a day, day after day?"

She paused. "I don't know," she answered honestly. "I've never tried."

"Well, I have." He let her go and started walking. "So you ride."

She nudged the gelding after him. She watched him striding through the grass, his long legs swinging into an effortless rhythm. There was so much she didn't know about this man, so much she wanted to know.

"You never told me how long you've been with Henry," she said at last, when she could no longer contain herself.

"About six months," he said, not looking at her. "Why do you ask?"

Instead of answering, she said, "Why Henry?"

He glanced up at her, a smile curling his lips as his

head fell back. "Why not Henry? He's the greatest king in Christendom. And only a king can give me what I want."

"What do you want?" she asked quietly.

The smile hardened, although his voice stayed light as he answered her. "Land. Titles. What every younger son turned knight-errant wants."

She kept her gaze on his face. "Your brother left a son and heir of his own, didn't he?"

He swung his head away from her, so that she could see only the sharp line of his cheekbone. "He doesn't matter. I want nothing from the de Jarnacs," he said, his tone suddenly harsh. "I will be the man I make myself."

The silence that followed was hard and brittle and unwelcoming of disturbance. She rode beside him, her hands clenched tight about the reins. She felt restless and unsettled, wanting to know more but reluctant to press on. In the end, he was the one who spoke next.

"Why are you still unwed at the age of nineteen?" he asked suddenly, surprising her.

The rain had eased up, and she pushed back the hood of her cloak before she answered. "I told you, I was betrothed as a child to Ivor of Chauvigny. He went on Crusade, while I was sent to his mother to be trained at the courts of Aquitaine and Poitou, and to await his return. Only, he wasn't particularly anxious to come back. He was gone for six years and finally died in Antioch."

"If I remember correctly, my dear Atticus," de Jarnac said, the warmth of amusement returning to his voice, "you told me *Elise* had been betrothed to Ivor of Chauvigny."

Recalling her earlier deception, Attica felt her cheeks heat. "I spoke of myself."

"Hmph." He kept his gaze on the distant hills. "So it was

after the death of Chauvigny that your father betrothed
you to Fulk of Salers?"

"Yes."

Something in her voice brought his head around, his
eyes narrowing as he stared up at her. "He must be a hard
man, your father, to use his only daughter so."

Her throat felt suddenly thick and tight. "My family has
many estates in eastern Brittany, but they are scattered and
not easily defended, and the times are troubled. The
d'Alérions need this alliance with Salers, and my person
and the three castles I bring as my dowry are what secured
it." She paused, lifting her head to let the damp wind fan
her cheeks as she drew the cold air deep into her lungs. "I
have never doubted my father's love. But I have always
known his first loyalty is to his house, and to his lord,
Henry. He expects no less from me."

"And your mother?"

Attica shook her head. "It was my mother who first suggested the alliance." A bitter smile tugged at her lips, then
faded. "My betrothal is one of the few things Blanche Blissot and Robert d'Alérion ever did agree on. I told you they
despise each other. Now that my father's age and illness
have freed her from the constraints of childbearing, they are
rarely together. She spends most of her time at the southern
courts, while he travels between his various castles and
hunting lodges in Normandy."

She was aware of de Jarnac's hard, intense gaze upon
her. "Is your mother as loyal to Henry as old Robert
d'Alérion?" he said.

Her horse stumbled in the sodden grass, and she pulled
it up sharply. "I don't know. Why do you ask?"

But he only shrugged and squinted away into the distance.

Attica let her fingertips trail down the fiery lightning

bolt emblazoned across the front of de Jarnac's shield, hanging against the roan's side. "When did Sergei leave for La Ferté-Bernard?" she asked after a moment.

"Yesterday afternoon." He slanted a grin up at her. "Unlike me, Sergei guessed the truth about your sex from the very beginning. He simply didn't tell me."

"Why not?"

He laughed out loud but didn't answer her.

They were traveling now through thin woodland of oak and birch with an undergrowth of bracken and fern and wide stretches of soft green grass. At the base of the slope, to her right, she could see a small hamlet of crude huts huddled against the cold, the dense gray smoke of their hearth fires curling up from holes in the thatched roofs. Encircling the village, a thick, protective hedge of brambles showed a prickly face to the world.

"Tell me more about him," she said. "About Sergei, I mean."

She watched de Jarnac's brows draw together in a frown of concentration. "If you're asking me to explain him, I'm not sure I can. I'm beginning to think that sometimes, when something truly horrid happens to people—particularly if they're sensitive to begin with—it can alter their perception in some way. A way that enables them to see things the rest of us tend to miss. But explain it?" He shook his head. "I can't."

She stared down at the high, bold line of his cheekbone, at the wind-tossed wildness of his dark hair blowing against the tanned column of his throat. He was no longer looking at her but at the gorse-covered cliff above, hovering dark and silent in the gloom.

"So what happened to Sergei?" she asked, remembering the squire's haunted eyes. "What happened to him that was so horrid?"

De Jarnac's head swung around to look at her again. "His town was attacked by nomads from the east. Mongols, he told me his mother called them—and every man, woman, and child in Christendom should get down on their knees each night and pray to God that scourge never reaches our borders."

"Why?" she asked breathlessly. "What do they do?"

She saw his nostrils flare. "They're herdsmen, Attica. From the steppes. They don't believe in cities, and so they . . . destroy them." He tightened his jaw. "Destroy them with a savagery the world doesn't often endure."

Looking at him now, she could see no emotion in the hard planes of his face. But Attica found she could scarcely speak for the tightening of her chest. "And Sergei saw it all happen?"

De Jarnac met her gaze steadily. "You wouldn't want to even imagine the things he saw. He and his mother were the only survivors out of a population of several thousand."

She lifted her head, listening to the wind blowing through the grass and scattered trees, and the tired clomp of the roan's mud-splattered hooves on the sodden earth. The things he spoke of, they had happened so far away and so long ago. Yet it seemed in that moment as if the horror of those dreadful events reached across the distance of time and space to touch her with a chill of fear and the sickness of despair. She wondered how anyone could endure such a thing and survive. A child. A woman.

A woman, put up for sale at an Eastern slave auction.

She dropped her gaze to the reins twisted through her fingers. This was one of the dark, secret things she wanted to know about this man; she wanted to know about the

woman he had bought in the slave market of Aleppo. She
wanted to know about Sergei's mother.

But when she cast another look at the dark knight beside
her, she saw that his attention had been caught by a line of
horsemen that had suddenly appeared on the crest of the
low ridge on the far side of the vale. He pulled the gelding
into a copse of birches and waited, his hand over the roan's
muzzle, until the riders disappeared over the rise.

By then, the moment had been lost, and they pushed on.

Early in the afternoon they came to a stream and paused
beside its grassy banks to rest for a while. The rain had
stopped by then. Attica swung off her wet cloak and tied it
to the back of the saddle, while de Jarnac sat on a water-
darkened log near the streambed and pulled off his boots
with a quickly concealed wince.

"We've only seen those few horsemen," she said, coming to sit beside him. "And we don't know for certain they
were Renouf's men. Perhaps no one is following us."

He grunted and raised the wineskin they'd brought
from the woman at the cottage. "They're out there. Renouf
knows where we're going, so he'll have sent most of his
men on the direct roads east to Le Mans. But he's bound
to have small groups of knights out covering the country to
the north and south, too."

Attica wrapped her arms around her bent legs, hugging
them close. The rain might have stopped, but she was still
wet and cold and already beginning to feel stiff from the
hours she'd spent in the saddle. "Who is the Saintly Guido?"
she asked, resting her chin on her knees,

"What?"

"The Saintly Guido. Olivier de Harcourt mentioned him,

and when I told you of it on the road to Laval, it seemed to mean something to you."

De Jarnac rubbed his cramped toes. "He was the singing master of a Benedictine monastery in Italy. Guido of Arezzo. He came up with the system of notation for writing down music."

"Music?" She frowned, trying to remember. "But there is no seventh note."

He shrugged. "Guido's system used six notes. But if a seventh has been added . . ." He shook his head.

"But what has any of this to do with Henry and Philip?" she asked, leaning forward.

De Jarnac held her gaze for a long, intense moment, then turned away, reaching for his boots. "Philip has always had a fondness for codes. I suppose it goes with his fondness for treachery and intrigue." He paused to ease his right foot into the wet leather of his boot. "At first, he used just simple ciphers, where the normal alphabet is replaced by another. But such ciphers are fairly easy to break, so now he's had someone develop a new code." He slammed his heel down into the boot. "A musical code."

"A musical code?" She studied his strong-boned profile as he reached for his second boot. "But . . . how is that possible? Even with the addition of a seventh, there wouldn't be enough notes. Not in a useable range."

"No." He stretched to his feet and swooped to pick up the wine skin. "Which is why I think they're using a code that relies on the length of the notes, not just on their pitch."

Her head fell back. "But there is no way to indicate the length of notes, is there?"

He shrugged, turning away. "Not that I know."

She watched as he crouched down to refill the skin

with water from the stream. The rain-cooled breeze gusted around them, bringing the scent of wet grass and earth, and the scolding churr of wrens in the copse of birches farther down the slope.

She was suddenly intensely aware of their isolation here, in the wilds of Maine, and of the hours and days she would be spending alone with him. The hours, the days, and the nights. She found herself watching the way his tunic molded itself to the muscles of his broad back and the veins in his strong hands stood out against the hard sinew as he dunked the bag beneath the surface of the stream. She swung her gaze away to the distant mountains lost in the misty shroud of low-lying clouds.

"When you were in Brittany and Ireland," she asked suddenly, "did the things you heard lead you to suspect John's loyalty to King Henry?"

He glanced at her over his shoulder. "I know there have been messages sent back and forth between Paris and John's court. But no, I didn't discover any real proof that John has decided to join the rebellion."

"Yet the letters patent from the breviary would prove it, wouldn't they?"

"To my way of thinking, yes." He stood, his back to her, his attention still focused on the wineskin in his hands. "But I don't know about Henry. After all, he's not only a king; he's also a father. He'd probably argue that the letters only prove how much Philip is willing to offer. There's no real evidence that John intends to accept."

"I don't understand how a son could turn against his own father the way Henry's sons have turned on him," she said softly. "What kind of men must they be, to rebel against the very man who gave them life? To conspire with his enemies?"

She was startled by the abruptness with which de Jarnac spun about. She saw the taut set of his shoulders, saw the sudden flare of an old, old pain in the depths of his vivid green eyes. Pain, and something else, something she thought might have been guilt, although she couldn't be certain because in the next instant his lids drooped and his lips curled into a bitter line. "Perhaps you were more fortunate in your sire than some of us," he said, and swung away to catch up the roan's reins.

She stared after him, her heart aching in her chest, a rush of unshed tears stinging her nose as she wondered what long-ago wound had cut so deeply that it still festered raw and bleeding in the depths of this man's dark soul.

CHAPTER
FOURTEEN

They were plodding up a long, grassy slope, wet and slippery with rain, Attica on the roan, de Jarnac walking beside her, when she saw his head jerk up, his eyes narrowing as he scanned the horizon.

She followed his gaze, her heart slamming up against her rib cage at the sight of two mailed knights, cresting the hill above them.

"Nom de Dieu," de Jarnac swore under his breath. Yanking Sergei's sword free of its scabbard, he leapt up behind her and grabbed the roan's reins from her hands just as one of the knights shouted out a challenge.

"Hold on," he told her on a quick expulsion of breath as the roan shied badly. She clutched at the pommel, flattening herself back against his chest as he swung his great shield around in front of them both. Up ahead, the knights were still collecting for their attack when de Jarnac sank his spurs into the roan's sides and charged.

The roan's hooves pounded into the sodden grass as the horse strained forward, its great head rising and falling with each upward lunge. Looking up, she saw that one of the knights, the one on the dark bay horse, had already pulled his sword and sent his mount plunging down the slope toward them. She couldn't see his face, only his dark helmet and the jutting flare of his nose guard as he rode at them, filling her terrified gaze with a vision of slashing hooves and red-rimmed nostrils and a deadly length of naked, polished steel held high. Attica squeezed her eyes shut and prayed.

The shock of the two horses coming together reverberated through her. She heard the thud of iron against iron, heard de Jarnac's breath, harsh against her ear as he twisted and thrust. The gelding lunged sideways, stumbling. De Jarnac pulled it up, and Attica's eyes flew open. She saw de Jarnac's blade, dripping blood, and the dark bay shying away, riderless.

"Get down and grab that horse!" de Jarnac shouted, practically throwing her sideways from the saddle. She hit the ground hard, rolling away from the gelding's flashing hooves as de Jarnac, swearing loudly, jerked the roan back toward the top of the hill and spurred it on.

She picked herself up and wiped her stinging, grass-stained palms on her surcoat. She would not look at the crumpled, bloody body of the knight, dark against the lush green grass of the hillside. His bay horse stood at his side, quivering. When Attica reached for it, it shied violently, its head flung back, its eyes wide, its ears flat to the poll.

"Easy, boy," she whispered. "Nice, pretty boy."

From the hill above, she heard the clash of swords. Someone screamed. Attica didn't dare look up. "Whoa, boy," she said again, her voice shaky.

Watching her warily, the horse snorted and tossed its head. Attica leapt forward, just catching the reins below the bit as the big stallion sidled away, dragging her with it a few steps. She'd never liked the knights' big warhorses, but she grabbed a fistful of mane and hauled herself into the saddle of this one. She noticed something dark and wet

staining the wooden pommel. It was a moment before she
realized it was blood. Shuddering, she gathered the reins
and turned the big destrier toward where de Jarnac waited,
a dark, solitary silhouette against a rain-drenched sky.

The second knight's destrier had strained one of its
hocks and was limping badly, so they left it there, on that
bloody hillside. Before they left, de Jarnac stripped the
helm and hauberk from one of the knights and took them
for himself. He also took the knight's tunic to replace his
own torn and muddied one.

They made better time after that, with the two horses.
She was glad when he took the big bay stallion and gave
her back the smaller roan. She preferred the roan. And
she didn't like the stains left on the knight's saddle by his
knight's blood.

The rain started up again for a while. But the cloud
cover was already breaking up, and in late afternoon the
rain petered out and the sun shone fitfully through shifting
white clouds.

They rested the horses again, then pushed on, speaking
little, the atmosphere between them strained and tense
until de Jarnac finally broke it by saying, "It bothers you,
doesn't it? Those two knights I killed?"

She lifted her head, her gaze locking with his. "Yes."

"Why?" He searched her face, as if he could find the answer written on her features. "You didn't seem particularly
distressed by the death of the *routiers*. You killed one of
them yourself."

She struggled with the effort to put the troubled ache
inside her into words. "The *routiers* were outside the law.
They attacked me for their own gain, their own greed. But
those knights . . ." She stared down at the reins threaded

between her fingers. "Those knights were simply following the orders of their lord. They weren't vicious, murdering thieves, only brave, loyal men. And they died for it."

"Would you rather we had died?"

"No, but—"

He pressed his lips together, and she saw the hardness in him, the cynicism left by the years he'd spent fighting in Outremer and across the battlefields of Europe. "That's what most battles come down to, Attica. Brave knights killing other brave knights because they happen to be loyal to different lords. Or to different versions of the same God."

She let her breath out in a long sigh. She felt a tearing away of something inside her, another part of the woman she had been. "I know you are right. Only I've never been quite so close to the killing before."

He gave her an unexpectedly gentle, understanding smile and gathered his reins. "The road is good here, and the land flat. Let's stretch their legs, shall we?"

With an answering smile, she touched her heels to the roan's sides and let the wind blow away her troubled thoughts.

They stopped frequently to water and rest the horses, and allow them to graze. But they always pushed on.

As twilight descended on the high, thinly wooded slopes, the wind kicked up again, damp and cold with the threat of more rain. Attica clutched at her saddle's wooden pommel with numb fingers, her body stiff and aching and so chilled, she had to clench her teeth to keep them from chattering. She was so intent on simply enduring that she was only dimly aware of it when the horses finally stopped.

She felt de Jarnac's arms around her, easing her from

the saddle and cradling her close to his chest as he carried her through the darkness. "Where are we?" she asked, too exhausted even to lift her head.

"It looks like an abandoned shepherd's hut." He ducked through a low doorway. "Part of the roof has fallen in, but there's enough left to keep us dry, should it come on to rain again. And we can light a fire."

He laid her gently on the leaf-littered earth floor beside a sunken, clay-lined hearth. She tried to push herself up on her elbows, but it was so difficult even to keep her eyes open.

"Go to sleep, Attica," he said softly, his hand gentle on her hair.

She awoke to find herself staring at a warm, crackling fire.

She lay still for a moment, letting her gaze drift around the small, crude hut. It had been built of thick, curving branches, the cruck frame filled in with woven reeds plastered with mud and straw. But much of the daub had fallen away with age and lack of repair, and she could see black sky sprinkled with a hazy pattern of cloud wisps and stars where some of the roof thatching had collapsed into the far corner.

A whisper of movement brought her attention back to the fire.

He sat beside the hearth, his forearms resting on his bent knees, his head turned as he stared thoughtfully at the dancing flames. Firelight glinted a hellish orange across his sharp features. He looked so big and strong and fiercely beautiful, she thought she could look at him forever. The wind moaned through the tall grass outside, bringing her again that awareness of their isolation, that warm breathlessness that tingled her skin and set off a peculiar hum low in her belly.

She must have made some slight sound, for he turned his head to find her watching him, and smiled. "So you're awake, are you?"

She pushed herself up into a sitting position. "You should not have let me sleep. I would have helped you with the horses."

He didn't say anything, only looked at her, his eyes dark and glowing in a way that told her he, too, felt the intimacy of their situation, the vastness of the dark velvet night wrapping itself around this small, fire-lit hut.

He turned to stretch toward one of the saddlebags. "Are you hungry?"

"No. I know I should be, but I am not."

"Eat anyway." He swung back to hand her some of the rye bread and cheese they'd found in the dead knights' bags. "You'll feel better."

"I feel better already, since I slept." But she took the bread and made herself tear off a chunk. It tasted dry, and she had to work hard to swallow it. "Do you think there are more of them out there?" she asked, reaching for a wineskin.

"There'll be more." He leaned forward to grasp another log and toss it onto the flames. The wet wood hissed, and he stared at it for a moment, watching it send up a plume of wet smoke. The wind rustled the thatch overhead, bringing the scent of wet leaves and grass.

"Tell me about Sergei's mother," she said suddenly.

He swung his head to look at her. The fire glazed the hard planes of his face, but his eyes were dark, their secrets hidden from her. He stared at her for so long, she didn't think he was going to answer her. Then he turned back to the fire. "What do you want to know?"

She studied his profile, the lean line of his cheek, the deep creases left beside his eyes by years of squinting into the desert sun. "What was her name?"

"Maria. Her name was Maria."

She bent her knees, drawing them up close to her chest with one arm, while she continued to nibble on the bread and cheese he'd given her. "Did she look like Sergei?"

He held himself very still. "In a way. She was small like Sergei. Slight. And fair, with that pale, snow-white skin that never shows the touch of the sun."

"She sounds beautiful."

His lips lifted in a sad, sweet smile she'd never seen before. "She was."

Something caught at her heart, something as sad and sweet as his smile. "You loved her," she said softly.

He brought his gaze back to her face, his eyes hooded. "No. I was fond of her. But I have never loved any woman."

Attica reached for the wineskin, surprised to see her hand trembling. "So you bought her simply to share your bed?"

His grin flashed wide. "I bought her to cook my meals and keep my clothes clean."

"She was your slave. A beautiful slave. You mean you didn't—" She broke off, unable to put her thoughts into words.

He ducked his head, the smile lingering on his lips. "I'm not saying I didn't want her, Attica. But I didn't force myself on her, if that's what you're asking. She came to me of her own free will, and not until I had owned her for six months."

He reached for another piece of wood, but instead of tossing it on the fire, he held it in his hands, his fingers moving restlessly over the rough bark. "We were in Syria at the time. There'd been a skirmish that day, with some of Saladin's men." She watched his chest lift as he drew in a deep breath, then let it out, slowly. "I had a friend. Ponce. We'd been together ever since I left Anjou."

"He was one of the squires who dared you to try the stilts," she said, remembering.

"That's right." A brief, sad smile flashed across his face, then faded. "Ponce was disemboweled in the fighting." His throat worked as he swallowed. "A man can take hours to die, Attica, with his guts hanging out. His blood turns the earth beneath him to mud, and still he lives. And no matter how brave he is, after a while he just can't take the pain without screaming. Not near the end."

She held her breath, listening to the crackle of the fire and the moan of the wind. De Jarnac's voice rolled on, as flat and emotionless as his face. "I held him in my arms until he died. And then . . . I don't remember exactly what I did. I only know that after a time Maria came to me." He tossed the stick on the fire.

The last of the bread and cheese seemed to stick in Attica's throat. She swallowed hard. "She'd grown to love you."

He shook his head. "No. She was fond enough of me to want to help ease my pain. And she needed something that I could give her. But she never let herself love me. She didn't even speak to me. Ever."

Attica's hand jerked in surprise, so that she almost spilled the wine. "She couldn't speak?"

"She could speak. I'd hear her talking to Sergei while she worked or murmuring to him when she put him to bed. At first, she knew only her own language, of course. But even after she learned French and Arabic, she never spoke to anyone but Sergei. I think she'd lived through so much horror and loss that she simply withdrew to someplace deep inside of her. The only person she let close to her was Sergei. She had such a fierce love for him, it was almost frightening. She lived for him."

Attica replaced the stopper in the wineskin and set it carefully aside. "She wouldn't speak to you, yet she touched you? She took you into her body?"

He shrugged. "Like I said, I could give her something she needed . . . human warmth and a kind of comfort, I suppose. I think she let me come as close to her as she dared. But somehow, by not speaking to me, she kept me out of her heart."

An ache built in Attica's chest. She tried to push it out with a sigh, but it didn't work. "And how did you keep her out of your heart, Damion?"

He stared into the fire, the flickering light playing over the harsh planes of his cheeks, the tight line of his jaw.

"She must have come close to you, Damion. You mourned her when she died. And you have kept her son with you to this day."

He tilted his head to look at her over the tensed muscle of his arm, propped on his knee. "She came close. I could let her, you see."

The pain in Attica's chest tightened until she thought it might kill her. "Because she put up all the barriers?" she whispered.

His eyes blazed at her, dark and fierce. "No. Because she was not the comte d'Alérion's daughter, betrothed to the viscomte de Salers."

For one intense moment she stared at him. He sat very still, his arms on his bent knees, his chest lifting with his soft breathing. Beside him, the fire crackled and spat as a fresh breeze gusted through the empty doorway.

She pushed up from the floor and went to stand at the entrance to the hut. The high, sparsely wooded hills spilled out before her in wildly shifting patterns of moonlight and wind-tossed shadows. She felt as if the dark, stormy night called to her, to something deep inside her, lured her with a beckoning sense of abandonment as dangerous and compelling as the man behind her. The woman she had been even two days ago would have resisted. But she was different now.

She braced one hand against the rough wooden door frame, her gaze still fixed on the endless hills. "If the viscomte and viscomtesse de Salers have taken up arms against Henry," she said, "my father may not allow this betrothal to stand. He is Henry's man and always will be."

She heard a whisper of movement as he came to stand behind her, his hands on her shoulders. His thumbs brushed the bare, sensitive flesh at the base of her neck. She trembled.

"And if," he said, his breath warm against her ear, "*if*, mind you, your betrothal comes to naught, think you that old Robert d'Alérion would then wed you to me?"

"He might," she said in a small voice.

His hands tightened on her shoulders, swinging her around until she looked up into his fierce, closed face. "I am a younger son, Attica. A younger son, with my own way still to make in this world."

"No." She shook her head, her hands splayed against his broad chest. She could feel the painful thump of his heart reverberating against her palms. "You're more than that. So much more than that."

A ghost of a smile touched his beautiful lips. "Oh, I'm not completely penniless. I've an insignificant manor left me by Hugh de Jarnac, and a small amount of wealth accumulated from tournaments and ransoms and my share of the booty from more sacked towns than I care to remember. But mighty noblemen such as your father do not wed their daughters to men such as me."

The truth of his words cut at her, ripped at her heart, until she felt as if she were bleeding inside, dying inside. *"Oh, God."* The words tore out of her throat. "I never minded before. But I do now. I do now." Her hands clutched at his shoulders, clenched in the cloth of his tunic until they cramped.

"Ah, Attica." He cupped the back of her head, pulling her up against his chest, holding her so fiercely, it almost hurt. She felt him press his cheek to the hair at the top of her head. Heard the ache in his voice as he said her name, over and over. Heard the ache turn raw.

And darken with desire.

CHAPTER
FIFTEEN

It had been a mistake to touch her, a mistake to take her in his arms, to feel the gently yielding warmth of her woman's body so close to his.

Damion felt the gusting of the wind through the open doorway beside them. The wind, bringing with it the freshness of rain-washed night air and the darkly sparkling promise of star-spangled infinity. On a night such as this, he thought, a man could forget the harsh realities of his world, forget his own code, his own promises to himself. On a night such as this, a man could forget himself.

With a groan, he rubbed his open mouth against her soft hair, his eyes sliding closed as he breathed in the scent of her, the scent of the road and night rain and this woman's own sweetness. He let his hands slip slowly, dangerously, down her slim, strong back once before bringing them up again to grip her shoulders.

He meant to set her away from him. He would have set her away from him. Only then her head fell back, her lips parting as she stared up at him, and he was caught by the dark turbulence of her eyes.

His gaze locked fast with hers. He dipped his head and brushed her lips with his gently. And at the touch of her sweet, soft lips, he was lost. Lost in the taste of her, the heat of her, the heat of their desire, their hunger.

He moved his mouth over hers, deepening the kiss as she opened her mouth to him, her tongue tangling with his, her arms curling up around his neck to clutch him to her tighter, tighter. He slipped his hands down her sides to find her hips and pull her up against the hard curve of his pelvis as he braced his legs wide. She pressed herself against him. Pressed, pressed. But it wasn't enough. Wasn't enough.

With a harsh murmur, he tore at the laces of her tunic and shirt, impatient to fill his hands with the naked swell of her breasts. When he touched her there, she made such a breathy, erotic noise deep in her throat as she clutched him to her that he felt his blood roaring hot through his veins, felt his unwanted, dangerous love for this woman flare up bright and fierce in his heart. Felt what was left of his self-control slipping, slipping.

He wanted to bear her down into the softly rustling leaves that littered the floor of the hut. He wanted to rip away this rough barrier of cloth between them and press the length of his naked body against her softly pale woman's flesh. He wanted to touch her in all the secret, burning places he knew she yearned to be touched. Touch her with his hands, with his lips, with his tongue. Feel her long, slim legs wrap around his waist, holding him to her as he buried himself inside her. He wanted to make her his, *his*, forever.

His.

Except that, for them, there could be no forever. And if he made her his now, the future would hold nothing for either of them except unbearable heartache. Or death.

He knew it, and yet for one quivering, savage moment,

he hovered on the edge, almost beyond stopping, his lips drifting down the white arch of her throat as she flung back her head. He heard the rush of her breath, hot and fast against his ear. Felt the rapid pounding of her heart beneath his splayed fingers as he cupped her bare, trembling breast. Cupped it, then let his hand slide away.

He kissed her hair, her ear—anything but her mouth. He didn't dare kiss her mouth. "Attica. *Mon amante,*" he murmured, his face buried in the soft curve of her neck. *Beloved.* His body shook with want and denial as he held her, his hands clenching in her hair. "We can't do this. We can't."

She curled her hands around his wrists, her head turning until she was looking at him with wide, solemn eyes. "I love you," she said, her lips trembling and tempting, oh so tempting. "Duty and honor may dictate my future. But I would have this moment."

Sweet Jesus, he thought, staring into the luminous depths of her beautiful brown eyes. *I'm only a man. Only a man . . .* He felt his breath shudder in his chest, hurting him.

He cradled one of her hands in his, pressed a kiss to her palm. "I love you, Attica." He curled his fingers around hers until her hand became a fist, hers inside of his. He felt her hand tremble within his grip, but he couldn't look at her, couldn't look at her beautiful, beloved face. "I love your spirit, your strength, your fierce and noble sense of honor. I love you in every way known to man." He paused, working hard to get the words out. "Which means I love you too much to destroy your life by making love to your body now."

"My life is already destroyed," she whispered harshly.

"No." He squeezed her hand, then let her go. "No," he said again, backing away from her, away from the pain and

longing he could see now in her face. "Not completely.
But if we do this, it will be."

The night wind sighed around them, ruffled the boyishly short curls that framed her face. "Then I would destroy it."

"But don't you see?" He took another step back, then
another. He was outside now, outside with the wind and
the stars and all the lonely pain of his forever. "Don't you
see?" he said again. "I love you too much to let you."

He couldn't quite bring himself to turn around and leave
her. He could only back away from her, one step at a time,
until she was lost in the shadows of the night.

He spent the hours left until dawn in the lean-to where
he'd stabled the horses. He sat with his spine pressed against
one of the roughly peeled logs that framed the doorway,
his head tilted back, his eyes half closed as he watched the
gradual lightening of the sky in the east.

His desire for her burned like a fever in his blood, tormented him like a hot coal in the depths of his belly that
left him restless, unable to sleep. Once, in that hour when
birdsong fills the air and dawn sweetens the world, the
need to go to her and hold her—just hold her—was so
strong, he had to grip the log behind his head, his fingers
digging in the soft wood to keep himself from rising and
crossing the short distance that separated them. Because
he knew that if he touched her now, he would never be able
to stop with a simple touch.

He knew, as well, that he could not trust himself to be
alone with her like that at night again, and that he would
need to stay as far away from her during the day as their
circumstances allowed. The knowledge that she would give
herself freely to him only increased the pressure on him to

keep it from happening. Not simply because, if his suspicions about her brother were correct, she might never forgive Damion for what he would have to do. But also because he knew, as she did not, the tragedy that could flow from an illicit love such as theirs.

They spent the next night in a forester's cottage, and the night after that in the guest house of an isolated monastery.

It didn't take Attica long to notice how careful Damion was not to touch her when they were alone during the day. Or the way that, when night began to fall, he always made certain there were other people around them.

With each day they moved into higher, wilder country, the fields of ripening hay and peas becoming more and more interspersed with tracts of dense virgin forest and more open bocage. Once, they sheltered beneath a ridge and watched two horsemen pick their way along the swift-flowing stream below. But they were too far away for Attica to be able to tell if they were her uncle's men or not.

The morning of the fourth day found them climbing a long, gentle slope covered with bracken and fern scattered with tall pink foxgloves and white marguerites. The sun shone golden and warm out of a soft blue sky, and they paused beside a gurgling brook to rest the horses and eat some of the honey cakes they'd brought from the last village.

"A day like this," Attica said, smiling as she lifted her face to the gentle June sun, "when the air is so sweet with the scent of grass, and the larks are singing in the tops of the trees . . ." She closed her eyes and breathed deeply, as if she could draw the magic of this moment into her very soul. "A day like this makes you realize what a joy it is simply to be alive. It's as if the whole world—as if God himself—were smiling. Do you feel it?"

She opened her eyes and turned her head to find him watching her. He lay sprawled on his side, facing her, one elbow bent beneath him, the other wrist resting slackly on his bent knee. And in his eyes flickered a raw, painful hunger he wasn't quite quick enough to hide.

She felt the smile slowly fade from her lips. The sun still poured over her and the larks still sang, but she was aware only of this fiercely beautiful man and of how desperately she wanted him. How much she wanted him in her life. Not just for this one memorable moment but for all the days and years that stretched out before her.

The warm mountain breeze eddied around them, ruffling the collar of his shirt where it shone white against the dark flesh of his neck. She ached with the desire to reach out, to touch him, to go to him now on this sun-kissed hillside and forget at least for a few, tender, stolen hours the unshakable call of duty and the bridegroom who awaited her at the end of her journey.

They stared at each other, and the wind gusted up stronger, carrying to them the distant scent of stale smoke mixed with the faint, unmistakable stench of death.

"What is it?" Attica asked as de Jarnac's head snapped around, his hand creeping almost unconsciously to his sword hilt.

"Mount up," he said curtly, uncoiling from the grass in one lithe, controlled motion. "Quickly."

They spurred their horses to the top of the hill, where a stand of mixed larch and ash grew thick enough to offer shelter. From there they could look down on what must once have been a prosperous village, nestled beside a rocky stream at one end of a broad valley patchworked with cultivated fields, lush pasturage, and orchards. Only now the fields were trampled and burned, the trees bare of fruit, the houses reduced to blackened rubble. The smell of burned thatch and charred flesh hung heavy in the air.

"Mother of God," whispered Attica, her horrified gaze sliding over the smoke-hazed ruin of the valley. "Who has done this? *Routiers?*"

"No. This is the work of an army, Attica. An army on the march."

She swung her head to look at him. His eyes had narrowed to thin slits, the powerful bones of his face standing out stark against his flesh as he stared down at the destruction before them. "The conference must have already collapsed," he said, the big bay stallion shifting restlessly beneath him. "This is the result."

"Philip did this? Philip and Richard?"

He nodded, gathering his reins.

She lifted her gaze to the horizon, but all she could see was desolation. The acrid stench of burnt wood stung her nostrils, making them quiver. "But . . . where is Henry?"

"I don't know." He spurred his horse forward. "Let's go down and see what we can find out."

They rode through an unearthly silence, filled only with the creak of their saddle leather, the thud of the horses' hooves in the packed dirt of the road, and the buffeting of the warm wind. Even the birds seemed to have fallen silent.

They splashed across the ford at a canter. Beside the stream lay the smoking ruins of a mill, the fresh green banks of the gently lapping mill pond splattered with the white of spilt flour and the red of the miller's blood. Attica turned her head away, her hand coming up to cover her mouth.

"My God," she whispered, staring down at the wind-ruffled feathers of a headless duck. "Why? Why do this?"

"To demoralize. To spread terror. To apply pressure where the enemy is weakest."

He urged his horse forward, carefully skirting a broken cart that lay on its side, its upthrust wheel creaking mournfully as it spun slowly in the wind.

They passed the remnants of the manor house, its wooden upper stories a mere pile of blackened timbers collapsed upon the stone undercroft. Bloated carcasses of pigs littered the yard and ruined outbuildings. The air hummed with the buzzing of flies.

"Is there no one left alive?" Attica asked, letting the roan pick its own way through the rubble-strewn track as she scanned the burned-out husks of what had once been houses and one small wooden church.

"The lord of the manor and his family were probably led off as captives to be ransomed. If they were lucky." He checked his horse, his head falling back as he watched a wood pigeon suddenly take flight. "Everyone else who isn't dead is likely hiding."

A gray striped cat with four white socks rubbed against the foundation stones of the village fountain, its mew plaintive. Attica reined the roan in beside it, but the cat took off, its paws scrambling over a broken crate.

"Don't look in the well," said de Jarnac sharply as she was about to do just that.

She twisted in the saddle to stare at him. He sat at ease in his saddle, one hand resting on his hip, a dark, hard-faced knight on a dark war horse. The wind gusted around her, enveloping her in a swirl of white ash. She heard the jingle of the bit as the roan shook its head, impatient with the flies. And she realized her eyes were so dry that they hurt as if she had cried for hours, although she hadn't shed a tear.

Something of her thoughts must have shown on her face, because he said, "You're right; I know what to expect because I've done this. What did you think war is, Attica? Knights in burnished armor charging each other beneath billowing pennants? It is, sometimes. But more often than not, this"—he swept his arm in a wide arc—"*this* is the face of war."

"Please," she said hoarsely. "Can't we—"

She broke off as a pitiful wail pierced the wind-blown silence. Her head whipped around, her gaze probing the piles of trampled and rotting cabbages, the smashed earthenware, the broken benches and bits of fencing that littered the nearest toft. "What was that? It sounded like a baby."

"A lamb, probably." He slowly turned the big destrier, his hand on the hilt of his sword, his careful gaze sweeping over the devastated village.

"No. It was a child. I'm certain of it."

And then she saw him: a small boy of perhaps two, naked except for a shirt. He came crawling out from beneath the shattered remnants of a hovel and staggered toward them, his mouth open in an endless, undulating cry, his fisted hands rubbing his eyes, his tears leaving tracks down his filthy cheeks.

At the edge of the toft, he paused, his chest rising on a shuddered breath. Then, before Attica could move toward him, the boy surged forward in a sudden rush. Startled, the big bay warhorse reared up, its great hooves slashing the air. The boy, running heedlessly forward, disappeared beneath the plunging stallion.

Attica bit back a scream as de Jarnac, swearing, twisted sideways and swooped down, bending dangerously, unbelievably low from the saddle. He came up with the squalling child held by the scruff of his collar. She let out her breath in a relieved rush. *"Grace à Dieu."*

"Huh." De Jarnac's startlingly green eyes gleamed at her over the dark, matted head of the baby. "Instead of sitting there thanking God, perhaps you could try telling me what we're going to do with a baby? *A baby,* for the love of Mary."

The child had latched on to the front of de Jarnac's hauberk with two frantic fists and buried its face into the knight's broad shoulder. Small shudders still shook the boy's thin frame, but he seemed reassured by the gentle strength of the brawny arm that held him so securely; the wailing ceased abruptly.

Attica smiled softly. "I think he likes you."

A slow flush spread over the knight's high cheekbones. "Well, he'd best learn to like you instead. I can't even get at my sword, let alone swing it, with him in the way."

Still smiling, she urged the roan closer and stretched out her arms toward the baby. "Here. Hand him to me." The boy began to whimper again as de Jarnac loosed the little fists' hold on his mail and she lifted the child gently onto her saddle bow. *"Tout va bien, mon petit,"* she whispered, trying to cradle the now howling, thrashing child to her. "It's all right."

"You're not holding him right," said de Jarnac. "Put one arm under his rump and use the other hand against his back to keep him steady."

She adjusted her grip as instructed. With a gurgled

hiccup, the child burrowed his face into her chest and quieted.

She laughed. "It worked." Her head fell back, her gaze meeting his over the child's head. She saw a muscle bunch in his cheek. And then it was as if a sad kind of tenderness relaxed the harsh lines of his face, and he smiled.

Attica felt her heartbeat slow as the moment stretched out, became poignant and aching with things unsaid and impossible. Her skin grew warm, her breath easing out of her parted lips in a painful sigh. And she wanted, wanted—

"No!"

The sound of a frantic, high-pitched scream brought both their heads around.

A woman with unkempt dark hair and a contorted, grief-ravaged face came running down the road, her skirts kilted up, her arms waving frantically. "No! Don't take him!" She stumbled over a broken plow and went sprawling, but picked herself up and kept running. "He's mine; he's my Folcard. Oh, please don't take him."

She stumbled to a halt some few feet from them, her chest heaving with the effort to suck in wind, her hands twisting in the skirt of her filthy, torn dress. Scratches covered her face and bare forearms; bits of dried leaves and twigs matted her hair. Her dark eyes were wide and wild in a pale face. "Please," she said again, sinking to her knees, her cupped hands coming up beseechingly. "He's my Folcard. I left him here, in the house." She nodded toward the pile of smoldering rubble beside them. "I left him and my Cecily with their papa while I went into the fields. But then the soldiers came, and I hid in the woods, and . . ." A shudder shook her shoulders, and she brought up her hands to cover her face. *"Oh, God."*

"Be at peace, woman," said de Jarnac. "We do not mean to steal your child. Get up."

Her face wary and uncertain, the woman staggered to her feet as Attica urged the roan forward and held out the little boy. Folcard took one look at his mother and began to scream hysterically, his little legs pumping in the air, his arms waving so frantically, Attica almost dropped him.

The woman snatched the child to her as if she thought Attica might change her mind and take him back. "Folcard," she said on a harsh expulsion of breath. "Folcard." Sinking to her knees in the mud of the road, she buried her face in the child's neck and wept.

De Jarnac's big destrier fidgeted as he glanced around uncomfortably. "Madame?" he said after a moment. "What can you tell us of the army that did this?"

For a moment, Attica didn't think the woman was capable of answering. She simply rocked back and forth, her baby clutched to her chest, her eyes squeezed shut as she said his name over and over.

"My good woman," said de Jarnac.

The woman's head fell back, her eyes opening, as if she had only just become aware that they were still there. "The army?" Her face contorted horribly. "God save us. They say that the conference at La Ferté-Bernard has collapsed; that's why Philip's army is on the march. He has taken La Ferté-Bernard and Montford—and Beaumont and Ballon as well. But we never expected them to come here. Not here."

Unable to look at the woman's grief-stricken face, Attica let her gaze wander—then regretted it when her attention was caught by a pair of large, wooden-soled shoes thrusting out from beneath the burned timbers of the house beside them. When she looked closer, she could make out stout legs, encased in torn hose and lying deathly still.

Here, surely, was the woman's husband. And the little hand just visible beside his must belong to Cecily. Swallowing hard, Attica jerked her gaze away.

"And King Henry?" de Jarnac was asking. His voice sounded rough and impersonal, but the woman responded to it.

"Henry?" The woman's face hardened with something that might have been anger. "They say he has fled to Le Mans."

De Jarnac lifted his head, his gaze sweeping the hills on the far side of the valley as he gathered his reins.

"What are we going to do?" asked Attica, watching him. "We can't simply ride off and leave her here alone with the child."

His head swiveled toward her, his eyes narrowing. "What do you suggest?" he asked dryly. "That we take her with us?" But he dropped his gaze to the woman in the road. "Are there others of the village left alive?"

Struggling to swallow a sob, the woman nodded. "Those who were in the fields. Most of us fled to the woods. It was only those still in the village . . ." She turned to stare at what was left of her home, and Attica saw the woman's face crumple, become old.

How will she bear it? Attica thought. *How does anyone bear such anguish and loss and horror? How?*

"Attica. Attica?"

She realized he'd said her name twice. She looked up into his face to find him watching her with narrowed, empty eyes. The wind blew his dark hair against the hard masculine planes of his face, and he was like a stranger to her. A cold, deadly stranger.

I've done this, he'd said, his big hand with its blood-stained glove sweeping in an arc over the burned hovels, the slaughtered livestock, the slaughtered children. *I've done this.* She sucked in a breath of tainted air that seemed to shudder her frame. *Oh, God* . . .

"We must go," he said, a strange, bitter glitter kindling in the depths of his eyes, as if he knew what she was thinking. But then, perhaps he did. He said her thoughts always showed on her face.

Her throat felt too tight to speak. Gathering her reins, she nodded, her knees urging the roan forward.

They rode in silence between the rows of smoldering cottages, past the sprawled, bloody, violated bodies of the men, women, and children who had once lived in them. Past the guard dogs with their ripped bellies, and the bags of spilled grain, soaked with blood, and the broken sickles and hoes.

Eventually the scenes of violence faded into the distance. Yet long after they'd left the ruined valley and begun to climb through the sweet green grass of the hills, she imagined she could still smell the place. The stench of burned thatch and rotting flesh seemed to cling to her, choking her. She swallowed hard, squeezing her eyes shut against the rising nausea, then opened them again abruptly when her mind's eye began to replay for her that hideous panorama of spilled blood and mindless destruction and grotesquely mutilated bodies.

And one little girl's small, lifeless hand.

With a strangled cry, she reined in, practically throwing herself from the saddle. She took two stumbling steps away, then hunched over and vomited into the daisy-strewn grass of the hillside.

Her body quivered painfully with each heave. Her throat burned, and she had to brace her hands against her spread knees to steady herself. She felt hot and shivery at the same time, and it was as if the warm blue sky and wind-feathered trees had disappeared and her world had narrowed down to the memories of that village and her own physical reaction to them.

She heard footsteps behind her, felt strong arms come around her waist from behind, warm and comforting. The low murmur of his voice was gentle and soothing in her ear. When the sickness she couldn't seem to control hit her again, she wrapped her hands around his brawny forearms and let him support her while the shudders wracked her frame.

And then, when it was all over, she turned in his arms and wept.

They rode in a silence filled only with the squeak of saddle leather and the muffled clomp of their horses' hooves hitting the soft grass. In the end, it came to be too much for her, and she swung her head to look at him. "What do we do now?" she asked.

He squinted up at the sun, and she realized he'd changed their bearing. Whereas before they'd been headed east, now they were tracking south. "We ride to Le Mans. And hope there's not an army in our way." He cast her a quick, appraising glance. "Are you all right?"

She felt her cheeks heat with a flush. "I'm all right," she said, her voice raspy. "It won't happen again."

"No. That's the kind of reaction you have only once."

She looked at him. He sat his horse with the graceful ease of a born horseman, one gloved hand resting on his lean hip, his back straight and tall. She could not begin to imagine this hard, ruthless man vomiting with shock at the sight of a dead child.

"Did you have it? That kind of reaction, I mean."

He met her gaze squarely, his lips curling up into that mocking smile of his. But in his face she thought she could trace the shadow of an old vulnerability, a phantom that was there and then gone. "Everyone does," he said simply, and spurred the destrier on ahead.

Toward sunset, they dropped down from a hillside thickly wooded with intermingled beech and birch, and came into a stretch of open meadow near a stream.

A party of some fifteen or twenty men and women wearing the somber gray robes and broad hats of pilgrims were camped on the high ground just beyond the ford. They looked up, their faces wary, as Damion spurred his horse across the stream, with Attica behind him. Smoke drifted up from several scattered cooking fires, wafted by a breeze carrying the rich aromas of burning wood and roasting meat and simmering potage.

One man moved away from the others, a man wearing the rusty black habit of a priest. Faint strands of gray streaked the dark brown of his hair, but his frame was big boned and tough, his face sun darkened, his eyes hard. He looked more like a middle-aged knight than a priest, and as he moved, Damion noticed that the man's right sleeve swung empty at his side.

"Good evening, Father," said Damion, reining in the bay charger. "We come in peace and mean you no harm."

The priest regarded him through still, enigmatic gray eyes. "You'll be wanting to camp with us for the night." He swept his hand in a welcoming gesture toward the fires. "Come and join us in our evening meal. A strong sword arm would be most welcome, should any straggling soldiers chance to pass our way."

Damion reached down to pat his horse's sweaty neck. "You have encountered Philip's army?"

"*Dieu merci,* no; but we have seen their work." The priest shook back the left sleeve of his habit to extend a hand rough with old calluses left by years of swordplay. "I am Father Sebastian. I was leading this group of good pilgrims from Caen to the shrine of Saint Martin in Tours." A faint smile touched his lips. "However, it seems our timing was infelicitous. They say that Henry has retreated to Le Mans, and Philip marches on Tours at this very moment."

"So I had heard." Resting one elbow on his high pommel, Damion bent to clasp the man's left hand in his own. "Damion de Jarnac." He nodded toward Attica, who was doing her best to hover inconspicuously in the background. "And this is Atticus d'Alérion, my squire."

"De Jarnac?" The older man's powerful grip tightened, and he did not immediately release Damion's hand. "Ah, I thought so. You have much the look of your brother."

Damion flung back his head, his jaw clenching with the effort to control himself beneath the priest's watchful eye. "You knew Simon?"

"Before I took the cloth, I was a man of the sword. Your brother and I were squires together."

Damion eased his hand from the man's grasp and straightened to gather the bay's reins. "I will understand," he said, his gaze focused fiercely on the man's face, "if you preferred that we ride on."

Father Sebastian laid a restraining hand on the bay's bridle. "My son, whatever I might have been in the past, I am now a man of God. And God's mercy is as infinite as his capacity to forgive. Please. Get down and join us. Later, perhaps, we shall speak of your brother. I have stories to tell that you might not have heard."

CHAPTER
SIXTEEN

Darkness fell quickly on the meadow.

The setting sun streaked the sky with long, rippling trails of gold and pink and vivid orange that faded almost abruptly to aquamarine, then to a deep, rich purple sprinkled with stars. The air filled with the *creak-creak* of crickets and the lower, more somber croaking of a frog in the stream, while from somewhere in the wood-covered hills behind them came the trill of a solitary nightingale so achingly beautiful that Attica felt her heart catch.

She sat in the warm glow of one of the pilgrims' fires, a horn of ale clutched almost forgotten in her hand as she sleepily admired the way the ruddy light of the dancing flames glinted on the auburn highlights in de Jarnac's dark hair and glazed the powerful bones of his face. One of the pilgrims—a slim, fair-haired boy of about sixteen with a harp slung over his shoulder—had cornered the knight shortly after supper and proceeded to talk his ear off about *vers* and plainchant and cansos. Quietly amused, Attica simply leaned back against her saddle and listened.

"If there is a way to indicate the length of notes," said the harpist, his fair eyebrows drawn together in earnest concentration, "I do not know it. But as to the other, I have heard something. . . ."

De Jarnac, his head nodding encouragingly, drained his wine cup and reached for more. He had been drinking steadily through the evening, Attica had noticed, although it didn't seem to have affected him in any way—except, perhaps, to intensify that coiled, almost lethal quality that hung about him always.

She sensed a wild, restless edge to him tonight that worried her. It was as if the mention of his brother had laid open an old, festering wound deep inside him. Glancing down, he caught her watching him and flashed her a wide, reckless smile. But his eyes remained brooding and dangerous.

Her gaze sought out Father Sebastian where he crouched on the far side of the fire before an old woman so bent and crippled, she could walk only with the aid of two canes. He had one of the woman's twisted feet in his lap and was massaging the instep while he spoke to her, his voice a gentle murmur on the night wind.

He must make a good priest, Attica thought, this man who knew life in all its joys and sorrows and agonies, who knew all the weaknesses and temptations and failings of men, yet still believed in the mercy of God and knew how to forgive.

And she found herself wondering exactly what Damion de Jarnac had done, that needed God's forgiveness.

"I have heard of an abbot in Rome who has improved upon the brilliant system of notation created by the Saintly Guido," continued the fair-haired stripling in an eager voice. "I believe he has added a seventh note, a *si*—named, of course, for Sancte Ioannes. . . ."

Her attention caught, Attica swung her head to look at the young harpist who stood on the far side of de Jarnac. She had assumed Damion to be simply enduring the youth's

enthusiastic discourse on music. Now she realized she'd
been wrong. Far from humoring him, de Jarnac had been
systematically and very deliberately pumping the young
harpist for information.

She drained the remaining ale in her cup and set it aside.
She would have spoken then, only she realized de Jarnac's
body had suddenly tensed, his head lifting as his fierce
gaze fixed on something across the fire.

She swung about to follow his gaze and saw that Father
Sebastian had left the crippled woman and now stood alone
on the edge of the fire's light. His long black habit flapped
in the wind as he stood, motionless and silent, as if waiting
for someone.

De Jarnac set aside the wine ewer and cup. "Excuse
me," he said to the boy, although his gaze never left the
dark, one-armed figure across the fire.

Attica started to scramble to her feet, but de Jarnac put
his hand on her shoulder, stopping her. "It's late. You
should sleep," he said quietly, not looking at her any more
than he'd looked at the young musician.

She stared up into his taut, shadowed face. "So should
you."

He shook his head. "There is someone with whom I
must speak first."

His hand left her shoulder. She watched him walk away
from her, the fire gleaming on the gilded spurs at his
bootheels. Just beyond the circle of light, he paused beside
the priest. She couldn't be certain, but she didn't think anything was said between them. Still, they turned together
and walked off into the night, a tall, devil-haunted young
knight who did not believe in the mercy of God, and the
knight-turned-priest, who did.

* * *

Enthroned in the carved chair she had brought from Châteauhaut, Yvette let her bemused gaze drift over the collection of swords, daggers, maces, and lances that decorated the inner wall of Renouf Blissot's solar at Laval Castle. She could appreciate their fine workmanship, and she knew the value of their inlaid gold and silver and precious jewels, but she could see no beauty in these objects of death. It seemed a strange decoration.

"Part of your collection appears to be missing," she said, noticing an empty hook.

"My niece took it," said Renouf Blissot. "I suppose I should consider myself fortunate she didn't leave it in my back."

Yvette brought her attention back to the small, dark-haired man who sat on a three-legged stool beside the exquisite silver candelabra that graced the oak table in the center of the room. He was a handsome man, Renouf Blissot, with his slim, wiry body and flashing gray eyes. But obviously not, she thought with a sigh, as competent as one would think in looking at him.

"How difficult is it?" Gaspard demanded, flinging his arms wide in that way he had as he paced up and down the solar, creating enough wind with his passing to flicker the torches in their wall brackets. "How difficult is it to keep one nineteen-year-old woman securely locked up?"

Renouf propped his elbows on the table and rested his chin in his hands. "You tell me, Gaspard," he said, his sardonic gaze following the other man's energetic perambulations. "You lost her before I did."

Gaspard whirled to point an accusatory finger at Yvette. "I told you. Didn't I tell you we should have come quicker? Why you must drag half the contents of the castle about with you, every time you travel—"

Yvette selected a sweetmeat from the silver tray at her side and popped it into her mouth. "Do sit down, Gaspard. You're fatiguing yourself unnecessarily."

"They fled east, of course," said Renouf Blissot, swiveling sideways to stretch his legs out before him. "Toward La Ferté-Bernard. A few days ago they killed two of my knights—at least, one assumes it was de Jarnac's handiwork. Whoever it was took one horse and one set of armor, and left the rest. No one has seen them since." He shifted his gaze toward Yvette. "Did you know of Richard and Philip's plans for the conference?"

"No. De Harcourt spoke to us of the alliance against Henry, but only in the most general terms."

Renouf grunted. "Too bad he wasn't as discreet with Attica."

"Do you know what documents he carried in that breviary?" Gaspard asked, helping himself to a cup of wine.

The castellan shook his head. "No. But if they were for John, the results could be disastrous if they fall into the wrong hands."

"I think we must assume they already have," said Yvette, pushing to her feet. "It's late. I shall retire now to that pleasant chamber you have prepared for us." She glanced at her husband, who had his nose deep in a wine cup. "Don't stay up late, Gaspard. We leave early."

Gaspard sucked in a quick breath of surprise that caused him to inhale some of the wine and fall to coughing. "Leave?" he said when he was able.

Yvette paused with her hand on the solar door. "If Attica has fled to Henry, it may not be easy to get her back. We'll continue on to La Ferté-Bernard and lay our case before Philip. He is, after all, Henry's liege."

"But I don't want her now," said Fulk, rising suddenly

from the window embrasure where he had been playing with a couple of half-grown puppies. "You can't expect me to wed her now, after she's been with this knight." His lip curled as if he had smelled something foul. "Another man's leavings?"

"Don't be a fool," snapped Yvette. "You repudiate Attica now and we will have Robert d'Alérion as our sworn enemy rather than our ally." She let go of the door to point a warning finger at her son. "You'll wed her all right, boy. Even if she's quick with child by this rogue knight, you will wed her, and make no mistake about that."

Attica awoke to the dark stillness that comes over the world in those hours just before the first lightening of dawn.

The fire had burned down to a pile of pale white ashes, but the night was not cold. She rolled onto her back, her head turning against the soft velvet of the folded surcoat she used as a pillow, her gaze searching for de Jarnac's familiar form beside her.

She was alone.

Pushing herself up on her elbows, she drew in a deep breath of night-scented air, her eyes narrowing as she searched the huddled, sleeping forms of the pilgrims. Impossible to tell if Father Sebastian was among them. She lay down again, trying to close her eyes and go back to sleep. But she could not rest easy.

Sitting up quietly, she pulled on her boots and then, wrapping the cloak around her, arose from the hard ground. She walked with no particular destination in mind, her footsteps carrying her almost aimlessly toward the stream.

Away from the camp, the night seemed even darker and lonelier. She could hear the wind stirring the trees up on the hill and sighing through the meadow grass. But the creatures of the night had all quieted. It was as if the world held its breath, waiting for the new day.

She saw him then, a solitary figure standing tall and broad-shouldered on a low rise overlooking the stream. She walked toward him, her footfalls muffled by the long, dew-dampened meadow grass. He had his back to her. He didn't turn as she came up behind him, but he knew she was there, for he said, his tone harsh, "You shouldn't be out here."

The very air between them seemed to crackle and heat with a mutually intense physical awareness, an aching need that brought a flush to her face and made her body suddenly, quiveringly sensitive. She knew she hovered on the edge of something beautiful and dangerous, knew she should turn around and leave him here, alone in the darkness, before it was too late. Instead, she took a step that brought her right up beside him. "Everyone in the camp is asleep."

He stood perfectly still. "That's not what I meant, and you know it."

She stared up at his hard profile. "I don't believe you'll hurt me," she said, although it was a lie. He had already hurt her by riding into her world and showing her what life and love could be like. What it could be like if she were someone else. He would hurt her even more the day her honor and sense of duty forced her to say good-bye to him.

He looked at her then, and she saw something flash in his eyes, something wild and dangerous that was there, then hidden beneath the deceptively lazy droop of his lids. "It would hurt you," he said, his voice low and rough. "What we would do together. It could destroy you."

"I know," she said simply.

The breeze, restless and cool and scented with ripe grass

and damp earth, danced around them to flutter her short hair against her face. He reached out, his battle-hardened hand gently brushing her cheek as he tucked the stray curls behind her ear.

He stared down at her, and his face took on that intense, heated look she'd come to know. She stood breathless and still beneath his touch, her heart beating so hard and fast, she could feel her pulse thrumming against his fingertips as they lingered at the tender flesh at the side of her neck.

"I know," she said again, her voice an aching whisper. "And I don't care."

She saw his head jerk, his nostrils flaring wide and proud. "You think you know." His hand clenched in the hair at the base of her head to draw her closer, until she could feel the heat of his body, enveloping her, see the fire in his eyes, scorching her. "You think you know, and you think you don't care. But you can't begin to imagine what could come of this."

"Perhaps not." She breathed in the scent of him, the scent of woodsmoke and leather and deadly polished steel. "But I know what my life will be like without this. I don't think I could bear it." She leaned into him, her hands splayed against his strong chest. She could feel the fine trembling going on inside him, feel the battle he fought with himself. The strain of it accentuated the harsh lines of his face, making him look more dangerous and beautiful than ever.

She saw his jaw tighten, the creases in his cheeks deepening as he held himself rigid beneath her touch. "Attica, please . . ."

She pressed her fingertips to his lips, stopping his words, tracing the line of that hard mouth, watching it part on a harshly expelled breath. *"Damion,"* she whispered, her hands sliding over his beard-stubbled cheeks to bracket his face, her gaze locking with his. She could see her own desire, reflected in the glowing depths of his eyes. See the need.

And then it was as if something within him tore loose, something that had been holding him back. With a harsh groan, he swept his hands down her spine and crushed her to him, his mouth slamming down on hers. She opened her mouth to his kiss, to him, and heard a low, primitive growl reverberate in the depths of his chest as he moved his lips across hers, deepened the kiss, filled her being with the feel of him, the taste of him, the essence of him.

And the essence of him was fire. She clung to him, breathed in that fire, so raw and passionate, it swept away all control. His tongue mated with hers, and the kiss became something urgent, something all-consuming. It was as if he entered her blood stream, pounded through her, became part of her.

With a low, keening moan, she pressed herself against him, her arms twining around his neck, her breasts flattening against his hard chest. She was desperate to get closer to him, hated the clothes that kept them apart. She wanted to slide her naked body against his, to run her fingers over his smooth, hot flesh, to touch him, all of him.

She knew he had the same need, for his hands were all over her. Through the cloth of her tunic, his fingers found her taut nipples and coaxed from them an exquisite sensation somewhere between pain and ecstasy.

He tore his mouth from hers, his lips and tongue trailing fire down her throat, sucking, licking, stoking that clenching need deep, deep in her belly. Her breath caught on a small cry, her head falling back, her eyes wide and glazed as she stared at the night sky above them. She thought she would surely die if he didn't do something, something to ease this coiling tension within her.

"Attica . . ." His voice was a warm, tortured whisper against the wet flesh of her throat as he suddenly held himself so still, she could feel the tiny, violent shudders ripping through him.

She clutched him to her, her hands clenching his tunic. "No. Don't stop. Not this time."

He raised his head to look down at her, color riding high on the sharp line of his cheekbones, his eyes dark with anguish. "I'm not worth this sacrifice. This risk." He shook his head from side to side. "You don't really know me. You don't know the things I've done."

Her head jerked in denial, her breath as raspy as his. "I know you. I know you've killed. I've *seen* you kill."

He closed his war-scarred hands over hers. "You don't know the worst of it."

She raised their entwined hands to her lips and kissed his clenched knuckles, her eyes locked with his. "Don't you see? It doesn't matter. None of it matters."

He tightened his grip on her until it almost hurt, then let her go. "It matters to me."

"Why?" She felt a rush of panic squeeze her. She wanted to pound her fists against his broad, fighting-man's chest. She wanted to take his head in her arms and cradle him against her breast like a hurt and needy child. She wanted to do something—anything to stop him from turning away from her like this. "Why?" she said again. "Because you think it your *duty* to protect me? From *you*?"

He stood with his body held taut, his features lost to her sight by distance and the shadows of the night. "Yes."

A ragged laugh tore out of her, a laugh that twisted and caught on the pain in her chest so that it came out sounding almost like a sob. "Behold my black knight." She hugged herself to keep from shaking. "My dark horseman, who claims to scorn the conventions of chivalry, when in reality he is all that is good and noble and honorable—"

His head jerked. "Don't try to make me into something I'm not."

"No. Listen to me. You think that whatever you did to your brother changes all that, makes it meaningless. But it doesn't. It doesn't."

In the sudden silence that followed her words, she could hear the gentle gurgle of the stream running broad and quiet with barely enough current here to send the water lapping against the sandy banks beside them. She saw his chest lift on an indrawn breath, saw his throat work as he swallowed hard. He swung abruptly away from her to go stand at the edge of the water. The air stirred around them, cool and sweet with dew. She stood very still, waiting.

"When my mother was fourteen," he said after a moment, his deep, rich voice floating to her on a waft of breeze, "her family betrothed her to a man she'd never met. A man she'd never even seen before."

He fell silent again, the night filling with tension, with the strain it took for him to say the things he was saying. "Your father?" she asked quietly.

He pushed his breath out through his teeth in a painful sigh. "Hugh de Jarnac. He was practically old enough to be her grandfather, but the alliance was considered valuable to her family, and because she believed in honor and duty, she did not object."

"What was he like?"

He lifted his hand, as if reaching for something, then let it fall. "I don't remember him much. To me, he was always a distant, imposing figure, gruff-voiced, mean-tempered. I stayed out of his way. He was killed on a hunt when I was nine. I think I was relieved."

She thought about her own father, the laughing, indulgent Robert d'Alérion. It was her mother Attica had stayed away from—and still did. "And your brother?" she asked.

The wind died suddenly, leaving the atmosphere oddly calm and hushed. "My mother was Hugh's second wife. He had a son already, by his first wife, a son who was a year older than my mother. His name was Simon."

She went to stand beside him at the water's edge, close, but not touching him, not even looking at him. "So your father already had an heir."

"Two, actually. Simon had been married, young, to a woman from Poitiers. She died in childbirth, giving him a son. Simon never remarried."

She looked at him then, and the fading starlight revealed to her a face almost frighteningly cold and remote. "Did he love his dead wife so much?"

A fierce smile curled de Jarnac's lips, showing his teeth. "Hardly. He never remarried because he was in love with my mother. His father's wife. And she loved him."

Attica sucked in a quick, shocked breath. "Oh, how awful for her," she whispered, her voice grating painfully in her tight throat. "How awful for them both." She knew well that such a love was doomed; for a woman to marry her dead husband's son was forbidden. In the eyes of the church, such a union was considered incestuous, and punishable by death.

She couldn't seem to stop herself from reaching out to him. She was afraid he'd scorn her attempt to touch him, but he took her hand, his fingers entwining with hers to draw her closer. "What did they do?" she asked.

His hand still linked with hers, he brought his arms

around her from behind, holding her back to his chest so that she could not see his face. "After Hugh's death, my mother's family wanted her to return to them, with her dower portion, but she refused. She claimed she stayed to help raise her son and her husband's grandson. But it wasn't long before there were . . . rumors."

She tipped her head back against his shoulder, her hands clutching at his wrists. "Did you know? Did you know how they felt about each other?"

He tightened his arms around her waist, rested his cheek against her hair. "Not at first. I was young, and they were discreet. Eventually, I was sent as page to the house of my uncle, and somehow he managed to keep me from hearing about it. For a time. But then, the spring after I turned thirteen, some of the older squires cornered me in the stables and taunted me with it. I half killed them."

He fell silent for a moment. She felt his breath warm against the side of her face, felt the quiver that ran through him. "I almost killed those squires for what they said, yet I think that even then, deep down in my gut, I knew it for the truth. And I knew that I couldn't rest until I looked into my mother's face and watched her reaction to what I'd heard.

"My uncle tried to stop me. I simply knocked him out of my way. I took one of his horses and rode for home."

She knew now what he was going to say, and she had to clench her teeth together to keep from begging him not to say it.

"There was a terrible storm that night. Rain poured in sheets out of the sky, but the lightning was so fierce and continuous, it lit up the countryside almost as if it were daylight. I reached the castle just before dawn. I pounded on the postern gate until the guard opened up for me, but the way the thunder was rumbling, no one else heard me arrive.

"I couldn't wait until morning to confront her. I ran up the stairs and threw open the doors to the hall. It woke up the men sleeping around the hearth, but I didn't care. I stormed into her chamber and . . . found them."

Wordlessly, she turned in his arms so she could look into his drawn, pale face with its glittering, haunted eyes. He threaded his fingers through the hair at her temples, stroking her, stroking, although he kept his gaze fixed on some distant point beyond the western hills.

"I was only thirteen, Attica. I was too young to understand what they meant to each other. All I knew was that my mother had betrayed the memory of her husband, while my brother had betrayed his father, and me, and defiled my mother."

Unable to continue looking at him, Attica buried her face against his chest, her throat so raw it ached. "Oh, God. Oh, God, no."

She felt the pounding of his heart reverberating against her cheek. "I drew my sword and challenged him to fight me right there, in my mother's chamber. He refused, of course. But I was determined to make him fight me. I kept chasing him around the room, swinging my sword at him. He was naked. He grabbed stools, cloaks, anything he could—to use as a shield. But he refused to pick up his own sword and fight back. My mother was crying—screaming— *begging* me to stop."

Attica closed her eyes, her imagination conjuring up for her the crash of thunder, the flickering firelight glittering on Damion's rain-soaked cloak and gleaming along naked steel; the beautiful woman, wide-eyed and wild with fear for the two men she loved most.

"She finally quit trying to reason with me and struck me on the shoulder with a water ewer. I think she was hoping to knock the sword out of my hand, but all she did was make me stagger . . . at exactly the same moment as Simon lunged at me to try to wrest the sword from my grip." His hands were at her back now, moving in slow, relentless circles, holding her pressed blindly to him. She felt his chest lift as he breathed. "The sword drove straight into his chest."

She tipped her head back, her throat tight, her words coming out in a hoarse whisper. "You didn't kill him deliberately."

He gazed down at her, his face drawn and fierce. "Yes I did. I wanted to kill him."

She shook her head. "Not like that."

"No. But he was still dead." She watched the muscles in his taut neck work as he swallowed. "He was only twenty-nine years old, Attica. Two years older than I am now."

"What happened to your mother?" she asked quietly.

His face suddenly went cold, remote. "She retired to a convent."

She let her hand creep around his neck to touch him there, at the nape of his neck, with gentle fingers. "And you took the Cross?"

He nodded. "I left my uncle's house and joined Sir Rauve."

"Have you seen her since? Your mother, I mean."

"No."

The pain she felt for him was suddenly too much to bear. A rush of tears swelled her throat, spilled from beneath her hastily lowered lashes. "Oh, Damion . . ."

He brushed his knuckles across her cheek. "Don't weep for me, Attica. It's their tragedy, not mine. I was too young

then to understand the forces of hopeless passion and ir-
resistible longing that drove them. But I understand it now.
God help me, I understand it now."

He moved his hand, tracing her features with the tips of
battle-scarred fingers that slid gently over her eyelids, down
the curve of her cheek, to linger at her lips. She watched a
kind of tautness come over his face, a lean, hungry look that
she recognized as the hunger of a man for a woman. He
stared at her, his eyes glowing as fierce as lightning. Then
he sucked in a ragged sigh that shuddered his chest, his
eyes squeezing shut as his hand fell limply to his side.
"You need to go back now."

She stood unmoving before him, her heart pounding,
her body trembling with yearning and love and a strange,
determined boldness. Slowly, she reached up her hand to
undo the clasp at her throat and let her cloak fall in a
whisper to her feet. Her girdle followed, landing with a
soft thump in the thick grass.

The sky was black above them, the stars fading with the
coming of dawn. The wind stirred the dying night around
them. She watched the white cloth of his ruined shirt flutter against the darkness of his bare neck, saw the pulse beating there wildly at the base of his throat.

She loosed the laces of her tunic and jerked it over
her head.

"Attica," he said, his voice low and breathy as she untied
the points of her chausses. "Please don't do this."

She lifted her head, her gaze locking with his as she
worked methodically, stripping off boots, hose, braies,
and shirt, until only the white swath of cloth that bound
her breasts remained. Slowly, she unwound the binding,
let it flutter to her feet like a wide, pale ribbon.

She stood naked before him. The night air skimmed

over her bare flesh, raising the fine hairs, filling her with a wild sense of freedom, of excitement. He held himself utterly still. But his eyes . . . his eyes burned.

She reached out to him. She took his hand in hers and put it on her breast so that his palm cupped her fullness. "Feel my breasts," she whispered, "heavy and ripe for you."

His hand jerked in hers, and she tightened her fingers around him, eased his hand lower, skimming down over the bare flesh of her quivering belly, down between her thighs to where she burned. "Feel my body," she said hoarsely, "open for you."

The pale glimmer of starshine showed her the beloved planes of his face, sharp and fierce with need. She could feel the hard trembling going on inside of him as he fought to hold himself away from her. Felt, too, the moment when he lost that fight.

A groan tore out of him as he hauled her into his arms, his mouth slamming down on hers. His kiss was rough, hungry, consuming, a swirling onslaught of tongue and need and blind, hot passion. "Oh, God, Attica," he said, his lips moving against hers, his breath coming in rough gasps, his hands sweeping urgently over her naked body. "I don't think I can be gentle."

She clung to him, her fingers digging into the tight muscles of his shoulders, her teeth nipping at his lower lip. "I don't need you to be gentle." She wrapped her arms around his neck to pull his head down to her. "I simply need you."

CHAPTER
SEVENTEEN

He bore her down into the tumbled pile of clothing at their feet, his hard man's body settling between her sprawled thighs. Stars sparkled at her from out of a graying sky. Then he loomed over her to fill her view of the world, a dark knight with a harsh face and eyes that glowed with passion and love, so much love.

She wrapped her arms around his waist, her hands reveling in the feel of the taut muscles of his back beneath the cloth of his tunic as she drew him down to her. He laid his palm against her cheek, his thumb brushing back and forth beneath her chin, his mouth hovering just above hers. She could feel the need trembling inside him, feel his chest expanding against hers with each ragged breath.

"I've wanted you so very badly," he said, his breath washing warm over her face.

She stared up at him, her heart pounding, her body aching with need. "I'm not afraid."

He bent and covered her mouth with his, his lips soft but urgent as he turned his head back and forth, slanting his mouth against hers. She felt his fingers tangling in the hair at the side of her head, holding her steady as he deepened the kiss, filling her with his tongue, tracing the line of her lips, making love to her mouth with a kind of wild desperation.

The wind eddied around them, sweet with the scent of meadow grass and stream-lapped sand and fresh with the promise of dawn. With a harsh murmur, he shifted his weight to one braced forearm, his lips still fastened to hers even as his hand swept down her body to close over her breast.

His touch on her breasts was as rough and hungry as his kiss, filling her with a need that burned, burned. His thumb swept her nipples and she gasped, squirming beneath him, her hands skimming over his back, impatient with the clothes that kept her from touching him the way he was touching her. She tugged at them, but already his hand had left her breasts to move possessively over the sensitive skin of her belly and slide between her parted thighs. He touched her there, spreading her wide, and it was as if he had enflamed every nerve of her body. She gasped into his mouth, her eyes flying wide in surprise. Then she felt his finger slip inside her, and she gasped again, her eyes squeezing shut, her body arching, her head falling back beneath a rush of intense, unbelievable sensation.

"God, Attica, I'm sorry, but I can't . . ." He tore his mouth from hers, his eyes dark with a fierce, raw need as he reared up, his hands fumbling beneath tunic and shirt to yank at the ties of his braies. She saw a shudder rip through him; then his hands were at her hips, gripping her, lifting her, his face hard, intent.

She wrapped her hands around the tight, bulging muscles of his arms, her throat dry as she sucked in air. She felt something incredibly smooth and unexpectedly hard push against the soft flesh between her thighs, and as much as she wanted this, she found she had to hold herself suddenly very still to keep from flinching away.

She saw a muscle bunch along his tight jaw. He leaned forward, his dark eyes riveted on hers. He caught her hands in his, stretched her arms over her head, pinned her beneath his weight. And pushed himself inside her.

She cried out. He caught her cry with his mouth, holding himself steady as she instinctively reared up against him. "Shhh," he said, kissing her mouth, her cheeks, her sweat slicked forehead. She quivered beneath him, feeling him within her, feeling his hardness, his heat, stretching her, filling her. "It's only me," he whispered, and to her surprise, she felt a shaky laugh ease out of her.

He kissed her again, his hair falling forward to brush her cheek. When her trembling began to ease, he moved, pulling partway out of her only to thrust in again, deeper, harder. And she caught her breath in wonder because what she felt was not pain so much as a strange, pleasurable kind of pressure. A pleasure that coiled and built with each thrust and drag until she wanted to scream with it, scream with joyous rapture and the unbearable agony of their love.

"Please," she said, her fingers digging into his shoulders, holding his chest pressed to her breasts as he moved so deep within her. "Oh, please." She felt as if she were reaching for something, something that hovered bright and promising, just out of her grasp.

"Ducemente, mon amanate," he whispered, nuzzling her hair, his breath coming in hard, fast pants. He eased his hand between their bodies until it rested low on her belly, the heel of his hand pressing against her mound. Pressing, pressing, pressing her between the hardness of his hand and the hardness of his body thrusting into her, thrusting all the way to her heart.

She felt her love for him explode within her, an all-consuming, fiery wash of unbearably exquisite delight. As though through a dim haze, she saw his head fall back, his eyes squeezing shut, his face contorting as if in pain. She felt him give one last, violent thrust, deep within her. Then he reared back, the sweat-sheened muscles of his throat taut and bulging as he pulled himself out of her.

Gasping, she clutched at his arms, holding him as the shudders ripped through him. She knew he spilled his seed outside of her to keep from giving her his child. She knew it, but that did nothing to ease the sad, empty ache within her.

He wanted to hold her forever. Simply hold her.

He rolled onto his back and gathered her in his arms so that she lay on her side with her head nestled in the crook of his shoulder, one hand flung across his heaving chest. His breath still came in ragged gasps. When he reached to smooth her hair from her damp forehead, his fingers shook.

He'd known this about love. That it could run so strong and deep that when combined with the heat of desire, it became dangerously overwhelming. He'd known this, yet he'd thought himself somehow different, thought he could resist. Now he knew himself humbled. And very afraid.

He felt her breasts press against him as she drew in a deep breath and pushed it out in a sigh. "I keep thinking I should feel guilt," she said, her voice hushed. She turned, resting her bare forearms upon his chest so she could lift herself up and look into his face, her eyes wide and dark with emotion. "But all I feel is joy. A terrible joy."

He could see her well now in the gathering light. He let his gaze rove over the delicate bones of her face, the high, wide brow and long, aristocratic nose, the full, trembling lips and proud, strong chin. He thought he could look at her forever. He wanted to look at her forever. He wanted to look into the faces of his children, his grandchildren, and see her features, her essence, mingled with his for all time. The thought of a life without her suddenly seemed almost more than he could bear.

A terrible joy. Yes, he thought; as great as it is, this joy is terrible, for it brings with it such fear of loss and the promise of unbearable pain.

He heard a lark's song floating sweet yet oddly sad from the wooded hills above. The morning air seemed to hurt his skin, hurt his chest as he drew in breath. With a fearful sense of urgency, he drew her up so that she lay along the length of his body. He caught her face between his hands, his lips capturing hers in a deep, desperate kiss. He had known these things about love, he thought, but he hadn't really understood. Hadn't understood at all.

"It will be daybreak soon," she said, a smile in her voice as her mouth moved against his.

"Do you think the good pilgrims might be shocked"— he ran his tongue along her lower lip—"finding us like this?"

She touched his cheek and smiled. "I think they might."

He sighed, his hands coursing down her bare back to cup her bottom. "I want to make love to you for hours, Attica. Slowly this time. I want to touch you all over. With my hands. With my lips. With my tongue." He rubbed his partially open mouth against hers.

The lark sang again.

"Tonight," she said with a laugh as he groaned and pressed his forehead against hers.

"And in a bed," he added, the grass rustling beneath him

as he shifted uncomfortably. "Tonight we need to find a bed."

A reddish glow stained the pale horizon as they walked back to the pilgrims' camp. The lush, knee-high meadow grass whispered about them, its sweet scent reminding Attica of summers past and the lost, happy hours of her childhood. She tightened her grip on Damion's hand. He turned his head to her and smiled.

Love bloomed in her heart, filling her with wild joy and an aching dread that tugged at her happiness. She told herself Stephen would support her when she approached their father on the subject of her marriage. She told herself that a man as loyal to his liege lord as Robert d'Alérion would never honor a marriage alliance made with a house that could turn traitor. She told herself that Old King Henry would reward Damion for his loyalty, reward him so handsomely that her father would see an alliance with him as valuable. She told herself these things because she needed to be able to hope. If she couldn't hope, she thought, she just might curl up into a little ball and die.

The pungent smell of woodsmoke drifted across the meadow along with the crackle of recently kindled fires and the faint murmur of anxious voices. She hadn't expected to find the camp already astir. Beside her, Damion stopped abruptly, his eyes narrowing as he gazed at the far hills.

Apprehension bloomed within her, deep and ominous. "What is it?" she asked, touching his arm.

He nodded toward the distant red glow. "The sun doesn't rise in the south, Attica."

She followed his gaze, her grip on him tightening. "What can it mean?"

He shook his head, but something in his face told her he knew. He knew only too well.

"Damion—" She broke off at the sight of a weary horse, its heaving flanks stained dark and flecked with foam, its head hanging in exhaustion as it was led toward the river. She saw a grim-faced, dusty man slumped beside one of the fires, talking to Father Sebastian. The one-armed priest looked up and saw them. He nodded at something the man said, then touched his shoulder as if in comfort and walked toward them.

"Surely that cannot be Tours?" Damion asked as the one-armed priest came up to them. "It is too near."

The older man shook his head. "No. It seems Philip's move against Tours was only a feint. He has turned and attacked Henry at Le Mans instead." Attica saw dark shadows shift, deep in the older man's eyes, as if he were remembering other cities, cities he himself had helped to sack. "They say the citadel still holds out. But the city itself is in flames."

"And Henry?" Attica asked.

The priest turned to her. "He rides for Normandy. The nobles here have all deserted him, all but for the handful of his household knights who ride with him."

Stephen, she thought, fear stealing her breath so that she could only nod when the priest excused himself and returned to the anxious pilgrims.

"Don't worry about Stephen," Damion said, as if she had spoken aloud. "Henry must have managed to escape Le Mans before Philip's forces were able to lay siege to the city. Stephen will be with him."

She turned to stare again at that hellish glow in the south. She was aware of a fine trembling within her, as if her entire world were shaking apart. "What do we do now?"

"Ride for Normandy. What else?"

He took her hand in his and together they walked toward the stretch of meadow where the tethered horses grazed in the pale light of early dawn. All around them the birds were awakening, fluttering through the dark silhouettes of the trees to rise up against the pearly sky, their voices blending into the heartrending song of dawn. Attica let her head fall back, watching them. She didn't understand how the world around her could seem so comfortingly calm and familiar, the new day so full of glorious promise, when her life as she knew it was collapsing.

"There is a convent," Damion said slowly, "not far from here. Sainte-Geneviève-sur-Sarthe." He paused, his head turned toward where the roan grazed, its tail flicking back and forth. "I would go there before we turn north."

She looked at him in surprise. "A convent?"

An odd tension vibrated in the air as she waited for him to answer her. "The abbess is Isabelle d'Anjou," he said at last, the name coming out unnaturally harsh and strained. "I need to talk to her. About this French code."

Once, Isabelle d'Anjou had been a famous patroness of troubadours; more than a patroness—a poet and musician in her own right. Something niggled at Attica's memory, something that sent an indefinable frisson of uneasiness over her. "I had thought Isabelle d'Anjou dead since I was a small child," she said, reaching out to run her hand over the roan's warm, satiny withers.

"No. She only took the veil."

The roan lifted its head and swung about to nuzzle Attica's hair, its breath blowing hot and grassy against her face. Attica caught the horse's nose in her hands. "You know her?"

"I know her." He sounded as if he would like to have

left it at that, but he seemed to think he should perhaps say more. "If there is a system to indicate the length of notes, she will have heard of it."

"Henry has been defeated," Attica said, her gaze fixed firmly on the horse beside her. "What difference can deciphering the French code possibly make now?"

"It's not over yet. If Henry rides to Normandy, it is because he intends to raise an army there. There and in England. He'll not give up. Not as long as he lives."

Her fingers trembled slightly as she let them trail over the roan's velvety soft muzzle. *If she couldn't hope . . .* Her chest suddenly felt tight, as if she had forgotten to breathe. But when she sucked in a deep draught of air, it only hurt worse. "If Henry is deposed," she said softly, "my father will need the marriage alliance with Salers to secure his favor with Richard. He will never allow me to break my betrothal."

"Then I'll just have to make sure Henry isn't deposed, won't I?"

She had been avoiding looking at him, but she couldn't seem to stop herself from turning now. He stared back at her, his green eyes brittle, the bones of his face standing out painfully sharp beneath the dark skin. She wished she hadn't looked.

She swung away from him to stand very still, her shoulders taut, her gaze fixed on a pair of pure white geese, their wings beating the clear dawn air as they rose from the surface of the slowly flowing stream. She was aware of him coming up behind her, although he didn't touch her in any way. Together they watched the geese take flight to soar above the meadow.

"They say geese mate for life. If they lose their mate,

they don't take another. They simply live the rest of their lives alone." He paused. "Have you heard that?"

"Yes." She reached for his hand as the sun burst up over the hills in the east to send a wealth of golden light spilling across the meadow.

He laced his fingers with hers and drew her around until she was looking up into his hard, beautiful face. "You are my mate for life, Attica. No matter what happens, I'll never love another."

He dipped his head to take her mouth in a warmly gentle kiss that ended all too quickly. As they turned to lead the horses back to camp, she looked for the geese. But the sky was empty and it was as if they had never been.

They made a wide arc around the city of Le Mans to come upon the convent of Sainte-Geneviève late in the afternoon.

The abbey clung to the side of a hill overlooking the Sarthe and, stretching beyond that, the gentle green valley of the Loire. The house was Benedictine now, but the huddle of ancient, low stone buildings was older than that. There had been a colony of women occupying the site since the fifth century, when, shortly after the death of a revered anchorite named Geneviève, a series of miracles had begun to occur among those who prayed in the holy woman's candlelit grotto.

Attica steadied the tired roan as they descended the steep path to the abbey, her gaze drifting over the simple stone structures built in terraced steps down the slope of the hillside. She found herself wondering what had driven a beautiful, wealthy, and renowned woman such as Isabelle d'Anjou to seek such a refuge.

Sainte-Geneviève-sur-Sarthe was known for its devotion and piety, not for its wealth or influence. Yet in her former life, Isabelle d'Anjou had been a grand noblewoman, great-niece of William of Aquitaine and wife of a powerful lord of Poitou, to whose court she had attracted the most learned men and talented musicians, poets, and artists of her day. It was difficult to imagine such a worldly woman in this bucolic setting.

They were nearing the convent gatehouse now. In the forecourt, Damion pulled off his helm and pushed back the hood of his hauberk, then dismounted to approach the porter on foot. Attica smiled. Even on foot and without his helm, he still seemed a frighteningly incongruous figure in this place of peace. The metal of the helm had left dark smudges on his nose and cheekbones, making him look fierce and dangerous.

She heard the scramble of tiny hooves as a herd of sheep came bounding up the rocky, sunlit hillside toward the gate, their woolly backs flashing white in the golden sunlight, their incessant bleating mingling with the *wop-wop* of a windmill's sails spinning in the fresh breeze. In anticipation of the flock's arrival, the convent's wooden gates stood open. But when Attica and Damion led their horses beneath the low arch, they found the entrance to the abbey's inner court suddenly blocked by the forbidding bulk of one of the largest nuns Attica had ever seen. Planting her black booted feet wide, the sister crossed her arms over her massive, black wool covered bosom and lowered her head to glare at them with a scowl that squashed three rippling chins against the white of her wimple.

"Good sister," said de Jarnac, the first of the bleating, milling sheep trotting through the archway as he flashed the forbidding-looking nun his most charming smile. "We have come to see your abbess. If you would—"

"Men of war are not welcome in this house. Pilgrims

may enter, and those seeking alms may enter." The nun paused, her beady dark eyes sweeping over him contemptuously. "But not men of war."

De Jarnac's head reared back, his nostrils flaring. Thigh deep now in sheep, Attica had to wipe her sleeve across her face to hide an inappropriate grin as she watched him struggle to rein in his quick spurt of anger and keep that winsome smile in place. "Good sister." He spread his arms wide as if in surrender. One of the sheep butted into him, hard enough to make him stagger. "I would willingly remove my sword and dagger and leave them in your keeping. If you would be so kind as to send word to your abbess—"

A disdainful grunt rumbled up from the depths of the nun's impressive chest. "Even without your sword and dagger, you are still a man of war. You are not welcome here. Be gone."

Surrounded by sheep, the woman made as if to turn away, but Damion's cold, angry hiss stopped her, his hand gripping the hilt of his sword as if he meant to draw the blade and skewer her with it. "God rot you, Sister. You come back here."

The nun whirled around, her eyes and mouth both opening wide as she skittered backward, the skirts of her long black habit flapping about her in the breeze like the wings of a startled crow floundering in the midst of a sea of bunching, bawling sheep.

"You will put down your sword and cease to abuse my nun," said a calm, cultured voice behind Attica.

She spun around to find herself confronting a tall, elegant woman wearing the black habit, white wimple, and black veil of the order. She had startling green eyes and a beautiful, unlined face, although she was not young. Attica stared at the woman's proud, aristocratic nose and wide cheekbones, and felt her grip on her reins tighten until the edges of the leather bit into her palm.

The woman looked not at Attica but at the dark, dangerous knight at her side. That smooth, ageless face showed no trace of emotion. Yet nothing could disguise the shock and quick spurt of hope that flared up, painful and bright, in the depths of those unusual green eyes. As Attica watched, hope gave way first to disbelief, then to certainty, and, finally, to a wild, fierce leap of joy quickly contained by wariness.

"Damion," whispered the abbess, the simple silver crucifix at her chest rising as she sucked in a sharp breath of air.

Attica turned to find de Jarnac's gaze riveted on the abbess. The breeze ruffled the dark hair that hung down over the neck of the hauberk he'd taken from the man he had killed. He held himself stiff and unmoving, his face as blank and emotionless as that of the woman he confronted. Then he swallowed, and the sinews of his throat strained painfully beneath his dark skin.

He took a step forward, then another. He reached out, his strong, battle-hardened hands closing over the slim white fingers of the woman before him. "Madam." Slowly, he sank to his knees, his head bowing as he brought her hand to his lips. "I have come to beg your forgiveness."

"My son, my son . . ." She paused, her voice trembling, her hand twisting to grip his. "It is enough that you have come."

CHAPTER
EIGHTEEN

She was a stranger to him, this pious woman in the simple, austere habit of a Benedictine nun. Once she had been his mother. She had laughed with joy and pride as she watched him take his first steps, had guided his small fingers across the strings of a harp, had argued passionately with him about the conflict between Saint Bernard and Peter Abelard. Once he had hated her for betraying her husband.

Once he had killed the man she loved.

She looked up from the mulled wine she was preparing over a brazier in her abbess's quarters. The golden light of late afternoon streamed through the high windows to glance across the features of her face. Fourteen years. He hadn't seen her for fourteen years, yet she was still beautiful. Still wary of him.

"Why now?" she said. "Why now, after so many years?"

Damion sat on a crude stool beside the brazier, his eyes carefully narrowed to concealing slits as he watched her stir the wine. They were alone. Isabelle had invited his "squire" to join them for refreshment in the abbatia as well, but Attica had politely declined, saying quietly, "I think you need to see your mother alone."

He'd caught her hand as she turned to go. "I should have

warned you. I'm sorry. I don't know why I found the words so difficult to say."

But she'd only pressed his hand, a smile gentle on her lips as her anxious gaze searched his face. "Don't you, Damion? I do."

Now he sucked in a deep breath rich with the sweet spicy scent of cinnamon and cloves and forced himself to answer the mother he'd been avoiding for fourteen years. "I've come for two reasons. One is personal, the other on King Henry's business."

"Ah." She poured the wine into two simple wooden cups and handed him one. "Let's take care of Henry first, shall we?"

Carefully sipping the hot, spicy wine, he told her what he knew of Philip's code and what he didn't know.

"I've learned much of the principle behind it," he said, "but without a system for indicating the length of the notes, it seems unworkable."

"There is such a system," she said when he had finished. "It was developed by a Benedictine nun in Catalonia. But it is not well known."

He stared at her over the rim of his cup. "Do you know it?"

She held his gaze steadily for a long moment, as if considering her reply. Rising gracefully from beside the brazier, she went to take a wax tablet and stylus from a shelf built into the plastered stone wall, near the arched plank door. "I will write it out for you," she said, resting the tablet on a small oak table.

She bent over the tablet and he set aside his wine cup to go stand beside her, his weight braced on one palm as he leaned over the table to study the symbols she etched on the tablet. "Yes," he said after a moment. "I see how such a notation system could be used to develop a code."

The abbess pushed the tablet toward him. "Yet knowing the notation system is not the same as knowing the code."

"No." He took the tablet in his hand. "But I have heard one of the melodies for which I later obtained the decoded message. If I match the message to its melody written out using this notation system, the code will be obvious."

"Hmm," said the abbess, sounding unconvinced. "And if Philip wishes to communicate with an unmusical conspirator who lacks your ability to remember a melody he hears only once or twice?"

He glanced up to flash her a wide smile. "Then I suppose the conspirator would need a jongleur to remember the melody and write it down for him. Your hypothetically unmusical conspirator would only need the key."

She sat very still, gazing back at him with troubled eyes. "I have heard Henry intends to reward you for your services by giving you the hand of his ward Rosamund, thus making you the Earl of Carlyle."

He straightened with a jerk, the tablet settling back onto the table with a clatter. "How the devil did you hear that?"

She lifted one delicately arched eyebrow. "The devil had nothing to do with it, *mon fils*. The English king's chaplain is my cousin. Or had you forgotten?"

Damion kept his voice level with difficulty. "Let us hope the man is not usually so indiscreet."

"Not usually. But he knows I am always eager to hear whatever news I can of you."

She said it simply enough, her hands folded quietly against the rough cloth of her habit, the serenity of her features never faltering. But in her words he heard fourteen years' worth of pain and longing and endless, desperate hope, and he felt regret lay a bitter hand on his heart.

"I'm sorry," he said softly.

The silence in the room stretched out, became something heavy and onerous. "Why have you finally come, Damion? Why now?"

There were so many things he wanted to say to her. Too many. Too many things he had no idea how to say. The words seemed to clog his throat until it hurt and he had to turn away, walking to stare out the small window to the court below.

These were the parts of the monastery where outsiders were permitted: the almonry, hospital, stables, and guesthouse, all clustered near the gatehouse and abbess's quarters. He thought he might see Attica, but the yard lay empty except for the long shadows thrown by the westering sun.

"Tell me, Damion: If you are set to marry one of Henry's wards, what, then, is your interest in the young woman who accompanies you here?" Isabelle asked, her voice deceptively soft.

He spun to face her. "How did you know?"

"You mean, how did I know she is a woman?" She gave him a slow, almost indulgent smile. "Her heart is in her eyes each time she looks at you, Damion." The smile broadened. "I decided either you had developed some peculiar tendencies while in the East, or your young squire with the big brown eyes and long legs must not be a squire at all."

He huffed a laugh and went to lift the mulling pan from the edge of the brazier. "Like some more wine?"

She shook her head as he carefully poured a stream of the hot liquid into his own cup. "I take it the lady in question is not Rosamund of Carlyle?"

He set the posnet down beside the brazier. "No. She is the comte d'Alérion's daughter, Attica."

"Ah. I did not think she had about her the look of a common ditch wife." The abbess tilted her head to regard him with all the worldly shrewdness of a great-granddaughter of the Duke of Aquitaine. "How long has she been traveling alone in your company?"

Damion propped his shoulders against the roughly plastered wall and blew gently on his cup before taking a deep swallow of the hot, spicy wine. "More than a week."

He heard the swift, startled catch of her breath. "Then I hope for the sake of your neck that you have not already plighted your troth to Henry's ward. For d'Alérion will surely demand you marry his daughter."

Damion met his mother's penetrating gaze. "I pray to God and all the saints that he will. For God knows I will never love another."

He saw understanding dawn in the depths of her eyes. Understanding, followed swiftly by concern and a deep, soul-felt compassion. "So that is why you have come," she said softly. "Oh, Damion, don't tell me she is betrothed already."

He nodded, feeling the reality of it, the gut-wrenching possibilities of it, rip through him to tear at his insides. "To a thirteen-year-old boy named Fulk the Fat, son of the viscomte de Salers."

"But surely neither the boy nor his parents will want the match now?"

"Now that I have sullied her virtue, you mean?" He shook his head. "The Alérions are a powerful house, and part of Attica's dowry consists of three castles of considerable strategic importance to Salers. For such a combination, Yvette of Salers would marry her son to a harlot with a harelip."

"And d'Alérion?"

Damion pushed away from the wall with a quick, violent motion. "Salers seems to have defected to Richard, which means that if Henry triumphs, d'Alérion may well wish himself out of such an alliance, for he is Henry's man. But if the Old King is defeated . . . Well, Robert will need ties to Richard's camp."

He paused in his restless prowling to glance out the window again. One of the novices had come into the outer courtyard, a tall young woman who moved with an innate grace that was beautiful to see. Beautiful and familiar, for he knew who she was even before she turned, her head coming up as she watched a robin take flight.

He knew she had only borrowed the dress of a novice, so that she might move more properly among this community of sequestered women. Yet there was something so disturbing, so terrifying, even, about the sight of Attica in a nun's habit that he had to grip the stone windowsill to keep from crying out in protest.

His mother's voice came from behind him. "You did not tell her that I would be here?"

He shook his head.

There was a pause. Then Isabelle said quietly, "Does she know?"

He understood what she was asking. Through the window, he could see the familiar figure hesitate, then sink down onto a low wooden bench beneath the spreading limbs of the old oak tree that shaded the courtyard. The novice's robes flowed around her, black and enveloping, and he felt his grip on the windowsill tighten. "She knows I killed Simon de Jarnac and why. That is all."

A silence descended on the room, a silence full of old memories and old hurts and a breathless, anxious waiting.

He swung his head slowly to look at the woman beside the table.

She sat with her hands folded in the lap of her habit, her back straight and tall, her head high. At forty-two, she was still beautiful, still brilliant, still glowing with an almost palpable vitality that made him wonder how she bore this narrow, cloistered life to which she had condemned herself. She had been fifteen when she had borne him, twenty-eight when he killed the only man she had ever loved, the man she loved more than life, more than honor, more than God. Twenty-eight when she came here as a humble novice, abjuring the world and all her wealth, abjuring life as she'd known it.

"Do you still miss him?" he asked quietly.

Her lips parted, as if she gasped in pain. "With every breath."

He swallowed, hard, but did not look away. "Why did you come here? As an act of contrition for what you'd done?"

He watched in surprise as a wry smile lit up her eyes. "Oh, no. I came here seeking peace."

"And did you find it?"

She hesitated. "Of a sort."

He felt his chest lift on a sigh. "Then I rejoice for you."

He went to her, sinking down on his heels beside her, his hands closing over hers. Her fingers felt cool and fragile to his touch, and very small. He didn't remember her being so small.

"There is no way to ask a person's forgiveness for what I have done, but I am sorry," he said, his gaze caught with hers. "Sorry for killing him, and sorry for turning away from you afterward in hurt and anger. But more than anything, I'm sorry for not understanding . . ." His voice roughened, broke, so that he had to swallow again before he could go on. "I'm sorry for not understanding that you were driven by something beyond your control."

"Damion." Her hands twisted beneath his to grip him tightly. She stared at him forever, her eyes dark green pools of so many emotions. "I have prayed every day that you might find it in your heart to forgive me. But not like this. I would a thousand times rather that you had never come to understand my pain than that you should experience it yourself."

He felt his lips lift in a sad smile. "Perhaps it is my penance."

"Perhaps. Let us pray that it is only a penance and not your fate."

It was the abbey's chaplain, riding his donkey up from the village, who brought the news that Old King Henry no longer rode toward Normandy but had turned south, to Chinon.

The fat little priest was still drinking Isabelle's wine and exclaiming over the unexpected turn of events when Damion left the abbess's quarters and went in search of Attica. She was no longer in the courtyard. The rich, golden light of evening soaked the walls of the surrounding stone buildings and spilled over the trees and grass of the hillside beyond. He climbed the broad, shallow steps to the western facade of the church, pushed open the door, and went inside.

He stepped into a dim, hushed world of incense and beeswax, of row after row of thick sandstone pillars and soaring vaults and great, echoing spaces. Steep steps, cut into the rock of the hill itself and worn shiny with the devout feet of the centuries led down from the nave to the cave of the holy anchorite, preserved below. He went slowly down them, his booted footfalls and rasping spurs falling harshly into the ancient stillness.

She knelt on the flagstone floor, the dark skirts of her novice's robes pooling around her feet, her head bowed in prayer. Blessed candles blazed on the altar of Sainte-Geneviève, their hazy smoke curling up to a low ceiling blackened by hundreds of years' worth of candles. In the faint light she seemed oddly ephemeral and beyond his grasp, simply one in an endless procession of black-clad, celibate women who had knelt here in prayer through the ages. As she made the sign of the cross and rose, the black cloth of her veil fell forward to hide her features and he felt it again, that unsettling whisper of shifting time, as if he looked at a vision of the future. A future that terrified him.

She turned, a brilliant smile lighting up her face at the sight of him. The disturbing illusion shattered, became but a memory. Yet as he took her hand and walked with her up the stairs and into the sunshine, the memory lingered, cold and heavy on his heart.

"Chinon?" She stared at Damion with wide, incredulous eyes. "Henry rides to Chinon? But . . . why?"

Around them, the long, ripening grass of the meadow swayed golden and sweet in the early evening breeze. After leaving the church they had come here, to the meadow below the cluster of monastery buildings. Here he had told her some—although not quite all—of what had passed in the abbess's quarters. Then he told her of the chaplain's news.

She stood very still, looking out over the broad valley of the Loire below. He watched her eyes narrow with concentration, as if she thought she could somehow *see* the reason—find it there, a week's ride to the south, where the castle of Chinon stood tall and strong on its bluff above the Vienne River. "Why?" she said again.

"I don't know. It's the last thing I would have expected Henry to do." He came up behind her, his arms sliding around her waist to draw her slim, warm body back against him. From here they could see the haze of smoke and dust that hung over the valley like a shroud of war. He rested his chin on her shoulder. She tilted her head sideways, and he rubbed his partially open mouth against her soft cheek.

He ached for her, ached with the need to lay her down in the sweet, flower-strewn grass and make love to her slowly, tenderly, the way he had sworn he would do. Instead, he was leaving her.

"I want to leave for Chinon at first light," he said, his grip on her tightening as he breathed in the scent of her, the scent of sunlight and fresh air and woman. It was so hard, so hard to get out what he had to say next. "I would ask that you stay here."

She swung to face him, her lips parting in surprise and hurt, her chest heaving as if he'd just kicked her in the stomach. "No. I want to be with you."

He snagged her arm when she would have jerked back. "Attica. Listen to me. Whatever is happening, Henry needs what I can tell him about Philip's code, and he needs it as quickly as possible. I can travel much faster if I'm alone." He paused. "Faster and safer."

She searched his face, her beautiful brown eyes sad but resigned, for he had used the one argument he knew she wouldn't fight against. And he felt like the lowest kind of scoundrel for doing it, because he wasn't being entirely honest with her about all of his reasons for not wanting her with him. But he would do anything to keep her out of danger.

"I don't want you to go," she said, her voice low and broken. "I don't want you to leave me."

He entwined her fingers with his, drawing her up to him. "I know. I don't want to leave you." He touched her cheeks, his fingers tracing the features of her face. His thumb snagged on the edge of her wimple, and with a guttural exclamation of impatience, he tore away both wimple and veil. Thrusting his spread hands through the hair at the side of her head, he framed her cheeks with his palms, held her steady for his kiss.

He took her mouth in a deep, violent kiss full of longing and need and hopeless love, all tangled up with a man's surging desires and a deep, nameless fear that tore through him, lending a note of savagery to the way he moved his lips across hers and thrust his tongue between her lips. She let out a low whimper, only instead of pulling away from him, she leaned into him, her fingers digging into his shoulders, her body pressing urgently against his. She tasted of passion and heartbreak and fear, and he never, never wanted to let her go.

The church bell began to ring, tolling the evening office, the great, hollow clang ringing out over the hillside. He didn't want to stop kissing her. His mouth left hers slowly, reluctantly, coming back again, then again, their breath mingling hot and damp, their eyes fixed with longing and need and the aching knowledge that he rode into danger, that this might be virtually the last time they ever kissed, ever touched. For one sharp, howling moment, he wondered wildly if he could bear it.

"You'll be careful," she said, her chest heaving, her eyes wide and shiny with unshed tears, her gaze traveling over his face, as if desperate to memorize each feature. "You will."

He rubbed his open mouth against hers. "I will. I will."

The stillness of dawn hung heavily over the mountainside, the air cool and damp with mist. Damion worked quickly, running the brush over the bay destrier's withers and flanks, the lantern hanging from a hook on the side of the stall casting a warm pool of golden light that left most of the stables in darkness.

He was reaching for the saddle blanket when the sound of footsteps approaching the stable door brought his head around. A darkly robed figure appeared out of the luminous mist. He had been expecting Attica. Instead, it was Isabelle d'Anjou who paused at the edge of the lantern light.

The big destrier swung his head, snorting out a breath, his hooves moving restlessly in the straw. "Where is your 'squire'?" she asked, faintly smiling.

"In the kitchen, doubtless packing my saddlebags with enough food to keep a small army happy." Damion tossed the blanket over the horse's broad back. "Why?"

She came to stand on the big stallion's far side, her head thrown back, her hands thrust deep into the opposite sleeves for warmth. "Because I want to know what it is you're not telling me."

He smoothed the blanket in place, deliberately giving her his most charming smile. "What makes you think I'm not telling you something?"

"That smile, for one thing," she said, making him laugh. "Attica may believe you told me everything last night. I know you held something back."

He swung away to grab his saddle and settle it on the destrier's big back. Last night, after vespers, he and Attica had spent hours in the abbess's quarters. Together, they had told Isabelle about Attica's flight, first from Salers, then from the protection of her own uncle. But he had sensed, even then, that Isabelle knew he was hiding something.

She said, "Damion, if you are going to leave that poor child with me, I think I need to know." She paused. "In case you don't come back."

He tossed the stirrup up and reached for the girth. "All right." He yanked the girth tight, then reached across the withers to hook the breastplate to the far side of the saddle. Straightening, he met her gaze steadily across the horse's high back. "Last night, when we told you about the Parisian courtier, and the viscomtesse de Salers, and the castellan of Laval, do you remember what you said?"

"I said you made it sound as if every noble from Brittany to Maine has been plotting against Henry."

He nodded. "It sounds ridiculously improbable"—he settled the reins around the stallion's neck and slipped the bit into its mouth—"until you think, what is the connection between Salers and Laval and the king?"

"Stephen d'Alérion," she said.

He nodded, lifting the bridle's headpiece up over the horse's ears and easing out the forelock. "Not only that, Stephen is one of only three or four men who know the real reason behind my journey to Brittany and Ireland." He buckled the throatlatch and reached for the noseband.

"Yet you say the castellan of Laval knew of it?"

Damion nodded.

His mother studied him with bright, intelligent eyes. "Attica doesn't realize you suspect her brother?"

He turned away. "No."

"I think you're making a mistake by not telling her."

He huffed a humorless laugh. "Do you honestly think she'd agree to stay here if she did know?"

Isabelle shook her head. "No." She lifted the lantern from its hook, her gaze searching his face. "Tell me, Damion: If it comes to a choice between your loyalty to Henry, and her brother's life, which will you choose?"

Through the stable's open doors he could see the sky bleaching white now with the rising of the sun. A cock crowed, undulating its jubilant cry to the morning. Damion gathered the reins in his hand and wheeled the warhorse to face the open door. His chest felt oddly tight. He sucked in a deep breath of air rich with the familiar scents of ripe hay and warm horseflesh. And still he felt it, that inner torment, tearing him apart.

He lifted his head, his gaze searching the swirling mist. He could hear her now, hear Attica running across the courtyard toward him. Running to him, because she didn't know. She didn't know what he was about to do.

He was aware of Isabelle, coming to stand beside him, although he didn't look at her and he didn't answer her question. There was no need. They both knew his choice had already been made.

CHAPTER
NINETEEN

Attica raced up the tightly spiraling staircase, her lungs straining to suck in air. The leather soles of her shoes slapped the endlessly circling stone steps, her outflung hands pushing off the curving stone walls as she tore up the church tower. Round and around she ran, hot, sweating, grazing her knuckles, as she hurried to reach the top of the tower in time to catch one last glimpse of him.

She burst through to the upper landing, the cool mist slapping her in the face as she lunged to the arched opening that overlooked the valley below. Her hands curling over the stone windowsill, she stared out over the clustered rooftops of the monastery to where the road wound down the mountainside and disappeared into a thick stand of pine.

He was there, at the edge of the wood, a solitary rider mounted on a great dark charger. Wisps of mist still trailed through the trees, but the sun was up now, shining out of a blue sky, glinting off the burnished steel of his helmet.

"Damion," she called, leaning out the opening, her arms waving.

He swung about, the restless horse dancing beneath him, his head falling back as he stared up at the monastery. His cloak billowed out around him in the breeze and the dark stallion reared up, its great hooves slashing the sky.

She saw him raise his hand in a brief salute, saw him wheel and touch his heels to the horse's sides. She heard the thud of hooves, echoing up the hill, saw the swish of the bay's dark tail. Then horse and rider disappeared into the forest, leaving the mountainside silent and empty.

Her hand fell slowly back to her side. A sob burned in her chest. She sucked in air, trying to ease the pain before it escaped as a wail. She pressed her fist to her lips, aware of light footfalls and the soft swish of robes behind her.

A cool hand touched her shoulder. "Come, my child," said Isabelle d'Anjou.

Attica turned and went into his mother's arms.

"I understand Damion told you what happened that night," said Isabelle d'Anjou, the skirt of her black habit fluttering in the breeze as she stood looking out over the quietly lapping waters of the pond. "That night fourteen years ago."

From her seat on a nearby low stone wall, Attica stared at the abbess, standing so straight and self-composed and at peace. After Damion rode away they had come here, to the reed-edged pond that helped to supply the convent's table with fish. The sun had burned away all traces of the mist by now, but the air was still fresh and clean. The sharp slap of ducks hitting the water as they came in to land mingled with the other sounds drifting down the hill from the monastery buildings—the lowing of cows waiting to be milked, the baaing of sheep jostling through the gate on the way to the high meadows. But they were too far away from anyone else for their words to be overheard, and suddenly Attica knew that was why they had come here.

She said, "He had an idea that if I knew what he'd

done—knew the truth of it—then I would turn away from him. But he was wrong."

The figure beside the pond did not move. "Damion didn't tell you the truth, Attica. Or at least not all of it. He couldn't, you see, for he is bound by a sworn oath."

The sun shone warm on Attica's back, but she felt a chill deep within. She didn't think she wanted to hear what Damion's mother was about to say. "You don't need to tell me," said Attica swiftly.

Isabelle turned, showing a face as impassive and uncompromising as Damion's own. "But I do. I'm the only one who can. He made that oath to me."

She held Attica's gaze a moment longer, then swung away again to look out over the distant valley. She stood very still, staring at the horizon. But Attica had the impression she looked far beyond it, into the past.

"I was fourteen years old the day I first set eyes on Simon de Jarnac," said Isabelle, her voice measured and calm. "He was in the party that came to my home to escort me to Poitiers, where I was to marry his father, Hugh.

"The night before we were to leave it had snowed. As I came down the steps to the litter, I was aware of someone stepping forward to help me. It was Simon, but I didn't take his hand; I didn't even look at him. Not then. I needed all of my willpower and concentration simply to force myself to get into that litter."

It was a scene Attica could imagine only too easily. The freezing morning, the light fall of snow blanketing the castle, the horses' hooves restless on the frozen earth, their breath steamy in the cold air. The young girl, sick with the knowledge that she was leaving her home forever, frightened of the future that had been thrust upon her.

"And then, two steps from the bottom, I slipped." Isabelle

swallowed, her smooth white throat working with the effort of what she had to say. "I slipped, and Simon caught me in his arms. It was so sudden, we both laughed. He was only fifteen himself, but already as big and tall as a man, and fiercely, wonderfully beautiful. I looked up into his eyes and I was lost. Forever."

Attica felt the shock of Isabelle's words rip through her. For some reason, she had assumed that the love between Isabelle d'Anjou and her husband's son had grown after Hugh's death. For if it had begun earlier, if it had been there from the beginning, then their relationship had been not only incestuous but adulterous as well.

"What did you do?" Attica asked quietly.

"I did what I had to do, of course. I climbed into the litter, and I traveled to Poitiers, and I married Hugh. Only I couldn't seem to stop myself from looking at Simon, and it wasn't long before I realized that Simon was looking back."

Attica sat very still, watching the drab brown ducks floating on the pond, their paddling feet sending gentle ripples undulating over the surface of the placid water.

"There are many kinds of love," said the abbess quietly. "Ours was deep and rich and profoundly spiritual, yet it was also . . . hungry. That wild hunger that burns and torments day and night, that steals the will, saps resolve. We fought it. For a time. But we were very young, and Hugh would go off for weeks, often months, leaving us alone."

Attica curled her fingers over the sharp rocks at her sides. "You don't need to tell me this."

"No," said Isabelle. "You need to know." She thrust her hands deep into her sleeves. "For there came a day, you see, when we simply couldn't stop ourselves. Afterward, we were horrified by what we had done. I had betrayed my husband, and Simon had betrayed his own father. Yet as wretched and guilt stricken as we were, we knew that as long as we were around each other, it would inevitably happen again. So he went away.

"He went away, and he stayed away until Hugh de Jarnac died. I sometimes think it broke Hugh's heart, Simon leaving like that. He couldn't understand, you see, what had driven Simon away."

Attica stared out over the meadow, where tiny blue and white butterflies danced among the daisies and buttercups and yarrow. "He never knew?"

"No. Although he always suspected that Damion was not his own son." She lifted her head, her face strained now by a softly tragic expression. "It's why he was so hard on Damion when he was young, why he made certain Damion's inheritance would consist of only one small manor."

Attica made a curious sound in her throat, her hand coming up as if she could ward off what she was about to hear.

"And Hugh was right," continued the abbess, her voice calm and flat. "He wasn't Damion's father; he was his grandfather." She paused, and in the sudden stillness Attica could hear the buzzing of the honey bees in the meadow and the slapping of the wind-whipped water against the pond's edge. "Simon wasn't Damion's brother, Attica; he was his father. The man Damion killed on that dreadful stormy night was his own father."

"Damion knows?" whispered Attica.

"He knows." The black veil fell forward, hiding Isabelle's face as she bowed her head. "Simon told him right before he died."

The men sprawled naked and bloody at the edge of the road, the afternoon sun hot on their pale dead flesh. They had been stripped of everything—armor, boots, even braies. Attica only knew they had once been knights because she drew rein and forced herself to look at their faces. Just in case.

She twisted away, nausea roiling in her stomach, one hand gripping the wooden pommel before her. *Thank God, thank God, thank God,* neither of those bloated, hideous faces belonged to the man she loved. Yet she knew them; they were two of the knights who had been sent after her from Châteauhaut.

The sudden trill of a blackbird deep in the forest brought her head up. An unearthly stillness hung over the glade, broken only by the shrill buzzing of the flies. Tugging her left rein, she drew the gray around in a tight circle, her anxious gaze scanning the quietly drooping branches of scrub oak and ash, all her muscles so tense that she was quivering.

"If I were anyone else, lordling, you would be dead meat right now."

Attica gasped, her heart seeming to stop beating only to start up again and slam against her ribs, hard. "*Damion.* Thank God."

The bay destrier appeared from beneath the trees, the knight in the saddle looking tall and lean and grim faced. "*Cross of Christ, Attica.*" He rode at her, his big warhorse looming over the smaller gray until he was close enough that she could see the deeply accentuated lines bracketing his lips, see the dilated pupils in his hard green eyes. "What in the name of all that's holy are you *doing* here?"

She met his gaze squarely. "Looking for you."

She heard his saddle leather creak as he reached out one gloved hand to grasp her behind the head. "Are you mad?" He tightened his grip, forcing her head around so that she had no choice but to look at the mutilated, discolored bodies of the dead knights. "Look at those men." He held her brutally when she would have jerked away. "Don't you realize what could have happened to you before you found me? What can *still* happen to you, by God?"

She wrenched out of his grip, her stomach heaving. "I know."

His dark eyes blazed at her from out of a harsh, tight face. "Then why the devil did you leave Sainte-Geneviève?"

She met his gaze squarely. "Because I know the main reason you wanted me to stay was to keep me out of danger. Because I realized I'd rather be with you and in danger than at the convent and safe. Because in less than a month I may be Fulk the Fat's bride, and I don't want to spend the rest of my life remembering the little time we had together, and wishing I had found the courage to seize a few days more."

A strange tightness came over his face, as if he were able to contain a rush of unwanted emotions only with effort. "Christ, Attica," he said, his voice unexpectedly gentle, almost hushed. "We could die before we get to Chinon."

She swallowed, a queer smile trembling her lips. "It's worth it."

"You're mad," he said on a rough expulsion of breath. Leaning forward, he caught her face between his hands and seized her mouth in a long, desperate kiss. "I shouldn't be glad you're here." His breath rushed warm and moist against her face as he kissed her eyes, her forehead, her nose. "I shouldn't be. But I am. God help me, I am."

Near dusk, they came upon a small manor house set in the midst of lush, gently rolling fields and scattered small copses of beech and poplar. It seemed a prosperous manor, from the looks of it, sturdily built of tuff and slate and surrounded by a high wooden palisade. But when they urged their horses at a slow walk through the untended gate-house, they found the yard lying silent and empty before them, the open gate swinging in the warm wind as if the last person through it had left so quickly he hadn't both-ered to secure it.

A swift search of the nearby village located the steward, who told them the lord and his family had retreated to a less comfortable but more heavily fortified manor up in the hills. Most of the lord's servants had fled as well, he said, along with any from the village who could. No one, it seemed, knew which way the French or English king would be marching next, but no one wanted to be in their way.

"I'm certain my lord would make you welcome, were he here," said the steward, pulling at one earlobe as he cast nervous sidelong glances at Damion's long sword.

And so they stayed. By the light of a single lamp, they ate their supper on the cool earthen floor of the absent lord's kitchen. They sat cross-legged, knee to knee, while they ate sausages and figs and crusty day-old bread washed down with fresh buttermilk. As they ate, Damion watched the flickering light cast temptingly mysterious shadows across Attica's downturned face. He remembered the way her breasts felt in his hands, the way she quivered when he eased his hand down her flat stomach. He thought about how badly he wanted to touch her, to taste her, to take her—but slowly this time, the way he had promised.

She wiped her fingers daintily, her head lifting so that she looked into his face. She smiled at him with her eyes, and he took her hand. Together they rose and crossed the yard to the small hall. Hand in hand, they climbed the wooden steps to the single solar above, a small but com-fortable chamber wainscoted with painted wooden panels.

Damion had expected the lord to have taken his bed when he fled, but it still stood upon a dais in the chamber, a massive oaken frame hung with fine green wool drapes and piled high with a feather mattress and a marten fur coverlet that gleamed in the light of his torch.

"Ah," he said, thrusting the torch into a bracket. "I've been wanting to find us a bed, and here it is."

Her laughter joined his as she caught both his hands in hers, pulling him to her. "It's like an enchanted house that has been waiting here. Just for us."

He drew her closer, their hands still joined between them. "And we shall make this as our wedding night." His gaze locked with hers, he lifted her hand to his lips and kissed the finger that led to her heart. "With my body, I thee worship," he said solemnly. "And with my heart, I thee endow."

He watched her move about the room, lighting the lamps and torches and candles, her gaze coming back to him over and over again. He shut the door behind them with one booted foot, shutting out the warm wind that flickered the cressets and stirred the short curls about her soft white neck as she turned to face him. A kind of hushed wonder hung about them, a stillness as complete as if they were indeed alone in the world. It was what they needed, he thought: an enchanted world of their own, a world without duty and advantageous marriage alliances, without traitorous brothers and dangerous, conflicting loyalties. Without agonizing, fateful choices.

She stood motionless in the center of the chamber, her eyes huge in a pale face, her chest rising and falling with each breath. She looked slender and oddly vulnerable in her short cropped hair and borrowed men's clothing. And he loved her so much in that moment, he ached with it.

"It's strange," she said. "I wasn't nervous, before, in the meadow." She smiled at him shyly. "But I am now."

He crossed to stand before her, close enough that he could have touched her, although he did not. "So am I," he whispered, returning her smile.

She breathed, her nostrils flaring. "Will you take off your clothes?"

His gaze caught hers and held it as he took a step back, his hands unbuckling his belt and letting it drop to the floor. His boots followed, then his chausses, the rushes whispering at his feet. He untied the laces at his neck, drawing tunic and shirt over his head at the same time. He tossed them aside and stood before her bare-chested, his eyes recapturing hers as his hands dropped to the fastening of his braies.

He saw her suck in a deep breath that lifted her breasts, the torchlight flaring in the dark pupils of her eyes as he untied his braies and shoved them down over hip and buttocks until he stood naked before her, the air cool and sweet against his hot skin.

She reached out, slowly, to lay her palm flat against his bare chest. He stood utterly still beneath her touch. Slowly, she slid her hand to his shoulder, down his upper arm, to his chest again. She said, "It's a wicked thing, I know, the pleasure I take in your body. The way I long to see you. To touch you." She sighed. "I can't seem to help it."

He carefully untied the laces at her throat. "How can it be wicked when our bodies are God's handiwork? Shouldn't we appreciate what he has made?"

A smile lit up her features. "I think he made you very fine." Her breath hitched as he ran his hands down her breasts to unfasten her belt and strip away her tunic.

He undressed her slowly, his hands gentle but sure, until at last they both stood naked in the glowing light of the torches. She took his hands and put them on her slim waist. He drew her to him, enfolding her in his arms as he buried his face in her hair. She smelled of the sun and the open air and herself, and he breathed deeply, his eyes squeezing shut at the simple, sweet joy of having her in his arms. A joy so piercing he ached.

He snagged his fingers in her hair, pressed a kiss against the smooth flesh of her neck. He felt her shudder, her hands gripping his shoulders as she turned her head, her lips seeking his.

He took her mouth in a hot, wet kiss of passion and possession and wild, desperate longing. Then he bent, catching her behind the knees to swing her up into his arms and carry her to that big, curtained bed.

Together they fell across the coverlet, the fur cool and sleek and wickedly sensual against his bare flesh. He rolled with her until she lay flat on her back and he above her, their lips close but not touching, his gaze locked with hers, their breath rasping shallow and rapid, their bodies pressed intimately together.

He was shaking with the urge to spread her legs wide and simply bury himself inside her. But more than his own pleasure he wanted hers. Dipping his head, he rubbed his open mouth against hers, then shifted his weight to the side, keeping one leg thrown possessively over her as he touched her.

He touched her with his eyes, and his hands, and his lips. He traced the curve of first one breast, then the other, with his tongue. He sucked one wine-red peak into his mouth and smiled against her wet flesh as she cried out in pleasure, her head falling back, her neck gleaming white in the torchlight, her back lifting off the bed as she arched up against him.

He made love to her breasts, explored all her secret places—the soft flesh below her ear, the intriguing hollows beside her pelvic bones, the silken skin behind her knees. She touched him, too, learned his man's body and what brought a catch of pleasure to his throat. He watched her face tighten with desire, her eyes go wide with wonder. Then he knelt between her legs, and she tangled her fingers in his hair, holding his head to her, gasping as he touched her there, where her legs met. Touched her and kissed her and delighted her.

Beneath his spread hands, the flesh of her buttocks quivered, grew damp with arousal. When neither of them could stand it anymore, he slid his body up hers until he covered her, his weight braced on his outflung arms so that he could watch her face as he entered her.

She stared up at him, her eyes dark and wide and shining with love, her splayed hands gripping his shoulders, her fingers digging into the taut muscles of his back.

"We are one," he said, his voice rough as he moved within her, his breath rasping in his throat, the muscles of his arms quivering with the need for control. "Feel me, a part of you."

She sighed his name, her arms twining about his neck, her long legs coming up to wrap around his hips and hold him close to her, drawing him deeper, deeper inside her. He made love to her with his body, with his mouth, with the sweet words he whispered until passion overwhelmed them and speech became impossible. And then, when it was time, he withdrew himself from her and they were two again.

They were two, and though he held her in his arms, pulling her tight up against him, she wept, and the night around them seemed suddenly cool and dark and lonely.

* * *

He awoke in the early hours of the dawn to find her watching him, her eyes wide and solemn. He pulled her to him, and she came hotly into his arms. He took her in swift, savage lust, a coupling of gasping breaths and wet, sucking bodies, of desperate need and unsure tomorrows.

Then they rose and put on their clothes and left the hall.

The sun was just stirring over the eastern hills as they turned their horses south and rode away.

For four days they rode through the soft, luminous landscape that stretched to the Loire River and beyond. They passed wet pastures hedged with ash, splashed through marshes and heaths and wet woodlands, cut across vast undulating planes scattered with wary villages and guarded manors. The nights they spent wherever they could be alone. It was as if they moved through their own private world. A world about to end as, on the morning of the fifth day, they came to the plateau of Chinon.

Attica reined in, her head falling back as she stared up at the distant castle. Built high on a bluff, it seemed to loom over the village and river below it, a beautiful if threateningly massive fortress of sun-soaked, golden-white walls and round towers that thrust up against a hard blue sky.

"I don't want you to misunderstand me on this," said Damion suddenly, his gaze still fixed on the distant castle, "but I would ask that you not tell Stephen what I have learned of Philip's code."

Her sudden jerk startled the roan, so that it moved restlessly beneath her. *"Mother of God—"* She sucked in a quick breath and steadied her horse. "Surely you do not suspect him? *Stephen?"*

"No, of course not," he said, a muscle tightening along his jaw. "But you know as well as I do that Stephen's face is almost as easy to read as yours. I fear he would find such information difficult to keep to himself."

She let her gaze drop to the reins threaded between her fingers. As much as she didn't like it, in her heart she knew what he said was true. Stephen's eyes always blazed with wild excitement whenever he found himself embarked on what he considered a great adventure. "You're right. I won't tell him."

"Thank you." He paused. "Attica?"

She glanced up to find him watching her, his features oddly strained. The wind gusted around them, rustling the leaves of the walnut trees overhead and lifting his hair where it lay against his forehead. His face looked gaunt, tight with an agony that mirrored her own.

"No matter what happens, I will always love you," he said.

"I know," she said, her chest tight with pain as she watched him knee his horse forward. Toward Chinon.

She wasn't surprised, somehow, when Sergei met them some half a league from the castle.

They came upon him sitting at the edge of a flower-strewn meadow, his horse's reins in his hand, his back against the trunk of an old walnut tree, his chin resting on his chest as if he dozed. As Attica drew rein, he awoke with a jerk.

"You're late," he said, pushing up with a wide, engaging grin. "I expected you an hour ago."

She threw a quick glance at Damion, whose eyes crinkled with secret amusement. They would have reached Chinon an hour earlier if they hadn't decided to pause beside a pretty and very secluded pond.

"How is Henry?" Damion asked as Sergei scrambled up onto the back of his palfrey and urged the bay up beside them.

"Ill. Very ill," said Sergei, his face suddenly serious. "It's why he's come here, rather than fleeing to Normandy and England as he first planned. If he is to die, then he wants to die in Anjou."

"I suppose it's natural." Damion tilted his head back as he let his gaze rove thoughtfully over the approaching battlements. "He was born in Anjou."

"And my brother?" Attica asked.

"He's well, my lady. He was at the king's side in the flight from Le Mans. I fear our departure was less than organized," he added almost apologetically to Damion. "But I managed to save all your horses, sire. And your trunks." He cast a critical glance over his lord's bedraggled appearance. "You look in sore need of a change of clothes."

Damion laughed, while Sergei turned his strange eyes toward Attica. "I've found you a gown, too, my lady, although I had to get someone to sew a band around the hem to make it long enough."

Attica smiled her thanks. She didn't ask how he'd known she was coming, when she was supposed to have stayed in Laval.

She let her reins go slack, the roan ambling along behind the other horses as she listened with only half an ear to Damion's rapid questions and Sergei's slow, careful responses. She felt as if she were tightening up inside, tighter and tighter, the closer they came to Chinon. By the time they passed through the castle's arched gateway, she felt almost sick with mingling hope and dread.

"Don't despair, my lady," said Sergei softly, his eyes warm with concern as he helped her dismount near the stables. She looked at him in surprise, but he was already turning away to address the slim, dark-haired lad who came to help with the horses.

"Run and fetch the comte d'Alérion," Sergei said in a low voice.

"There is no need," said the lad, nodding up the hill. "He comes hither."

"My father is here?" Joy leapt in Attica's heart as she swung about, her gaze searching the crowded castle ward for the imposing figure of Robert d'Alérion.

Instead she saw a tall, slender young man with fair hair, his even features set in unusually serious lines as he walked toward her. "But that's not the comte d'Alérion," she said, laughing with delight at the sight of her brother's handsome, beloved face. "That's—"

She broke off as the significance of the title struck her, her throat suddenly raw, her heart pounding so hard it was like a buzz in her ears. She walked up to him.

"Stephen? Where is Papa?" She searched his face, her head shaking back and forth in insistent, useless denial. "Tell me it isn't true. Oh, please God, tell me it isn't true."

He stared down at her, his eyes liquid with his own pain. He opened his mouth and took a deep breath, then couldn't seem to get the words out. But it didn't matter anymore because she could see the truth in his eyes.

The pain of it hit her with a physical blow that doubled her over, her arms crossing at her stomach as she tried to suck in air. She felt Stephen's hand on her shoulder but she jerked away from him, suddenly, irrationally furious with him. Then her rage collapsed and she whirled back to bury her face against his chest, her fingers clutching at the fine cloth of his tunic. "Oh, Papa," she whispered. "Papa, Papa."

Stephen hesitated a moment, then folded his arms around her and held her awkwardly as the tears came and she wept for their dead father.

CHAPTER
TWENTY

Attica stood on the battlements of Chinon castle, her head held high, a hot, dry wind rushing out of the west to slap her cheeks and sting her eyes.

She felt a stranger to herself. She was not this grieving woman, staring unseeingly over the sun-drenched slate rooftops of the town of Chinon below. She found it impossible to believe that a few weeks' ride to the north, at his favorite hunting lodge in Normandy, Robert d'Alérion did not still live. Impossible to believe she would never again hear his great, booming voice, or see his swift smile, that she would have to go on missing him like this for the rest of her life. The awful finality of it crushed her; it was simply too much to bear.

"He died in Normandy," said Stephen, coming up beside her. "Weeks ago. I sent word to Salers as soon as the news came." He braced his arms against the parapet edging the chateau's high wall walk and leaned into them. "Obviously, by the time my messenger arrived, you had already gone."

Something in his voice made her turn her head to look at him. "You sound as if you think I should not have left. As if I should have stayed at Châteauhaut and let Henry be taken at La Ferté-Bernard."

She watched the sudden rise of color to her brother's

high cheekbones. "No, of course not. But . . . God's teeth! I've feared you dead. Anything could have happened to you out there. Anything." His gaze swept her, from the short curls flying about her face to her torn chausses, before he turned his head away again, his jaw held tight. "I know what kind of man Damion de Jarnac is, so you need not fear I suspect you of any impropriety. But you have been alone with him for the better part of two weeks, Attica. You must surely realize that people are talking—" He broke off and swallowed hard. "Thank God Fulk of Salers hasn't decided to repudiate you. By rights he could have done so, you know. *And* demanded to keep your dowry."

She held herself very still. From the bailey below came the high-pitched whirling screech of a grinding wheel sharpening a sword. A tumult filled the air: the hoarse shouts of men stockpiling baskets of stones for use as missiles, the squeal of pigs about to be butchered, the rumble of carts bringing in bags of rye and barrels of salted fish and all the other supplies the garrison of a castle under siege might need.

"How do you know Fulk has no wish to repudiate me?" she asked quietly.

Stephen pushed himself upright and swung to face her. "Because Yvette is here with Philip in Anjou, demanding that you be returned for your wedding."

Attica searched her brother's tightly held features. "You would have this betrothal stand? You would ally our house with those capable of conspiring against their liege lord?"

His face suddenly went white. "The marriage alliance has already been made, Attica. Even Henry understands that. Were we to try to withdraw from it now, we should have Salers as our enemy rather than our ally. And if that were to happen, we could easily end up losing every estate we have in Brittany. Of course this betrothal must stand."

She stared at him, noticing for the first time how these past months had changed him. He'd grown leaner, she thought; leaner and harder. He was only twenty-one, yet the two parallel lines that used to appear between his eyes only when he was worried or concentrating had become permanent now.

She said, "You told me once that you did not favor this scheme of Father's, to wed me to Fulk. That you thought it wrong of him to ask such a thing of me."

He shoved the splayed fingers of one hand through his fine, tousled hair, sweeping it back from his forehead in a distracted gesture she remembered from their childhood. "I did think so at the time—as your brother. But now, as the comte d'Alérion, I understand why Father felt he had to do it."

"Stephen," she said, her voice low and throbbing with controlled emotion. "I do not wish to marry Fulk of Salers."

She saw something blaze up, hot and intransigent, in the depths of his normally gentle gray eyes. "You agreed to this betrothal, Attica."

I agreed only because I didn't know, she wanted to scream. *I didn't know, then, what I would be giving up. I didn't know.*

"You agreed to it," he said again, leaning into her, "and you said your betrothal vows. This marriage is as if done, Attica. As your soul belongs to God, your loyalty and your body belong to the man who will be your lord and husband. And whether you wish it or not, sister, that man is Fulk."

From where he stood beside the king, Damion could see her with her brother up on the battlements. He didn't like the angry set of d'Alérion's shoulders or the controlled way Attica held herself, as if she were reaching down inside herself for the strength to endure.

If he had to, thought Damion, he would fight the world to make her his. But he didn't see how he was going to fight Attica herself.

"You have served me well, de Jarnac," said Henry, giving Damion's shoulder a staggering buffet that jerked his attention back to the king. "Were it not for the warning brought by your squire, Philip and Richard should have taken me at La Ferté-Bernard like a pigeon in a knave's net. You shall be rewarded well."

"It is Attica d'Alérion who deserves your thanks, not I, Your Grace. She's the one who first discovered the plot against you, and risked much to warn you of it."

"So your squire tells me." A peculiarly harried expression came over the old king's face. "Although if she could have contrived to warn me without bringing the viscomtesse de Salers down on my head, I should have been even more grateful." Crossing his boxer's arms across his broad chest, he went to stand at the edge of the terrace, his bowed horseman's legs braced wide as he watched some of his knights tilting at the quintain in the yard below. The afternoon wind tossed his short-cropped hair about his head, the bold ginger threaded now with gray and thinning noticeably at the back. "Tell me truly," he said after a moment. "Has my son John joined the others against me?"

"I know he has been approached," said Damion, choosing his words very, very carefully.

Henry's hand closed into a tight fist that jerked up, then relaxed. "Well, he would be, wouldn't he? The question is, were the letters patent you discovered confirmation of an agreement already reached or simply a temptation to treason?"

"That I do not know, Your Grace."

A liver-colored bitch, one of the many hounds always to

be found cavorting at Henry's heels, jumped up to put her front paws on the king's thigh, and whimper. He fondled her ears absently, his attention swinging back to the men. The air filled with dust and the thunder of galloping hooves, the *thwunk* of lances hitting the quintain, the men's hoarse shouts of encouragement. "Look at them," said Henry. Beneath its scattering of freckles, his skin showed gray and pasty in the golden sunshine. "You say one of them may be conspiring with Richard against me." He pulled the hound's ears thoughtfully. "But you don't tell me which one."

Damion thrust his fingertips beneath his belt as he considered his next words. "There may be a way to discover it," he said, his gaze on the practice yard. He would not look at the battlements above, would not think of the possibility that the man betraying Henry—betraying them all—could be Attica's brother. "Philip communicates with his adherents by means of a musical code. A code I have broken."

"A musical code?" Snapping his fingers to call the hound, Henry turned to stroll along the river wall. Illness had slowed his characteristically restless, impetuous movements, Damion noticed; the king walked as if breathless and in pain. Any other man would have taken to his bed long since, but not Henry. "Is such a thing possible?" he asked.

"Yes," said Damion as they crossed the drawbridge to the central fortress, chickens squawking and fluttering out of the way of Henry's ponderous stride. "The genius of the system lies in the ability of its messengers to pass unremarked from place to place. I understand there is a band of wandering minstrels in the castle right now, preparing to perform at tonight's banquet."

Henry stopped so abruptly that the small page following behind with a cup of ale almost ran into the king's heels. "God's bones," he roared, his eyes flashing with a quick flare of temper. "I shall have them seized and put to the torture immediately. If there is a traitor in my household, I shall know his name before nightfall. His name, and his game."

"Your Grace," said Damion calmly, "the minstrels know their songs, but not the messages they contain or even the code itself. It's doubtful they know who amongst all those seated at your table is actually in contact with Philip."

Henry rested his fists on his hips, his round head jutting forward intimidatingly. "Are you saying I should let the knaves go?"

"I am saying that if you allow the jongleurs to play unmolested, then Philip will remain none the wiser to what we have discovered and we may continue to intercept his messages."

The king grunted in disbelief. "Out of an entire evening's entertainment, how can you possibly know which melody contains a message?"

"The coded melodies always begin with the same series of notes. I'll know."

"Huh." Henry seized the cup of ale from the trembling boy and drank deeply, his eyes narrowing in thought. "You will sit beside me at the banquet tonight, de Jarnac," he said after a moment, wiping his mouth with the back of his hand. "We will let these damned traitorous jongleurs play. And then perhaps we shall see whether or not one of my men deserves to have his head on a pike, decorating my castle gate."

"Yes, Your Grace," said Damion, bowing. For one moment he allowed his gaze to drift back to the battlements. But Attica and her brother had disappeared.

She sat beside the grassy banks of the castle's moat, her heart heavy with worry as she watched a couple of knaves

work to haul in the wicker eel traps and empty them into
baskets. It was early evening now, the light spilling across
the countryside in a rich, golden flood.

The water here ran clear, kept fresh by a stream that
spilled into the Vienne. She drew her knees up to her chest,
conscious of the heavy folds of soft midnight blue wool
about her ankles, the weight of her woman's girdle lying
low on her hips. It seemed strange, somehow, to be dressed
as a woman again. She felt feminine, almost beautiful even,
and yet, disturbingly, less free. A breeze swelled, shifting
the tall reeds beside her with a faint sigh that sounded sweet
and soft and vaguely melancholy.

And she knew he was there.

She turned her head, a smile touching her lips as she
watched de Jarnac cut across the meadow, his stride lean
and long-legged, the wind stirring the dark hair on his bare
head. He wore a woolen tunic of rich brown trimmed at the
neck and cuffs with bands of fine cream work embroidery.
His chainse showed white at his throat, contrasting vividly
with the dark tan of his skin. He looked magnificent.

He sank down into the grass at her side, a sparkle lighting up the depths of his green eyes as he let his gaze travel
over her own finery in a way that reminded her how sel-
dom he had seen her dressed as a woman. "Sergei said I
should find you here."

She wrapped her arms around her legs, hugging them
closer. "I won't ask how Sergei knew."

Damion laughed softly. "No, don't." He sobered quickly,
his gaze searching her face. "I take it your brother still favors your betrothal to Fulk?"

She nodded, turning half away to stare off across the river.
"I will speak to him again tomorrow, after he has had time to
think about it more calmly. He is angry now. He's been so

afraid that something must have happened to me on the road here." She paused. "I have not told him of our feelings for one another. I fear that would only enrage him further."

There was a heavy silence. Then de Jarnac said, "And if Stephen still insists you fulfill the marriage agreement? Have you thought what you will do then, Attica?"

She hugged herself tighter, as if she could somehow hold herself together, as if she could keep her world—keep *herself* from flying apart. "Then I shall approach Henry and throw myself on his mercy." Stephen would never forgive her for it, of course. Her heart ached with the pain that thought brought, but she knew she could bear it, if the alternative was to lose Damion. The problem was, she didn't know what she would do if Henry refused to support her. She was afraid Damion would ask her that, but he didn't.

"Attica?"

She swung her head to find him watching her, his face taut with desire and need. Reaching up, he touched her cheek with his fingertips, his eyes taking on that hooded, sleepy look she knew so well. His head dipped toward her. Beside them, one of the knaves called out to the other, then laughed as the eel trap they were emptying fell into the water with a splash. Damion flashed her a quick smile and let his hand drop.

"I must get back," he said, pushing to his feet. "Henry is an impatient taskmaster."

She rested her chin on her hands, her breath easing out of her in a long sigh as she watched him stand up. "I was sitting here, wishing we'd never had to come to this place. That we could simply have kept riding, just the two of us, forever."

"Our forever will come," he said. "You'll see." But then he left her there, to her thoughts, and to the lonely whispers of the wind.

*   *   *

She stayed beside the stream for a long time, reluctant to return to the crowded ladies' chamber where she had been given a place. Slowly, the shadows began to lengthen and the church bells to ring. She knew it was time to go.

She had just risen to her feet when she heard a woman's voice behind her saying, "I've been looking for you."

Attica turned to find herself confronting a handsome woman in her early twenties, richly gowned in crimson silk trimmed with gold braid. "I have brought you this," said the woman, holding out a circlet of fine gold, wrought into the shape of entwined leaves and flowers with centers of precious and semiprecious stones. Standing on tiptoe, the woman placed the circlet on Attica's short-cropped hair, then stepped back, her head tilting critically to one side. "There, the effect with the curls around your face is quite pretty."

Attica put up one hand to touch the gold circlet. "But you mustn't lend me something so fine."

The woman smiled and shook her head. "It's not a loan. It's a gift from Henry. An expression of his gratitude for your loyalty and courage." She held out her hand. "I am Alice of France. I hear your name has been joined to mine on the list of reluctant brides to be handed over to their anxious grooms."

Attica was surprised into letting out a quick laugh that ended on a wry note. So this was Alice, Princess of France. Daughter of the late French king Louis VII, and sister to his son and heir, Philip II, she had been betrothed as an infant to Richard. Only that had been twenty years ago, and the marriage had never taken place. Henry simply kept her at his court, ignoring Philip's demands that Alice either be made a bride or be returned to Paris along with her dowry—

a particularly strategic and therefore valuable bit of French soil within a day's march of Paris.

Some said Henry delayed Alice's marriage because he wanted her wed to his son John, whom he doted on, rather than to Richard, who was already too dangerous. But others whispered that Henry delayed Alice's marriage so that he could keep her in his own kingly bed. . . .

Puzzled, Attica searched the princess's face. "I don't understand. Are you saying Salers has applied to Philip for aid in securing my return?"

Alice nodded, and the two women turned to walk together along the water's edge. "The viscomtesse accuses Henry of deliberately withholding her son's betrothed. She wants you back, and Philip is standing behind her demand."

At the other woman's words, Attica had the strangest sensation, as if the world around her had suddenly dimmed and blurred. She was aware only of the slow, heavy beating of her own heart, sending the blood pounding through her body until she felt as if she were shaking, shaking on the inside with a terror such as she had never known. If her betrothal had become a matter of state . . .

In the meadow beyond the castle, some boys were playing knight, the smaller boys mounted on the shoulders of the bigger ones, each pair trying to unhorse their opponent. The two women stopped to watch, the French princess laughing gaily when one of the half-grown "knights" went sprawling into the grass. Then she glanced at Attica, and the laughter faded from her lips.

"*Mon Dieu,* you *are* reluctant, aren't you?" She reached out gently to touch Attica's hand. "I see it in your eyes. I'm sorry. I only made a jest before."

Shaking her head, her throat suddenly too full of tears to risk saying anything, Attica swung her betraying face away.

"It is not, in truth, a proper subject for jests," said the French princess, her voice suddenly and surprisingly harsh. "We women are not born to find happiness in this world, are we? Only to do our duty and bring honor and glory to our house." She stared off across the river, her last words little more than a whisper. "However miserable it may make us."

Attica looked down into the other woman's face and saw the strain of worry there, and the sadness, and a trace of the anger the French princess probably didn't acknowledge even to herself. "Will Henry do this thing?" Attica asked quietly. "Will he hand you over to Philip as part of a peace settlement?"

A pair of wild geese flew above them, the sinking sun touching their outstretched wings with gold. Alice tilted back her head, watching them a moment, her features carefully erased of all emotions before answering. "If he decides it is in the best interests of his people, then, yes, Henry will do it." She brought her gaze back to Attica's. "To me, and to you."

The weight of the delicate band of gold on Attica's head suddenly felt unbearably heavy, weighing her down. She understood now the meaning of this precious gift. She understood that Henry Plantagenet had paid what he considered his debt to her. Now, if she wished to escape her marriage to Fulk, she could expect no support from him. For the sake of peace, he would see her returned to Salers— against her will, even, if that became necessary.

Overhead, the geese dipped and wheeled, their twinned voices filling the evening sky. But Attica could not bear to look at them.

* * *

"I hate these damned banquets," growled Henry, his hands curling around the carved arms of his high-backed chair. "It's inhuman, expecting a man to sit still for so long."

Seated at the place of honor on the king's right, Damion laughed softly, while Alice put her hand on Henry's arm and said, "If you had any sense, you'd be in bed."

Henry growled again.

Torchlight gleamed on upraised brass as some half a dozen liveried trumpeters stepped forward. A fanfare rang out, bouncing off the vaulted stone ceiling of the hall and heralding the entry of a procession of pages bearing basins, ewers of water, and cloths.

Only by leaning forward was Damion able to look down the long swath of white linen-covered table to where Attica sat on the king's far side, beyond the French princess. She had her head turned, listening to something Stephen was saying. Damion willed her to glance his way. She did not.

The noise of the crowded hall swirled around him; voices rose in greeting and laughter, benches and stools scraped over the rough floor, dogs barked and chased one another beneath tables. But he was aware only of the honey-haired woman with big brown eyes and a sad, winsome smile who would not turn and look at him.

She wore a gown of soft midnight blue wool that molded itself to her high, round breasts and bared the long, smooth line of her neck. A gossamer white veil held in place by a circlet of jeweled gold framed her face in graceful folds that fell back when she raised her goblet to her lips. He watched her throat work as she drank, watched her neck arch and her breasts lift, and felt his need for her fill him until he was shaking with it, shaking with his want.

He wanted to bury his face there, in the curve of her neck, and breathe in the heady fragrance of her hair. He wanted to take her hand and lead her someplace far away from this noisy, crowded hall, someplace where he could undress her slowly and wondrously, where he could lay her down and make sweet, wild love to her. He wanted to make her his, all his, forever and ever. He wanted these things with a savageness that tore at his gut and filled him with terror. Because he was so afraid, so achingly afraid—

"I don't think you're a very gallant knight," said a young, petulant female voice at his side.

He turned to find himself staring down into the malevolent blue eyes of a pale-haired, flat-chested girl of perhaps thirteen years who sat on his other side, her head held high and haughty.

"I beg your pardon, my lady." He flashed the disagreeable little girl his most charming smile.

The girl tossed her long, straight hair so that it floated in a silken cloud around her thin shoulders. "I am Lady Rosamund of Carlyle," she said, "and this is Lady Ermengart."

Murmuring politely, Damion raised his gaze to the stern-faced woman who sat on the child's far side.

"You can't say you don't remember me, monsieur le chevalier," continued the king's ward.

Damion shook his head, not knowing whether he wanted to laugh or groan. Because the truth was, he had forgotten all about the king's ward, had forgotten that Henry had promised to reward him for his loyalty and service by giving him Rosamund of Carlyle and the rich English earldom that came with her. Everything Damion had ever wanted suddenly lay within his grasp.

But, it was no longer what he wanted.

"I am better born than you are, you know," said the girl petulantly.

Damion reached for his wine and drank deeply, his eyes

meeting hers over the rim of his cup. "Alas," he said with a sigh, "'Tis sad, but true."

"Lady Ermengart says most ladies are better born than their husbands. The problem is too many ladies and not enough husbands."

Damion felt his smile fade as he reached for his cup again. So someone had already told the girl what was planned for her, and she wasn't very happy about it. Another unwilling bride to be thrust into the arms of a man more interested in her lands than her person. He almost felt sorry for her.

Rosamund fixed him with a critical stare. "How old are you, anyway?"

He was surprised into letting out a short bark of laughter. "Last time I stopped to think about it, I was seven and twenty."

The girl sniffed, turning away to rinse her fingers daintily in the rose-scented water presented to her by a page on bended knee.

"I suppose that sounds terribly old to you, doesn't it?" Damion said.

She reached for the towel to dry her hands. "Actually, no. I was hoping for an old man, so that I should soon be a widow. I think I should far rather be a widow than a wife."

Caught in the act of taking another drink, Damion choked.

"Still," said the girl thoughtfully, "you might very well die in war, or at a tournament."

Damion pulled back his lips from his teeth in a smile that was not at all charming. "One can always pray," he said, then ostentatiously bowed his head as the king's chaplain began to say grace.

The smell of roasted meat drifted into the hall, mingling with the scents of smoke and dog and hot, sweating men. Another flourish of trumpets announced the arrival, amid murmurs of appreciation, of a boar's head to the high table. As the stewards carved, other dishes appeared, the servers kept running with slices for the diners. There was a crane with rose leaves and capons in saffron; partridges with coriander and venison in broth; herring, mackerel, and cod in exotic sauces; braised leeks and onions; a seemingly endless procession of dishes that dragged on and on.

At last, the tinkling of little musical bells announced the arrival of a flat-nosed fool clad in a parti-color tunic of red and green, who capered before them as the servants began to clear the first course. Suddenly he stopped, his head tilted at a queer angle, his gap-toothed mouth pulling into a wide smile as he paused to fondle his bauble. "Sire," he said, bowing with stately grace toward the king. Only he bowed so low that his nose touched the knees of his colorful hose and he staggered, raising a light chuckle from the diners. He straightened with a start, bristling with comic indignation. "You mock me. You mock. But I think if everyone here knew what some of you do beneath those boards and cloths—" he shook his bauble at them and tssked— "we would all be mocking you."

A chorus of laughter went up around the room while Lady Rosamund scowled and said, "I don't understand. There's no one under the tables yet except the dogs."

Swallowing his amusement, Damion turned his head and found Attica watching him, her eyes big and dark and hurting.

She had never been any good at hiding her thoughts or feelings from him. And so he knew, then, that someone must have told her about Rosamund of Carlyle, and he knew why she had been avoiding looking at him. He wanted to go to her, to take her in his arms and kiss away her needless pain and fear. He wanted to tell her that it wasn't true, what she was thinking, that he had no intention of taking this ill-natured child beside him to wife. That it was she, Attica, he wanted and meant to have.

But, he couldn't go to her because he was tied here, to the king's side. And the strum of a gittern told him that the first jongleur was about to perform.

The night was dark and nearly moonless, the only light the cold, silver glimmer of distant stars arcing high and indifferent above the quieting castle. Attica paused at the edge of the bailey, her face to the wind as she let the fresh air drive away the scents of roast meat and spilled wine and stale woodsmoke that seemed to cling about her still, even though it had been an hour or more since she'd left the banqueting hall.

Hugging her mantle close, she had just turned to make her way back to the women's chamber when steel-like fingers reached out of the darkness to crush her wrist in a hard grip and pull her behind the shadowy corner of the stables. She opened her mouth to scream, gasping as a roughly callused palm clamped over her face. Wild with terror, she fumbled with her free hand for her dagger and heard a familiar, amused voice say, "Would you skewer me with your short blade, then, lordling?"

His hold on her relaxed, and she whirled in his arms to throw herself against his chest. "Mother of God, you terrified me. What are you doing here? I thought you with the king."

He pressed a kiss to the top of her head. "And what are you doing here, wandering alone about the bailey while all the rest of the castle settles down to sleep?"

"Wishing you were with me," she said, lifting her face to him.

He took her mouth in a long, hot, searing kiss that ended

all too soon. "I should beat you, you know." His arms tightened fiercely around her. "How could you believe even for one moment that I intend to marry that spoiled child?"

"Huh," said Attica, remembering Lady Rosamund's petite, wraithlike figure and long, fair hair. "She is pretty."

"If you like your females pale and tiny and young. Very young. I don't." His lips curled up into a smile that tugged at her heart and made her feel warm inside. "Especially when those females want to be widows. All Lady Rosamund could talk about at supper was the various ways in which I might die and leave her in that happy state."

Attica let out a soft laugh. "She didn't."

"She did."

She rested her forearms on his chest, her spine arching as she leaned back in his arms so that she could see his face better. "Marriage to Rosamund would make you Earl of Carlyle."

"And marriage to Fulk would make you viscomtesse de Salers someday. Why should I be tempted when you are not?"

She clenched her fists in the fine cloth of his tunic, shaking him. "Damion, be serious."

"I am serious. I've never been more serious in my life."

She sucked in a deep breath, trying to summon up her strength and courage, because she felt so weak and ill at the thought of what she was about to say that she could barely push the words out. "If I am wed to Fulk of Salers, then you must take Rosamund of Carlyle to wife."

She felt him stiffen beneath her touch, his hands coming up to tighten on her shoulders as he seized her in a sudden, almost violent grip. "Why?" He stared down at her, a dangerous glitter flashing in the depths of his dark eyes. "So that if I can't have you, I'll at least be able to console myself with an earldom? Is that what you're saying?"

He took a step back, his arms falling away from her as a fierce, frightening hardness came over his face. "You're actually thinking of going ahead with it, aren't you? You're thinking of marrying that thirteen-year-old boy."

"Damion—" She reached for him, but he jerked out of her grasp. She brought her hands up together, pleading with him. "Please try to understand. I stood before God and made a vow—"

"A vow you were ready enough to break a few hours ago, if only Stephen or King Henry would have supported you. So what happened to change your mind?"

"I haven't changed my mind. But how can I wed you if both my family and my lord would see me given to another?"

"You can come away with me."

His words hung in the air, frightening, tempting, and damning. She felt an aching rush in her chest, as if her heart were torn and bleeding inside of her. She couldn't bear to look at him; it hurt too much, knowing she might lose him. But she couldn't bear to look away, either. "Don't you understand? If I run away with you, I will dishonor not only myself but my family as well. I don't know if I could live with that."

She heard the hissing intake of his breath. He stared down at her, his face cold and tense. "Oh, I understand all right. But you could live without me, is that what you're saying?"

"*No.*"

"That's what it sounds like to me."

"I *love* you," she said, her voice thick with tears she didn't dare let fall, for fear that once they started she'd never be able to stop them.

"But not enough."

She brought her hands back together to press them to her chest. "How can you say that? I love you more than my own *life*. But how can I betray my family and my lord both? Simply for my own selfish happiness?"

"So you would betray me instead?"

Her breath caught in a loud gasp as he spun away from her, his head thrown back, his eyes squeezing shut, his jaw tightening. "I'm not some chivalric knight out of a troubadour's idealized romance, Attica. My love for you might be pure and sweet and holy, but it's also earthy and passionate and physical." His eyes came open slowly as he swung his head to look at her over his shoulder. She was shocked to see a gleam of wetness there, faintly visible in the cold starlight. Shocked to hear the rough, raw pain in his voice as he said, "I'm not the kind of man who can love you chastely from afar, Attica. Don't ask it of me."

"Damion—" She went to him, her cheek pressed to his hard chest, her arms coming up to wrap around his taut neck. For one endless moment, he held himself aloof. Then a groan tore up from inside him and he swept her into his arms. His hand fisted in her hair to yank her head back, his mouth taking hers in a deep, violent kiss that left her so shaken, she might have fallen if he hadn't been holding her. She clung to him, listening to the wind ruffle the thatch of the stable roof beside them, and the soft nicker of a horse, moving restlessly in its stall.

"Mother of God, Damion. What am I to do?" She buried her face in the soft cloth of his tunic, her hands clutching him, holding him to her. "What am I to do?"

He held her close. But he didn't answer her. And she knew that was his way of telling her the choice was hers, and she was going to have to be the one to make it.

CHAPTER
TWENTY-ONE

As the comte d'Alérion, Stephen had been given a small chamber to himself in one of the towers of the eastern fortress.

She found him there in the early morning. The sun streamed through the lancet windows high in the wall, heating a room almost as austere and simple as a monk's cell. He had been sitting at a table, working. He'd stripped off his tunic, and his shirt was awry and his fair hair tousled, as if he'd been clutching it the way he used to do when they were children and his tutor had set him a particularly difficult passage of Latin to translate.

"Oh, it's you," he said with brotherly negligence when he answered her knock at his door. He swung away from her, his hand indicating one of the stools near the table. "Come in. Sit."

She stood just inside the closed door, her hands gripped together before her. "Stephen . . . I've come to ask you—to beg you—" She sucked in a deep breath and pushed the words out in a rush. "Please don't make me marry Fulk of Salers."

He stared at her across the width of the chamber, his thin face troubled. Wordlessly, he went to the table where a ewer and cups stood near a wax tablet and lute, and poured himself a drink. "Do you want some?" he asked, glancing up at her as if in an afterthought.

She shook her head and watched as he raised the cup to his lips and swallowed. The silence between them stretched out, became taut.

"Attica . . ." He pinched the bridge of his nose between thumb and forefinger, a sigh lifting his narrow chest. "Please try to understand. Even if I wanted to release you from this betrothal, I couldn't. It's all gotten tangled up in the negotiations between Philip and Henry. It's out of my hands."

She took a step toward him. "If you were to speak to Henry, to ask him—"

He let out a humorless laugh as his hand fell away from his face. "God's death, Attica. The man is willing to give Alice to Richard, if that's what it takes to reach a settlement with Philip. Do you honestly think he would allow consideration for your personal inclinations to sway him?"

She felt the harsh reality of what he was saying, the implications of it, deep within her, deep enough to bruise her very bones and leave her aching. She wrapped her arms around her waist, hugging herself, but the ache remained, ominous and frightening.

Stephen turned away, draining his wine. "It isn't as if you love another," he said, setting the cup away from him.

She came up beside him, hope flaring anew in her heart. "Would it make a difference if I did?"

He shook his head, a sad smile curling his lips as he stared down at his empty cup. "No. It would only make the situation more tragic."

He looked up then, and their gazes met and held in a long silence filled with a lifetime of shared memories, good and bad. "Do you ever wish," she said suddenly, her voice such a broken tear it didn't sound like her own voice at all, "did you ever wish that you'd been born someone else, not a d'Alérion at all?"

Something shifted deep in his eyes, something secret and shadowed and wretchedly unhappy. But he only shook his head.

Chased by a welling of desperation and confusion, Attica ran. She ran the way she hadn't run since she was a child, arms reaching, legs stretching high and wide to swallow the distance. The sun beat down hot and golden on her shoulders, and the wind whipped her short curls about her face. She knew people turned to stare, but she ran anyway, through the cobbled tunnel of the barbican and into the open country beyond.

The air was sweeter here, scented with the ripe goodness of the wheat and barley in the fields where peasants straightened their backs to watch her pass. She ran until she reached an open meadow beside the river. Sucking in air, her face damp and hot, she waded deep into the high grass and sank down into it, letting it part and close around her.

She folded her arms on her upraised knees, her head bent, her forehead pressing into her bony wrists. As her breath steadied, she became aware of a deep shuddering within her that she knew had nothing to do with her running.

The chattering call of a tern sounded from someplace nearby. She lifted her head, her gaze drawn to the sandbar of the slow-moving river beside her, but the dense leaves and drooping branches of a big willow hanging over the water hid the bird from sight.

She felt so terribly alone, sitting there in the sun-spangled field beneath the vast blue sky. Alone and lost. "Oh, Papa," she whispered, missing him with a sudden, swift awareness of loss that took her breath away. She wished she had him here now to wrap one of his great arms around her and somehow lead her back to the sense of order and security and certainty that had been hers as a child. She closed her eyes, picturing Robert d'Alérion's big, bearlike frame and open, pleasant face. He had always seemed so sure of himself, so grounded in what was right and true and noble.

Yet he must have known this dilemma, she thought, this wrenching agony of being pulled apart by conflicting loyalties and impossible choices. She wondered if he had suffered when he betrothed her to Fulk, if he had felt the pain of putting his loyalty to his land and his house ahead of his love for his own daughter. He certainly hadn't let it stop him from sacrificing her.

She let her head fall back, her eyes wide and painfully dry as she stared up at the vast blue sky above. But she was still alone. Alone and torn apart by indecision and the bitter knowledge that whatever she chose, the result would be heartache and loss.

Damion stood with one shoulder propped against the bare stone wall at the entrance to the narrow window embrasure, a lute dangling forgotten from one hand as he watched Henry pause beside the mews in the yard below, his old falconer at his side, a hawk on his wrist. In the chamber behind Damion, Sergei moved about softly, gathering up clothes and bits of armor from Damion's corner of the Knights' Tower. The room was crowded with cots and wooden crosses hung with mail shirts, and smelled strongly of sweat and horses and liniment. But for the moment, they were alone.

Sergei put away the leather gloves he'd been cleaning, and came to stand beside him. "You've deciphered the message from last night's performance."

Damion sucked in a deep breath, then let it out slowly,

his gaze still fixed on the bailey below. "Two days from now, Henry will visit the Shrine of the Virgin at Loudun, to pray for his health. None but the king's inner circle have been told of his intention, yet Richard knows of it. There will be some ruse to draw off the main body of knights, thus reducing Henry's escort. Richard and his men will be waiting at a stream a league or so from the castle."

"An ambush?"

Damion nodded. "Henry will ride straight into it. Everything has been arranged. The message only confirms the details."

Sergei sank down on the bare stone seat opposite him, a troubled frown drawing his brows together. "There is nothing in the message to indicate who the traitor might be?"

Damion shook his head. "No. It could be one of half a dozen men. All were at the banquet last night."

"What will you do?"

Damion swung to face his squire. "Tell Henry, of course. He may simply decide to cancel his visit to the shrine. But I suspect it more likely he'll play along in the hopes of trapping this traitor."

Sergei's dark, exotic eyes shimmered with some emotion that was there and then gone. "And if the traitor is Stephen d'Alérion?"

Damion's hand tightened around the neck of the lute, drawing it up. Wordlessly, he swept his right fingers over the strings to produce a harsh, discordant sound.

"You could warn him," said Sergei leaning forward. "Find some way to let him know that the code has been broken, the plan betrayed. Give him a chance to flee before he is caught."

Damion looked up. "Could I? And if he's not the only traitor next to Henry, then what? We would have lost our means of monitoring the conspirators' movements, so that the next time they decided to strike at Henry, they would likely succeed." Once more, Damion drew his fingers across the lute, then thrust it aside. "No. If Stephen has turned traitor, then the most I can do is hope that in the turmoil of battle I can find some way to let him escape. For Attica's sake."

Sergei's gaze dropped to the lute, although he made no move to pick it up. "And if you fail? If her brother is killed? She may never forgive you for it. You realize that, don't you?"

Damion felt the pain of it, the awful truth of it, like a sword thrust to his heart. "I know," he said on a harsh expulsion of breath. "God help me, I know. But if I were to sacrifice Henry for such a reason, I could never forgive myself."

Attica stood in the lower bailey, her hand clutching the throat latch of her cloak as she watched the royal caval-cade prepare to move off. The morning mist that hung heavily over the river was thinner here, drifting through the yard in insubstantial wisps that curled around the horses' darkly restless legs and obscured the jutting stone parapets looming above.

The yard was full of mounted knights, the damp air ring-ing with the tramp of horses' hooves, the creak of saddle leather and jingle of mail, the low murmurs of men. She saw the king emerge, cloaked and hooded against the cold and leaning heavily on Alice's arm as she helped him down the steps from the hall and into the litter. His condition had worsened, someone had said, which was why he had agreed to use a litter to make this pilgrimage to the Shrine of the Virgin near Loudun. He must be very ill indeed, At-tica thought.

The men in the yard began to separate into two parties. Only some six or eight knights, led by Stephen, would actually be escorting the king to Loudun, for word had come that morning of a threat against one of Henry's loyal castles on the Vienne, and Damion was leading most of the knights and a number of sergeants south to its relief.

A dark warhorse reared before her, its great hooves slashing the gray sky. Attica took a step back, her breath hitching in her chest as she looked up into Damion's glinting eyes. The cold steel and jutting nosepiece of his helm seemed to accentuate the sharp bones of his face, making him look fierce, frightening. He held his shield before him, the jagged flash of lightning standing out bold and bloodred against the black background.

She hadn't seen him since the night of the banquet, had avoided seeing him, avoided letting him see her. She was afraid he'd look into her woman's eyes and *know*. Know that hours spent prostrate on the chapel floor in prayer had brought her neither peace nor relief. Know that she still felt torn apart by conflicting loyalties and agonizing choices. Know that she might decide, in the end, that the impossible choice was the one she must make. But, oh God . . .

He was her heart and soul, her passion and joy, her life. She looked at him, and all the torn, tormented bits inside her twisted, hurt. Hurt like a slow, living death.

He brought the big stallion under control, one forearm resting on the saddle's high pommel as he leaned into it, his face hard and unsmiling. "You've been avoiding me, Attica. Why?"

The wind blew, flapping the hem of her cloak out, making the stallion snort and throw its head. "I've needed to think."

He tightened his hold on the reins. "And have you? Thought, I mean."

She glanced beyond him, to where Sergei waited, a sad, anxious look shadowing his young face. She tried to smile at him, only she couldn't. She stared into his dark, exotic eyes, and it was as if the shouting men and trampling horses around them faded queerly into a soundless world where movement slowed and noise dimmed to faint distant echoes that roused some nameless, unreasonable terror from deep within her.

"I suppose I have my answer," Damion said, his voice brutally clear and cold, although not so cold she couldn't hear the raw thread of pain within it.

She jerked her gaze back to stare up at him, her chest rising and falling with her suddenly agitated breathing. "Damion—" She took a step forward, reaching for him, but he turned his stallion away.

She folded her arms across her chest, the mist cool and damp against her face as she watched him ride away from her. She wanted to call him back, but she knew there was nothing she could say to him. And she wondered, in despair, if her decision had already been made and she was only trying to find the courage to admit it.

"Attica?"

She turned, looking up as Stephen reined in beside her. "Wish me well," he said, curbing the impatient capering of his big, dun-colored stallion. His cheeks were flushed, his eyes bright with the kind of wild excitement she remembered from their childhood whenever he'd been about to embark on some mad, dangerous adventure.

"Of course I wish you well," she said, and this time when she tried to summon up a smile, it came.

She followed the men through the gateway to the grassy

hillside to watch them ride away. But the mist swallowed them almost at once, and they were lost to her sight.

She returned to the yard to find Alice still there, beside the hall, her head bowed, her shoulders slumped in exhaustion.

With so many of the men gone, the castle servants were busy throwing open shutters and sweeping out old rushes to be replaced with new. Their shouts and laughter mingled with the rumble of hand carts and the banging of the wheelwright's hammer and the screech of strutting peacocks to fill the bailey with a tumult of sound and activity. But the French princess sat alone on a bench against the hall's side wall, one hand held up to cover her eyes.

"Alice?" Attica touched her arm. "Are you all right?"

The other woman looked up, startled, showing a face strained by sleeplessness and worry. "Oh, I'm fine," she said, visibly struggling to regain her normal composure. "Simply tired. Henry was so dreadfully sick last night, he's only now fallen into a fitful sleep." She gave a shaky half laugh that ended in a kind of sob. "Imagine *Henry* spending the day in bed. A man who never even sat down in his life but to eat or ride a horse."

Attica sank onto the bench beside the other woman. "But . . . how can this be? Henry has gone to the Shrine of the Virgin."

Alice shook her head. "No, that wasn't the king, only his old falconer, wrapped up in Henry's robes."

"I don't understand," said Attica, a nameless sense of unease hovering over her.

"Someone near to Henry has been betraying his movements to Richard. There was to be an ambush, at a stream east of the castle."

"And now?"

The other woman's face set into hard lines. "Now, it is Richard and his supporters who shall find themselves ambushed, for de Jarnac does not ride south, as all think."

Attica stared off across the bailey, where a squire was leading a limping horse toward the farrier. She was remembering the night of the banquet and the intent look on de Jarnac's face as he watched the jongleurs. If he had learned something of the conspirators' plans that night, he had said nothing of it to her. But then, they had hardly seen each other. And even then, she thought, they had had other things on their minds. . . .

The French princess went back into the hall soon after that, while Attica wandered about the bailey, too troubled to return to the crowded ladies' chamber. In the end she found herself outside Stephen's tower room, not quite knowing how she came to be there.

Lifting her hand to the latch, she pushed the door open. The room hadn't been Stephen's for long, yet he had stamped it as his, the cool, damp air holding the faint, ecclesiastical fragrances of incense and beeswax mixing strangely with the scents of horses and dogs and leather and polished steel. She went to stand in the middle of the chamber, her eyes squeezing closed against a sudden rush of tears.

"Oh, Stephen," she whispered, her heart heavy with the burden of what she knew she must do. "I'm sorry." She sucked in a deep breath, then let it out slowly, feeling the pain of her decision settle deep into her soul where, she knew, it would always lie. "I'm sorry," she whispered again, "but you ask too much of me. More than you have a right to do."

She couldn't have said exactly when she had made her choice. Perhaps she had always known what she would do in the end. It had only taken her this long to admit it.

She opened her eyes, her breath easing out of her in a

long sigh. She saw his lute, still lying on the table, and she went to it, her fingers trailing across the strings, the sweet notes falling sad and lonely into the stillness of the moment.

> *You are my hope*
> *My life*
> *My love.*

Suddenly, her hand froze, her attention arrested by the sight of the wax tablet Stephen had been working on when she'd disturbed him the other morning. A wax tablet covered with a pattern of musical notes of the kind developed by a Benedictine nun of Catalonia and used as a code by those conspiring against Henry with Philip of France.

Somehow, she made herself walk with proper decorum and what seemed like agonizing slowness toward the stables. Her legs were trembling, her breath coming shallow and rapid, the noise and movement of the yard whirling in a giddy blur around her. A woman peeling rushes to be soaked in fat for rushlights looked up and called to her. Attica quickened her step.

She felt such a deep, white anger toward Stephen for what he was doing that she was shaking with it. But he was her brother, her blood, the companion of her childhood and the hope of her house. Even though what he did was wrong and dishonorable, she could not let him die.

She could not let Damion kill him.

She flung herself through the stable doors into a cool dimness scented with horses and hay and fresh manure. "Mary, Mother of God," she whispered in prayer as she led de Jarnac's black Arab out of its stall and saddled it with swift efficiency, "please." *Please let me catch up with them in time. Please don't let them kill each other. Please, please, please.*

Gathering the reins, she was just hauling herself into the saddle when one of the castle grooms came through a door in the back. "*Alons*, what are you doing?"

She dug her heels into the Arab's sides to send the horse flying through the open doors and cantering across the packed earth of the yard. Chickens and pigs scattered, squawking and squealing and causing a charcoal burner to upset his cart. Someone shouted, but she pressed on, the stallion's hooves slipping and clattering over the cobbles through the barbican.

They burst out into the light again. The mist had burned off by now, the sun rising golden and hot in a clear blue sky. The west wind caught at her hair and billowed the skirt of her dress out behind her as she sent the horse plunging down the steep slope, through the narrow, winding streets of the town. She chafed, furious, frightened, as she stood at the river's edge, the Arab's reins gripped in her sweating fist as she waited for the ferryman to come back from the far shore and carry her across the Vienne.

All the while she waited, all the while the ferryman worked to haul her across the water, she was thinking. How much distance would a litter supposedly carrying a sick king cover in an hour? A league? Two? How far from the castle would Richard lay his ambush? An hour? More? The ferry hadn't even reached the opposite shore when she leapt off it, splashing through the shallow water and driving the stallion on, on.

She had chosen the Arab because of his speed and his endurance and his heart, and he gave her all she asked for and more. Dust billowed up behind them as they raced through fields of ripening wheat and rye, past ancient vineyards and groves of walnut trees. The stallion's neck grew dark and shiny with sweat. The hot air buffeted her face and ears, the world narrowing down to the rush of the wind and the creak of the saddle leather and the relentless pounding of the Arab's hooves churning up the road.

An hour or so later, she had slowed the stallion to a walk to rest him on a long uphill stretch when the gusting wind carried to her the unmistakable, blood-chilling sounds of battle—the scream of horses, the throaty shouts of men, the clash of steel. Attica flung up her head, her heels digging into the Arab's sides just as a trumpet rang out, sounding three piercing notes.

She surged over the crest of the hill, then reined in hard, her heart slamming into her throat as she looked down on a wild melee of helmed and mailed knights, their horses plunging and squealing, their swords flashing in the sun as the blades rose and fell, hacking, hacking. Dust and the smell of blood hung thick in the air. Beneath her, the Arab capered impatiently as she sought helplessly to pick out the familiar forms of her brother and the man she loved from amongst that surging mass of horseflesh and mail and death.

Richard's men had lain their ambush in the thick copse of trees that shadowed the stream at the foot of the hill. But they had been expecting only a small royal escort and were far outnumbered. Already they were breaking away in groups of twos and threes, scattering across the fields, fading back into the darkness of the woods.

As Attica watched, one knight, mounted on a familiar dun, his shield gone, spurred up the hill toward her. Behind him galloped a dark-helmed knight riding a black destrier and clutching a shield blazing with a distinctive red bolt of lightning. She had a strange sense of time spinning out of control, of having been here, seen this, all before. And then she realized that she had, that this was the way she had first seen Damion de Jarnac, his shield gripped before him, his sword raised as he swept down on the *routiers*. Only this time he rode not to rescue her but to kill the brother she had risked everything to save.

She cried out his name, but it was lost in the tumult of battle and the squeal of the warhorse as de Jarnac reined in his stallion hard enough to set it back on its hocks, as if he'd suddenly realized the identity of the man he pursued and decided to let him escape. Attica's breath eased out of her in relief, only to catch again in dismay as she saw Stephen abruptly draw in rein and wheel. His lance was gone as well as his shield, but he raised his sword, defiantly yelling his war cry as he set his spurs to his horse and sent it charging at the black knight. Damion hesitated, then spurred his own charger forward. The earth thundered, the stallions' pounding hooves sending up chips of sod as the men hurtled toward each other.

"No!" Attica screamed, frozen with horror.

The two warhorses came together with a brutal crash. The dun squealed, going down on its side, its hooves flailing, the knight on its back hitting the ground with a ringing crash that sent his helm flying off.

The black destrier wheeled, half rearing up as the dark knight threw himself from the saddle. Stephen lay still, one leg twisted unnaturally beneath him, broken. He lifted his head, his hand groping for the sword he had lost. But the black knight was already upon him, his sword raised high, ready to deliver the coup de grâce—just as Attica sent the Arab flying down the slope, a hopeless cry of denial and impending loss tearing from her lips.

CHAPTER
TWENTY-TWO

Damion held his blade poised, ready to thrust. Beneath the steel of his helm, his face dripped sweat, his breath came hot and fast in his throat. But his hands were steady as he brought the tip of his sword to the fallen man's throat.

The wind gusted round him, bringing him the drumming of hoofbeats and the sound of Attica's voice, pleading, *"Don't. Oh, God. Damion, no."*

His head came up, his eyes narrowing at the sight of the Arab's flaring nostrils and flashing hooves. She flew down the hill toward them. He could see her golden brown hair gleaming warm in the sun, the skirt of her dark blue dress billowing out around her as she leaned low over the black stallion's sweat-stained neck.

Deliberately, Damion brought his gaze back to the man on the ground before him. His grip on the sword tightened for the kill. Only he couldn't do it. He couldn't kill Attica's brother.

"Do it," said Stephen, his voice harsh, his breath ragged enough to quiver the chain mail at his breast. "For God's sake, kill me."

Damion shook his head, his blade swinging away. "I cannot."

A queer smile curled the fallen man's lips. "What would you do?" He jerked his head to where the king's men were regrouping, rounding up their prisoners. With a broken leg, d'Alérion could never escape now. "Let them take me back to Henry, to face a traitor's death? Do you think Attica will thank you for your mercy? Will she thank you when she's forced to watch them cut off my balls and pull out my guts? Will she thank you while I'm swinging at the end of a hangman's noose? Will she be pleased, do you think, when I'm drawn and quartered like a butchered hog?" The fierce smile faded, overcome by a wild-eyed, trembling look of pleading. "For the love of God, kill me now."

Damion brought the point of his blade to hover just above the place where the pulse beat in Stephen's bare neck. Stephen's eyes squeezed shut, his throat working as he swallowed. "Tell her . . ." A hint of a boyish smile flashed, disappeared. "Tell Attica she would have made a better knight than I have."

"Damion—Oh, God, Damion, don't!" Attica screamed. Dirt and small bits of stone sprayed through the air as she reined in the Arab and threw herself from the stallion's back. Without looking up, Damion drove the blade home. Stephen convulsed once, then lay still.

"Stephen." Attica's voice turned into a thin wail that blew away in the hot, dusty wind. She fell to her knees beside her brother, her face twisting with anguish as a dry, gut-wrenching sob tore up from deep inside her. "Stephen," she whispered. "Oh, God. Stephen, no."

She reached out, her hands trembling. She touched her fingertips to his face, cradled his cheeks in her palms. "Stephen, don't be dead. Please don't be dead." With a moan, she gathered him up against her breast, her slim young body bent and shivering as she rocked back and forth on her heels, her brother held close. Blood drenched his mail, streamed down his neck and over her hands and arms to soak into the fine cloth of her skirt, turning it dark and wet. "No," she said again, shaking her head from side to side. *"No."*

Damion stared at her. The sky above suddenly seemed too blue, the sun shining on the bright green grass of the hillside too vivid to bear. He wanted to say something, anything, to ease her pain. But there was nothing he could say that would comfort her, and his throat felt too impossibly tight to let him push out any words, even if he'd had them to say.

Her head fell back, showing him a pale, haunted face and bruised, horrified eyes. He could count the beats of her heart in the blue veins visible beneath the fragile skin at her temples as she stared up at him. The wind blew between them, hot and dry and scented with death. "You knew," she said, sucking in a deep breath that shuddered in her chest. "You knew it was Stephen."

"No." He sheathed his sword. "Not until today."

"Yet you suspected him. You suspected him from the very beginning."

"When I first met you on the road, yes. But after that, not until I spoke to your uncle in Laval."

A shudder shook her slim frame. "You lied to me. Before we reached the castle, when you asked me not to tell Stephen what we knew of the code. You *lied*." Her gaze slid away from him, back to Stephen. With careful tenderness, she laid her brother's body on the grass as if he were a sleeping child. She sat very still, her bloodstained hands flattened against her thighs, her head bowed.

"You lied to me," she said again, her voice a torn thread. "I could have warned him. But I didn't."

Damion felt the sun shining down hot on his mail. But inside he was cold. So very cold. "I couldn't let you."

"You couldn't let me?" She looked up at him, her lips twisting in scorn, her head jerking as if in denial. "*You couldn't let me?* God above. How could you *kill him*?" She surged to her feet, wide-eyed, a sob bursting from between her clenched teeth as she threw herself at him. *"You killed him."* She pounded her fists against his chest, the sharp links of his chain mail bruising and cutting her tender flesh, smearing them both with blood, her blood, and Stephen's. "You killed him." Her voice broke, became a sob. "You *killed* him. Oh, God. Why did you have to kill him?"

"Attica—" He tried to grasp her by the shoulders, but she jerked out of his reach. "Splendor of God, what would you have had me do? Take him to Chinon in chains to meet a traitor's death?"

She backed away from him, her eyes wide with pain and an anger that bordered dangerously near to hatred. *"You could have let him go."*

She swung away, her arms wrapping around her waist as she doubled over, an aching moan curling up from someplace deep inside her. "Oh, God. You killed him." Her legs buckled beneath her, and she sank to her knees in the grass. She pressed her hands flat to her face, her chest shuddering with the effort to draw in breath.

"I would have given up everything for you," she said, her hands sliding down to clench her skirt. "I would have betrayed my house, my liege lord, my vow to God, all for you. And you"—she let out a horrible laugh—"you kill my brother."

"I would die for you, Attica. Without hesitation or regret. But I couldn't let Henry die, not because of my love for you. I couldn't look the other way while Stephen betrayed his lord to his enemies."

She stared at him. Her hands had left smears of her brother's blood on her cheeks and neck, the red standing out starkly against the white of her skin. "You couldn't even look the other way while Stephen rode off?"

Damion tightened his jaw, unable to answer her. Because while it was true that, in the end, he had pulled up, it was also true that for a few, fatal heartbeats, the bloodlust of battle had pounded hot through him and he had begun to give chase.

A sob rasped painfully from her throat as she swung her face away from him, her eyes squeezing shut against the tears that now welled up hot and fast. He ached with the need to go to her, to enfold her in his arms and comfort her with his warmth and his strength and his love. But he knew this was one time his touch would bring her no ease.

His head lifted, his gaze caught by the flight of an egret that rose, white and graceful, from the reeds near the water's edge. He saw the lanner before the egret did, the hawk's dark wings spread wide, its curved beak bold against the blue sky as it hovered, then swooped, claws grasping. The egret let out a shrill cry and fell to earth, the lanner diving behind. And still Damion stared at the empty sky.

He was aware of Sergei reining in to slip from his saddle and go kneel beside Attica. The squire's hand touched her shoulder gently, and she turned to him, harsh sobs shaking her shoulders as she clutched him. Damion stood where he was, watching Attica turn away. Then he went to where Stephen lay, still, on the grass.

This at least, Damion thought, he could do for her.

* * *

Henry Plantagenet, King of England and Wales, and lord of more French lands than the French king himself, lay beneath a coverlet of thick marten fur in a bed curtained with scarlet silk. Though the summer evening was bright and warm, the shutters had been closed against the setting sun. A brazier glowed on the stone hearth in the chamber's corner, the bubbling contents of an earthenware pot nestled among the coals filling the room with a heavy, herb-scented heat.

Stepping into the faint glimmer of light thrown by the cresset lamp hanging by a chain from a bracket on the wall, Damion bowed. "You wished to see me, Your Grace?"

Henry struggled to push himself up on the pillows. "I hear Philip's armies are overrunning what's left of Maine and Touraine. Is it true?"

Damion met the English king's gaze unswervingly. "Yes, Your Grace."

A draft swung the cresset overhead, the light flickering over a face shockingly pinched by illness. The fingers of one of Henry's hands plucked restlessly at the edge of the camlet sheet as his gaze drifted away. "Perhaps it would have been for the best, after all, if Richard had succeeded in taking me today." A breath lifted his chest, then eased out in a long sigh. His gaze drifted away, and it was as if he spoke to himself, his words a broken murmur. "I've dedicated my life to bringing peace, prosperity, and justice to my lands. I don't want to spend what might be my last hours watching everything I've worked for destroyed."

He brought his gaze back to Damion, his face hardening, his voice turning bitter and cold. "I want you to send word to Richard and Philip. Tell them I've decided to agree to their terms. My subjects will swear allegiance to Richard, and he shall have Alice to wife on his return from his

Crusade." A growl rumbled his barrel chest as he added savagely, "If she's lucky, perhaps the treacherous bastard won't come back."

Damion glanced at the regal young woman who sat, quiet and unmoving, beside the king's sickbed. "Yes, Your Grace." He kept his face as much of a mask as he could make it. "And Attica d'Alérion?"

Henry swiped his hand through the air in an angry gesture. "She'll not reward Salers and his wife for their treason by making their son the new comte d'Alérion. Stephen d'Alérion's lands are declared forfeit by reason of his defection, and I'm settling them on you"—He gave Damion a considering look—"since you didn't seem overly enthusiastic about being the Earl of Carlyle."

"And the girl?" said Damion again. "Attica d'Alérion?"

"Salers can have her if he still wants her, but I doubt he will, now that she won't have the power of her brother behind her." Henry rubbed the back of his hand across his dry, cracked lips and nodded toward the silver ewer and delicate Venetian glass goblet resting on a nearby chest. "Pour me some wine," he said, his voice becoming raspy. "The girl can take the veil."

Damion moved to the heavy oak coffer decorated across its side panels with carved dragons and two-headed beasts devouring their own tails. "I would have her to wife, Your Grace," he said, his hand almost steady as he poured the wine and handed it to the king.

"Oh, you would, would you?" Henry took the wine, a faint gleam of amusement lighting up his eyes. "That does much to explain your lack of interest in Carlyle." He shrugged. "Go ahead and take the girl too, if you wish— that is assuming, of course, that she'll have you, with her brother's blood still fresh on your hands." Raising the goblet, he drank deeply, then sighed in satisfaction, his head sinking back into the pillow. "If I thank God for anything," he said, smiling faintly, "it's that He's had the mercy to let me fall ill in Anjou, where a sick man can at least be assured of drinking a good cup of wine." He cocked one gray eyebrow at Damion. "Ever spend much time in England?"

"Not a great deal, Your Grace."

Henry grunted in envy. "It's true what they say, you know: English wine can only be drunk with the eyes closed and the teeth clenched."

Damion laughed while Alice of France reached forward to pluck the wine goblet from the king's slack grasp. "You should rest now, Henry."

Henry threw a ferocious scowl at her and said, "Stop fussing over me, woman." To Damion he added, "Arrange the meeting with Philip and that bastard son of mine, so that we may exchange the kiss of peace. Only don't make the place of meeting too far."

"You'll go in a litter, in any case," said Alice hastily, pulling the covers up under his chin.

"God's righteous wounds, I'll do no such thing," he bellowed, his face suffusing with color as he struggled to sit up. "I'll ride there on my own horse, like the king I am. I'm not dead yet."

Heavy banks of clouds raced in from the west, blotting out the thin sliver of moon and the stars and stirring up a mournful wind that shrieked through the narrow streets of the darkened town.

Attica threw a quick, anxious glance behind her, grateful in spite of her fear for the protective cloak of black secrecy the night wrapped around them. Stumbling, she threw

out one hand, running it along the rough stone wall of the
building beside her, feeling her way carefully as she followed Sergei down the steep, refuse-strewn street.

As if he sensed her unease, Sergei's whisper floated
back to her from out of the darkness. "We're almost there,
my lady."

A wolf howled in the distance. Attica gripped together
the edges of her mantle with her free hand and tried not
to shiver.

It didn't seem right, somehow, that she should have to
creep through the darkness of the night as furtively as
a thief or a spy. There should be nothing wrong with a
woman wanting to give her brother a decent burial, nothing wrong with wanting to spare his body the final degra-
dation of the gibbet, nothing wrong with depriving Henry
of the pleasure of seeing Stephen's head on a pike, decorating the castle gate along with the heads of the other
rebel knights who had been killed today.

Unfortunately, Henry hadn't seen it that way. He'd been
furious to discover Stephen's body missing from among
those brought back to the castle. She wasn't exactly certain how Sergei had managed to spirit her brother away, although she knew she had Damion to thank for it.

Damion . . .

But the thought of him brought with it such a confused
welling of hot anger and desperate longing that she jerked
her mind away.

"Here," said Sergei, ducking suddenly through a small
arched doorway.

She followed him down a short flight of shallow steps,
for the priory of Saint-Rémy was an old one, and over the
centuries the level of the street outside had risen. She found
herself in the side aisle of a small church with barrel vaults

and twin arcades of squat sandstone arches, dimly lit by candles that glimmered over fresco-covered walls and ceilings.

A movement near the altar drew her attention to a monk who rose, genuflected, then came toward them, his hands together before him as if in prayer. "Welcome, daughter. Your brother lies there, in the Lady chapel."

But she had already seen him, a still, darkly robed form lying on a trestle table before a side altar.

She walked up to him on shaky legs, her breath rasping harshly as she gazed down on him. In place of his armor, he now wore the habit of an Augustinian monk, the cowl drawn up around his face like the hood of a mail hauberk. The monks had bathed the blood from him, and the cowl hid the gaping wound in his throat. In the gentle light of the candles, he looked so young, she thought; young and, oddly for one who had met such a violent death, at peace.

"You do not mind that we have dressed him as one of our order?" asked the monk, coming up quietly beside her.

"No." She reached out a trembling hand to touch the sleeve of his habit. "He was actually consecrated to God once. But our elder brother died, and so Stephen became our father's heir."

Yet he had never really delighted in the sport of knights, she remembered, even though he had done his best to live up to Robert d'Alérion's expectations. They had both been taught to bend themselves to their father's genial but implacable will, to put the needs of the house of Alérion ahead of their own wishes and desires.

Oh, Stephen, she thought. *My poor knighted monk.*

She sank to her knees beside his body, her hands folded together and resting on the cloth of his robes, her head bowed in prayer. She was aware of Sergei and the monk moving off down the nave, their voices lowered to soothing murmurs. She was glad they had not left her entirely alone.

She did not know how long she knelt there in prayer. She felt a touch on her shoulder and looked up into Sergei's anxious face. "We must get back, my lady. We must not risk letting your brother's location be known before the monks can bury him in the morning."

She crossed herself and rose stiffly to her feet, but she found she could not bear to leave him. She stood gazing down at his boyishly handsome face with its prominent cheekbones and delicately sculpted mouth. He would never grow old now, she thought. He would always look thus in her memory.

She was vaguely aware of Sergei stepping back, of a sudden charge of energy humming in the air, as if a flash of lightning were about to crackle through the chapel.

She lifted her head, her gaze locking with that of the man who now stood, tall and straight and silent, on the far side of the bier. He must have only just ridden in, she thought, for he still wore his hauberk, and his cheeks and nose still bore the faint black smudges left by his helm. The air around her filled with the scent of the night wind and warm horseflesh and cold steel.

"Why have you come?" she asked, her voice a harsh whisper.

He leaned toward her, his fingers curling over the edge of the bier, his face hard and intent. "I had to see you."

"Here?" Her hand swept through the air, flickering the candles that burned beside her brother's body.

"Yes, here." The dancing candlelight flared over the fierce bones of his face and glittered in the frightening depths of his beautiful, beloved eyes. "I thought you ought to know that Henry has declared Stephen's lands forfeit."

She was aware of a curious inner emptiness. She knew she should feel something—anger, dismay, perhaps even fear. As Robert d'Alérion's only surviving child, she would have inherited all his lands after her brother's death if Stephen hadn't died taking up arms against his liege lord. Yet she felt nothing. It was as if the losses she had already borne had hollowed her out inside, so that she couldn't care about anything.

"He has settled both lands and titles on me," Damion said, still staring at her hard.

She forced her lips into a travesty of a smile. "So now you have everything you've always wanted. Land. Titles. Power. Congratulations."

She saw his brows draw together in a confused frown, as if he couldn't understand her reaction. But then, she couldn't understand herself. She felt dead inside. As dead as her brother before her.

"No," Damion said, his head swinging sharply, once, from side to side. "Not everything. I don't have you, Attica. Henry has said I might take you to wife, but . . ." He paused, his breath pushing out in a long sigh. "It's your choice. You must agree to have me."

She stared at him, her heart beginning to pound wildly in her chest. For some reason, it hadn't occurred to her that with the death of both her brother and her father, she had become Henry's ward. Her mother might still be alive in Aquitaine, but women meant nothing in such matters. Attica was now in the king's gift. And Henry had given her to Damion.

She licked her suddenly dry lips. "And if I refuse?"

A muscle leapt in his tightened jaw. "Then you are to become a bride of Christ."

She spun away, the candles on the altar blurring into an arc of golden-white light as she brought her hands up to cover her mouth and nose.

His voice came from behind her. "Will you, Attica? Will you refuse me? Would you rather take the veil?"

She swung slowly back to face him, only to discover she could endure no more than one look at the intense longing burning in his eyes before she had to drop her gaze to her brother's peaceful features. "I would rather take the veil than marry anyone but you." She paused, trying to swallow the sob that burned like a live coal in her chest. "Except . . . how can I marry the man who killed my own brother?" She heard the swift intake of Damion's breath and pressed on, before she lost her courage.

"I love you, Damion. Beneath all the anger and hurt I'm feeling, I know the love is still there. But don't you see?" Somehow, she found the strength to look up at him again, although what she saw in his face almost destroyed her. "Don't you see?" she said again, her voice breaking. "Stephen's death will always lie between us. As surely as his body lies here between us now."

"Stephen lies here on his bier between us now, yes," said Damion, his hand stabbing downward, the color riding high on his cheekbones. "But tomorrow he will be in his grave. And if he continues to come between us, then it is only because you have willed it so, Attica d'Alérion."

"My lady," said Sergei, stepping forward again. "We must go."

For one intense, unforgettable moment she held Damion's gaze. Then she bent to kiss Stephen's cold cheek.

She turned away almost blindly, pushing a small leather

bag of coins into the monk's hand in alms. She was grateful when Sergei took her arm to guide her up the darkened
steps.

The door opened to the restless night, the air fresh and
cool and damp with the promise of rain. But at the top of
the steps she paused and glanced back for one brief instant
to see Damion still there, beside the bier, the candlelight
glimmering soft and golden over the sun-darkened planes
of his face as he gazed down at Stephen's body. And then
he did the strangest thing: That hard, dark knight sank to
his knees and bowed his head to pray.

The door slammed shut behind her, and she saw him
no more.

Outside, the night wind tore at her mantle, whipped at
her hair, thrashed the branches of the trees on the far side
of the priory's high wall. A shutter banged in the distance,
startling a dog into barking. She tipped back her head,
staring up at the storm-tossed sky with wide, painfully dry
eyes. Lightning cracked, splitting open the clouds, tearing
at her heart and laying bare her grieving soul.

Early the next morning, Attica stood on the wind-
blown battlements and watched Henry and a small party of
knights led by Damion de Jarnac ride forth from the castle
of Chinon, their horses richly caparisoned, their pennants
and banners snapping in the wind.

When they returned, the English king was no longer on
his horse but in a litter.

Rumors whipped around the castle. They said Henry
had reached a humiliating agreement with his son Richard
and the French king, then collapsed. They said Henry had
demanded that Richard and Philip furnish him with a list
of the names of those who had conspired against him.

They said Henry had cursed his son with the same breath as he had presented him with the kiss of peace.

They said Henry was dying.

Damion didn't see her again until early the following evening.

He came upon her in the chamber that had once belonged to Stephen d'Alérion. It looked as if she had been gathering her brother's things together into a neat pile on a narrow bed oddly reminiscent of what one might see in a monastic cell. But now she simply stood half-turned away from him in the center of the room, her hands thrust into her sleeves, her head thrown back, her eyes closed as if she were lost in thought. Or in prayer.

Pausing in the doorway, he let himself drink in the sight of her. She wore a plain, dark wool gown and a veil that covered her short hair. She looked thinner, he thought, and disturbingly pale. Then he must have made some small sound, or perhaps she simply sensed his presence, for she whirled suddenly to face him, one hand flying up to press against her breast.

"What are you doing here?" she demanded, her eyes wide, her body heartbreakingly tense.

He pushed away from the door frame and walked toward her. "I must speak with you."

She turned away from him. "We have nothing to say to each other."

"Sweet Jesus, Attica—" He caught her arm, but dropped it when she spun to confront him, her eyes blazing. He sucked in a deep, calming breath. "Will you listen to me? Henry isn't just ill. He's dying."

She shrugged, that brief flame of animation fading from her features. "Men die. At least Henry is old."

The cold, shattered look in her beautiful brown eyes was terrible to see. "For the love of God, Attica." He started to reach for her again, then thought better of it. "Try to understand. Time is running out for you. When Henry dies, Richard will become king. And Richard will give you as bride to Fulk of Salers. Make no mistake about that."

She walked away from him, toward the small window set deep into the tower's thick walls. The golden light of the late afternoon sun washed over her, illuminating that oddly calm, blank face. "I have decided to take the veil," she said, her voice as flat and emotionless as her features.

The veil. Oh, my God. A wild terror leapt within him, tore at his gut, chilled his soul. "Attica—" He took a step toward her, then stopped. "You don't need to do this. If you cannot bear the thought of being my wife in truth, then become my wife in name only. I am willing to swear upon every holy relic known to man that I will never touch you—that if you will it so, once we are wed I will simply ride away and leave you alone in possession of your lands. You need never see me again."

"Damion—"

"No, hear me out. Let me do this for you. As my wife, you would be safe from anyone's attempts to marry you off against your will. You have no need to take the veil."

She shook her head. "I will be no man's wife. Even a king cannot force a woman to marry when she has pledged herself to God."

"You underestimate the man who will be king," he said dryly.

Her chin lifted in that way she had. "I shall have the Pope behind me."

"The Pope is in Rome."

"But God is in my heart."

"Cross of Christ," he swore, bringing his fist down on the top of the small table beside him hard enough to make the few items scattered across its surface jump. "This is not God's will, and you know it. God gave us our love. He wouldn't have created something so beautiful between us if not for a purpose."

She walked toward him to pick up a small, ivory-fronted book from the top of the table. "Do you know what this is?" she asked softly, holding it out to him.

He shook his head.

"It's a book of days. I gave it to Stephen when he was knighted." She turned the book in her hand. "It's ironic, isn't it? I risked so much to come here, thinking to save my brother's life. Instead, I brought Stephen his murderer."

Her words hit Damion like a vicious blow, low to his gut. He braced his outstretched arms on the table between them and leaned into it, his voice coming out strained, almost savage. "I did not murder your brother and you know it, Attica d'Alérion. Stephen signed his own death warrant by the decisions he made and the actions he took."

"No," she said quietly. "Were it not for me, he would be alive today."

He straightened with a jerk and stepped around the table toward her. "Attica, don't blame yourself."

She backed away from him. "How can I not?" Silent tears coursed down her cheeks, although she seemed unaware of them. "Don't you see? If I hadn't listened when you asked me not to tell Stephen that we knew about the code, he'd still be alive. Now he's dead, and I . . ."

Her voice broke suddenly and she turned away, her shoulders hunching as she brought her hands up to her mouth.

"I betrayed him. I betrayed him as surely as he betrayed Henry. And in so doing, I have destroyed my entire house."

"What madness is this?" He seized her by the shoulders and swung her around again, his grip on her tightening when she would have wrenched away from him. "What do you think?" He searched her beautiful, beloved face. "What do you think? That the line between loyalty and betrayal is always clear and immutable and easy to follow? Well, let me tell you, it's not. It's shifting, and it's dim, and I swear at times it disappears altogether. There are times when we can only do what seems right in our hearts. And in your heart, you have betrayed no one."

"Haven't I?" She searched his face, her eyes dark and deep with anguish. "Isn't our very love a betrayal?"

His heart felt so heavy in his chest that it ached. "Don't say that. Attica . . ." His voice cracked, and he had to swallow before he could continue. "I will always love you. You are my heart, my life, my soul."

A sob shook her thin frame, and she bowed her head as if she could no longer bear to look at him. "Please leave me," she whispered. "If you love me, please just . . . go."

It was the hardest thing he'd ever done, to go away and leave her then. Outside, the yard lay oddly empty and silent in the rosy hues of the setting sun. He crossed the castle to the Knights' Tower, his footsteps echoing hollowly as he climbed the tight spiral of steps to his chamber. The room stood almost empty now, the cots stripped, the rough wooden crosses bare of their mail shirts and helms. Sergei must have been cleaning again, Damion thought idly, noticing the freshly strewn rushes and the lute that lay as if it had just been set down upon his bed.

Feeling like a dead man, he picked up the lute almost absently, turning it in his arms. It felt cool and strangely heavy in his hands. He touched his fingertips to the strings but could not bring himself to play it.

He had lost her. The knowledge of it echoed like a scream in his mind, an agony in his heart, an unbearable grief in his soul. He had lost her. With a shudder, he drew his finger, once, across the lute's strings, drawing forth an aching chord.

> *Without you,*
> *My sun dies*
> *My prayer falters*
> *My song ends . . .*

With a savage curse, he whirled to hurl the instrument against the bare stone wall. The impact smashed the delicately inlaid wood into a thousand splintered, irreparable shards that lay scattered among the rushes like the shattered dreams of a ruined man.

Damion stood just inside the curtained doorway of the king's chamber, a rolled parchment held loosely in one hand.

Henry's head turned on the fine linen of his pillow to display an ashen face, ravaged by pain. "Well?" he said, his once gruff, booming voice reduced to a faint scratching. "Has it come, then?"

Damion moved forward, slowly, and held out the scroll. "Yes, Sire."

Henry reached out a shaky hand, only to let it fall to his side again. "I can't read it. You must tell me. Is John's name there? Has he in truth betrayed me along with the rest?"

Damion stared down at the scroll in his hands. How do you tell a king that the son he loved above all others has betrayed him? he wondered. How do you break a dying man's heart?

The silence in the room hung heavy and damning. Henry let out his breath in a long, painful sigh. "It's true, then."

"Yes, Your Grace." He was aware of Henry's hands clenching at the bedcovers, but he could not bring himself to look directly at the old man's face.

"And why have you been chosen to bring me this news?" Henry asked after a moment, his voice brusque.

"Your son Geoffrey has gone to the priory to pray, while William Marshal sees to the defenses of the castle."

"No," said the Old King impatiently. "I mean the others. Where are the others?"

Damion let his face go blank. "The others?" he repeated, raising his eyebrows.

"So they've gone, have they?" Henry's mouth twisted into a bitter line. "Faster than a priest can chant matins. Scrambling over one another in their eagerness to gain favor with the new king." His gaze narrowed as he studied Damion's face. "They are wise, you know. I am an old man, and unwell, and soon Richard will be king. If not tomorrow, then the next day."

"Then tomorrow or the next day I will pledge Richard my fealty."

"You are a chivalric fool," said Henry.

Damion smiled. "I know."

Amusement flared in the older man's eyes, then faded as he reached out to clasp Damion's hand in a surprisingly strong grip. "I have promised you rich rewards, Damion de Jarnac," he said, his head lifting off the pillow. "But I fear I may not live long enough to see that you receive them. You should take Rosamund. With her safely wedded and bedded, Richard will have had no choice but to accept you as Earl of Carlyle."

"If I can't have Attica d'Alérion to wife, I will take no other," Damion said simply.

The Old King grunted. "You may feel that way now. But believe me, in another twenty years, you'll be glad enough to have Rosamund's estates and titles as your own, even if you have found no joy from having the girl herself in your bed."

Damion forced his lips into a travesty of a smile. "Perhaps I simply can't abide the thought of drinking English wine for the rest of my life."

Henry's eyes opened wide as he laughed out loud. But the laugh turned into a cough that rumbled in his throat like a death rattle.

Attica was at the priory of Saint Rémy, lighting a candle in the Lady chapel, when the bells began to ring. She raised her head, her hand tightening around the taper as she listened to the slow death knell.

One toll for each year of Henry Plantagenet's life.

CHAPTER
TWENTY-THREE

Damion stood beside the royal bier, his head bowed, his hands clasped behind his back. The sweet sound of nuns' voices singing Kyrie Eleison floated up to the soaring, honey-toned stone vaults of the abbey church. The scents of incense and beeswax and fear hung thick in the air.

They had traveled up the Vienne to the Abbey of Notre Dame de Fontevrault, a handful of loyal knights, one royal bastard, and the body of a dead king decked in royal robes and wearing a crown of gold. Now they waited, these men who had remained faithful to the Old King, to see what the new king would do with them.

The sound of a heavy booted tread echoed down the nave, punctuated with the clink and rasp of spurs. Richard, King of England and Wales, Duke of Normandy and Aquitaine, and Count of Anjou, had entered the church. He strode to the head of the bier, his face a frozen mask as he stared unflinchingly down at the father he had helped to kill. He had much the look of his father, Damion thought, this new king, although he was taller, and his features more fiercely drawn. He stood very still. Then a shiver of emotion contorted his face, and he dropped to his knees.

He did not pray for long. Pushing to his feet, he took one

last look at the dead king, then turned on his heel and left the church.

Damion did not look up. He had made his decisions, knowing well the probable outcome. Now he would bear the inevitable consequences. It was as simple as that.

"Monsieur le chevalier de Jarnac?" said a small man with a thin, pointed nose and an officious manner, stepping forward.

Damion raised his eyebrows. "Yes."

"King Richard commands your presence."

The hot July sun shone out of a clear blue sky, baking the broad riverside meadow where the new king had set up court for the day. Scores of milling boots and restlessly tapping slippers had quickly crushed the tender grass underfoot, grinding it into dust that drifted up to fill the air with a faint haze. Starched wimples and linen chainse began to wilt, lead-based makeup ran in white rivulets down ashen faces, slim courtiers swooned in unaffected faints.

Neither the heat nor the passing hours had any discernible effect on Richard, who plowed through the business of the day with cold efficiency. But then, thought Attica, he was sitting down, and beneath a canopy, too.

Sweltering herself in scarlet velvet heavily embroidered with silver thread, she moved restlessly around the edges of the crowd of gaily plumed lords and ladies, bright in their silks and satins and sparkling with jewels, who fluttered about the new king's faldstool like the hovering wings of some giant, gaudy peacock. She kept scanning the crowd for one familiar, beloved face, a face she was desperate to see just one more time. For Attica was in the king's gift, and she was here so that this new king could give her away.

Don't think about it, she told herself, her hands curling into fists she hid beneath the rich cloth of her skirts. *You can't avoid it, so all you can do is face it with dignity and courage.*

But her courage and dignity were both fading fast beneath the strain of this interminable wait and a rising spiral of fear. Fear that something had happened to Damion, that Richard had already dealt with the dark knight in some hideous way, that she would never see him again.

She found her gaze drifting desperately to the calming silver sheen of the Loire, just visible through a thin screen of trees. Her head held high, her gaze focused on the cloudless sky, Attica backed away from the royal assemblage. Backed until she was far enough away simply to turn around and walk rapidly through the grove of scrub brush and elms that lined the river.

Sliding down a grassy embankment, she came to a gravel shore lapped by the gentle waters of the Loire and sheltered by a big old elm that leaned out over the river at a drunken angle. With a sigh, she sank down on a driftwood log and hunched over, hugging herself, trying to stop the fine trembling going on inside her as the fear she'd held in check now reared up, fierce and all-consuming.

Oh, God, she thought, *let him be all right. Please let him be all right.* He had betrayed her trust and killed her only brother. And still she loved him, still she would give anything to see him safe and well.

With a stifled moan, she pressed her hands against the bones of her face. Pressed and pressed. And saw, through her splayed fingers, the unsmiling face of Damion de Jarnac's enigmatic young squire, dressed for court.

"Sergei," she said, dropping her hands, her breath leaving in her chest in a painful rush. "Is he here? Is he all right?"

"He is coming," said the squire enigmatically. He stood some five or six feet before her, a burgundy colored, jauntily plumed cap dangling from one hand to lay against his leg, an unusually solemn expression pulling at his young-old face. "How can you still blame him?" demanded Sergei, exactly as if she had spoken her thoughts aloud. "I could understand it at first, when you were still struggling to come to terms with your brother's death. But you should have seen some reason by now."

Attica felt angry color rise to her cheeks. She made no effort to pretend not to understand his meaning. "Damion could have told me, Sergei. He could have told me he suspected Stephen."

"Could he have indeed?" The boy took a step toward her, the expression on his face furious enough to make her draw back unconsciously. "And what would you have done if he had told you? Would you have gone to Stephen and warned him his treason was about to be exposed?"

She opened her mouth to say yes, then shut it again.

"That's right," said Sergei, his changeling eyes narrowing down to two accusatory slits. "You have to think about what Stephen would have done, don't you? Oh, he might simply have slipped out of Chinon in the dead of the night and fled to Richard. But then again, he might have decided to use the dead of night to slip a dagger into de Jarnac's back instead."

"Stephen wouldn't have done that."

"Wouldn't he?" The squire moved to prop one booted foot on the end of her log and lean into it. Lean into her. "Could you have been certain enough of that to risk de Jarnac's life on it?"

She lifted her chin. "I needn't have told him de Jarnac was involved."

"No? So you imagine, do you, that even if you hadn't told Stephen where the exposure was likely to come from, he couldn't have figured it out?" He dropped his foot to crouch on the gravel before her, his head coming level with her own, the anger fading to be replaced by a boyish earnestness. "Don't you see, my lady? If de Jarnac *had* told you, you'd have been faced with a terrible choice. You'd have had to decide whom to betray, your brother or the man you loved."

She heard the wind rustling through the spreading limbs of the elm overhead. She didn't look up.

"He spared you that," said Sergei. "He kept his suspicions to himself, hoping he was wrong, hoping that even if he wasn't, he might somehow manage to help Stephen avoid suffering the consequences of what he'd done. But de Jarnac couldn't simply close his eyes and stand back while your brother brought down the king. He wouldn't be the man you love, were he capable of that."

She shook her head, her jaw tight. "You forget, Sergei; I was *there*. I saw Damion spur his horse after Stephen—"

"And you saw him rein in, too. Perhaps it's because you're a woman, or because you've never been in a battle, but any man would understand what happens to a knight fighting hand to hand like that. De Jarnac might have begun to give chase, but he pulled up. That's what's important. Stephen could have ridden away. It was his choice to turn and fight. What do you think de Jarnac should have done? Stood there and let Stephen kill him?"

"No," she said, her voice a raw whisper.

The squire's strange, changeling eyes captured hers, refusing to let her look away. "It was a mad thing, what Stephen did. He must have known he was likely to die."

Attica swallowed a painful lump in her throat. She had

replayed that scene on the road to Loudun over and over in her mind. And although it made no sense, the more she thought about it, the more convinced she became that Stephen had wanted to die, had made up his mind to die. She didn't want to believe it, she'd raged against it, and still . . . *Oh, Stephen,* she thought, squeezing her eyes shut against a threatening sting of tears. *Why?*

"What will Richard do to him?" she asked, opening her eyes to stare out over the silver-brown, placidly drifting waters of the Loire. "To de Jarnac, I mean."

Sergei shrugged, his gaze swinging away to where a small page was scrambling down the riverbank toward them. "I don't know. He can be a cruel, brutal man, Richard, especially when he's thirsty for revenge."

Attica turned. The page, a small, round-cheeked boy of no more than nine or ten, was out of breath, his fair hair tumbling over his eyes as he bowed low. "My lady Attica d'Alérion?"

Attica shakily rose to her feet. "Yes?"

"King Richard commands your presence."

Her face a serene mask, her heart thumping so wildly in her chest that she wondered it didn't kill her, Attica d'Alérion walked toward the English king.

The staring crowd of courtiers parted before her, but she was careful to look only straight ahead. She noticed Gaspard Beringer, standing to one side, his fair-headed handsomeness arresting even in this crowd of primped and pampered nobility. Next to him, Yvette looked like a small round partridge, the disconcertingly predatory gleam in her sharp eyes camouflaged for the moment by maternal concern, for she was busy fanning Fulk's face. Fulk, normally so pale, had a tendency to flush bright red in the heat. He would have had his birthday by now, Attica realized with a start, seeing him. He was fourteen and ready to be wed.

She sucked in a deep breath at the thought, and when one breath wasn't enough, she took another and then another. Still she felt as if she couldn't get enough air, as if a great weight pressed on her chest, crushing her, crushing. Her step faltered, and she would have stumbled if the page hadn't grabbed her elbow to steady her.

"Come, daughter," said Richard, stretching out his hand to her. "Come sit beside us." He smiled at her, but his grip on her hand was uncompromising as he pulled her down to settle on the cushion at his feet.

"With the death of your father and brother, you have become our ward, Attica d'Alérion," he said, his voice deeper, less hurried than his father's. "You needn't fear that we will be careless of the trust imposed upon us. On the question of your brother's lands which have been declared forfeit, we settle them on you again, in recognition of your family's long allegiance to us."

Attica sat very still, her hands clenched together in her lap, her head bowed as she concentrated on the seemingly impossible task of maintaining her composure. At the king's words, she felt nothing, neither surprise nor pleasure, for whether she was forced to wed Fulk or allowed to seek refuge in a convent, the lands would not be hers. She wished they could have gone to Damion.

"The question of your marriage appears more complicated," continued Richard, "for our father promised you to Damion de Jarnac, while Robert d'Alérion betrothed you to Fulk of Salers. Is this correct?"

She swallowed, trying to remove the treacherous lump that had appeared in her throat. "Yes, Your Grace."

At a barely perceptible movement of one ringed, royal finger, a herald's voice boomed out, *"Fulk Beringer, of Salers."* A page prodded Fulk forward until he stood, red-faced and sweating, some ten feet in front of the king. No one offered Fulk a cushion.

"Damion de Jarnac," boomed the voice again.

Attica's head came up, her breath catching with joyful anticipation.

He was there, at the edge of the meadow, seemingly un-aware of the ripple of interest that passed through the crowd of tired, jaded courtiers. His head held high, his gaze steady and calm, Damion approached the king with a sure, measured tread. He wore a dark, midnight blue tunic and embroidered velvet surcoat worthy of a courtier, but no one seeing this man could ever mistake him for anything but the knight he was. It was there in the lean, athletic grace of his stride, in the breadth of his shoulders, in the unself-conscious pride with which he bowed low before the new English king. For a moment, she thought he must not have seen her, seated at the king's feet, for he didn't look at her, only stared at the man before him. But then she saw the pulse beating hard and fast in his neck, and she knew by the stiff way he held himself that he was as aware of her as he was of him.

Heedless of whoever might be watching her, Attica let herself drink in the sight of him. She knew him so well, knew the hard lines of his dark, taut profile and the gentle curve of his lips. She knew what those lips tasted like, knew the soft touch of his battle-hardened hands on her body. It brought her such a sad, sweet ache, looking at him. But she couldn't bear to turn away. The desperation of her fear for him had washed away the lingering remnants of her hurt and anger. Now she knew only a profound sense of loss and the bitter taste of regret.

Beside her, Richard put his fingertips together and leaned forward in his chair, as if the knight before him piqued his interest as well as the crowd's. "You have caused us much grief these last months, Damion de Jarnac," he said.

Damion smiled. "Yes, Your Grace."

To Attica's surprise, an answering gleam lit the young king's eyes. "While others betrayed our father and scrambled to gain favor in foreign courts, you stayed at his side. Such loyalty and courage is as rare as it is admirable, and well deserving of reward." Richard shifted his weight to rest one arm along the side of his chair, while Attica, who hadn't even realized she'd been holding her breath, let it go in a long sigh that left her feeling almost dizzy with relief.

"Unfortunately," continued the English king, "the lands and titles of the comte d'Alérion have been restored to the comte's rightful heir, Attica d'Alérion, so that we are unable to confirm the gift granted you by the late king. However . . ." Richard paused, drawing out the moment in a way that told Attica he was enjoying this. ". . . there remains the question of the lady Attica herself, who has been promised to both you and to Fulk of Salers."

"But she is *betrothed* to me," said Fulk, stepping forward impetuously, only to be brought up short by a pair of crossed pikes that caused him to lose whatever color the heat had brought to his face.

Richard's eyebrows lifted. From the crowd came a maternal, warning hiss.

"I beg your pardon, Your Grace," Fulk stammered, his head bowing.

Richard continued. "We could, of course, emulate King Solomon of old and offer to split the lady in two with our sword. But we think . . ." He fingered his beard, as if considering the problem. "Yes, we really think we prefer to allow the lady to choose."

Attica's head whipped around, her eyes widening in shock as she stared at him.

"Stand up, daughter," he said, his hand cupping her elbow to urge her to her feet.

"If I might interrupt, Your Grace?" said Damion.

Attica froze, while Richard's eyebrows lifted again.

His hands on his hips, his head thrown back, Damion said, "Your late father offered the lady Attica a third choice, that of becoming a bride of Christ. I would ask that she be given that option now."

For the first time, Damion's gaze met hers, and everything that was in his heart spilled into his eyes. She saw his love for her, so much love it made her chest ache to see it, and she saw the pain of the sacrifice he'd just made by insuring she had a safe refuge if her anger and hurt were still too great to enable her to choose him.

Yet she also saw a desperate flicker of hope. Hope, almost drowned out by a deep, lingering hurt that both startled her and shamed her. She'd been hurting so much herself these past few days that she hadn't realized he'd been hurting, too. Hadn't realized that she had hurt him.

"Very well," said Richard. "She may have the veil as a third choice." His hand tightened on her arm, drawing her around to face him. "Lady Attica?"

She sank into a deep curtsy, although her knees felt so shaky, she feared they might collapse beneath her. "Your Grace."

He smiled at her. "You have three alternatives, Lady Attica: Which will you choose?"

She spun around, her hands fisting in her heavy velvet

skirts, her heart pounding in her chest. All her life, she had been taught to think of others, not of herself; to serve the interests of her house and conform always to the expectations of her parents. She had chafed against the restrictions they imposed upon her, but she had always sought to do her duty, had always buried her own wants and needs and desires in the name of honor and loyalty. Now suddenly everything she wanted was within her grasp. All she had to do was reach for it.

Already her heart was flying across the meadow to the man she loved. It was a strangely difficult thing to do, to put one foot in front of the other. But the second step was easier, and the third required no conscious thought. She was only vaguely aware of Yvette's angry, blotched face; of Gaspard's mouth, working soundlessly in consternation and confusion; of Fulk, looking sulky and hot.

And then she was running, running like the child she had once been, with the sky blue above her and the wind fresh in her face. She saw the leap of guarded hope in Damion's eyes, followed by a sweet exultation that swept his face. With a deep, joyous laugh, he caught her up in his arms, lifting her feet off the ground, her momentum spinning them round and round. She braced her forearms on his shoulders, her back arching so she could look down into his face. "I choose you," she said, her eyes misting with sudden, unshed tears, her laughter joining his to float up, up to the cloudless heavens. "Forever. Forever and ever."

EPILOGUE

Normandy, 1199

Lilting and clear, the sweet notes of the familiar melody drifted away on the fresh sea breeze. The day was glorious, Attica thought, glorious and fine, the sun warm, the sky a vivid blue. She drew the clean April air deep into her lungs, her gaze lingering on the distant swell of white-capped waves rolling in toward the rocky shore below. Even as a child, this daisy-strewn hillside overlooking the sea had been one of her favorite places at this, the d'Alérions' greatest castle. She still came here often, whenever they were in residence. She would bring her sons, and a hamper and cloth, and spend the afternoon at peace with her memories.

Sighing contentedly, she turned her head, a smile touching her lips as she watched her older son's fine-boned, sure hands move nimbly over the strings of the lute. "You have your grandmother's gift," she said softly. "Your grandmother's and your father's."

"Father?" Stephen de Jarnac looked up, his fingers suspended over the strings, his bright green eyes widening in surprise. "But Father doesn't play."

"Not anymore." Attica shifted awkwardly, for she was

401

big with child, and she found it hard to sit anywhere for very long. "But he did once." Her smile turned wistful at the memory. "Like an angel."

"Then why doesn't he play now?" asked six-year-old Simon, tweaking the instrument from his older brother's slack grasp.

"I suppose because he no longer finds joy in it," she said, gently but firmly separating the squabbling brothers. "Or perhaps," she added, half to herself, "he is afraid to allow himself to find joy in it."

"Father? Afraid?" Stephen scoffed. "Father isn't afraid of anything."

"Even the bravest man is afraid of losing the ones he loves," she said quietly.

Stephen stared at her, his young face unnaturally solemn. The wind gusted up from the sea, loud and blustery, then dropped again. In the sudden silence, they could hear the sound of a horse's hooves coming toward them fast. Attica glanced up to see a horse and rider cresting the hill above them—a dark, desert-bred horse, carrying a tall, dark knight who reined in sharply to swing out of the saddle with a lean, athletic grace that still took her breath away. Still, after all these years.

"It's Papa," shrieked Simon. The boys jumped up, the lute thrust aside, forgotten, as they ran to him. Attica stayed where she was and watched her husband come at her, enjoying the way the wind lifted his dark hair from the collar of his rich velvet mantle, and the sight of the sun shining warm and golden over the strong bones of his face. Across a distance filled with the call of gulls and the sounds of the sea, his gaze met hers, and his eyes smiled.

"Wait for me," called Simon in frustration as he lagged behind his older brother. Laughing, Damion tore his gaze from hers and reached to lift his younger son high into the air. Then he swung the little boy up onto his shoulder, so that he had a free hand to ruffle Stephen's dark head when the older boy leaned into him. Watching them, Attica felt her heart fill with such joy, she thought it might burst.

He spent a moment listening to the boys' excited chatter, then left them to care for the Arab and walked up to her.

"I didn't think you were coming, *monsieur le comte*," she began teasingly. But the welcoming smile faded from her lips as she searched his face. "What is it?"

"A messenger just rode in, from Aquitaine." Stripping off his gloves, he dropped smoothly onto the cloth beside her and plucked the jug of cider from the hamper. "Richard the Lionhearted has been hit by a crossbow bolt, at the siege of Châlus, and is not expected to recover. Which means"—he paused to fill a horn with cider and throw it back with a quick flick of his wrist—"that John will be the new Duke of Normandy and Aquitaine, and King of England."

A sick, hollow feeling yawned deep within her. "What will you do?"

Damion poured himself another cupful and raised it to his lips. "They say Philip is in Paris. I would go and pledge him my fealty." His gaze met hers questioningly over the rim of the cup. "Do you think me disloyal?"

Attica shook her head. "No. Richard was a hard, brutal man, but at least when he rebelled against his father, he did it openly. *And* he proved himself to be a strong lord. But John . . ." She hesitated, choosing her words carefully. "John is devious and weak. In the end, he will lose this land to Philip. I would not see you sacrifice everything, simply out of a sense of loyalty to such a man."

Tossing the cup aside, Damion reached for her, a wry

smile twisting his lips. "I fear you have been married to me for too long."

"No, not nearly long enough," she said as he came to sit behind her, her back against his chest so that he could put his arms around her. "I intend to keep you tied to my side until you're too lame and battle weary to sit a horse, and I'm a withered old crone worn out from breeding."

Laughing, he placed his spread hands high on her swollen belly. "And how is my daughter today?"

Father Sergei had told them this baby would be a girl, and Attica believed him, for Sergei had always known such things, even before he'd become a priest. "Your daughter is restless," she said, just as the baby kicked hard enough to make Damion laugh again.

He turned his face into Attica's hair. "My daughter is always restless."

"Music soothes her." Attica nudged the discarded lute toward him. "Why don't you play for her?"

Damion went suddenly, utterly still.

She turned in his arms, her hand coming up to touch his cheek. "It's been ten years, Damion. Henry and my brother are long in their graves, and soon Richard will join them. What happened all those years ago at Chinon . . . it belongs to the past. But your music . . ." She paused, struggling to put her thoughts into words. "Your music was a gift from God. A gift, like our love. And like our love, God gave it to you for a purpose."

"A purpose?" The exhalation of his breath wafted warm and moist against her knuckles as he brought her hand to his mouth. "Because of music, I almost lost you." He turned her hand in his and pressed a kiss to her palm.

She shook her head. "Because of music, you were able to save a dying old man from treachery." She traced the hard, proud curve of his lips with her fingertips. "Don't you see? No matter what happens, you'll never really lose me, Damion. You are my soul. And you always will be."

High on the hill above the sea, the two brothers paused in the midst of arguing over who should hold the Arab's reins, their heads turning together at the sound of an unknown, haunting melody plucked from a lute with such unearthly skill that it stole their breath. "It's Father," whispered Simon in awe, while Stephen only stared, his eyes shining with some emotion he could not have named.

"I die for you," sang Damion, his gaze locked fast with his wife's. *"You are my hope, my life, my love."*

After a moment, her voice joined his.

> *"Give me yourself.*
> *If not your body,*
> *Then your heart.*
> *Make me your soul."*

Low and sweet, the music rose up into the cloudless sky, their voices entwining with the warmth of the sun and the excited laughter of their children to weave a garland of healing joy that wrapped around them like the springtime fragrance of a lover's bower. And then their song turned into laughter, and the laughter drifted out to sea to be brought back to them on the surge of the endless, cleansing tide.

AUTHOR'S
NOTE

The historical events against which this story is played out—the revolt of Richard, the conference at La Ferté-Bernard, the burning of Le Mans and the retreat of Henry II to Chinon—are portrayed for the most part as recorded in the chronicles, although some have been compressed in time and space. Likewise, the Saintly Guido is a historical figure, although the Catalonian nun is not.

It is important to remember that the Normans and Angevins of twelfth-century France, like the gently-born across the Channel in England, spoke an archaic form of French. Rather than invent some anachronistic, pseudo-medieval English, I have, for the most part, simply translated the characters' speech into modern English or, in some cases, modern French.

I would like to thank John Galbraith of Catholic Online for his help in fixing medieval church dates. The song in old Provençal sung by the trouver in the inn is by Arnaut and can be found in René Lavaud, *Les Poésies d'Arnaut Daniel* (Toulouse, 1910). Damion's love song, although inspired by contemporary models, is my own.

If you enjoyed *THE LAST KNIGHT*
you won't want to miss
Candice Proctor's
other fabulous romances...

SEPTEMBER MOON

Patrick O'Reilly loves life in the wilderness. All he
needs is his land, his work, and the company of the children he adores. The last thing he wants is the prim and
proper Englishwoman, Amanda Davenport, who arrives
to care for his unruly children, yet he finds himself inex-
plicably drawn to this proud woman and the fire he
knows exists beneath her refined exterior...

THE BEQUEST

When Gabrielle Antoine arrives in the rough mining
town, the convent-bred beauty is shocked by the deca-
dence she finds there—and stunned to learn she has just
inherited a bordello from the mother she never knew.
Worse, her mother's business partner, Jordan Hays—a
rugged, cynical loner—embodies everything Gabrielle
fears . . . and secretly desires. Soon Gabrielle finds herself swept away by a passion as tempting as sin itself...

NIGHT IN EDEN

Bryony Wentworth's life is shattered when she is unjustly
accused and sentenced to indentured servitude in New
South Wales. Broken in body—but not in spirit—she
fights for light, and for her life, wanting no part of the man
who would save her, Captain Hayden St. John. But the
mother in her cannot turn away from Hayden's needy
infant and the woman in her cannot deny her passion for
the rugged, enigmatic man she is bound to serve.

Published by The Ballantine Publishing Group.
Available in your local bookstore.

Mary Jo Putney

THE WILD CHILD — now available in paperback!
Bribed by Kyle, his twin brother, Dominic Renbourne agrees to take his twin's place for a few weeks at Warfield Manor, where he is to pay court to Lady Meriel Grahame, the orphaned heiress Kyle intends to marry. The last thing Dominic expects is to be entranced by a silent sprite whose ethereal beauty is as intoxicating as the flowers and trees that surround her. Despite his longing, Dominic's sense of duty keeps him away from his brother's future bride, but Meriel's untamed spirit proves more powerful than Dominic can resist . . .

THE CHINA BRIDE

Born to a Scottish father and now living in China, Troth Montgomery never imagined that one day she would leave the Orient, arriving in bitter winter at the estate of a stranger—the brother of the man who had briefly been her husband. Now, as the widow of Kyle Renbourne, Viscount of Maxwell, Troth is entitled to the home she always dreamed of but remains haunted by the memory of a dashing husband and the brief, forbidden love they shared. Then Kyle seemingly returns from the dead, his mind and body badly wounded. Bitterly aware that she will never be a fitting English wife, Troth defiantly embraces her foreign traditions, hoping that the ancient arts of her ancestors will restore Kyle's spirit and her own battered heart.

Published by The Ballantine Publishing Group.
Available in your local bookstore.